BY THE PACT

BOOK 1 OF PACTS ARCANE AND OTHERWISE

JOANNA MACIEJEWSKA

By the Pact

Pacts Arcane and Otherwise: Book 1

Editing by Arran McNicol

Cover art and design by Joanna Maciejewska and Inq So

ISBN (paperback) 978-1-7346067-2-0

ISBN (hardcover) 978-1-960158-05-5

ISBN (ebook) 978-1-7346067-1-3

Published by Joanna Maciejewska
PO Box 243
Bushland
Texas 79012, United States
info@authorjm.com

Printed and bound by IngramSpark.
Australia: Ingram Content Group AU Pty Ltd, Melbourne, Victoria. US: Lightning Source LLC, La Vergne, Tennessee / Allentown, Pennsylvania / Jackson, Tennessee, United States. UK: Lightning Source UK Ltd, Milton

Keynes, United Kingdom. Europe: Lightning Source UK Ltd, with facilities in Germany, France, and Spain.
The authorized representative in the European Economic Area is Lightning Source France, 1 Av. Johannes Gutenberg, 78310 Maurepas, France.
compliance@lightningsource.fr

ALSO BY THE AUTHOR:

Pacts Arcane and Otherwise

By the Pact

Scars of Stone

Shadows over Kaighal

Demon Siege

Shadows of Eireland

Humanborn

Myth-Touched

Snakebitten

Other books

Memories of Sorcery and Sand

Collections

Scourges, Spells, and Serenades

To Inq
Who can now say, "I told you so."

1

As soon as Kamira kicked sand into the dark hole in the desert, she knew she'd found the right place. The golden grains rolled down and stopped at the edge of a tunnel leading deep into the ground. At least she hoped it was, because after two days of pointlessly crawling into random holes that always turned out to be dead ends, her patience and good mood were both running thin.

Half-crumbled ruins jutting out of the sand like skeletons of creatures long dead did little to improve her state. Every stone, charred or glazed into glass, reminded her that the surrounding desert was the result of a single mistake, a mistake that her predecessors made in their blind pride. Even over four hundred years later, people weren't willing to forgive a whole kingdom lost, and the blame for the past deeds traveled down the line of teachers and students of a once-respected school.

She shrugged off those thoughts as she circled the hole searching for the source of magic that barred the sands' entry. Her shadow shifted, mimicking both the movement of her sleek figure and the shape of her messy hair that she liked to adorn with feathers and bones. Back in the city, she'd add even more decorations, enjoying the many flinches her appearance spurred in the common folk. Over the years, the whisper "demonologist" behind her back aroused amusement instead of ire, and she'd long stopped bothering to explain her actual title or that she was nothing like arcanists of the past. Catering to common fears and misconceptions often brought unexpected benefits, and if nothing else, it made people leave her be. Only those who wanted to conduct business bothered her, and Kamira appreciated the peace and quiet of being alone.

Mostly alone, she concluded at the sound of footsteps.

"You found it." Veelk stopped beside her.

If she was the epitome of what people thought a demonologist should look like, complete with her gaunt, close to malnourished features adding a sinister undercurrent to her grouchy personality, Veelk reflected the commoners' idea of a tribal warrior. Tall and muscular, with a hairless head and an intricate net of scars marking his copper-hued skin, he often took advantage of anyone who assumed he was an uneducated savage. He surprised them with his wit, leaving many of people speechless, but when the ways of civilized men failed, he never lamented resorting to his keshal. His tribe's traditional spear had a blade at each end of the haft—one narrow and one wide, both as sharp as his tongue.

"I hope so," she muttered. "Otherwise, we're going to crawl in the dirt, risking the desert collapsing on us, only to find another dead end with an equally dead body."

Veelk grinned, unmoved as usual. "If you ever stop complaining, I'll know a demon has taken you." He approached the hole and carelessly threw a rock inside. Instead of bouncing or rolling, it sank into the black.

While he listened, Kamira bit her tongue before reminding him demon possessions were deemed impossible. After three years of traveling together, such a comment was nothing more than bait or distraction, or possibly both, since Veelk rarely passed on the opportunity to tease her as if trying to cure her inherent grumpiness.

"It's deep." Veelk glanced at her. "For once, that mage's source might have actually been right about the location."

Kamira groaned, since it meant they'd both have to climb down, because there was no chance Veelk would go down to check it only to come back up to help her, always eager to give her exercise opportunities. She eyed the opening in the ground with hate. "I regret we took the job."

"No, you don't." As he squatted by the opening in the ground, the keshal strapped to his back towered over him. "Think of all that you might find in there. All the knowledge that will be yours to keep."

She sneered, meeting his bait with hers. "All the knowledge I won't be able to carry out?"

Veelk's glance over his shoulder made it clear he didn't fall for it. "I would consider carrying some for you if you stopped complaining and started moving. Or, at least, did both at the same time."

With a chuckle, she made her way to him. If she found any tomes worth taking, it would be Veelk's turn to complain about lugging the ancient scribbles, which he was certain to call them. But if she wanted her meager payback, she needed to make it down the tunnel, otherwise the only spoils he'd carry out would be the items that looked most valuable, and even if old books fetched a good price among collectors, they didn't look as enticing as jewels or gold.

It didn't require much focus to summon a lumisphere, and with the nudge of her will, she sent it down. As it sank, its warm light revealed a partially crumbling tower. Where the Cataclysm damaged the structure, its large stones shifted or broke off, creating an irregular pattern of ledges that seemed stable enough to allow careful descent. She inspected the inner walls with interest, but no obvious arcane markings presented themselves. She wanted to believe the structure was sturdy on its own, but more sand trickled from the edges, and as it stopped short of falling, it reminded her that magic had its part in securing the opening. Unless the arcanists of the past were subtle with their art, someone ensured the remains of the old tower didn't collapse or get buried by the desert entirely.

Veelk made his way down, and after he checked the first ledge was stable, he helped Kamira. While she was finding her footing, he dropped to another ledge, so she called her lumisphere back and inspected the walls with renewed interest. Whoever wanted the tunnel sand-free must have been carving the runes around it while balancing on the uneven surfaces, and this meant a rushed job that would be hard to conceal. Yet the porous walls revealed nothing, not a single mark nor even a portion of an arcanist's circle.

Disappointed, she followed her companion down. As they descended, the air cooled and carried a breeze that made Kamira pause.

"You sense that too, don't you?" Veelk threw her a glance.

She nodded. "Demon magic." She didn't need to explain that it wasn't the traditional magic that arcanists channeled through their pacts with demons.

Veelk dropped off to another ledge. "Lingering from the Cataclysm?" he asked while she made her way down to him.

A simple "yes" was all she needed to lull their instinctual concerns. After all, the original Towers were the epicenter of the Cataclysm, and the place where the arcanists of old laid down their lives fighting a demon who had betrayed their trust. Or, if the high mages got their version of history: where the arcanists paid dearly for attempting to summon a powerful demon in the flesh.

But the truth was that she couldn't be certain. Magic didn't linger in places unless it was spelled into artifacts or arcane circles. And the pure demonic nature of the energy suggested that no arcanist had a hand in its making. At the same time, this was the place of a grand battle, and no one knew what happened when a demon was slain. Maybe his magic did continue to haunt the place of his final rest.

"So it's a no." Veelk tensed, glaring at the tunnel's dark bottom with wariness.

All she could give him was a shrug as she approached the edge, letting him help her down. The grim aura of the tower must have been getting on his nerves too, since he offered not even a single remark at her lack of climbing prowess. They descended in silence, and the drift carried the faint magic from beneath in waves that made her think of steady breaths. The image that followed, of a powerful creature lurking in the darkness below, sent a shiver down her spine, but she didn't share her thoughts with Veelk. He needed to be focused on real threats instead of entertaining her doubts.

Feeling solid ground beneath her feet when they reached the dusted floor at the bottom of the tower brought no relief. Even the notion of familiarity the structure had for one who had spent years in the High Towers, like Kamira, couldn't ease her thoughts. As she ran her hand against the half-crumbled reliefs depicting the great deeds of the arcanists of old, a pang of regret struck her. The mighty figures adorned in what was now considered tribal fashion were forever captured in stone performing incredible feats of magic. So much had been lost over the centuries, so much knowledge and power, and with the high mages dictating the rules for years after the original Towers' destruction, no arcanist since had been commemorated, nor their deeds depicted in such a way.

"Some demon gnawing on your brain?"

Kamira snapped out of her thoughts. "Not since yesterday." She inspected the corridor and pointed to the left, picking the direction at random. "Should be this way." Even if she knew where the teachers' quarters were supposed to be, entering the ruins through an unknown tower meant she first needed to find a point of reference; a bigger hall or a stairway would do. Until then, one way was as good as another.

Veelk inspected her as if estimating her confidence and headed down the dusty corridor. She allowed him to get ahead in case the builders or recent visitors left any nasty surprises amongst the rubble. With the tribal scars protecting him, he could withstand most magical assaults, and he had a better chance of avoiding or destroying traps than she did. She smiled at that, because on rare occasions her magic came to aid as she shielded him from afar. Tackling the largest piles of rubble from caved-in walls, she tried to shake off the nagging feeling of uneasiness. The exploration wasn't going at all as she had imagined. For years, she'd dreamed of delving into the old structure and discovering the long-forgotten secrets of the most skilled arcanists of all time; instead, she only found a longing to get back to the surface.

Veelk looked back over his shoulder. "You shouldn't be so—"

He never froze, just shifted instantly from a casual gesture to a battle-ready stance, keshal unstrapped, staring back the way they had come. Kamira ducked out of the way almost flat against the wall. The darkness behind them was so thick that it filled the corridor like black fog. Out of it emerged creatures with crude crystal bodies, and she gasped. Even in her homeland, where arcanists placed demon-imbued stones on statues and animated them, no one ever attempted to craft a construct from the stones themselves. Their creator must have been both skilled and powerful, and she tensed. The limitations of her own pact had become clear in comparison.

The creatures moved at a slow pace, but their bulky mass blocked the way out if Kamira and Veelk wanted to retreat to the point of descent. Kamira moved behind Veelk, studying their crystalline skin. Besides directing sheer power at them, more than she could ever channel, she couldn't think of any way to stop them.

Veelk lunged and thrust at the one to their left. The keshal's blade glanced off its body, as somewhat expected, and the construct retaliated. Kamira stumbled backward trying to get out of Veelk's way as the crystalline claws cut through the air.

"Better start running." Veelk held his defensive stance, dodging just out of their reach only when he had to. "And pray to your demon to give you some magic."

"I don't pray to any demon," she muttered out of habit.

"The running part still stands."

His tone may have seemed carefree, but she knew he meant it. Even if there wasn't any way to defeat the creatures, they could at least outrun them.

"Suzhaul's curse!" Veelk's shout startled her, and before she knew what all was happening, he threw her against the wall.

Kamira narrowly dodged the giant crystal body

thundering past, its swift movements and pivot both apparent and unexpected. *So much for their slowness,* she thought with her back to the stones. She searched the hallway as Veelk leapt and spun with narrow swings and powerful thrusts back and forth in front of her to hold the constructs at bay on both sides. Further down the corridor, a destroyed portion of the wall seemed to open into a natural tunnel. It could be unstable or a dead end, but trying to outrun the creatures would likely be suicide, so they had to risk it.

"There!" She ducked as Veelk's weapon drew an arc in the air, delivering another blow. It didn't escape her that blood trickled down his arm. The gash seemed shallow enough, but over time the creatures would wear him down.

He glanced at the tunnel and nodded. "Go."

Without hesitation, she slid along the wall while the closest construct was preoccupied with its main opponent. She didn't look back until she reached the tunnel. Veelk was right behind her, so she ducked into the uneven, damp walls of the tunnel. Her fingers dug into the thick soil as she fell to her knees to crawl through, and her lumisphere flickered when several lumps of wet sand loosened from the low ceiling, but the tunnel seemed stable enough, and the air inside smelled fresh. A short distance farther, and she was able to stand up, but the rumble behind her held her breath of relief.

Too big to follow them inside, the creatures kept clawing and pounding at the corridor's stone wall, disturbing the wet earth with steady tremors.

"We better get going," she muttered.

The image of the desert collapsing all around them always accompanied her whenever they delved into underground, forgotten ruins, and even though she'd learned to brush away such concerns, she couldn't fight her own imagination. At least the air, though filled with the scent of wet ground and traces of unsettling magic, moved with a slight breeze, offering comfort and reminding her that she wasn't buried alive or stuck in a giant sandworm, if such things could exist. One glance back, though, where the creatures relentlessly fought against the stone, made her take back that last thought. If someone was capable of creating constructs like that, sandworms seemed just as possible.

Upon Veelk's insistent gaze, she sent her lumisphere ahead, and he squeezed past her. Even with the tunnel being taller, he couldn't fully straighten up, but his keshal remained at the ready nonetheless. The path weaved through the ground, and as it sloped downward, Kamira paused to look back. Maybe the creatures had abandoned their pursuit, and the exit would be clear again. Backtracking seemed a better idea than venturing deeper into the ground, possibly away from their goal if the tunnel didn't lead back to the structure.

"There's an opening ahead." Veelk slowed down.

Kamira didn't have to ask why he stopped. The familiar, unsettling magic emanated from the tunnel's end, more intense than back in the corridor. She swallowed the suggestion to turn around and instead sent her lumisphere in. Its faint light revealed a spacious chamber, partially covered with rubble and sand, especially by the walls, where the desert broke through the tall windows, but the patch of dark opposite them suggested another exit. Deeper in the chamber stood a strange milk-white crystal reaching high up to the ceiling.

"I've never seen anything like that." She stared in awe, but the magic surrounding it resembled the one radiating from the constructs earlier, and it had the same malicious flavor she'd been tasting in the air since they had entered the ruins. "Ready?"

Veelk poked his head into the chamber. "Do you really think the arcanists would leave traps in a place like this?"

"It's not the traps I'm worried about." Kamira indicated the crystal with a slight point of her chin. "With all the weird magic around, this must be some remains of the battle that took place here before..." Her voice creaked, but she didn't need to finish. Veelk knew the tale of the Cataclysm. "Besides, I'm not sure how, but the constructs we've met are connected to this thing." Looking back at the tunnel and the shape of its walls, she'd think the crystal creatures could have been the ones to dig it out... if they were small enough to fit in.

Veelk arched his eyebrow in a mockery of polite interest. "If it comes alive when I enter, leave it to me and get to that exit."

At the thought of her companion facing a construct of that size, Kamira opened her mouth to protest, but in the end, all he had to do was hold its attention and survive while she made it through the chamber. "Ready when you are."

As soon as he exited the tunnel, Veelk stretched his back and flexed his muscles, twirling his keshal. Kamira stood in silence, but nothing happened, and after several drawn-out heartbeats, he glanced back at her and smiled.

"There's something around the stone." He took cautious steps toward it, and she could swear no speck of dust rose at his passage. "The markings are odd, but look a bit like a summoning circle. Old arcanist ways, maybe?"

"Maybe. Stay away." She entered the chamber, eying the crystal, but it didn't react to her presence. It must have been as Veelk said: a dormant relict from the Cataclysm, harmless but still echoing with past magic.

"You aren't going to inspect it?" Veelk asked as she made her way through the chamber.

Her hesitation didn't last long as another gust of magic breeze swept over her. No discovery could be tempting enough to take such a risk. It was one thing to venture into half-buried ruins in search of artifacts, avoiding traps left by the previous explorers or maybe even the place's lost owners, but entirely different than willingly facing the unknown aftermath of the magical battle from centuries ago. "I'd rather get out of here before we have to fight something as nasty as those things. Let's see if that exit connects to the surfa—"

"It doesn't, little mage." The deep, masculine voice echoed from the stone through the room. "But you won't need it anyway."

Kamira curled as convulsions shook her body, unable to call for help. She fought for words, but only a vicious cough came out of her mouth. Veelk shot to her side. He stood with his arms wide, facing the crystal as if barring the way, and the net of scars on his skin lit up with a golden glow, absorbing the energy and disrupting its flow.

"Step aside, mage killer. I have no quarrel with you," came the voice again. "But I'll kill you if you keep protecting that pitiful *gaharra*."

Kamira allowed herself a sigh of relief as the debilitating pain faded enough to move, but she didn't waste time. Veelk could only protect her for so long, so with trembling hands, she drew several symbols in the dust around her. Even shaky lines on an uneven surface would suffice... With one mental command, she activated her meager circle, and a wall of energy rose around her, cutting off the pain and malicious magic.

"Done," she said, and Veelk stepped aside.

"Ah, a pactee... That I did not expect." The crystal vibrated as the voice continued.

At Veelk's questioning gaze, Kamira said, "It's an old name for an arcanist. I thought your folk would know."

He didn't take the bait, but the corner of his mouth creased into a smile, letting her know he appreciated the attempt. Had they not been in a life-threatening situation, he'd likely have reciprocated with a witty remark. Instead, he turned toward the crystal with his keshal at the ready.

"I have no quarrel with you, mage killer," repeated the voice.

"But I have quarrel with you."

Laughter echoed through the chamber, and the lumisphere trembled in the waves of magic that followed the sound. "Your people were always brave, but in the end, Suzhaul picks no weaklings."

Kamira and Veelk exchanged surprised glances, since the name was not common knowledge, at least in their world. Kamira stiffened. The truth she'd been refusing to consider forced its way back into her thoughts. It wasn't a human they were dealing with. And if a demon indeed resided within the crystal, it meant the tales of the past weren't as accurate as the high mages claimed them to be.

Curling her hands into fists before they trembled too much, she said, "You're Veranesh." Of course, it could have been another demon, but it seemed much too coincidental.

Another burst of laughter sent ripples through the waves of magic washing over the chamber. "So mages told stories? Delightful. What were they? Tell me."

Kamira pressed her lips into a tight line. The odds of

surviving disappeared like water in the desert sun, but she couldn't give up, not yet.

"Kam?" Veelk prodded her.

"He's the one who destroyed these Towers and all the lands around them. A cautionary tale for those who dare to choose the arcanist path." She tried to control her voice, but fear tainted her words. "The purest of evil, the most malicious of the kind... You know how it goes."

"They left out some details, but didn't exaggerate much." An arc of blue lightning flashed within the crystal as Veranesh spoke, and revealed a dark silhouette of a massive body with blurred shapes of wings and claws.

"They did forget to mention you're still here," Kamira replied, but her gaze darted to Veelk.

He gave a slight nod, and as soon as the demon spoke, he began moving slowly through the chamber.

"That's indeed something they wouldn't like to reveal," Veranesh said. "I'd guess their so-called victory over me was too big of an event to admit the truth. So what happened? They pronounced themselves saviors?"

If anyone asked Kamira, talking to demons was like willingly walking into an assassin's blade. She might have made a pact with one, but both she and her demon were happy enough to reap the benefits of the pact without engaging in too many conversations. Yet this time it meant keeping Veranesh distracted. She'd rather not risk he'd be able to breach her lousy circle.

"Something like that," she replied. "Hunted down a few surviving arcanists, chastised others, and spread the demon hate. Come to think of it, they might have been right, at least in the last part, don't you agree?"

"From their perspective, most definitely," Veranesh said. "But that's a long discussion, and meanwhile you could try something... unwise. I wouldn't bother with a mage, but a pactee is a different matter. I shall make you an offer, but if you try to leave this chamber, you'll die. And with you—a large part of this land."

She swallowed at the thought of the Cataclysm that destroyed the continent centuries ago. She had to keep him talking and ease his suspicions, so agreeing to anything was out of the question. "You're bluffing."

"Am I now? I had four hundred human years to devise this spell, and it's the key to my freedom."

Veelk had stopped and was standing midway between Kamira and what they hoped was a way out, relaxed but ready. All Kamira had to do was get to the exit while Veelk kept the demon's attention, but Veranesh's suspicion made such a simple task seem impossible.

"It's hard to believe in your generous nature," she said. "You must have a reason to keep me in here, and it's not the caring for my life, so cut the game."

Veranesh spoke, but she didn't listen. At his first word, she sprang to her feet, and even though her instincts screamed against the dissolution of the circle, she gave up her protection and dashed toward the exit. At the same time, Veelk mocked an attack at the crystal.

"What a pity," Veranesh said.

Before Kamira realized the shift in magic, her lumisphere dispersed, drowning the chamber in darkness, and she collapsed to the ground, shrieking. This time the attack felt different. The physical pain mixed with the sudden emptiness within her, and even though the torture took away her focus, it couldn't conceal the hollow space in her mind... the space where her magic and pact used to be.

Veelk abandoned the pretense of the attack and made it

back to her. He dropped to his knees and curled around her, yet she kept shivering and moaning.

"I admire the perseverance and will to fight, but it's time you stopped, pactee. My offer only lasts as long as my patience." The darkness lit up with the blue glow of the crystal. Within it, the dark silhouette brightened, illuminating a humanoid figure with birdlike features: a long, pointy nose, clawed fingers, and furled wings.

"Let Kamira live," Veelk said with a trembling voice.

"Very well."

Kamira sighed with relief when the pain faded, but the feeling of emptiness persisted. Whatever Veranesh did to her, it affected her pact.

"You couldn't have shielded her, mage killer," the demon said in an almost comforting tone. "The spell was already on her. I'm merely executing it."

Veelk narrowed his eyes. "How did you know?"

"Suzhaul used to discuss his ideas with me, and I made some suggestions. Glad to see he put them to good use." Sarcasm rang in the demon's voice.

Kamira sighed and sat up. Despite Veranesh's claim, Veelk still held his arm around her. "He broke it," she whispered. "He broke my pact." It couldn't have been possible. Only the demon and the arcanist who made the pact could break it.

"I thought that would get your attention." Veranesh must have heard her. "Are you ready to listen?"

Her expression hardened as she squeezed Veelk's muscular arm and replied, "Fine, demon. Let's hear your lies."

"Very wise. The spell I put on you will release upon your death. It'll sow destruction across the land and free me from this place. But since you're a pactee, I'll give you a choice.

You can die here and now, and maybe spare some lives, or you can leave, live your life freely... and die somewhere else, some other time, in a place possibly more crowded than here. I'm patient enough to wait a bit longer from my freedom."

Kamira huffed. "That's not much of a choice, even if you actually promised me my whole lifetime."

Veelk had an unspoken question in his eyes, and she shrugged in reply. She'd called the demon's bluff once and paid for it. It wasn't wise to risk it again.

The demon laughed. "I see you've dealt with my kind before. I suppose I could offer you another way."

She saw that coming. If he didn't want something from her, she would be dead already. "I'm all ears."

"I'll let you live, and you find a way to free me."

"Out of the question." She never believed the Cataclysm was the fault of the arcanists of old, and to help Veranesh would mean betraying their sacrifice.

Veelk replied at the same time, "Agreed."

She sent the mage killer an angry glare, but his expression made it clear that arguments were pointless.

"Garivan," Veelk said. "Go by the rule."

If she had her magic, she wouldn't resist the urge to burn his eyes out... even if it wasn't exactly possible with the scars protecting him. Of course, she couldn't claim she didn't remember Garivan, because the memory of the betrayal they'd suffered remained as clear as ever. Yet it didn't mean Veelk had the right to call upon the promise they'd made back then in such circumstances. "No heroics, survival first" had no place in a confrontation with a powerful demon.

"How about you do me a favor, mage killer, and find a few small creatures," Veranesh said before she could present her arguments to Veelk. "They'll be useful, should we come to an agreement. And while she isn't distracted by your presence, I'll discuss the details with the pactee."

Veelk tensed. "I'm not leaving unless you guarantee her life."

Veranesh looked down at him, his sharp features hardening. "You're becoming tiresome, mage killer. Had I no respect for Suzhaul and arcanists of old, I'd no longer bother with either of you. Comply or watch her die."

Kamira shivered. The sudden shift in the demon's mood brought back the fear. "Veelk, just take supplies and go." They couldn't win this game. With her magic gone, she could do as much as throw obscenities at the demon. The unpleasant memory of her pact being severed overwhelmed her, and she forced herself to focus on the problem. Veelk was right: survival first, even if in the end it meant she had to pretend to make a deal.

Veelk smiled as if he knew to what conclusion she arrived, and after giving the demon a short nod, he left the chamber.

"So, how come you became a pactee?" Veranesh asked. "My spell wouldn't have worked on you if you didn't have traces of what they call high magic, but you didn't use it to fight me."

She could ignore his question, but if they both remained silent, it wouldn't help her figure out how to alter the odds. "I studied with them for a while, but when I disagreed with one of them, they kicked me out. So I found an arcanist to teach me and a demon to make a pact. No glory, no pretty title, but enough to get by."

"Enough to get by... Do you regret?"

She shook her head as she pondered what sounded like genuine interest in the demon's voice. "The look on the face of the fourth archmage when I told him what I thought of him... It was worth it. I'd do it again," she said with confidence.

"Please, continue."

Her eyes opened wide. Demons couldn't read minds, so Veranesh must have learned it from her expression or was wise enough to understand there were no simple answers to questions about regrets like that.

This time she didn't answer in an instant, and memories swarmed her.

The thrill of making a pact. Meeting Veelk and the friendship with a mage killer that grew so unexpectedly. The satisfaction of seeing the morbid look on her father's face when he learned she'd become what common folk called a demonologist. The anger at the unjust treatment she suffered, both from the high mages and anyone who despised arcanists. The foolish hope that one day she'd make a name for herself. The feeling of freedom from the High Towers' rules. The unfulfilled ambitions. She thought about it all often, about the choices she made and consequences she had to face, and in the end she always concluded that no, she didn't regret.

"There's more," she admitted. "But it's a long story." One she wouldn't be sharing with a cunning and deceptive demon.

"And you're willing to end it here?"

She gave him a bitter glare. "Eventually everyone meets their match."

Veranesh huffed. "I didn't expect empty words like that. I won't accept them from a pactee who only moments ago was ready to fight to the end."

"I did fight to the end, but I'm not a pactee anymore. I have no magic left." She stared at him, putting forth all the effort she could muster to look like someone resigned to their fate.

"I see." In the crystal's blue light, Veranesh's smile seemed sinister. "You're hoping the sands will bury us. That it'll give the high mages enough time to find a way to defeat me."

She pressed her lips together and looked away, but to her surprise, the demon chuckled.

"It seems that we have more in common than you'd think, you and me," he continued, amused. "If you agree to help me, I'll not only give you your magic back, but also promise you get to see the high mages fall."

"Why not kill me now? Why risk it?" There had to be a reason for Veranesh to prefer her alive. If he really desired his freedom, he shouldn't have bothered with all the talk. Two human lives must be nothing in comparison to regaining his freedom after centuries in that crystal.

Veranesh offered a predatory smile. "Because I enjoy the thrill, and to see what you're going to do, what you'll learn, and what decisions you'll make... That's something I haven't experienced in a long time. And if you fail or try to turn against me, I still get my freedom."

"I didn't make my pact yesterday, demon." Kamira grimaced. "There's another reason you want me to live."

His eyes lit up, and their color resembled honey. "I want my revenge. I want to watch my enemies fall when they think nothing threatens them. I want to hit them when they least expect it. And for that, I need someone to prepare everything and free me in the right way... and at the right time." He smiled and stared at Kamira. "The chance of bringing high mages to their end... It's worth the risk, don't you think?"

"It is." She wasn't lying. Survival aside, the prospect of

bringing the high mages down, of seeing them helpless and humiliated... The prospect of exposing their lies and corruption... It was worth the risk of agreeing to the demon's terms.

Veranesh regarded her with his eyes narrowed accompanied by the corner of his lip curling, as if he'd expected such response, as if she proved they were indeed alike. "Will you find a way to free me then?"

"I will."

2

The silence enveloped him. No sounds of battle, no buildings collapsing, and no blasts of magic disturbed it, just the quiet squeaking of wood and distant splashing. Their soothing rhythm made Ryell open his eyes, his thoughts heavy with the realization of where he was... where he shouldn't be.

The small cabin's only furniture was a table and a hammock, but he didn't expect anything more from the scabby caravel he remembered from the burning port. Not only had it escaped the siege, but it was still seaworthy, and that within itself felt like the one last blessing from the Light.

"Lie still," said a man. "Your wounds will open."

As the man entered the cabin, Ryell recognized Tyddes, one of the merchants who'd tried to reach the port during the siege. Dark circles framed his eyes, and his pale face matched his unkempt clothing and short brown hair.

"No." Ryell's response was nothing more than a whisper. "I need to go back! My orders..."

"The city had already fallen when we left." Tyddes didn't

hide his pain. "No point in dyin' on that wharf..." He regarded Ryell in silence, gratitude as clear as his tiredness. "You saved my son's life, all of our lives. We couldn't have left you there."

Ryell gave him a slow nod. He couldn't blame the merchant for doing what felt right. "Anyone else make it?"

Silence sufficed for a reply, and Ryell closed his eyes, his chest heavy. Faws, Helkus, and others... Their faces remained fresh in his memory, and their smiles concealed their weariness. The last time he saw them, they'd prepared to fight to the end together, and all of them did, except for Ryell. He should have died there too, on the crumbling walls of his homeland's capital.

More memories swarmed his thoughts like carnivorous fish. His muscles tensed as he recalled the countless battles with armies of twisted creatures and the powerful demons commanding from afar, making their servant demonologists summon even more monsters. His thoughts resembled streams of blood marking the battlefields as he reminisced on the defeats that forced retreat after retreat until nothing was left but the capital. The siege lasted months, pushing the refugees to the brink of desperation as the magical barrier that protected them weakened steadily over the weeks. With only the ocean behind them... Ryell exhaled at the memory of the capital's final days, when its white marble turned red.

"They were brave warriors," Tyddes said. "The queen will honor their sacrifice."

Two of his words felt like a slap on the cheek, and Ryell's vision blurred with rage. *The queen.* Until the last moments of the siege, he'd hoped Cahala qi'Devanshari hadn't made it from the fallen city, that she died when the palace collapsed under enemy fire. Ryell clenched his jaw so hard his teeth gritted.

"You shouldn't be so hard on yourself." Tyddes offered a compassionate glance—to Ryell's relief, misinterpreting the situation. "They'll live in your memories, and maybe one day you'll go back to our land and avenge them."

Avenge them... This suggestion brought comfort even if Ryell had something else in mind than picturing himself as the commander leading Devanshari soldiers against demons. He took a deep breath. He was meant to die with the others, and if by the Light's whim he survived, there must have been a reason. He'd get that treacherous gaharra. He'd make her pay.

Tyddes smiled as if sensing the shift in Ryell's mood. "We'll signal the queen's ship. I'm sure they have more suitable quarters for a hero like you."

"No need, my friend." Ryell stopped him with a gesture, his heart racing all of a sudden. The queen couldn't know he survived. "I'll stay here. I promised to get you to safety, and I'll see it through, even if it means sharing hardships with you."

The merchant's face changed, and only guilt rang in his voice when he replied, "I don't want to sound ungrateful, but we have very meager supplies of the Light's essence. If we were to share them with yet another person... It's already dire as it is. The queen's ship must have a bigger stock, and they'd surely spare some for a war hero."

Ryell closed his eyes, considering his choices. His body already ached with longing for the essence, but he'd spent years on the border, away from the capital and Hajihali itself. This alone should have made him more resistant to its power and to the addiction, and the rage that burnt through his body at every thought of the queen should help divert his thoughts from the physical symptoms. Of course, the need for the artifact's magic ran deep in his people's veins, and the price for keeping his body starved for the Light would likely be high, but well worth paying if he could hide away from the queen's eyes.

"I'd like to stay here." He chose his words with caution. "I can do without the essence; we were trained for it. I don't want to be treated like a hero when so many of my comrades have fallen. I'd rather see to your safe passage and make sure their sacrifice wasn't in vain."

Tyddes's face softened. "I'm sure we can arrange that. I'll let the royal ship know, so they can spare some of their supplies—"

"Don't tell them I'm here." Ryell sat up, despite his body rebelling against the sudden movement and screaming the extent of his wounds. "They mustn't know." He leaned forward, ignoring his chest's pain. With Tyddes so insistent, he had no choice but share at least a portion of his knowledge. "Can you keep a secret?"

The merchant gave him a startled gaze and nodded with hesitation, as if hoping he could have denied Ryell.

Ryell lowered his voice. "I think there's a traitor in the queen's entourage. Someone who helped the enemy and might be threatening our lady's life."

"A traitor!" Tyddes covered his mouth, and his eyes widened. "This needs to be reported."

"In due time. Acting too soon would alert the traitor."

Tyddes shifted uneasily. "But I... I don't think I'm..."

Ryell shook his head. "I don't expect anything from you, my friend, but you're the only one I can trust. If the traitor learns I'm alive, something might happen before I can present the evidence. You know yourself how things can be." The moment he spoke, he knew he'd struck the right chord.

Even if Tyddes tried to remain an honest merchant and a man of his word, he must have witnessed underhanded dealings and dirty politics. He must have known what happened to all the inconvenient witnesses, unruly protesters, and political opposition. Mentioning that the traitor was close to the queen implied there was enough power and influence at play to threaten Ryell.

"I understand. I'll tell others you're wounded and mourning, and you wish to be alone. They should understand."

Ryell hid his relief. One wrong word, and his hopes for revenge could have been crushed. "Thank you, my friend. I'll be forever in your debt." It served his plan well that Tyddes preferred to avoid details. It seemed better if the poor man had no idea how deep the treachery ran.

"A man who risked his life to save my only child needn't speak of debts. It's the least I can do." Tyddes headed for the door. "Rest now, please. Your wounds need to heal."

All Ryell could muster was an absent-minded nod as the merchant left. He hardly remembered anything from the pier, only the sight of his sword and the wave of demonlings rushing toward him. The sailors on the caravel threw burning oil jugs in vain attempts to keep the monsters away, and the thick smoke concealed the port, forcing Ryell to focus on the creatures before him. Even if the images of the fight remained blurry, the pain of his flesh ripped by claws remained vivid. He stood on that pier alone, so how did he end up on board? The merchants must have gone back for him after he collapsed, and he swallowed heavily at the thought that some might have died while trying to keep him out of death's clutches. He couldn't bring them back to life, but he could bring the traitor to justice, even if it meant he'd have to make a stand against the queen herself.

≈

PRINCE ALLYV SAT in the corner, putting all his effort into pretending he was reading the book of Devanshari history rather than paying attention to what was going on in the cabin. The poor chamberlain didn't need any more humiliation presenting his plea to what seemed like two of the most hardhearted people in the whole ragtag fleet. Allyv cringed at the thought that one of them was the mother he used to admire.

Cahala qi'Devanshari yawned and stretched on a pile of cushions. Her eyes skimmed past the three men in her presence, her face frozen in an expression of utter disinterest, and in that moment she resembled a spoiled child, not the queen of a once powerful nation.

"You bore us with details, chamberlain," she said in a low, deep voice. "We will not spare any essence for other ships. They need to survive on what they took with them. Bother us no more with it."

She waved her hand at the chamberlain, and the jewels of her ring matched the red of the chamberlain's face. The elderly man bowed and left without a word, clearly dissatisfied, and Allyv couldn't blame him. Even on a ship away from the ruined city and surrounded by no more than a handful of her subjects, Cahala still insisted on maintaining all the privileges and pleasures of the luxurious life now past. Maybe it was her way of ignoring the reality and pretending the months of suffering and loss had never happened, but Allyv found it hard to justify her behavior. Their people needed her more than ever, and she was turning a blind eye to their plight.

"He might stir unrest." Phuran approached from the queen's side as he spoke.

Allyv could never bring himself to like Phuran, no matter how much dedication to the crown that man had shown. Something in his moves reminded Allyv of a snake in the trees, slithering ever so slowly toward its victim. Before the demons attacked, gossip circled in the palace about people who displeased Cahala and then suffered mysterious accidents. Phuran's name often accompanied those whispers along with words of caution, but no one of the court dared to speak their suspicions aloud, and Allyv never found anything to confirm his concerns.

"He'll do what he's told," Cahala replied. "At least for the duration of the travel. As much as he tries to pose as strong, he needs the essence no less than anyone else. He won't risk cutting off his own supplies. Once we reach the other continent, he might look for some other solutions... But won't we all?"

Phuran bowed. "Some solutions might prove riskier than others, and an aging body might not take them well."

"That would be a terrible loss to our people," Cahala cautioned him with the wave of her finger. "We're not only the elite now; we're all that's left of the Devanshari nation. We need to preserve whatever we can of our heritage until we can retake our lands or settle somewhere else."

"Indeed, my queen." Phuran bowed again. "This is a crucial time, and no divide should come from one man's hurt feelings."

Cahala smiled. "That is true. Should such need come, we will ensure that our people stay united and strong, and you will be the executioner of our decisions."

"I live for the Light's grace," Phuran replied.

Allyv resisted grimacing. He would be surprised if that man had ever seen the true Light or followed any of the honorable and righteous principles that were the foundation of the Devanshari.

Phuran left the cabin, and the dark, simple robes concealed both his body and his weapons. One of the man's arms looked stiff, but Allyv knew better than to fall for such a deception. He'd seen Phuran in a fight one night when the assassins came, and the queen's adviser proved much less a cripple than he pretended to be. Allyv swallowed at the thought that both he and his mother owed this man their lives. It seemed ungrateful to harbor loathing instead of gratitude, but one good deed could hardly be enough to erase all other, less scrupulous deeds.

"This man does nothing but search for excuses to kill people, mother," Allyv said, breaking the silence.

"He's burdened with our safety. And he serves us well."

He should have known Cahala wouldn't listen, but the months of siege and days of sea travel brought him to the edge. "He's turning your people against you!" His voice rose with ire. "If this continues, there won't be anything left of Devanshari before we reach Tyorane. And who knows what challenges await us on that savage continent?"

Cahala rose from her cushions and stared into his eyes. "There's nothing left of the Devanshari already," she said. "Look around you! A lousy fleet of ships full of merchants scared for their lives and a few of the court members who were smart enough to leave on time."

Or rather, who had enough money to pay for the passage while others couldn't, Allyv didn't dare say aloud. His mother was as fierce in her anger as she was beautiful in her grace.

"But you gave them hope! You promised we'd go to Gildya to build a new Hajihali! And with it, we'll build our new home." Allyv's own voice sounded weak to him, as if he wasn't a young man ready to face the responsibilities, but a complaining child.

"And go to Gildya we will." Cahala's expression softened. She touched his face, and a warm hue changed the icy blue of her eyes. "But first, we need to ensure our survival. With your father gone, you're our people's future. We want that future to be strong and confident, not starved from lack of the essence because we supported some lowlife merchants."

Allyv wanted to break away from her hand, to shout his disobedience, but all he could muster was "I understand," because he understood that if he were to do nothing for his people, there would be no future for Devanshari, no future for him. Just a king with no land and no people. His mother, so wrapped up in her own pleasure and survival, had forgotten that ruling meant more.

Cahala nodded, and Allyv turned away, unable to endure her smug, satisfied smile. While she lay back on the cushions, sipping wine and playing with her necklace, he stood up.

"I'll go for some air and leave you to your thoughts, Mother." He needed to get away from her poisonous words before he lost the last crumbs of hope he'd clung to since the fall of the capital.

"Go." She barely paid any attention to him.

Allyv left and made his way to the upper deck, forcing uneasy smiles whenever a member of the crew or servant walked by, all concerned and searching for reassurances. Outside, salty wind filled his lungs with the odor of fish and seaweed. Was that what sailors' freedom smelled like? Their weathered faces and tanned skin mislead him at first, but they were also of the Devanshari people. Yet they seemed to do without the essence. If they could survive away from the Light's power, maybe there was a way to cure his people of their affliction. Maybe there was no need to build a new Hajihali and once more bind Devanshari to an artifact that lured the demons toward their lands.

The memory of Hajihali's warming light and its gentle magic seeping through his homelands, protecting the Devanshari and bringing health and prosperity, filled Allyv with longing. His stomach clenched in the familiar craving, because even the essence, the liquid-like concentrate of Hajihali's light, couldn't substitute the feeling of the artifact's ambient power. Rebuilding Hajihali seemed the most logical solution... but it felt like repeating the very mistakes that brought misery and destruction upon the Devanshari. If he wanted his nation to truly be free, he needed to take another path, a more difficult one.

"We need to find the cure," he whispered. The wind carried his words away the moment they slipped from his lips, as if sealing a promise, and Allyv finally realized his purpose.

MYRKAN INHALED DEEPLY, and the odor of burnt flesh filled his nose. He relished the moment, and his claws flexed at the memories of ripping humans apart and destroying their pitiful city.

Asayalari, the lowest among the yalari, scoured the ruins and ensured the city's complete destruction. The white marble of the rich residences lay crumbled and smoldering, their gilded ornaments shattered as a reminder to those who thought of opposing Myrkan's kin. Further away from the palace, where the poor once lived, charred stumps marked the remains of their wooden houses.

Every now and then, screams rose from the distance as

the asayalari got their claws on a living victim, but otherwise the fallen city remained quiet. Myrkan smirked at that: the capital of Devanshari finally belonged to yalari. Yet the war itself was enjoyable. Humans bled their last drops of blood in vain attempts to push away the ones they called demons, but they didn't pose a real threat. The worst part was the wait to wear their magic barrier down and push them deeper and deeper into their land until only one city remained. After that, when they had nowhere to run and their protection waned, yalari made quick work of them. Myrkan's tongue moved when he recalled the metallic taste in his mouth, when his sharp teeth dug deep into his victims. He might be a kanyalari—the highest among the yalari, cunning and calculating—but his instincts still demanded the thrill of the hunt.

The familiar sound of claws biting into the stone alerted him of another yalari's approach, but to turn would show weakness. Instead, he threw a question: "The artifact?"

"It's done." Fyertash crested the rubble and balanced with ease on the uneven surface. "The pactees accompanied by asayalari squads are now seeking out libraries and temples to destroy any records of it."

From a distance, Fyertash could have been taken for Myrkan's twin with his long face and hooked nose, but no yalari would consider another to be a brother, and Myrkan had no doubt the covenant between him and the handful of other yalari was coming to an end. They were all determined to see the artifact destroyed, but with it gone, each would focus on their own interests and wouldn't hesitate to go against former allies if needed.

"They may have taken some," Myrkan said.

"I doubt they burdened themselves with writings when

they ran for their lives." Fyertash glanced at him with little concern. "Couldn't your spy...?"

Myrkan huffed and shook his head. "She's out of my reach now." He rubbed his chin. "We need eyes across the waters."

"That's something we'll have to discuss with others." Yet Fyertash didn't move from his spot.

Myrkan tensed as his instincts sharpened in anticipation of assault, even if his voice of reason suggested that Fyertash would not attack openly. The cunning yalari had barely enough power to be considered equal to Myrkan, let alone other kanyalari, so he'd likely use deception and subterfuge instead, maybe pitting Myrkan against another of their kin. Yet a preemptive strike would reveal Myrkan's weakness.

Before he could decide on the best reaction, a sudden pain twisted his stomach.

With his vision blurred, he frantically searched for the assassin even if his chances for survival became slim. Fyertash must have been acting as a distraction, allowing the real assassin to sneak up from behind Myrkan... but Fyertash clutched his guts in pain as well.

The sensation passed, and Myrkan regained his composure first. "Looks like we aren't done here after all." He inhaled the breeze coming from the ruined port, and the faint scent of magic confirmed his suspicions and—though he wouldn't admit it openly—brought concerns. Two hundred years by yalari count, twice as much by human, passed without incident, so what changed?

Fyertash huffed as he regained his poise and then grimaced, looking at the sea, undoubtedly concerned with similar thoughts. "If we're to launch another invasion, we'll need to prepare, replenish the ranks of asayalari, and find new pactees... then find a way for them to cross the water."

"It's just a disruption or a failed attempt, so we have time. And if it's a trap, all the more we shouldn't rush." Myrkan rubbed his chin. "I think we have to remind our human allies of the agreement made centuries ago, and find out why they failed on their end."

"I'd suggest sending Uganel. He's good in human games and illusion, so he'll gather information without giving away too much." Fyertash flashed a cunning smile. "It would also help to maintain... the cooperative mood among those remaining here."

Myrkan gave him a restrained smile. Uganel was last one to join their covenant. He skimped on resources and constantly antagonized everyone, going as far as questioning Myrkan's leadership that others had reluctantly accepted. Sending Uganel overseas would limit his influence and indeed would help maintain control. Such suggestion also revealed the depth of Fyertash's insight, and Myrkan searched his face for hidden intents, but the other yalari revealed nothing except anticipation and excitement. Fyertash could have been looking for a closer alliance, since, with his meager power, hardly anyone respected his insights, and listening to him seemed like a better choice than turning him down, at least for the time being.

Later on, when all was done and their covenant became obsolete, Myrkan would consider destroying Fyertash, not for concern of his meager power, but for his adept ability to play others thus threatening to turn traitor or rival.

After all, no yalari ever had a brother.

3

When Veelk re-entered the chamber, Kamira was backing away from the demon. He stopped in the entrance, hoping to gauge the threat, but she seemed unharmed, and no malicious magic lingered in the air.

"You're insane! I'm not going to do it!" Kamira's shouts matched the horror on her face. "This is not what we agreed on!"

"I promised you your magic back." Veranesh's calm voice suggested no immediate danger. "How can I keep my part of the agreement if you're refusing it?" The light still emanated from the crystal, drowning the chamber in a cold blue.

"This isn't my magic! I want my pact back! I want my demon back!" Even though Kamira spoke with force, Veelk caught the panicky undertones in her words.

"That's impossible." Veranesh's calm voice, on the other hand, suggested he either didn't notice or didn't care about her reaction. "You'll have a new pact."

Holding in a smirk, Veelk entered the chamber. "Negotiations going well, I take it?"

Kamira's bewildered gaze sought his eyes. "He wants to

make a pact with me, and I keep telling him it's impossible."
She glanced at the demon, not bothering to hide her
contempt. "His idea of an agreement is to kill me."

"I've never seen a ritual that would cause a pactee's
death." Veranesh's mockery echoed within the walls.
"Unless they did something foolish, like slicing their veins
open."

She let out a groan, then took a deep breath. "You're too
powerful for me. If we make a pact, I'll die the first time I
cast a spell. I need... someone with less power."

Even though frustration still emanated from her, Veelk
gave a nod to her somewhat composed explanation. It
seemed that no matter her feelings toward the demon, she
was willing to make things work, and that meant they'd
both stay alive for a little longer. Unless, of course, either she
or Veranesh lost their patience, and Veelk wasn't sure the
demon would be the first one to give up. When it came to
dealing with stubborn people—and demons—his
companion rarely exercised her otherwise praiseworthy
discipline.

Veranesh's laughter filled the chamber, and Kamira gave
him a nasty look, the one Veelk knew she reserved for the
people she really wanted dead. Many of them, in fact, were
those stubborn ones who refused the reason.

"If you prefer a more promising arcanist, I can always try
to find you one," she grumbled.

"I think you have enough promise within you. I wouldn't
waste my time otherwise." Amusement still lingered in
Veranesh's words.

Kamira huffed. "You don't understand. I had a pact with
a minor demon."

"Have you ever tried to summon a more powerful one?"

"I was told that no powerful demon would make a pact

with me." She looked away, and Veelk had no doubt it wasn't easy to admit, especially for someone who'd turned down all the prestige and true power and was left with scraps of magic from a mediocre pact.

Veranesh's lips stretched into a grin, making his expression almost amiable. "Told by your own yalari, I presume?"

Silence followed as Kamira stared at the demon, dumbfounded. Then she cursed, and Veelk smirked at her creative use of the arcane language to express her anger.

"That lying, treacherous... Of course she'd tell me that. I'm such a fool."

Veelk refrained from a comment, and Veranesh seemed to have enough sensibleness to remain silent as well, so Kamira muttered to herself for a while, and the aggravated tone of her voice left no doubt about what she wished for her former pact demon.

"You'll have to get used to such power, but until you do, I'll make sure you don't draw too much and kill yourself by chance," the demon said when Kamira's bickering hushed. "Any kanyalari can do that. Only the minor yalari can't control how much you draw."

She nodded but kept eying the demon with suspicion. "You could be deceiving me as well, since you're of the same kind. But I'll make a pact with you."

Veranesh arched his eyebrow. "Now that's quite trusting. I expected more arguments."

"If you wanted me dead, you wouldn't have to trick me in the pact, and I need my magic back, or I'll be useless." Kamira shrugged.

Veelk smirked at that. They both suspected Veranesh was lying to them, but magic was only magic, no matter which demon granted it. And with it at her disposal, they could find a way to thwart Veranesh's plans, whatever they were.

Kamira fished out a piece of chalk from her bag and found a rubble-free spot on the floor. In the blue light, she drew symbol after symbol.

Veelk took that time to approach Veranesh. "I've found the creatures you asked for. Two nightflies and a lizard, stunned but alive."

"Leave them by my prison, mage killer. I'll do the rest."

Veelk didn't ask any questions as he set them down. The sooner they were done, the sooner they could get away from the wretched being.

Kamira seemed preoccupied with her task, and he had to admit that with all her loathing comments toward demons, she respected the old ways, the ways of arcanists: her circle was perfect, with each line carefully drawn and each symbol in the right place, and all of it done in a half-ruined chamber filled with rubble, dirt, and barely enough light. Such dedication and precision would've seen great achievements had she stayed in the High Towers, and Veelk smiled at the thought. Had she not shunned the high magic and became an arcanist, she would have never saved his life. Instead, he might have taken hers.

But there she was, an arcanist, and a bloody good one. On that, Veelk and the demon agreed.

Kamira finished the drawing, and when she started the incantation, the magic condensed in the chamber and tingled Veelk's skin. Deep in the scars left by his tribe's ritual, another demon's power stirred, ready to protect him from harm, but no attack came. Instead, Veelk watched a display of magic, light, and gestures while Kamira performed the demon summoning. The trapped demon observed her efforts with a hint of a smile—a benevolent benefactor rather than a creature of pure evil.

What game are you playing? Veelk had no interest in demons and their dealings, except for the one who protected his tribe, but years of traveling with Kamira made him suspicious of those otherworldly beings no less that she was. Besides, Veranesh somehow knew of Suzhaul and his secrets, and that posed questions Veelk needed answering. But first, they had to make it out of the ruins alive.

"I accept the pact," Veranesh said when Kamira finished.

The light dimmed and the magic died out when a single blue ray struck Kamira's body, connecting her for a heartbeat to the trapped demon.

"My gifts for you are ready. Come and collect." Veranesh barely moved within the crystal, but his claw indicated an object on the floor. "There should be some crystal pieces broken off around my prison. Take them as well. They're as good as strong imbued stones."

Kamira didn't move from her spot, inspecting her own hands as if they'd become strange beings, and with visible hesitation summoned a lumisphere. The gasp she let out told Veelk the new pact made all the difference in the power at her disposal.

Veelk circled the crystal, picking up its chips from the ground. When he found the nightflies and the lizard, his eyebrows arched, and he waved at Kamira to have a look at their crystalline bodies.

She gave the creatures one glance and turned her wide eyes toward Veranesh. "Those things outside... It was you."

"I rarely get visitors, so I wanted to make sure you came by," Veranesh replied. "Unfortunately, they're too unstable to be of more use. The small ones will last, though." As the demon spoke, the nightflies' long bodies curled into wristbands. The lizard's head stretched to a point, while the tail straightened, and its limbs froze into the hilts of a dagger. "The lizard blade is for you, mage killer, and the bracelets are for my pactee. Go on, put them on."

A doubtful stare was the only answer Kamira gave, and Veelk expected nothing else. The demon would be lucky if she held them long enough to shove them deep into one of their backpacks, never to be seen or worn.

Veranesh sighed. "You're the most stubborn human I've ever met."

The nightflies fluttered their crystal wings, tearing away from Veelk's hands, and flew to Kamira. She lifted her forearms in an instinctive defense, as lousy as the rest of her fighting skills, and the creatures' long bodies wrapped around her wrists, becoming bracelets. Veelk inspected them with his eyes narrowed, but from afar they emanated no magic, and had it come to that, he'd be able to break them off Kamira's forearms.

"Only you can awaken them again," Veranesh said. "They can be your weapons or spies. Or you can talk to me through them should you decide my knowledge is worth your trust."

Kamira inspected the jewelry with a grimace. Veelk would be surprised if she ever decided to use them, maybe except to get them off her... and for that she'd likely ask for help of his muscles rather than give the demon the satisfaction of awakening the creatures.

"Your dagger is simple, mage killer," Veranesh continued, "but I think you'll find it useful. The blade can't be stopped by any high magic, and will cut even through a mage's barrier if needed."

Veelk arched his eyebrow at such a bold claim but secured the weapon to his belt. "I appreciate the gift."

Kamira got back to her feet, giving the nightflies a last contemptuous glare, as if they were shackles. "So, where do I start?"

Veelk turned his head away from the crystal to hide his smile. Kamira must already have an idea what to do next, but apparently she wasn't beyond fishing for knowledge, even if she distrusted Veranesh.

"You will have to discover how my trap was devised and understand its working," the demon replied. "While you search for answers, be sure to use the magic you have now. I'm certain you'll have to become more skillful than you are now if you want to survive setting me free." He offered a crooked smile. "And it goes without saying that you should tell no one of your new pact or of me."

Veelk exchanged glances with Kamira. "We'll have to kill that mage," he murmured.

"A mage?" Veranesh asked.

The downward arc of Kamira's lips made it clear what she thought of his questions, but she replied, "He sent us here to find a book of old masters. I wouldn't be surprised he knew about you."

"It's likely," Veranesh agreed. "It might be worth finding that book."

"We'll look for it on our way out," Veelk replied in a rush. The sooner they left, the fewer chances the demon would change his mind.

"Very well." Veranesh offered a sardonic smile as if Veelk's urgency didn't escape him. "Don't let my pactee die. I still have that spell on her." His eyes glowed when they focused on Kamira. "Good luck, pactee. Succeed, and I'll keep my word. You'll have all my magic at your disposal for as long as you live, and you get to call yourself the savior of this land."

His chuckle echoed within the chamber, and Veelk shared the demon's amusement. If they kept their part of the deal, Kamira would likely be known as the evil arcanist who brought Veranesh back, not as the savior. But Veranesh himself must have also known that they'd do anything in their power to thwart his plans, and ultimately keep him where he was, within the crystal prison.

Veelk waited for Kamira to join him at the exit from the chamber, and together they entered a half-collapsed corridor. The lumisphere glowed over Kamira's shoulder as if nothing had happened, though the silence of unspoken thoughts haunted their passage.

Veelk broke it first after they put some distance between them and Veranesh. "Don't you think he was a bit too friendly for the pure evil he's said to be?"

"Demons are deceitful," she replied in her habitual tone. "But I think there's more to it. I find it hard to believe Yoreus had no idea about the demon, but all the stories say that Veranesh was destroyed, not trapped."

"High mages not willing to admit their failure?" After what they'd been through, such a lousy attempt at humor could hardly be enough, but he preferred Kamira irked than somber.

"Or making sure no one searches for him." Of course, she ignored the jab at her former colleagues. "Madmen, worshipers, power-thirsty arcanists... I can even imagine Gildya wanting to free the demon just to make high mages' lives a bit harder." She slowed down, choosing her steps carefully in the rubble. "One thing he got right: we'll need to know more if we're to play the game, like what happened, how and why he was trapped, and what his real reason is for keeping me alive."

"And how he knew of Suzhaul," Veelk added.

She threw him an inquisitive glance. "Afraid your tribe's secret isn't safe?"

Veelk shook his head. "It's as safe as it's always been. But knowing how he learned about Suzhaul might tell us of his true nature or which other demons are involved."

Kamira gave him an amused huff. "That's quite a bold statement, even for a tribesman on good terms with a powerful demon, probably the only good one out there."

"Mage killers are not chosen for their temperance and humility." Veelk threw her a playful sneer. He could suffer a bit of her teasing if it shifted her mood.

"Of that I'm sure. If pride could glow, I wouldn't need a lumisphere with you around," she said with an innocent expression. The corridor opened into another, wider and still intact. The lumisphere's light revealed broken mosaics on the floors and reliefs on the wall. "Come, let's find that book and anything worth selling before we find an exit."

Her words made it clear she'd rather spend time roaming the underground ruins in search for a way around than go through Veranesh's chamber again, and he wouldn't argue about it. As all of his tribesmen, he didn't believe in gods, especially the gods of luck, so he didn't fancy stretching the demon's patience either. At least he could hope that since Veranesh had gotten what he wanted, he wouldn't send his crystal monsters after them, and they likely were the only threat in the tunnels. Demons rarely shared their power and territory, even if it was to be with hyenas or snakes.

A gust of magical breeze teased Veelk's senses, filled with the same distorted magic he'd felt before. When he focused on Kamira, he sensed the same pure energy she'd had before, when her pact was with some insignificant demoness, and he narrowed his eyes, but he couldn't be certain whether it was her channeling that cleansed the magic she received, or whether that unpleasant distortion had its source somewhere other than Veranesh.

"Something wrong?" Kamira asked.

"No," he replied. The time for questions would be later, a safe distance from the demon and when they both could allow such distractions. "Lead the way." The sooner they found the book and were out of the ruins, the better.

THE TALL WALLS of Kaighal rose in the distance days before Kamira and Veelk got close to the city. The desert shifted into meager shrubbery, but the heat remained merciless, and she couldn't wait to get into the shade of the buildings, even if it also meant remaining in the shadow of High Towers. She cringed at the mere thought of the mages' pride, but in the end, Kaighal was her home more than her family's lands ever were, and if she wanted to forget about the building on top of the hill, overlooking the city, she could always get lost in its many narrow streets.

"You know... you could finally do something about that eyesore." Veelk must have caught what she was looking at.

She smirked. Fueled by her new pact, magic coursed through her body, ready to be channeled at her will, and over the weeks it had taken them to travel back from the ruined Towers, she'd grown used to her new limits... or rather the lack of them. Veranesh kept his promise, and he didn't allow her to drown in power she wouldn't be able to control, but beyond that, he didn't restrict her, and for the first time in forever, she'd been enjoying her daily magic practice routines.

Back on that first day, when they'd finally crawled out

from the tunnel, having found both the book they were searching for and a way around Veranesh's chamber, she didn't channel magic at all. She still recalled staring down the black hole, with the new pact demanding she made use of it, but instead she walked away. As much satisfaction as she'd have had using Veranesh's own magic to collapse the whole flerra of the desert upon him, such an act of defiance would gain her nothing. If disposing of the demon was that easy, high mages would have gotten rid of him centuries ago, and if she wanted her chance at double-crossing him, she couldn't indulge in petty desires for a payback that would give her intentions away.

But the High Towers were another matter. She doubted Veranesh cared what happened to the mages, so she allowed herself a moment to enjoy the image of crushing what they considered the symbol of their power.

"Tempting," she murmured. "Though I doubt one demon's power would be enough for eight archmages, let alone other teachers and pupils."

Veelk grinned at that. "You could just stand there and make the right impression while I dispose of them."

She rewarded him with a chuckle, and only then shook her head. Even if magic attacks didn't bother Veelk, there were other ways to kill, and desperate mages could try all of them while he attempted to cut through their ranks. And after he had insisted on survival, after she had made a pact with a powerful demon and agreed to do his bidding, throwing it all away for the fleeting feeling of satisfaction was nothing but foolish. Not to mention that if the archmages managed to take her down, and Veranesh told the truth about that destruction spell, her death would wipe out the city... wipe out her home.

"This is not how one would go about survival," she

replied. "And I don't think this is what he meant when he promised me revenge."

He shrugged in response, as if he hadn't expected her to agree in the first place. "We need to get rid of Yoreus anyway."

Kamira gave a nod to that. "But the way we planned." Three weeks of traveling back to Kaighal gave them enough time to plot a quiet murder, and after leafing through the book Yoreus desired so much, she wouldn't mind asking the mage a few questions beforehand. Her fingers brushed the bag slung across her body as she once more sought reasons someone like Yoreus would want to find Gayabal the Magnificent's journal... No doubt, Gayabal was one of the first high mages, the founder of their school, and the author of the theory of high magic. Yet all those things were deeds of the past, and she doubted Yoreus needed to go back to basics of the very art that elevated him above others.

Even if having such a book was a matter of prestige or superiority over his peers, Kamira couldn't help wondering why he wanted it so bad to risk the high mages' secret getting out. Unless, of course, he was planning to make sure she never spoke a word of it. She sneered. If Yoreus intended to get rid of her, he was in for a nasty surprise.

Her thoughts circled the journal again. Back in his day, Gayabal was looking for a way to make high magic something more than a desperate attempt to gain any power. She still remembered the boring classes in the High Towers on how long hours of preparation would allow one to reach through the veil separating the worlds and pull the magic out without a demon intermediary, and she could imagine Gayabal's frustration as he continued his studies. According to gossip, Gayabal's zealous approach to research was a result of a demon rejecting him a pact, but in the end, he succeeded in making high magic superior to its arcane predecessor. And with Yoreus's interest in the old mage's journal, Kamira couldn't shake the feeling that Gayabal's findings had to be connected to Veranesh's imprisoning.

"Having second thoughts?" Veelk asked.

Abandoning her contemplations, she shook her head. She would have lied if she claimed to have never taken someone's life, but it was always when she was defending herself or others, and once... once out of revenge. To assassinate a man who wasn't an immediate threat didn't sit well with her, and she filled the days of their journey arguing back and forth for Yoreus's death. But in the end, if she wanted to ensure no one knew she'd met Veranesh, the archmage had to die, and even if Veelk did the killing, the blood would stain her hands as well.

She still had a choice. She could turn back and deep in the desert allow Veranesh to kill her.

If she chose to live and to play the demon's game, Yoreus could be the first of many. At the same time, maybe in the end, she could prevent Veranesh from escaping. With growing frustration, Kamira chased those thoughts away. Doubts had already consumed too much of her time, taking her focus away from plans and plots. She'd do what was necessary to survive, like Veelk and she always did.

They approached the city gate. The guards who lazily inspected merchants and farmers entering didn't bother them, and the large stone arch's shadow swallowed Kamira. Once it spat her out on the other side, in Kaighal, her decision would be sealed.

4

The northeastern part of Kaighal stank with sweat, fish, and rotting seaweed. Not even the sea breeze improved the air in the poorest district of the port town, and Allyv hesitated before opening windows. The asylum—a bold name given to a half-crumbling townhouse—faced the sea, but somehow the wind always brought the worst stench along, challenging even the air inside, thick with dust and urine.

Allyv claimed the top floor for his bedroom and research lab, which at rare times also served as his office, and though the air didn't smell much better, every morning the sun sneaked in through the window and tickled his eyelids, bringing hope.

Stretching on the narrow bed, he inhaled the scent of hay in the mattress, one of the many things he had trouble getting used to. He never allowed himself a moment of nostalgia in the morning, afraid of losing focus. Instead, the memories of soft beds and fine clothes, the gourmet meals' aromas, and birdsong haunted him in the darkness when he tossed in the rough sheets begging for sleep.

He washed in the basin and stared at the face in the mirror, at the pale skin and sunken eyes surrounded by darkening circles, at the dry lips and famished cheeks, and the longer he looked, the less he remembered the proud and handsome prince of Devanshari that he once was. Others forgot as well, and even though most still addressed him "Lord Allyv" or "prince," the words started losing their meaning, drowned in the hopelessness of Kaighal's slum.

"This is not a place for a young lord." Hajha walked in carrying a tray. Her plump body had shrunk in the past weeks, but she still found enough energy to climb the stairs every morning, bringing breakfast to the man she'd cared for since he'd come to the world. "You need healthy food and fresh air, not stale bread and days spent in a stuffy room. You'll get sick, my prince."

His heart softened at the sound of her caring voice, but his expression remained firm and determined when he replied, "We're all sick, Hajha. I'm trying to fix it."

She found a free spot for the tray and walked around the room collecting dirty clothes and putting away sheets of paper covered with crisp Devanshari handwriting, his handwriting, while Allyv fished in a trunk for something to wear. He had never expected independence to be so mundane and challenging at the same time. Back at home, or even in Kaighal had he stayed with his mother's entourage, servants would have seen to his outfits, and the most effort he would have to make would be choosing which one to wear. At least Hajha ensured he had clean clothes to wear, otherwise he'd be even more a mockery of qi'Devanshari bloodline than he already was.

"You should get out more often, Prince Allyv." Hajha walked to the door but threw him one last pleading glance.

"Get some fresh air. Practice your fencing. Spend some time in the company of young ladies. You can't wither like that."

"I will, Hajha, I will." His response was reflective, addressing more the tone of her voice than the actual words to which, with each day passing, Allyv paid less and less attention. As much as Hajha cared for him, she seemed to forget he didn't have time for leisure. He leaned over the table, skimming through the previous day's notes. "As soon as I find the cure."

"At least eat your breakfast, then," she said, sounding defeated, and she left.

Allyv picked at the bread on the tray, taking bites as he reviewed his research. Its taste couldn't compare to Devanshari bakeries, and the texture lacked the spongy softness, instead irritating his throat when he swallowed. His eyes tirelessly followed the lines of text, searching for an answer. There had to be a solution somewhere in his notes.

Initial tests showed promise, and the herbal substitutes eased his patients' conditions, but finding the cure was just as distant as when he started, and the half-measures made him feel like he was only swapping one addiction for another. But at least it bought them more time.

With the next bite, his stomach twisted, and Allyv dropped to his knees, heaving. His vision blurred, his limbs refused to obey, and he fought to regain control. Dragging himself up drained what little energy remained, and the fog covering his eyes left him groping for his hip flask. Papers fell as he swept them from the table until his fingers closed on the familiar shape. Hands shaking, Allyv opened it and poured two drops of the essence into a mug of water. Resisting the urge to down the mixture in one gulp, he ensured the hip flask was closed and set it carefully to the side.

Then he lifted the mug. The clear liquid's faint glow carried promise, and relief washed through his body as soon as he took the first sip. His vision cleared, and so did his thoughts. But when he stared at the water in the mug, at the two meager drops of salvation he was steadily running out of, the words he said to Hajha came back. They were all sick.

The hip flask's contents tempted him, and it took Allyv all his will to focus his eyes on something else while his thoughts still circled the precious essence. He drifted off, and before he realized, his hands reached for the flask. One more drop wouldn't make a difference, and he needed it—he needed it to figure out the cure.

"Demon's rot!" Allyv clenched his fist and pushed away from the table and elixir, stumbling backward onto another table. The glass retorts of his meager laboratory clanged with protest. His eyes remained fixed on the flask as he steadied his breath and fought for clarity. He drank the rest of his water, its bland taste a reminder he was trying to cheat the addiction, but the trace of the essence still eased his tension. Yet, at the mere thought of the essence running out, his body trembled, and Allyv pushed away the images of going back to his mother, begging her for help. Not only would enduring such humiliation be a lethal strike to his pride, but Queen Cahala would also demand his obedience. Allyv grimaced at the memory of her expression when he announced he would pursue a different path. If she'd had another child, she would have disinherited him in an instant, of that he was certain.

With a sigh, he picked up some documents listing all the plants available in Tyorane. The cure had to wait. First he needed to make a replacement drug for his people.

~

SHYOLI QI'AYTRELLA CLOSED her hand around the imbued stone. Its coarse edges scratched against her delicate skin, but her hungering body sensed the magic hidden within its small shape. As she rushed through Kaighal's streets, the sun burnt her fair skin, deepening the longing for her home's shaded walkways. The sharp breath she drew made her grasp for memories of the air in Devanshari gardens as dust filled her nostrils and irritated her throat. Nothing on that Light-forsaken continent, the place of her family's exile, could bring her joy. Nothing except...

Her hand clutched the imbued stone, and her anticipation swelled. At first, she picked up her pace, but the flash of her father's expression forced a slower stride. She better made sure he didn't know where she'd gone. That meant deception, and a lady like her wouldn't run during her stroll around the town. She almost froze at the thought that her family's friends might be around, noticing her rush and fluster. With a heavy heart, Shyoli stopped at a small square, pretending to refresh herself by the fountain. If someone had already seen her, she could always claim some commoner frightened her or brought back the memories of the siege. Shyoli shuddered as the images swarmed her, uninvited, at the mere thought of the past. With a few splashes of cool water, she chased them away, focusing on the present conundrum.

She couldn't just barge into the house, holding the stone, and she couldn't sneak into her own home, either. Any gossip, let alone her father questioning her, could ruin her plan, and she clutched the stone harder. One look at the purse was enough to abandon the idea of hiding her treasure here. Even if she guarded it, one of those pesky little thieves Kaighal seemed ridden with could still snatch it and make away with the stone. And back at home, a maid could take it... No, impossible. She chided herself for similar distrusts. All the servants had been with her family for generations, and they stayed with them after the capital fell, out of gratitude for the passage on Fento qi'Aytrella's ship. Yet they were all Devanshari like she was, so they suffered away from the Light. Hunger for magic made loyalty all that more difficult in an already dire situation, and should one of them sense the imbued stone left in the purse, they could take it. No, Shyoli almost shook her head at the thought— she needed a better place to hide her treasure.

A street trader approached her, gesturing at tacky beads and mumbling something in the dialect that in Kaighal was considered a language. Shyoli grimaced as she waved him away.

"No, thank you, I don't need anything," she said insistently.

If she tried hard enough, she could understand most of what Tyorane's inhabitants said, but their words and intonation seemed crude in comparison to the flowing Devanshari speech. Sometimes, when the crowds' chatter reached her ears, she could hardly believe this was the same language, divided only by the distance and time's passing. At least the trader didn't bother her longer, reading enough displeasure on her face to walk away.

Free of distraction, she considered the stone once more. Her boots fit perfectly, and her sleeves seemed too risky to hold something so heavy, but the corset should keep it in place. She took out a laced scarf and gently patted her skin, wiping off water, sweat, and beauty powder alike, but she managed to discreetly squeeze the stone into her cleavage. At the image of the stone rolling down her body and falling out through the wide skirts, her eyes widened, and she ensured the corset's fastening held tight.

"That'll have to do."

One last look around, but no bright skin stood among the sea of browns, coppers, and grays, reassuring her that none of Devanshari were around. As she fixed the scarf around her neck, covering the ruined makeup, Shyoli couldn't resist a glance at her hands and a bitter realization that if they stayed in Tyorane long enough, their skin would darken as well. With her thoughts grimmer, she resumed her stroll, even more unnerving in its slowness when she reminded herself of the sun's destructive power. The corset pressed the stone against her body, and the gentle flow of magic intensified her hunger, turning a simple task into an ordeal. At least she wasn't that far from home.

The residence her father had bought in Kaighal waned in comparison to what Shyoli had at her disposal in Devanshari. Just two stories and several rooms, no ballroom nor private garden, though they still fared better than many of the less fortunate noble families. She shuddered at the thought they could have been forced to live in a townhouse or even worse, and she blessed her father's resourcefulness. Back when nobody believed the capital could fall, Fento qi'Aytrella was already preparing for departure, securing much of the family wealth and heirlooms. Of course, Shyoli was too busy attending social gatherings, discussing the imminent break of the siege and the royal forces' counterattack that would see young noblemen bathe in the glory of destroying the demon army and planning the months-long celebrations that would follow. In hindsight, she could see the childishness of such dreams, but didn't give much thought to her old friends. The wise ones fled in time, and soon enough, when the queen had the artifact rebuilt, they would restore their position and wealth, so she'd meet them in one social gathering or another, like she used to. Those who were fools and joined the fight for the city likely died and therefore deserved no place in her mind. Life has been difficult enough without conjuring the atrocities of war and death the qi'Aytrella family so narrowly escaped.

The sight of her residence's gate chased away grim memories, and as she approached, a brown skinned guard opened it. He offered but a small bow, and Shyoli grimaced. The lack of due respect brought her noble blood to boil. She'd have that rude man sent away, but the urge to complain to her father waned as the stone rubbing against her skin reminded her of more pressing matters.

Her maid waited in the main hall and picked up the hat Shyoli threw on the ground.

"Let no one bother me." In the safety of her home, she could finally pick up the pace. "The sun wore me down, and I want to rest."

Her boudoir windows, open yet curtained, offered both fresh air and escape from the heat outside. Instinct demanded she close the windows and draw the thicker curtains, but common sense advised against risking any attention. With the weather so hot, she hardly ever closed them, and if her father noticed, it would make him worry. Instead, she bent over her bed, breathing in and out, and tried to loosen the corset enough for the stone to fall out, but with it sitting firm, she soon turned to pulling on her clothes and pushing her hand into her cleavage. The rest of the beauty powder ran off her face as the unexpected exercise broke sweat, but it was a small price to pay to get the treasure in her grasp.

Finally away from prying eyes, Shyoli inspected it—a glimmer of triumph on her face reflected in its surface—and placed it at the bottom of a drinking glass. She poured water from the decanter, her hands trembling in anticipation, but the liquid remained crystal clear. Hesitant, she stirred it with her finger.

The conversation she'd overheard two days earlier didn't go into details, so she had no idea how long she was supposed to wait, and impatience got the better of her. As the liquid cooled her throat, the echo of magic traveled through her body, a faint wave unable to sate the hunger. The water tasted of disappointment. She touched the stone at the bottom of the glass, its energy still hidden within. It seemed that she should have kept it in the glass longer, but the thought of waiting overnight for the water to become infused with magic brought pain.

She put the glass away, trembling both from hunger and anger. Once more she sifted through her memories, remembering the argument her father had had with some of his friends. As stubborn as he was, Fento qi'Aytrella discarded their remedy, but the heated exchange and rounds of convincing stayed in Shyoli's mind, clear with the relief the men described. And the simple instructions that were yet another argument that her father discarded would serve her. She'd have to get the mortar and pestle from the kitchen and keep quiet when crushing the stone, but according to her father's friends, such effort was well worth the time. Her eyes widened at the idea as she figured out the best way to get what she needed. Soon, the hunger wringing her bowels would be sated.

5

When Kamira and Veelk walked into the tavern in the poorest of Kaighal's districts, few heads turned. So late into the evening, sailors and local thugs were too busy with their drinks to pay attention to new patrons, no matter how odd they looked, and too streetwise to stare at that oddness too long. In places like Seabird's Spit, curiosity could quickly escalate to death, and that Yoreus chose such a place for their meeting served Kamira's plans well. Last thing she needed was people paying close attention to her conversation with the mage.

As they made it between crude wooden tables, only a lone man continued to watch them. With his fair skin and blond hair, he couldn't have been from Kaighal, not even from anywhere in Tyorane. She'd seen the likes of him in the past, when circumstances pushed her and Veelk on a journey to the continent to the east, but she'd never visited the country of that man's origin, Devanshari. To her surprise, the stranger's eyes widened when he glanced past Veelk's keshal, and Kamira could have sworn a hint of recognition flashed on the man's face, as if he knew of mage killers.

Had she not been preoccupied, she would have sat down beside him to ask questions, as the knowledge of Veelk's kind was rare enough around, but dealing with Yoreus was more important than sating her curiosity, so she followed Veelk straight for the table in the back.

They ordered food, and as soon as the tavern maid served it, Veelk dug in. Kamira only played with her spoon, aware of the man at the other table still watching her. When she shifted in her seat, his eyes widened once more, and sudden anger twisted his face before he looked away. His hands clenched the table's hard wood, and the corner of his lips twitched before he downed his drink in a lousy attempt at pretending he didn't stare at her.

"An arcanist hater?" Veelk pointed at her pendant—which, unlike many other arcanists, she wore openly—reflecting the lamps' light.

She responded with a cringe. Kaighal was a free city. It might be the high mages' home, and the city council might dance on their strings, but the years of reprobation had long come and gone, and arcanists enjoyed the same freedom and privileges as anyone else in the city. Besides, even in other countries in Tyorane, she wouldn't be facing such blatant hate without a good reason. That reaction, along with his skin untouched by the sun, suggested he'd arrived in Kaighal recently. She smirked at the thought that he'd learn the local ways soon enough or risked a knife in the dark from someone who happened to have an arcanist in the family.

The door opening pulled her attention away from the stranger. The tall man who entered the tavern wore a long cloak despite the warm evening, but the cloth couldn't hide his posture and moves—those of someone with power and authority. Kamira exchanged a glance with Veelk. Archmage Yoreus had arrived, so the game of deception and provocation was about to start.

"Oh, look. He made it," she said as soon as Yoreus approached. "It must have been such a strain to walk over here all the way from the Towers."

"Ah, Kamira." He looked down at her with no sign the insult had hit. "And I see you still keep your tribal guard around." Uninvited, he sat down at their table.

"He's useful. That's more than I can say about you," Kamira baited. Usually, such insults were beneath her, as she preferred to discompose Yoreus in subtler ways, but her general antagonistic approach toward high mages should convince him that in foul mood she'd decided on a more direct approach.

Yoreus tensed but kept his composure. "I'm powerful. That's more than you can say about yourself."

She almost grinned at his predictable retaliation. High mages looking down on her had stopped bothering her a long time ago, but for the sake of deception, she could pretend to take offense. "I'm also lacking your irresistible charm." She weighed her reply with a generous amount of sarcasm, appropriate for a hurt person who was trying to get back at him.

"I'd share it with you"—the mage sent her a smile— "when you're done giving yourself to the cattle." He threw a condescending glance at Veelk.

Kamira almost burst out laughing at Yoreus's poor attempt, but Veelk dutifully took the cue. When he rose from his seat, his hands closed into maces of bone and muscles as if he really was an offended lover.

"Veelk, don't!" Kamira said, her tone firm and decisive,

even though deep inside she cheered on the archmage. With pride dictating his words, she didn't even have to push him too hard. "Wait for me outside," she said. If they wanted Yoreus to feel in control, Veelk had to leave, but had she shown up without him in the first place, Yoreus might have gotten suspicious.

Veelk grumbled a few words in a defiant tone, but he obeyed and left the table. Over Yoreus's shoulder, Kamira caught his amused expression as he gave her a short nod. The mere thought that she was Veelk's lover must have pushed his control to the limits, and once outside, he'd give in to hearty laughter. At the same time, Yoreus's misconceptions were not their problem, and if it could serve her goals, she'd let him keep them.

"So, where is it?" Yoreus whispered as soon as Veelk left.

Kamira huffed. She'd have preferred another round of insults, but knowing her past interactions with the archmage, another opportunity would present itself soon enough. "Probably buried in the sand. We never found any entrance going deep."

To her surprise, Yoreus lost his composure quicker than with her teasing. "You weren't looking hard enough! There had to be a way in! My information couldn't be wrong!"

She narrowed her eyes, curiosity reignited. There had to be something in that book if Yoreus desired it so much, and even if she had to spend days studying outdated high magic theories, she'd figure it out. Unless, of course, her plan succeeded; then she'd lure Yoreus out into a more discreet place and let Veelk do the questioning.

Upon Yoreus's insistent gaze, she focused back on the conversation. He clearly expected a reply, so she shrugged as she said, "Your information might have been outdated.

Wouldn't be surprised if some sandstorm buried the entrance."

"You need to go back. You need to try again!"

"Out of the question. We've already spent over seven weeks in that *flerra* of a desert. Not even if you paid me double. Find someone else to run your errands." In the past Kamira might have been happy enough with such errand running, mostly because she and Veelk got to keep all the findings Yoreus wasn't interested in, but he had to expect that she would refuse if there was nothing in it for her. And her plans aside, she wouldn't pass the opportunity to remind the archmage he had no power over her.

Yoreus regarded her with disgust, and she remembered that expression from her time in the High Towers. Except that she wasn't a student anymore, so the archmage's displeasure carried no weight. "That's... disappointing. I expected more from you."

"I hope you don't expect me to cry about it."

Her response earned her Yoreus's grimace. "What happened to you? You had such promise. It's sad you ended up as a minor arcanist with barely enough power to summon a lumisphere. Maybe you should reconsider—"

Even though she cared little for the belittling comments, she mustered some anger, because this was the opening she needed. "Reconsider *what*, exactly?" She huffed. "Maybe I should drag your sorry, fat hide outside and show you what a minor arcanist can do."

"Don't be ridiculous!" Yoreus laughed. "I admit Tijhran is a good teacher, but even the eighth archmage could beat him in a duel, and you're not half as good as your master."

She snorted. When it came to dueling, magic wasn't everything. High mages might have the advantage of the unlimited power, while pacts limited arcanists, but with the need to utter every single syllable of complicated spells, mages were slower to do anything, while a skilled arcanist could channel her magic with little focus. But educating Yoreus didn't seem like a way to her goal, so instead, she gave him a cunning smile. "I tell you what. Let's duel, then. If I defeat you, you will acknowledge my skill in public." If she led him to believe a hurt pride dictated her words, he wouldn't suspect deception. "And if you defeat me, I'll go back to High Towers and study... under you." He couldn't say no, not to such an offer. Not only would he be able to show his superiority, but she'd also be under his power for longer if he won. And he had all the reasons to believe that she wasn't a match for him.

Yoreus's eyes flashed with lust, and she couldn't decide whether it was mere desire to put her in her place, or if the archmage had more carnal interest in her as well. "I think I could spare some time to teach you a lesson." His condescending tone rang with anticipation.

"Shall we, then, archmage?" She indicated the back door.

The archmage gave a nod, his face spoiled by the smug smile of a victor, and Kamira matched his expression. As long as he believed she was so full of herself to underestimate him, he'd never see the trap springing. But before they got up from the table, the fair-skinned stranger approached them. He offered Kamira nothing more than a hateful glance and focused his attention on Yoreus.

He placed his hand on the archmage's shoulder. "You might want to reconsider that duel," he said with a singing and flowing accent, unlike any Kamira had heard in Tyorane.

"And who might you be?" Yoreus brushed his hand off.

"A man saving your life, I suppose. Ryell qi'Teshari, at your service." He followed with a bow.

"Ah, one of the Devanshari refugees." The archmage inspected him. "So tell me, Ryell, how are you going to save my life preventing a duel I can't possibly lose?"

Kamira stared at him no less inquisitively, but said nothing. The sooner this Ryell left, the better, but if she interfered, he'd likely accuse her of hiding something.

"Her companion is a mage killer," Ryell replied. "She's likely only a distraction to make you let your guard down."

Controlling her face, Kamira offered a polite arch of her eyebrow. Clearly this man had no love for Yoreus, yet he interfered. His earlier loathing glares suggested his only goal was to frustrate her. Demons take him and other arcanist haters!

"He's waiting outside, unaware of our conversation," Yoreus pointed out nonchalantly.

"Are you sure?" Ryell asked. "Think of it. Why would she want a duel she can't win?"

Cursing in her thoughts, Kamira forced a burst of laughter nonetheless. "You really think so, don't you? He might be an archmage, but he's all rusted in his arts, while I use my magic all the time to survive. I'd win."

She stared at Yoreus with confidence verging on a challenge, and his face reddened. He stood up abruptly, forcing Ryell to step back. "That's quite enough!" He looked at Kamira and gestured at the door.

Her words must have hurt his pride more than she thought, or her insult struck truth if emotions got the better of him. She nodded in agreement. The duel was on, and that was all she needed. If that Ryell was foolish enough to follow them, she would take care of him too.

"All you have to do is walk through the front door," Ryell

said, "and see if the mage killer is still there. But I bet my family ring he's not. He's waiting in that back alley to kill you when you storm out of here carelessly."

"How can you possibly know he's a mage killer?" The archmage's voice rang with suspicion.

"He carries their weapon," Ryell replied. "Royal guard studies mention them, though until I arrived in Kaighal, I considered them a legend."

Yoreus turned to Kamira, and his expression made it clear he was ready to give in. "Is that true?"

She mustered a shrug. "Like I'd know." It seemed the plan had failed, and all she could do was avert the archmage's suspicions. Better if he thought Veelk's calling was a coincidence and not a part of a plot against him. "For all I care, he could be the lost prince of Zemarion. I pay him for his muscles, not his talking."

"Maybe you should consider asking him before he kills you," Ryell said with a vile sneer. "Though he might actually do the world a favor by ridding it of demon-conspiring scum."

With Ryell's interference, she couldn't push too far. She stared at them both with contempt and said, "Why don't you take your new friend, Yoreus, and crawl back to the High Towers? I think I've had enough of your company for the day." She reached for her mug and took a sip. "By the pact, even this watered-down ale is better than suffering you two."

The archmage stiffened, giving testimony to her efforts' success, but Ryell pulled on his arm. "It's not worth your life," he said.

Yoreus hesitated again. "You said you're a royal guard? And a noble, judging from your name?" Another inspecting look accompanied the words, and as he threw glances between Ryell and Kamira, it became clear that he was weighing who you trust. "Very well, then—I'll take your advice." He turned to Kamira. "I don't know what you were trying to achieve, but if I learn you were plotting against me..."

"Don't you think that if I wanted to kill a high mage, it would rather be Kerl?" She threw him a challenging stare. Yoreus knew her history, so he had to realize he couldn't be the object of her hate. At least this once her past in the High Towers had come in handy, helping to conceal the truth. "I'm only here for your money, so if you ever have a job that is something more than pointless wandering the desert, you know where to find me."

Yoreus gave her a nod as if she'd eased his suspicions enough, and then he followed Ryell, who didn't even so much as look in her direction before leaving.

Kamira didn't move until they left, considering the outcome. Not only had her plan to lure Yoreus out failed, but Ryell's words also raised suspicion. Even if the archmage couldn't be certain she and Veelk had tried to kill him, and even if she succeeded in convincing him there was no plot, he'd still be on his guard. He likely wouldn't risk meeting with her again, if he decided to have any more work for her to begin with. As she played with her pendant and sipped the ale, she couldn't help hoping Yoreus would return, angry and demanding answers. At least it would give her the opening to walk out with him through the back door, and even if he expected an attack, with Veelk's skills and her new pact, they could take him down.

Playing all the scenarios in her head did little except lift her mood, because Yoreus didn't show again. With a heavy sigh, she stood up and headed for the back door.

⌇

THE BACK ALLEY smelled of rotten food and urine, and Kamira chose her steps carefully, hoping her boots wouldn't sink into something vile, even though the moonless night made the task close to impossible. The stench seemed to stick to her skin, making her yearn for another bath.

"What happened?"

She'd expected it but still twitched when Veelk's voice came from behind. By the pact, for someone so big to move so lightly was inhuman, and she had no doubt that he enjoyed giving her that slight jump to keep her on her toes, and—as he liked to say—to remind her of any dangers that lurked in the dark, ready to take advantage of an unsuspecting arcanist. She sneered at that thought. As unskilled in combat as she was, her survival instincts had never failed her, and she often had her barrier up even before she realized what the threat was. Of course, in the past, she could do little else with her magic being hardly sufficient for any casting, let alone extravagant use, but with Veranesh's power at her disposal, this changed, and the real reasons for getting rid of Yoreus aside, she regretted missing the chance to fight against him.

"There were unexpected complications." She let her displeasure weave through the words. "Remember that arcanist hater? He recognized you and warned Yoreus. I barely managed to convince the old fart I wasn't planning on killing him, and that I didn't know who you really are."

Veelk said a few words in his native tongue, and although Kamira didn't catch the meaning, the tone was enough of a tell. "Want to try again?"

As much as she wanted to give a nod, she shook her head. "The old crook will be jumping at every shadow now and likely won't take a step outside the Towers. Better wait it out and make him doubt there was any plot to begin with. If we act, we'd confirm his suspicions and risk an open war. I don't think I can take on all the archmages at once," she added jokingly.

"He might try something in return," he replied.

"I'm sure you can handle an assassin or two, should it come to that. You could use some fighting exercise." Kamira eyed his body as if finding flaws in the perfect mass of muscles. "You seem a bit out of shape."

The way Veelk arched his eyebrow made her expect a demand for proof, but instead he said, "No more than you are."

To him, any excuse to practice with his weapon or fists seemed good enough, and Kamira snickered. "I was never in shape. That's why I have you."

"A bit of exercise wouldn't hurt. If you got some muscles on that skin and bone of yours..."

"And make your life easier?" She laughed, then threw a dissatisfied glare at their surroundings. Getting used to the stench didn't mean she wanted to soak any more of it in. "Let's get out of here. I could use a bath and some good food."

"Then the Jagged Swordsman it is," Veelk said.

Without delay, they exited the alley. The light of a passing guard's lantern made the shadows dance. The main street boasted the lights powered by imbued stones, Gildya Magna's gift to Kaighal and a thorn in the High Towers' side, as high mages couldn't match such generosity, but the smaller streets and back alleys in the poorer districts were still drowned in darkness, luring the less noble of the city's inhabitants, and patrols still carried their own sources of light. The guard gave Veelk a long stare and his blade an even longer one, but then he rushed away. Alone, in the alley, he must have known better than to question a man without a reason, especially a large man with a deadly-looking weapon.

"What about that foreigner?" he asked once the guard was out of earshot.

Her forehead furrowed. "Been in a wrong place at the wrong time? He seemed to harbor ill feelings toward all arcanists."

"I'm not surprised. His people lost their land to demons."

"Really? I've heard about the siege but never thought it would be so serious. Devanshari had a powerful magic artifact at their disposal. They shouldn't have lost to a bunch of arcanists, even if they managed to put together a demonling army."

Veelk shrugged. "I heard it from Salgie. She was quite upset last night."

She couldn't resist throwing him a playful smile. "Really upset or wanted your good nature to take pity on her?"

As expected, his confidence never faded. "I made sure to cheer her up, be her worry true or not."

"It's the coins that made her happy, not you."

The grin she received in return reassured Kamira that her jab had missed, but she hadn't expected otherwise.

"But these were *my* coins."

Allowing herself a short laugh at his bold response lifted some of the frustration of the evening. Veelk's simple approach to life and pleasure always amazed her, and to be able to jest with him without reservation had brightened many of her days. No matter what problems Yoreus would cause, they would handle them, and if Ryell's hate toward arcanists turned more personal, she'd have no reservations about giving him more solid reasons for his feelings, likely the last ones he'd ever have. With a powerful demon to outsmart and a death spell to lift, she wouldn't let the rage-blinded Devanshari interfere.

"Tomorrow we head for Gaunash," she said. If anyone could point her in the right direction, it was her teacher. "So if you have any goodbyes to say, do that tonight." It didn't matter they would be gone for less than a week. Veelk never passed on the excuse to visit his favorite brothel.

"As soon as I make sure you're safe at the inn," he declared with a serious note that suggested he'd make no argument that Yoreus didn't have enough time to set up a trap. Then a playful spark flashed in his eye. "Unless, of course, you want to accompany me."

"I'll pass this time," she replied as if there was any time she didn't. As much as company was pleasant from time to time, she preferred someone to talk to about magic, and the otherwise fine men and women at Hircifa's Peony Garden lacked in that regard.

Veelk glared, and to her surprise, his displeasure seemed more serious this time. "You really should try to enjoy life a bit. You're getting grumpier and grumpier with every passing year."

"I have more and more problems every passing year."

"You make up these problems." He poked her shoulder. "The world won't crumble if you relax a bit. I'm sure the demon will understand."

Instead suggesting that guessing the extent of a demon's patience was at best risky, she said, "I'll drink some wine before bed. How's that?" Some topics seemed better left within jesting words, because if Veelk convinced himself she was unhappy, he'd enjoy trying to remedy that. She almost rolled her eyes at his last attempt and an unsuspecting suitor he'd sent her way.

"You Northerners really don't know how to have fun," Veelk said. "I'm surprised you didn't decide to spend the night in the temple, singing hymns and chewing on prayer beads."

The joke was too old to earn him anything more than an arched eyebrow. "That would be my late maternal grandmother, and I'm told to have taken after the paternal side of the family." Of course, as if to confirm her own words, her heritage and upbringing sneaked the tone of an irked noblewoman into her words. With all the knowledge of what the so-called deities were, no arcanist ever prayed, and even though in her homeland people worshiped the Four, she never brought herself to bow to the powerful demons who protected her brethren.

Veelk didn't reply, as if sensing her good mood went only so far after a failed plan, and she sent him a thankful smile. They made their way through the quieter streets of one of the residential districts where townhouses hugged each other, forming a maze of alleys and courtyards, and into the still-active merchant area where the lights of the inns, leisure houses, and other public places remained always lit. The guards became more frequent, but with wealthier people frequenting the district, they rarely had to do more than hush a loud patron who was singing on his way home.

They stopped under the iron sign fashioned into a warrior with a sword. Music and cheerful songs came from the inn, and Veelk hesitated.

"See you in the morning." Kamira playfully pushed him. Even if she preferred solitude, it didn't mean he should give up his pleasures. "And try to get some sleep between your exercises."

Veelk flashed a smile and walked away. If she was to believe gossip, Veelk had enough stamina to keep all of the girls from Hircifa's Peony Garden happy, and he was never stingy with his coins. She chuckled as she entered the inn. He surely had enough fun for both of them.

Lefna, the innkeeper's daughter who stood behind the counter, had a room key ready before Kamira even made it through the spacious dining hall. This late in the evening, many wooden tables stood empty, but Opyr couldn't complain about the lack of patrons, since most were wealthy enough, and the fame of his superb food and a careful choice of musicians and dancers always lured more guests in. And, of course, there were the likes of Kamira and Veelk, renting Opyr's rooms indefinitely and making their home in the inn. Every now and then, she pondered finding a place, but having one's own home required hassle and time, especially since some people could be displeased having an arcanist for a neighbor. A room in an inn seemed a reasonable compromise in that matter.

"Is master Veelk coming too?" Lefna's cheeks darkened with blush.

"Later or in the morning. He had some matters to see to." Kamira smiled at Lefna's dreamy sigh. Sure, Veelk couldn't complain about lack of attention, but he was both muscular and exotic enough to make up for the hairless scalp and the scars marking his body. Kamira inspected Lefna's full curves, pleasantly tanned face, and auburn hair. Not exactly Veelk's type, but close enough. "I'll mention you asked about him and make sure he stops by," she said.

Lefna's face brightened. "Thank you, my lady!"

Kamira huffed in amusement. No matter the familiarity she insisted on, somehow Opyr and Lefna had learned that she actually had the right to the title many merchants and innkeepers freely used to tickle their patrons' pride, and refused to simply call her by her name. "Not at all. Would you get someone to bring food up to my room if it's not too late? And a bottle of wine," she added, remembering the promise.

"Of course, my lady."

While Kamira climbed the stairs, she couldn't help wondering whether Veelk would consider Lefna attractive. As flirtatious as he was, so far he had never used his charm on Opyr's daughter. Maybe, like Kamira, he wasn't willing to give up good food and a bath chamber that boasted hot water heated with imbued stones if Opyr didn't like the idea of a casual romance between his only child and what many citizens of Kaighal considered an uncivilized tribal warrior.

The room was at the end of the corridor, and Kamira unlocked it with a smile. Early after she'd met Veelk, she insisted on sleeping in separate rooms, more to keep the distance from her self-proclaimed guard and discourage him from sticking around than anything else, but pragmatism soon took over. On the road, they shared the fire, often guarding each other's sleep, so it seemed like a silly notion to impose artificial boundaries in Kaighal. Besides, Veelk rarely spent nights in their room anyway, so paying for two would be a waste of coin that could be better spent.

The room greeted her with darkness, and she lit up a lumisphere as she walked in. Spacious and bright in the daytime, it had a table by the double window and two beds at the opposite walls. Two large chests held their spare clothes, with the more presentable outfits never worn and buried at the bottom, under the piles of weathered travel shirts and pants. Beside them lay their travel bags, still unpacked. The pile of books burdening her nightstand, which she meticulously collected throughout their journeys and exploration, was the only other personal touch to the room.

Below, a musician started a tune, and joyful chants followed, reminding her of the more discreet sounds of the desert. As much as she enjoyed the comforts of the city, she missed the wind and grit of the sand. But as she slouched on the floor by the bed's leg, she felt her thoughts drift, already looking for solutions to Yoreus's failed assassination and plotting the quickest route to Gaunash. Things to consider came one after another, and Kamira rubbed her temples with a heavy sigh.

Veelk was right: she should do something for fun.

A maid brought dinner, and Kamira ate it from the tray while sitting on the floor. After weeks of journeying, chairs seemed like strange and foreign creatures, inventions of torture over tired people, but she welcomed the cutlery and wet cloth for cleaning her hands. As she leaned over the tray, the smell of roasted kitsay, a small desert rodent, filled her nostrils with the pleasure of having real food. She savored the first bite, but then hunger took over.

Sated, Kamira took several swigs of wine straight from the bottle and stretched on the floor, enveloped by the scent of the wood. The music downstairs made her drift into thought but didn't lull her to sleep, and as always when her body was idle and rested, she found herself longing to practice magic. Master Tijhran claimed respectable arcanists never practiced their art drunk, and she snickered at the disapproval he'd dish out if he knew. Besides, respectable arcanists didn't do many things, from wandering the desert in search for trinkets that survived the Cataclysm through running errands for high mages, all the way to making deals with evil demons.

She hefted the bottle again and sat back up.

The power came in a gentle gust and enveloped her in a cocoon as she called up a barrier. The flow of energy, as smooth as a comb through perfect locks, allowed her to draw more at will, and Kamira once more realized the difference of having a pact with a higher demon. At the back of her mind, Veranesh's ghastly presence lingered, but he was neither trying to control the power nor restraining it like her previous demon used to. If anything, he offered even more with what felt like a faint warning to take only as much as she could handle.

With anticipation rising, she changed the flow of magic, and the barrier sparked with arcs of lightning. The wooden floor charred at their touch, so Kamira altered the energy's nature once more, and the barrier condensed into semi-translucent liquid. She reached out but lost her focus, and the barrier collapsed, drenching both her and the floor with water. At the back of her mind, Kamira could almost hear her teacher's scolding voice as he repeated his warnings about not performing arts drunk. Mindful of the inn's patrons, she put her hands to the floor, and with a controlled but strong burst of energy, she evaporated enough liquid to ensure nothing would drip on the people downstairs. The last thing she needed was causing Opyr trouble if someone complained about an arcanist staying in the Jagged Swordsman.

In the past, such a feat would drain most of the magic she had at her disposal through the pact, but this time energy remained as it was, plentiful and waiting for her command. She exhaled with a wide smile. Power. Real power she could use to practice and grow. Power given willingly, not drawn with difficulty. More than she could ever use, not a meager source that always drained too soon.

All she had to do was to learn to control it, and with her arcanist training, it would hardly be a challenge.

The cold touch of the water-washed crystals on her wrists reminded her that there were other things to explore. But curiosity aside, the nightflies reminded her about what came with the power she received, and her mood dimmed. At the same time, sooner or later she'd have to deal with the demon, and showing her excitement for his gifts could convince Veranesh she was willing to trust him and do his bidding. She hushed her arcanist's pride and voice of reason, both demanding she remain unyielding. If she wanted to live and ensure the demon remained trapped, playing the game of wits was inevitable. And if pretending to be drunk with power and willing to serve could help her gain knowledge, it was a small price to pay. After all, the High Towers taught her a lot about flattering and manipulating her teachers, and the demon would likely be no less benevolent to a servile and agreeable servant than the archmages were to their favorite students.

The nightflies remained coiled around her forearm, their crystal wings glistening with water, and Kamira realized that Veranesh had never bothered to instruct her how to control them. In a way, this reaffirmed his promise that only she could control them... if she figured out how.

She drew the energy again, directing its flow at the inanimate creatures, and spoke just one word.

"Fly?"

6

Archmage Yoreus poured himself more wine. The soft cushions he valued for their comfort made him sink into the armchair as if the burden of his thoughts weighed on his body. Atissa walked in, and her rocking steps brought beauty and harmony into the chaos of suspicions, fears, and decisions that plagued Yoreus's mind. She brushed her brown locks behind her ears and straightened invisible creases on the simple student robe she wore.

"He's asleep now, Father," she said with that sweet, soft voice he made her practice. "Why did you bring him here? He's just a refugee, even if he is of a noble ancestry. The Devanshari are of no consequence to us." She stopped several steps away, awaiting his permission.

"You shouldn't be so certain." He indicated the other armchair. He might have offered Ryell a place to stay out of gratitude, but before they had even made it to the High Towers, Yoreus had already considered all the possible advantages of his new acquaintance. Atissa had to learn to search for such possibilities as well, or she'd never keep up with other archmages or become one in the first place.

"There are enough of them in Kaighal to tip the balance between Gildya and the Towers, and their queen has taken interest in Gildya's work. She's a welcomed guest in their halls, and so is the coin I'm told she spares generously."

"But her resources are limited, and her goals are clear."

"Are they now?" Yoreus arched his eyebrows.

Atissa's confidence faltered, and she didn't reply right away, her furrowed forehead indicating that she'd taken his veiled warning.

"She promised her people new Haja... Hajee... a new artifact to feed them magic," she said with caution.

Yoreus smiled at his daughter weighing her words. She acted a bit defensive after her brash statement, but all in all, he'd trained her well. What she lacked the most was the experience, and going through such mental exercises could only get her so far. "And that makes her goals clear?" he asked when she didn't follow up.

Atissa shook her head. "Everyone can have a hidden agenda."

Yoreus nodded, hiding his displeasure. It was one of the first lessons he'd given her, and the most crucial one in a city like Kaighal, where both High Towers and Gildya Magna vied for power and control over the city council. Every time he had to remind her of it, his desire for Atissa to become an archmage faded, replaced by concerns. He only caught a few glimpses of the queen in the streets; first when she arrived in the city, and second when she headed for Gildya for the first time. Nothing he saw or knew indicated whether she was indeed only interested in recreating the artifact, or if she'd make a play for power, tipping the delicate balance of influence. He held off a sigh. It was time that, after too much frustrating prodding, his daughter arrived at the same conclusion.

"So what do you think Cahala qi'Devanshari really wants?"

"That we don't know."

He almost cheered when those words finally left Atissa's mouth. Brilliant and quick-learning, she'd grown prideful and confident, and to admit she had no knowledge of something became rarer and rarer. As much as Yoreus wanted the best for her, being an archmage required a clear mind and awareness of one's weaknesses more even than one's strengths. If Atissa continued to cater to her own arrogance, he would need to devise more cruel lessons. But he had still time, and he indicated for her to continue. Even without solid information, she could speculate.

"We can assume she's addicted to magic, just like all the Devanshari are. She'll likely be driven by the need to sate her craving."

Yoreus concealed a snicker when Atissa included him in her assumption. A defensive maneuver, but at least it indicated pride didn't blind her so much that she'd risk his anger. "Good," he said. "We also know she doesn't support her own son who pursues the more medical path, trying to ease his people's pain and cure the addiction."

Her forehead creased. "Is it even possible?"

Yoreus rubbed his chin. After centuries of being exposed to their artifact's energy, their bodies absorbing magic since birth, the Devanshari had become dependent on it. The addiction had been passed on for generations, and Yoreus had his doubts whether it could be cured at all, but he knew too little to be certain. If high mages got a chance to examine the refugees, maybe they'd find more definite answers, but Cahala qi'Devanshari allied herself with Gildya, and her son stayed away from High Towers as well. "It runs deep in their blood, maybe too deep. But young

Allyv seems determined. I'm sure we'll all benefit from his research."

Her face brightened. "That's why you secretly donated money to the prince's asylum." Her look of triumph faded as soon as her eyes sought his praising expression. "No. You gave him money to create counterbalance. To deepen the split between the mother and her son, and thus divide the Devanshari."

"Very good!" Yoreus toasted with his glass and indicated she should pour some for herself. The pride of her conclusions dimmed his earlier concerns. After all, aside from the initial overconfidence, she reasoned and speculated better than he could expect from someone so relatively inexperienced. "Weakened, they have less influence, and Kaighal will absorb them soon enough, as it always does with newcomers."

She glanced at the door leading to her room. "And that Ryell? Why is he here?"

"It seems he saved my life tonight," Yoreus said in a lighthearted tone, but the very memory of the events in the tavern brought his blood to boil. Even if Kamira spoke the truth, and a mage killer's presence was a mere coincidence, something in her behavior grated on his instincts. She had always been an unnerving student mage, and nothing had changed when she became an arcanist, but the way she'd taunted him back there made him think she was ready to fight him. And that led him back to suspicions, because she had no chance of winning.

Upon Atissa's inquisitive gaze, he forced his thoughts away from Kamira and back into the present.

"He had also seen what really happened in Devanshari capital, or to be more precise, *how* it happened," he added.

"Father?"

"Their artifact, Hajihali, was powerful, and so was the protective barrier it created. There were several demon invasions throughout their history, and one even succeeded in conquering some of the borderlands, but none ever got close to the capital city, let alone destroy it. I need to know how that was possible."

"Do you think demons will invade here next?" she asked.

Outside of his private chambers, she'd never admit to having similar fears, but here they could be honest with each other... At least as honest as an archmage could be with anyone, because Yoreus harbored secrets not meant even for his daughter.

"I believe the Devanshari artifact was their goal, and they might leave us alone. Bringing a demon army to this world must have been difficult, and there aren't that many arcanists who can replenish their troops. But needless to say, we have to stay vigilant." The news of invasion came unexpected, and Yoreus didn't like that the archmages had no warning of what was going on overseas. Even if they wouldn't be able to use such knowledge publicly, old alliances required such information to be passed on, and the silence worried him more than some kingdom's fall.

Atissa's inquisitive stare made it clear that she suspected there was more to it, but she didn't press. Good. Even if he'd failed in rooting out that foolish pride of hers, at least he'd managed to teach her that some things were only for the archmages' eyes and ears. He'd promised her she'd soon become one, but discrediting the eighth archmage required time, and Yoreus had more pressing matters to consider. Besides, Atissa could learn a bit more about patience—no harm in that.

"So Ryell will provide you with knowledge?" she changed the topic.

"He might be useful in other ways, too." Yoreus put the empty glass aside. "As a noble, he could be a negotiator between us and the royal family, should we need it, or we can use him to drive the wedge deeper into the Devanshari people." He stood up from his chair. "That's why he's going to stay here as my guest for a while, and I want you to help him with anything he needs. Wear your nicest dresses, smile, and make use of that sweet voice of yours. Make him feel welcome and comfortable."

"Do you want me to...?"

"If it comes to that, yes." Yoreus didn't hesitate. If she wasn't his daughter, she'd likely be sleeping her way up the Towers' hierarchy, and teachers and archmages weren't as young and good-looking as Ryell, so she should consider herself lucky. "Upon close contact, a faint magical aura might stimulate his instinct and redirect his addiction." If Atissa succeeded, they'd be able to control Ryell, and maybe find a way to extend such influence on others. "But don't rush. We have time."

"As you wish, Father."

Yoreus gave her a warm smile and brushed her cheek. Atissa, his dear Atissa, always willing to fulfill his wishes without a single word of protest, deserved his attention and praise. Her youthful overconfidence could be easily corrected, and with her as the eighth archmage, supporting all his decisions, he could easily gain significant advantage in the Towers' politics.

But before he put his grand plans in motions, he had to deal with that arcanist gaharra and her tribal dog first. No matter what Kamira's goals really were, Yoreus doubted they aligned with his. And if she'd lied about the old Towers, if she found the way in, she might have learned of things no arcanist should ever know. He turned away from Atissa to conceal the emotions that threatened his composure then headed for his private chamber. Sending Kamira to fetch the journal seemed like a reasonable risk at the time, but in hindsight, he regretted he hadn't sent common thugs instead.

"Get some sleep, my dear," he said over his shoulder. "You did well today."

He didn't wait to see Atissa's cheerful expression, his thoughts circling another woman. The sound of the closing door was like a seal to Kamira's fate. He'd learn how much she knew and what her plans were, and then he'd dispose of her.

IRTAN, the first archmage of the High Towers, woke from his slumber to the feeling of a magical disturbance. His aging body failed him in more ways than he'd care to admit, but his sense of energies, honed through the years of practicing the craft, never let him down, and he snapped his eyes open, staring into the darkness. No sound disturbed the silence, but he had no doubt that there was someone lurking in his private chamber.

"Who are you?" he asked. If it came to a fight, bed covers put him at a disadvantage even if his body didn't, but his voice remained every bit commanding. Spells didn't need spry muscles to kill. "Why are you here?"

"You should know who I am," the stranger said in a deep tone, "when I tell you I came to discuss the alliance forged a long time ago, one between high mages and us."

Irtan sat up, his fear mixed with curiosity. The stranger spoke about secrets not even all the archmages knew about, so he couldn't be human. But the demons had kept away from the High Towers for centuries... He had to muster his breath at the thought this could be connected with the fall of the Devanshari capital. Yet speculating what the demon wanted was pointless. At least the creature hadn't come to kill him, and any other issues he could deal with one way or another.

"Very well," Irtan replied. "Let me get some light, and we can talk—"

"Gather others first."

Irtan stumbled though the dark of his bedroom, donning a robe along the way. He'd much rather deal with the matter alone, but opposing a demon never ended well.

His day room drowned in the black, and since his guest didn't follow him out of the bedroom, Irtan lit all the lamps with a quick spell. Then he opened the door to the stairway. With his chambers at the top of the tallest tower came the peace and solitude he desired, but it also meant walking down several flights of stairs before he could find a servant at that time of the night, and for once he regretted not having a student he could send on such an errand. On the other hand, becoming a tutor meant allowing an unschooled youngster too close to all the secrets... both the archmages' and his own.

With that thought, he made his descent. Three stories down, he came across a patrol, senior students ensuring their younger peers didn't sneak about the Towers or ended up in a mischief unsuitable for future high mages. At the sight of him, the two young women and a man bobbed their heads in a slight bow as they stepped aside to let him pass. Not one smirked at the archmage night robe, and Irtan gave them a nod of approval.

"Go and wake up archmages Loktra and Yoreus," he said without a word of greeting. "Tell them it's a matter of the highest urgency, and that I expect them as soon as possible. And get someone to bring cafra juice and bread to my chambers."

Their confusion lasted only for a blink, and after muttering their acknowledgment, they rushed off, leaving Irtan smiling with satisfaction. Many students in the Towers, misguided by dreams of power and grandeur, were slow to pick up the most fundamental rule: one was to meet an archmage's wishes without hesitation, no matter how unusual they seemed.

As soon as his messengers disappeared, Irtan made his way back up. His body protested the continuous strain, but he wanted to ensure he would be back in his chambers before other archmages arrived. He didn't expect the demon to say anything until then—it was a matter of pride. If Yoreus or Loktra caught up with him in the stairs, nothing would make it clearer he was getting old, and Irtan preferred his position unchallenged. His forehead furrowed at the thought of the ambitious second archmage. Time would come, sooner than later, when Yoreus would make his play for power. At least dealing with the demon would put the Towers' politics aside for a while. Irtan snickered at a sudden thought. Maybe even it would teach the second archmage some humility, because no matter the power the high mages possessed, it all faded when confronted with one of the demon kind. And Irtan could bet all his magic that so far Yoreus hadn't had a chance to meet any of them. That alone was worth walking down and up the stairs in the middle of the night.

As he walked back to his day chamber, he said, "They should be here shortly."

No response came from the darkness of his bedroom, but the lingering disturbance in magic reassured Irtan that his demonic guest was still waiting. As he sat in one of the chairs arranged around a small table, a servant knocked and brought in refreshments. He glanced curiously at Irtan, but knew better than to ask, and left promptly.

Yoreus arrived shortly after that with no traces of sleep on his face and still wearing the day's attire, giving testimony to the second archmage's late night's work. Irtan made a mental note to discreetly inquire what had been keeping Yoreus up recently. Both ambitious and hardworking, he wouldn't have been wasting his nights on trivial or irrelevant matters.

Yoreus took the indicated seat. "You called for me?" Nothing in his posture revealed any emotions, not a spark of curiosity about the nature of such a summons nor a hint of frustration for having to answer it.

"I called for both of you. We have an unexpected guest who would like to speak with all of us."

Irtan didn't make any gesture, but Yoreus focused on the dark rectangle of the bedroom doorway, and understanding flashed on his face. He definitely was quick to catch on... or he might have expected such a visit if he knew something that Irtan didn't.

They waited for Loktra in silence, and the third archmage finally made her appearance. Her heavy eyelids and the slowed motion of her bulging limbs indicated that Loktra had been roused but had to yet wake up. She stumbled into the chamber, and a yawn froze on her face. It took only the time she needed to close the door behind her to gather her clarity, and Irtan almost smirked. Even if she wasn't as ambitious as Yoreus was, she wouldn't have become an archmage, climbing all the way to the third, if her mind wasn't sharp. If she made use of it more often, she'd keep the second archmage occupied enough and fearing for his position, leaving Yoreus no time to threaten Irtan's status. Perhaps a subtle prompt could reignite her craving for power, but that was a matter for another day.

"Good, we can start, then," the demon said from the doorway, turning the heads of all of them.

The demon pushed his body through the bedroom door, and the wooden frame creaked but didn't break only for his lack of wings. He wasn't much bigger than humans, but his elongated face was marked by a long and pointy nose, so reminiscent of a beak, and it left no doubt about his otherworldly origins. Were they alone, Irtan would gladly inquire of the demon about the summoning, since the last time the arcanists attempted such a feat ended in disaster, and after that, hardly anyone would dare to pursue such research anymore. But the demon's posture suggested it cared little for such idle talk, and other archmages didn't need to know of Irtan's curiosity about the matter. If need be, he had other ways to get that information.

He focused his attention back on the demon, who gave a loathing glare to a chair and squatted down beside the table. He wore a cloak that concealed his tail and a pair of wide trousers that suggested he knew his way around humans well enough.

"My name is Uganel." The demon's tail swayed as he spoke. "I'm here because of a disturbance around the yalari your predecessors trapped centuries ago. What do you know about it?"

Irtan shifted in his seat as both Yoreus and Loktra looked at him. "There was an unusual wave in the flow of magic some weeks ago, but we know nothing about it. No difficult spells were performed at the time, and we considered it a spontaneous event. Could it be something else?"

Uganel grimaced. "He might be trying to free himself."

"That should be impossible!" Loktra said. Irtan had to admit that she kept her composure better than he'd expected, and after the initial shock of seeing a demon, she showed no emotions unfit for an archmage. "As long as there are at least three to four archmages, he shouldn't be able to try anything."

Uganel huffed, and Loktra paled slightly. "Nothing is impossible with a yalari of his power. That's why we'd prefer him destroyed, not contained. As long as he lives, he's a threat to all of us."

Irtan narrowed his eyes. Veranesh's entrapment was part of the deal made centuries ago, and Uganel must have known that high mages would never agree to killing that demon. If he came with the intent of demanding Veranesh died, it would mean shattering the old alliance. Yet, unless demons acted first, Irtan preferred to avoid making the enemies of them.

"Could this be connected with what you did in Devanshari?" he steered the topic into another direction, hoping to gain some insight into the demons' motives in the process. "Cahala qi'Devanshari and a handful of her people fled over here." The foreign queen and her people, so small in numbers, couldn't affect Kaighal's politics in any significant way, but their presence could have interfered with demons' plans. He also needed to make sure Uganel understood that offering refuge to them was not meant to antagonize the demons.

"They know nothing of the events that happened in this land," Uganel replied.

"But they're trying to recreate the artifact," Irtan said. "And Cahala is a frequent visitor to Gildya Magna. It'd be foolish to assume she's not up to something after you destroyed her kingdom."

"If needed, we'll destroy it again," Uganel replied in a rough tone that suggested he'd take no more arguments. "She's of no consequence."

"Then there is no other trace." Irtan would much rather tell the demon he was worrying about nothing, but such a remark wouldn't go well with the proud being. Besides, as much as Irtan hated to admit it, even though demons were an instinctive and decisive kind, and they had the tendency to dispose quickly of enemies true or not, they wouldn't risk contacting high mages if they didn't perceive a real threat.

Yoreus cleared his throat. "There might be another one."

Uganel regarded the second archmage with narrowed eyes, and so did Irtan.

"Speak, mage," the demon said.

"Some time ago, a few months or so, an arcanist approached me. She's the traveling sort, often venturing into forgotten places to search for lost knowledge and ancient artifacts," Yoreus explained. "She intended to search the desert for any entryways to the old High Towers, and asked me whether I'd sponsor her travel in return for interesting findings."

Irtan inspected Yoreus at a strange note in his voice, but apart from it, nothing else indicated the second archmage wasn't sharing all the truth.

"I didn't know you dealt with arcanists," Loktra said, sour voice interrupting the tale.

"She's a useful tool, providing material for research." Yoreus stared back at the third mage with no reservations. "No one of importance, nor any significant power. I turned her down, since we don't need anyone digging out old secrets, but what if she found the money and a way in? Scrappers like her can be quite resourceful."

"If she got inside, she might have discovered something or even come across Veranesh himself." Irtan rubbed his chin. All the implications of an arcanist stumbling upon the archmages' secrets shifted the situation in unknown directions, some more dangerous than others. "We should find her and see how much she knows. Maybe offer her incentives to ensure... her willingness."

"No," Uganel said. "I'll find and question her. You high mages are supposed to ensure no one reaches Veranesh. If the desert is not enough, drown him under the sea or melt the sand into solid rock."

"We'll do what's necessary," Irtan promised. And only that which wouldn't get people questioning high mages and their motives, of course. "Yoreus, do you know that arcanist's name? And where to find her?"

The second archmage nodded. "Her name is Kamira, and from what I've gathered, she's a frequent visitor to Kaighal, though I don't know her current whereabouts."

That change in Yoreus's voice again... Irtan refrained from grimacing, this time certain the second archmage was hiding something.

"That's good enough. I'll find her." Uganel stood up and opened the window. "You make sure Veranesh stays where he is. You know the consequences." Without any parting words, he leapt into the darkness.

Irtan ensured the demon didn't linger outside and then closed the window. "I don't trust him." He sat back in his chair. "He might deal with the problems, but he'll have his own kin's interests in mind. Yoreus, I want you to keep an eye on that arcanist and, if she reappears in Kaighal, see what you can learn from her."

Yoreus's lips widened into a bitter half-smile. "She might be willing to do business with high mages, but she's not really on friendly terms with us."

"Oh, why is that?" asked Loktra.

Irtan squinted, pretending to fish for a faint memory, though he remembered the name well. "Someone by that name used to be a student here..."

"She got expelled after insulting the fourth archmage," Yoreus said. "I don't think I'll be able to get any information from her, and I have a feeling she'd rather side with demons than us, but I'll see what I can do."

There was more to that, but Irtan knew better than to press. He'd rather make the second archmage believe his lies were solid enough than give him a reason to guard his secrets even more. "Do what you need, and promise her whatever she wants—within reason, of course. I want to know what happened in the old Towers before the demon does."

Yoreus and Loktra both stood up and left, leaving Irtan to his thoughts. None too pleasant as he considered Yoreus's behavior during the meeting. The second archmage knew more than he let on, so he must have been playing his own game, and Irtan smiled. Yoreus had indeed been busy and made his move sooner and more discreetly than Irtan expected, and even the threat of Veranesh breaking free might not be enough to keep him in check.

The first mage adjusted in his seat. Interesting times were coming, and he needed to ensure that none of these interferences would affect his own plans.

And Kamira... When that daughter of a Tivarashan noble first arrived in the High Towers, he'd expected her to be a spoiled and lazy student. Yet she'd surprised them all with both perseverance and quick mind. All her teachers foretold a bright future for her, but in the end, her Tivarashan pride got in the way of advancement. Regardless, no matter what Yoreus said about her power and capabilities, Kamira's intellect could prove her a dangerous adversary, and Irtan smiled. If the second archmage went against her, some of Irtan's problems might solve themselves.

Interesting times, indeed.

IN THE VAST halls of Gildya Magna, gold marble columns stretched up like arms of giants and reached toward the barrel vault above. Polished floor tiles formed geometric shapes, but with all the people around, Cahala couldn't tell if there was anything more to the pattern. The corner of her mouth twitched when another person almost ran into her and scurried off with no more than a murmured apology. Back in her land, such behavior would justify a death sentence if she felt the incident spoiled her benevolent mood.

"We should have come with the full entourage." Phuran stayed behind her. "Maybe then those commoners would show appropriate respect."

"We'd waste our time in official meetings." Cahala hid her frustration. Even without an army of dames and servants, they should have seen her fair skin and superb outfit and stayed out of her way. "And we aren't interested in staying here a moment longer than necessary. Light bless us!" She pressed an embroidered cloth to her mouth. "What's that smell?"

"I believe it was the man who just passed us, my queen."

"Truly, we would expect the people of reason and

science to treat hygiene more seriously." The adepts from the Gildya seemed to cherish their superiority over their fellow men, a claim entirely unfounded if Cahala had a say, but their behavior revealed them for what they were: a pack of squabbling commoners who fought over scraps of knowledge that could let them crawl upward over their colleagues' bodies. They reminded her of dogs fighting over a piece of meat, and to even admit that she needed help from them was the single most humiliating experience of her life. She tensed to resist a shudder. Even if thoughts of all the events that led her to this moment haunted her, those barbarians wouldn't get the satisfaction of seeing her in distress.

She picked up her pace and headed straight for the double doors at the end of the main hall. Two guards wearing lavish armor covered with imbued stones let her through without a word, much to her satisfaction that at least someone in the building acted in an appropriate manner, but she still swallowed as even from a distance the magic within their jewels made her hunger grow more intense, reminding her that the essence supplies were waning fast.

Beyond the door, the multitude of colors and shapes filled the waiting hall. Odd sculptures, geometric tapestries, and miniature trees with their bark encrusted with imbued stones arranged in the round-shaped chamber provided space for strolls, and cushioned benches stood against the walls. At the far end, two spiral staircases led up to the Gildya Magna's most renowned members' offices, and Cahala headed that way without hesitation. No man nor law would force her to sit and wait like all those peasants.

Some supplicants threw her surprised glances, and her mood shifted with the taste of satisfaction. They surely couldn't have expected that Cahala qi'Devanshari, the queen of her people, would wait to be called in for a meeting? As she approached the stairway, an apprentice on the floor above—a woman in her twentieth summer or so—stared at her for a moment, but before Phuran scolded her for being disrespectful, a spark of recognition flashed in the apprentice's eyes, and she rushed away.

"Good," Cahala said. "Looks like this time our arrival might be announced, and we won't have to barge in."

They paused at the base of the steps, and Phuran offered his arm. Cahala accepted it before lifting the heavy folds of her gown. The expensive fabric whispered with every step, drawing the attention of the people waiting in the hall, and the queen let a gentle smile dance on her carmine lips. *Watch and admire, primitives. This is how royalty looks.*

Adept Davshil was waiting at the top of the stairs, bowing his head slightly. "Lady Cahala." His outfit of brown and gold reflected the most recent fashion in Tyorane, sewn from fine cloth and covered with embroidery. A heavy chain with Gildya's symbol rested on the man's wide chest, and the stones in his rings emanated gentle magic. Yet the expensive outfit did little to conceal his lowly heritage, apparent through his almond-hued skin characteristic for Kaighal's locals and a commoner's face that lacked the beauty and regular features that noble bloodlines boasted.

"Adept Davshil," Cahala returned the scant greeting. The fact he hadn't addressed her properly brought a tinge of frustration, but she needed him. She'd have time for pride later, once their business concluded. "We're here to inquire about the project that is dear to us."

"Of course, of course!" The smile stretched his face, but it couldn't soften its unpleasant, angular shape. "Please, come into my office."

Cahala followed him into a room of a moderate size filled with bookshelves, cabinets, and a large desk covered with scripts and blueprints. Davshil helped her to a chair, kicking a pile of papers to the side without even a hint of embarrassment.

"We'd like to hear what news you have," she said. The sooner she left this filthy place, the better.

"Ah, news. Yes." Another smile passed over his lips, but his eyes focused as he searched the blueprints. "After extensive research, we came across some information that makes us believe we'll be able to build what you're asking for, though the size might pose problems. If your people were able to provide any knowledge or scriptures on—"

"We have no such things," Cahala cut in. "We were more concerned about saving lives. Books can be written again, discoveries can be rediscovered, but a life taken is never to return."

"That's very true and wise." Davshil nodded with eagerness that reminded her of a servile puppy. Dogs, they were indeed dogs. "We'll work with the information we have. Some old research is most definitely connected to the matter and might prove useful in designing the artifact, though the technicalities of these texts still need to be deciphered. Our language hasn't changed much throughout the centuries, but the adepts of yore used different, less-refined names for the processes Gildya has been exploring and perfecting."

Cahala leaned closer to the desk. "Maybe you should ask the man who drew these? They look recent." Her almond-shaped nail pointed at the name and date scribbled in the edge of the blueprint. "Call for that Alluvendran. We'll be pleased to meet him."

"That's quite impossible." A blush covered Davshil's

face, and droplets of sweat gathered on his temples. Apparently, with all his shortcomings so far, at least he had the decency to feel embarrassed for refusing her request.

"How so?"

Silence fell, but Davshil gave in under Cahala's stare. "Alluvendran is being detained in Gildya's prison. He was a brilliant inventor in his time, very gifted," he explained reluctantly. "But his research took him down a path condemned by Gildya Magna, and he became a threat."

Cahala considered the information. "We understand. We still would like to meet that man, but if the Gildya is able to prepare a project for the new artifact and ensure its assembling, we won't insist on it. It's the ends that interests us, not the means."

"Most definitely!" Davshil relaxed. "I'm sure we'll be able to present the final project very soon! Though the new device might not be as big as the one the Devanshari had."

She discarded his comment with a wave of her hand. "Size is of less importance. If needed, we'll commission the construction of several more to meet the needs of our people."

"Oh, that's most commendable." Davshil's smile twitched. "I'll let my colleagues know to proceed with the design and ensure all of our resources are on it."

"We'll be waiting for the word." Cahala stood up. "As for the compensation for the Gildya," she added when the adept glanced at her nervously, "my adviser will take care of that. We'll cover the expense of both research and construction."

"That's most generous, most generous!" Davshil called out as Cahala headed for the door.

It might not be her throne room, but she still got to decide when the hearing was over, and a commoner such as

Davshil didn't deserve the time of extended and courteous farewells. He was nothing more than a servant tasked with work for which she chose to compensate him. Phuran said a few words to Davshil, and she had no doubt that a pouch exchanged hands, but he didn't dawdle. Before she made it to the stairs, he was already by her side, and they made their way back through Gildya's vast halls.

"He has no idea how to make us the artifact we desire," Cahala said when they walked out through the massive wooden door, into Kaighal's busy square. Even if any adepts were still around, it would be harder for them to eavesdrop on one of many conversations outside.

"My impression was the same, my queen," Phuran replied. "Shall we ask another adept to work on it?"

She shook her head, walking down the vast steps leading to Gildya Magna. For the commoners they were, the Gildya's members surely liked to give impression of wealth and power. "They're all worthless. We need someone who won't shy away from challenges. Someone ready to experiment and discover... See what you can learn about that Alluvendran: who he is, what his alleged crimes were, and where is he held."

"Yes, my queen." Phuran bowed, but as his back straightened, he suddenly froze, scanning the crowd in the square.

She knew that look. The sharp look of the assassin, and not the mellow expression of the adviser. "Is something wrong?" Words nearly refused to push through her clenched throat, but she forced them out. Whatever the threat, she needed to know.

"I thought I saw Ryell qi'Teshari among the commoners." Phuran turned to her, already relaxed.

Blood left Cahala's face and drowned her heart.

"Impossible." Her voice broke. "He was ordered to stay in Devanshari. He should have died in the siege. He can't be here." A deep breath did nothing to calm her, but it did remind her she needed to keep her appearances.

"If he's still alive, I'll find him." Phuran's voice left no doubt of his intention.

"Very well." Cahala gave her cheeks a gentle pinch to return the red lost. "Ensure that we never see his face again." She resumed the descent, her chin high again.

"Yes, my queen."

THE BRACELET CAME TO LIFE, and the nightfly's crystal wings flared with pure energy. It made no sound as it ascended, and Kamira watched its spins with fascination, then focused on controlling it. It yielded as she made it twist through the air with sharp turns, pressing the small creature's limits. Following her will, the nightfly spiraled down, breaking its descent at the last moment. It skimmed above the floor and shot up again.

"Amazing!" Kamira glanced at the other bracelet, but one seemed enough until she learned to control it.

"I see you're enjoying your gift."

Her heart skipped a beat, and she lost control of the nightfly, but instead of shattering on the floor, it hovered in front of her. After all, Veranesh did say they would be able to communicate through the bracelets, so it made sense he could also command them.

She held off the sarcastic reply that came to mind. "I do."

"You were about to say something else."

"I figured fighting with my demon isn't the best approach to a pact," Kamira replied, surprised he caught it.

The demoness she had a pact with previously couldn't discern subtle changes in Kamira's voice. The historic accounts of Veranesh being genuinely interested in humans and their world must be true, though why he would have such curiosity when he came to the world to destroy it was beyond her. "Besides, I fight with Veelk all the time, so I don't need to add to my daily punishment."

Veranesh laughed. "What a subtle way of telling me that we don't share a similar bond."

She fought to keep her face straight. The demon definitely knew enough about human nature and habits to proceed with caution. "So, what are you here for?" she asked, changing the topic. "To check on me?"

The nightfly flew several circles over her head before Veranesh replied, "To enjoy the meager substitute for freedom. To get to know the pactee with whom I entrusted my *true* freedom."

"You've done it before, haven't you?" The creatures back in the Towers were made of the same crystal, and he did admit to have used them—it became clear how.

"That's true. Though my constructs can't survive on their own for long. Neither can they go far."

She smiled as it became clear that he had ulterior motives in giving her the nightflies. "But now, with a pactee to sustain them, you can explore wherever I go. Cunning."

A hiss that came through the creature sounded much like disapproval. "These are gifts. You can use them however you see fit or not at all, and I'll not interfere. Though I can communicate through them, or if needed, control them when you're unable or unwilling."

She shifted on the floor when laughter shook her. "Why would I believe a higher demon would do a scout's or messenger's bidding for me?"

"Don't you think that after four hundred years in the same place I might be bored?" Amusement resonated through the nightfly's crystal body, but Kamira's silence was the only reply. "You still don't trust me, do you?" The previous jovial tone had faded from his voice.

She saw no reason to deny it. "No."

Convincing him of her trust might have gained her an upper hand, but after all that transpired back in the Towers, Veranesh would not believe any hasty reassurances. As much as going against a cunning opponent was unappealing, she had to appreciate the demon's insights. From what little she knew about his kind, not many of them bothered with understanding humans any more than it served their immediate goals.

"Fair enough, pactee." The nightfly glided down, toward her wrist. "I have time."

"Wait!" Kamira called out, and when the nightfly paused, it became clear she'd been played. "Curse you, demon, and your games."

Veranesh chuckled, and she found no anger in his voice. "I've seen the likes of you. Careful, suspicious, but always full of questions. You won't trust me, but it won't stop you from getting all the information you can giving back as little as possible."

Caught again, she reined in her frustration. "I apologize," she muttered. Veranesh reminded her of Master Tijhran, and her teacher always knew how to push her into a defensive stance. It didn't help either that the demon was right about her intentions.

"No need. I forced you into this pact, and you have indeed all the reasons to distrust me," Veranesh said. "But I won't answer your questions until you're ready... to accept that my replies might be honest."

She thought about it. "That makes sense." Not that she liked admitting it. At some point, she would have to figure out how to convince the demon he'd earned her trust, otherwise he'd never give her any answers.

"But I can still teach you," he said, to her surprise, "as a gesture of goodwill. If you wake up the other nightfly, I'll show you how to control it. With a trance, you might be able to look through its eyes and follow its flight."

She didn't even try to hide her excitement. Besides, it could serve her well. Showing genuine interest could convince Veranesh of her growing trust better than any attempt at deception. After all, the meager skill she had in the arts of manipulation paled in comparison to the demon's centuries of experience.

To her surprise, the demon proved to be a patient teacher, and Kamira found herself enjoying the lesson, more so when she shared the feeling of flying through the nightfly's eyes. They jumped between the creatures, swapping control while they spiraled and darted through the air. She chased Veranesh across the room and hid between the furniture, and not even once did the demon complain about the childishness of their game. Experiencing the flight for herself made her better understand the torture of his captivity, and against her better judgment, she insisted on prolonging the lesson.

"That's enough for tonight," Veranesh announced when instead of falling into a trance, Kamira dozed off. "You're tired and getting sloppy."

She yawned. Her body was stiff, and the drenched clothes she never bothered changing stuck to her skin rigidly, as they had already dried. Veranesh's nightfly still hovered nearby, and of all the sarcastic comments her mind conjured, none felt appealing enough to be voiced, not after all the knowledge and excitement the demon had gifted her. He might have been playing her, appealing to her compassionate side or looking to gain her trust... She almost slapped herself for such thoughts. Giving in to suspicions meant stooping to the same deception and lies that she'd abhorred during her studies in the High Towers, and which had driven her away from her homeland.

At the same time, she intended to find a way to betray him in the end. A demon that caused the Cataclysm and destroyed a kingdom couldn't be set free, not ever and not for any price. But at least until then, she could find balance between trust and distrust and stay honest to whatever was left of her pride, the same that made her abandon her ambitions and turn down a promising future as a mage, and that ultimately pushed her into a role of an insignificant arcanist. If she didn't want all these choices to be meaningless, if she wanted to keep her chin high up, she couldn't go down the spiral of endless lies until she had no other way.

Veranesh still kept the nightflies in the air, unmoved by her silence, and she called one of them to her wrist, where it froze back into a crystal bracelet. Then she cracked the window.

"Here's some trust, demon," she said before heading for bed.

7

The yalari sat among the rubble of the Devanshari's Great Palace in the scorched gardens where the artifact pedestal once stood. Even shattered, it continued to tease their senses, and Myrkan's four companions revealed their uneasiness with twitches and curled wings. Their instincts still demanded destruction, and the sight of the white marble, crumbled and marked with flames and blood, did little to ease their minds. Humans might not have been much of a challenge, after all, but their world still carried the notion of unknown threats. Over time, Myrkan grew used to those alien lands, but he understood the restlessness of his brethren.

"We're done here," Derazin said. "We should go back and ensure our domains are still intact."

His massive, obese body only enhanced his discomfort in the realm of humans. Back in the yalari's world, he could compensate his weight with the ever-present energies, but drawing on it here proved to be cumbersome to all of them. Out of his element and impaired, Derazin acted frantically and without confidence, and Myrkan kept calculating how to use it to his own advantage.

"Derazin's right. Uganel is dealing with all the other matters." Trupyad's habit of blindly supporting whomever spoke first make Myrkan regret he hadn't claimed seniority. The yalari's small, sleek frame moved like a snake. With not enough power to be considered a kanyalari, he was only invited to the covenant because of his knowledge of the arcanists who were willing to summon powerful yalari to their world. That alone, to Myrkan's regret, earned Trupyad a place among them and the right to have his say. "He'll deal with the gaharra who ran away and ensure the mages are keeping their part of the deal."

"And what if he doesn't?" Fyertash said in a confident tone, but the glance he threw at Myrkan gave him away. To think he was once a powerful kanyalari, with that weak spine of his, made Myrkan cringe. But at least he could count on Fyertash's support. "What if there are complications? It's human world, and we sent him to deal with a problem caused by a yalari who outwitted many of us in the past."

As Myrkan expected, such a remark didn't sit well with Derazin—after all, no one liked to be reminded of their defeats.

"We came here only to destroy the artifact." Derazin raised his voice as if that could convince anyone to his side. "It no longer draws energy and causes pain to all the yalari, so there's no reason to keep this going." His wide gesture indicated all of them.

"So eager to start infighting again?" Arujhan, the most powerful among them, joined in. His shape resembled that of a human, with eagle-like wings stretching proudly from his back. He looked at his long talons as if he could see himself in the shiny black surface.

"It's not about the artifact anymore." Myrkan stared at Derazin with a challenge. "We all felt Veranesh's power echo through this world. He must have found a way to shed the binding. And even if he's not free yet, relying on those indolent high mages could be our downfall."

"They aren't stupid. They wouldn't let him escape," Trupyad said. "Veranesh can try as much as he wants, but there's no way he can break free."

"There's always a way." Arujhan looked down at the sly yalari. "I agree with Myrkan. This isn't about the artifact anymore."

"So what do you propose? We follow Uganel and pay Veranesh a visit?" Derazin mocked. "Wouldn't *that* pose a threat?"

Myrkan stood up, drawing everyone's attention. He was, after all, the leader of this covenant, even if others were more powerful than him. "It's time we dealt with all the problems once and for all. With the gaharra who might try to rebuild the artifact, the yalari who should be destroyed instead of being trapped, and with the humans who become more and more of a threat without anyone to control them."

Derazin's jaw dropped. "You're thinking another invasion!"

"That's ridiculous!" Trupyad's voice echoed within the ruins, scattering carrion birds from the rubble. "And have you thought of what the Four will do if we march for the lands they consider theirs?"

Myrkan instinctively closed his fists, ready to crush the spineless yalari. The mention of the Four, the powerful yalari protecting a human kingdom spoiled his mood, but they could be used both as a threat and as an incentive.

"They won't do anything if we keep away from their borders," Fyertash replied, staring Trupyad down with his eyebrow arched. "And they do keep their humans in check, so there's nothing for us to do there."

Myrkan gave him a quick nod, but his attention shifted to the only demon who hadn't said anything about his plan yet, and sure enough, he caught Arujhan's openly calculating gaze.

"You intend to enslave humans," Arujhan said, as the others fell silent, "why not kill them?"

"They have their uses." Myrkan paced around his companions, holding off a smile at the suspicious glances when he passed behind their backs. Covenant or not, their bodies responded to what their instincts deemed a possible threat. Only Arujhan stared unmoved into the blue sky over the rubble. "We could benefit from the strength of their minds without entering pacts, without giving anything. Their devotion could tip the scales of the power struggle."

"Use them like that poor gaharra Pardayi does?" Derazin asked.

Myrkan huffed. "Pardayi only has a small temple and nearly begs humans for a petty handful of devotion." He spat, and the saliva landed by Trupyad's leg, close enough to be a clear message to the weak yalari. "I'm talking about whole nations bowing to us. About ensuring no yalari would stand against us... even the Four that you and Trupyad tremble so much about."

"A bold plan," Arujhan said. "And it requires armies we don't have. Many asayalari fell during the siege, and the pactees we used to summon them are exhausted."

"We've shown our power with the destruction of a human kingdom," Fyertash said. "We'll lure more pactees with promises of magic and get the army ready while Uganel deals with the most pressing matters."

Derazin looked down at the speaker, and his loathing expression reminded Myrkan that the two yalari had history. Details eluded his memory, but their mutual hostility was connected to a rebellion five centuries earlier, or ten centuries if he bothered counting in human years. Betrayal and fights were so common among his kind that Myrkan could hardly grasp a reason for them to hold on to grudges for so long.

"That's absurd." Derazin never took his eyes off Fyertash as he spoke, making it clear that he was ready to argue anything that came out of Fyertash's mouth. "Preparations would take weeks, if not months, and we'd still have to take the army across the sea. We should leave everything in Uganel's able hands. If you're worried, we can send someone to help him."

Myrkan jumped at the chance. "Are you volunteering, then?" The sarcastic comment brought the desired effect— Derazin looked away.

Arujhan stood up before any response could trigger more fighting. "Let's vote."

Myrkan looked at the yalari towering over them, and his teeth gritted while he sat down, but he knew better than to challenge openly. Arujhan was one of the most powerful yalari, with his domain stretching across the vast plains of their world. One day... One day Myrkan would wash that smug face of Arujhan's with his own blood, but until then, it was wiser for Myrkan to keep his head down. Arujhan made a habit of disposing of his opponents swiftly and before they rose to true power capable of threatening him.

Derazin said, "We're done here. Time to return to our realm."

"I think the same," Trupyad chimed in.

With a grimace of contempt, Fyertash stared at his predecessors. "If that gaharra rebuilds the artifact, we'll back where we started. We should finish it. All of it."

"You know my vote," Myrkan said when Arujhan finally looked at him.

"That I do. And I'll support it."

"What?" Derazin rose.

Arujhan walked over, his wings spread wide and body overwhelming the other yalari. "We've voted."

His words left the right impression, and Derazin returned to his spot, though with barely concealed dissatisfaction.

Myrkan expected the infighting to ensue as soon as they dissolved their covenant. Yalari rarely allied, and such alliances hardly ever lasted longer than necessary. All the more, he strove to understand Arujhan's motives to vote in his favor. After the deed was done, and the artifact didn't threaten them anymore, the most reasonable thing to do was to return to their realm and ensure their domains were safe... Myrkan almost grinned when the answer presented himself. Arujhan had enough power to discourage anyone from going after his lands or taking back what could be taken, while others' domains would slowly crumble without their presence, stolen away by their ambitious neighbors. The longer they stayed in the human world, the weaker they became, and that likely served Arujhan's plans well if he intended to take what was theirs, but Myrkan considered the risk worth taking. If they got rid of Veranesh and conquered human nations, he wouldn't need a yalari domain anymore. No more squabbles over crumbs with other yalari when he'd have all the humans to rule over.

Maybe he would even join forces with the Four, and ensure no other yalari ever considered coming to this world again.

That brought the most genuine smile to his face. Even if only through Arujhan's support, Myrkan had won against Derazin. "Let's start the preparations then."

With the votes cast, and neither Derazin nor Trupyad willing to openly contend Arujhan, all the yalari departed. Fyertash took off to inspect their remaining asayalari forces. Derazin hobbled toward the ruined port, since he was the craftiest among them and could salvage whatever was left from the Devanshari destroyed ships, and Trupyad scurried off to find more arcanists through his contacts. Myrkan hesitated, but he couldn't help Trupyad with his task, and reason dictated staying away from Derazin, so unless he wanted to roam the rubble pointlessly, joining Fyertash was the best choice.

"Myrkan."

Arujhan's voice stopped him from leaving, and Myrkan tensed. He knew the other yalari would demand repayment for his support in the voting, but he didn't expect such a conversation so soon.

"The high mages are losing their grip," Arujhan continued, "and we can't count on them keeping Veranesh imprisoned. He's more a threat than the Devanshari can ever be, even if they rebuild their artifact."

Myrkan nodded slowly, eyeing the other yalari. "A new artifact would just bring the frustration back, but Veranesh... He'd destroy us," he said, choosing a cautious reply. There had to be a reason for such obvious remarks, and he'd rather wait for Arujhan to reveal his intentions.

Arujhan huffed in amusement and stared toward the sea. "For what we did to him, he'd have us suffering for years. You'd beg him to finish you."

The tone of his voice made Myrkan shiver. A kanyalari speaking words padded with fear had to be taken seriously, and it gave him the opening he needed. "You have something in mind, don't you? That's why you supported me in the voting."

"I do." Arujhan looked at Derazin, whose massive silhouette towered over the rubble in the distance. "This temporary covenant won't last. It might be time to forge a new one."

"OUCH! You're pulling our hair, you stupid girl!" Cahala swatted at the maid's hand. "One would think you grew up in the woods, not in what is supposed to be one of the finest cities of this continent." Even saying that brought a cringe about, because her lodgings left much to be desired. Cramped in an ordinary residence with rooms resembling cargo crates instead of comfortable and spacious chambers, and a garden the size of a single flowerbed, she hardly could consider her surroundings "finest."

"I'm so sorry, my lady. I'll be more careful."

The fear and servility in the girl's voice soothed Cahala's mood only a little, because no matter how many times she expressed her displeasure or threatened to send them away, those Kaighalan servants never yielded to address her appropriately. She could understand none of them would call her their queen, but they never added "your majesty" to their responses either. Of course, she knew that in that semi-civilized town, citizens considered one's wealth first and ignored anyone's birthright all the same, but sharing the title with some lowlifes who happened to stumble across a coin or two only added insult to the injury.

The maid's wide eyes fixed on her made it clear the girl didn't realize how disrespectful she was, and Cahala sighed. Even if her servant deserved solid scolding, crying and apologizing would only delay everything.

"You better," Cahala replied. "Light bless us all, you wouldn't last a day in a minor Devanshari noble's house with your clumsy hands."

"Yes, my lady."

Cahala grimaced at the sudden cold tone in her servant's voice. People around here clearly didn't appreciate the opportunity of serving someone of royal blood. As the maid continued brushing, the queen let her thoughts drift toward home and Hajihali. The memory of its glow warming Devanshari hearts faded when confronted with her growing craving. The essence could only help so much, and its supply was fading.

A knock on the door brought Cahala back to reality, and she barked, "Enter!"

Phuran walked in, and his sight smoothed her creased forehead. Phuran never bothered her without a good reason, so she could at least hope for good news.

"My queen, Adept Davshil of Gildya Magna is here to see you," he said.

She clapped her hands. "Finally! We'll receive him in our leisure room as soon as this inept peasant is done with our hair." She scrutinized the hairdo in the mirror. "Never mind. This will do. A few months more and you might actually learn how to perform such a simple task." She waved the maid away with satisfaction when the gilded vanity mirror revealed the glint of the servant's tears before she bowed and rushed away.

In a better mood, Cahala sprayed her body with a mist

of flower water and walked over to the leisure room where the adept already awaited her.

The only furnishing was a cushioned bench and a low table, but the space still remained limited, and Adept Davshil didn't keep close to the door like any supplicant should to ensure a queen's comfort, and Cahala fought with the urge to turn away and leave at such a display of disrespect. Yet the contraption resting on the table and the craving twisting her bowels made her swallow her pride.

"My lady, I bring good news!" At least he had enough wits to bow before he pointed at the table. "I believe we've managed to recreate your lost artifact's function."

"This?" Cahala arched her eyebrow. "It's rather small."

Davshil fidgeted, but regained his composure in a heartbeat. "It's only a prototype, my lady, to ensure its properties match the ones you require. Shall I demonstrate?"

"Go ahead." She sat on the cushioned bench.

Davshil tinkered with the device, and each moment he took only heightened her ire. If that thing required so much work to be of use, it couldn't have been a replacement for the artifact. Yet when it finally hummed, the room filled with magic, and Cahala closed her eyes and relaxed. It had a different rhythm and felt less intense than what she remembered, but her body responded with immediate relief. A gentle smile danced on her lips.

"Yes. We are satisfied with Gildya's effort." She savored the moment. "We are satisfied with the device."

"On behalf of Gildya, I thank you, my lady." Davshil bowed. "I'm authorized to leave this device with you, if you so wish, and we can start manufacturing more. It's quite a simple concept, so the cost is not going to be high."

"That is pleasing to hear." Cahala never opened her eyes, enjoying the foreign pulse of magic. "As usual, discuss details with our adviser."

"As you wish, my lady. I'll instruct him about the device's care and leave a supply of imbued stones—"

"Imbued stones?" Her eyes snapped open.

"They power the device, my lady. We calculated that a medium stone can sustain the device for about a month."

Blood rushed through her veins, all the ire of the morning returning a thousand-fold. "Are you trying to jest us?! The artifact we had in Devanshari needed no foolish stones! It drew magic straight from the demon realm." Her voice rose as she spoke. "This is a mockery of the fine Devanshari arts and an attempt to enslave our people to Gildya! We will not stand for this!"

Davshil's face lost all color. "My lady, the artifact you had in Devanshari was ancient, and there are no writings of its construction." He took a hesitant step backward, as if the limited space of the room could impose any distance between them. "Gildya's sailing through uncharted waters, and this device is a huge step forward in attempts to recreate the artifact's true power. But it's going to take time and—"

"Then get back to work!" Cahala gestured at the door. "We do not wish to see you again until you have something of worth to show." Her shouts lured Phuran, and he stood by the open door, ready to dispose of any threat, real or not. His sight soothed her anger. "Pay this man whatever he's owed for that lousy bauble and see him to the door," she told him.

When they left, she fell back to the cushion, her anger evaporating as the device hummed and the magic soothed her body. The very thought of losing that feeling of easiness made her crumble like the walls of the Devanshari capital.

Those cursed demons... They had to come and destroy everything! Memories of the golden palace, of the respect and wealth she had, forced tears from her eyes, and she instinctively checked her surroundings to ensure no one could see her. She stared at the device, that imperfect, lousy bauble mocking the lost Light, and her vision blurred while the thought of being hungry again made her blood cold. She couldn't lose it again. She just couldn't.

When Phuran returned, she was sobbing into the armrest. Without a word, he dried her eyes with a silken sleeve before moving away and bowing as any loyal servant would.

"He's gone now, my queen," he said softly, though his face reflected no emotions. "And I bring a piece of what might be better news."

The last of her sob died in her throat, and she looked at him with hope. "You've found him?"

He offered his smile, the one that always preceded the announcement of things done, even those things that many of her other advisers would question. But they didn't get the same results Phuran did, and Cahala waited eagerly for his report.

"I've found them both. One of my spies discovered the whereabouts of the prisoner called Alluvendran, though reaching him might be difficult and will require some prior arrangements. Davshil spoke truth, my queen—this adept is heavily guarded."

She nodded without even asking whether it was possible to get to that adept. If Phuran bothered her with such information, he must have already been devising a suitable plan. "And Ryell? What about him?" she asked instead. That wretched royal guard who was no one, and who was supposed to be a dead no one, still haunted her with his presence. Even if he couldn't be a real threat to her, getting rid of him would ensure no disruptions to her plans.

"He's been seen around Gildya, most likely trying to gain information on you, my queen. I took the liberty of making sure he won't be of trouble to you."

She grimaced, because the meaning of his message was clear. "If he has others around when your killers come, his death might arouse questions. Maybe we should have him brought before us and judged as a Devanshari traitor instead."

Phuran shook his head. "I thought this bore too much risk. We don't know how much proof he has, and any manipulations of the trial would raise even more suspicions. No matter the verdict, some people could start doubting you, my queen. But I thought of another way."

Cahala couldn't help arching an eyebrow. "Now you've got our attention." Phuran's approach to getting rid of problems was always quite final, and he rarely settled for discrediting her opponents or thwarting their efforts, ensuring they never rose against her again.

His expression shifted, revealing both cruelty and satisfaction, as if the mere thought of his plan brought him pleasure. "On his way out, I mentioned to Adept Davshil a certain Devanshari rogue who makes bold accusations of Gildya's involvement in the attack on our land. I made it clear that you, my queen, can't act against your own people and suppress their right to express their concerns, but if the man happened to disappear, it would surely better the uneasy relations between Gildya and the Devanshari. And if anyone asks questions, they're free to accuse him of thieving from Gildya or any other crime."

She laughed and clapped her hands. "That's brilliant! Phuran, we're so lucky to have you."

"I'm happy to serve." He bowed.

With Ryell nigh out of the way, her focus shifted. She indicated for Phuran to sit beside her, a sign of her favor that she rarely offered to anyone but him. "Tell us more of Alluvendran," she said, her voice filled with excitement. "Where is he? What will we need? Is there going to be any danger?"

He took the seat, but his posture remained stiff, indicating readiness to spring back to his feet, and his dark blue eyes never lost focus. "He's kept in the woods to the north, near the Tivarashan border. Gildya used to have an outpost there that was supposedly abandoned years ago, but they've secretly changed it into a prison. It's full of guards in imbued armor, armed with Gildya's best weapons, and there is gossip of three golems. All that for one man."

"He must be quite powerful, then. It means we won't be wasting our time on him." She relaxed, considering their next steps. While the device Davshil delivered could only be considered a temporary solution, she appreciated the clarity of thought it offered along with providing much-needed relief. "We'll leave the planning to you, but we want to be present when that man is freed. We'll also need a discreet place away from Gildya's eyes, so Alluvendran can work undisturbed."

"Of course, my queen." He stood up. "I'll have everything arranged as soon as possible."

"Do not rush," Cahala cautioned him. "We can wait a bit longer, and the success is more important than time." Even if she had to rely on Davshil's trinket until then, it seemed capable of keeping her hunger for magic at bay.

"Yes, my queen."

As he left, she stretched back on the cushions, enjoying

the soothing flow of magic. The day was shaping to be much better than how it had started.

WITH HIS HANDS pressed to his forehead, Allyv sat at the table staring at the research notes. The letters danced in front of his eyes and blurred into meaningless babble. Retorts behind him stood forgotten, and the contents of their dirtied glass brought no solution. Countless combinations of ingredients and their proportions waited to be tested, and he wandered through them like a child through an ancient library. All he needed was one step, one discovery to set the research in the right direction, but all the attempts so far only made him doubt whether a replacement for liquefied magic could even exist.

The essence in his flask shrank every day, and he caught himself torn between trying to preserve it and ensuring his mind was clear enough to do the work. At that thought, he tilted the mug, but it didn't reveal any leftover liquid, so he poured more water from the jug. He downed it in one swig, but it contained no trace of the essence, and his gaze wandered toward the hip flask again. Before reaching out for it, he clenched his fist. He didn't have enough to be indulgent.

"Lord Allyv?" A knock on the door accompanied Gulir's voice. "There's someone to see you. A man named Fento qi'Aytrella."

Allyv jumped up at the name. "Tell him I'll be right there, and make sure he's comfortable waiting."

For Gulir, native to Kaighal, qi'Aytrella was nothing more than another Devanshari name, but the prince remembered well his father's closest friend and adviser.

The memory pushed others to the surface, carrying Allyv to the times before the demon attack took his father from him, but he chased them away and rushed over to the trunk, digging for his best shirt and searching the cluttered room for his shoes. His mind raced, and as much as he respected Fento, he grew anxious of such an unexpected visit. The nobleman didn't approve of the asylum, but generations of the fine Devanshari bloodline urged the qi'Aytrella family and many others to distance themselves from the commoners Allyv was surrounded with. Yet it would be so like his mother to send someone Allyv admired to convince him to abandon his pursuits. He let out a sigh. No matter what reason Fento had to visit, Allyv had to see him.

He ran this fingers through his blond hair, more out of a habit than an attempt to force them into place, and left the room. Rushing down the stairs, he caught glimpses of people roaming the floors, and the emptiness in their eyes brought a mix of pain and determination. His mother might be the queen, but she couldn't order him away from those who needed them, and no tricks or rhetoric would change his mind.

Several workers, some from Kaighal and some Devanshari less afflicted by the essence deprivation, interrupted their tasks to greet him, and he waved back, never stopping. Only when he reached the bottom floor did Allyv allow himself a moment of rest, and the hasty breath wheezed from his lungs. Hajha was right: wrapped up in his research, Allyv had forgotten to see to his body's fitness. Maybe later, in the afternoon... Before he could make any plans, his thoughts returned to the guest waiting for him.

He fashioned a warm smile and, with his back straight, walked into the reception area, but the words of greeting never left his mouth when Fento's desperate face made it clear he hadn't come as the queen's envoy.

"Help her, please!"

Behind him, limp in the chair, sat a copper-haired woman. Allyv remembered Shyoli qi'Aytrella from his childhood. They'd played in the palace gardens while their fathers discussed state affairs, and the memory of a cute, talkative girl contrasted with the sight of the quiet young woman whose complexion had lost its rosy hue. As a moan accompanied her shivering, Fento jumped to her side, holding her hand and whispering words of comfort.

With the two so close to each other, Allyv didn't need long to realize the father's state wasn't much better than his daughter's.

"What happened?" he asked. "She doesn't seem to be in withdrawal."

"She's not." Fento shook his head, his expression pained. "We have enough essence... enough to get by for a little longer. But we've tried to lower the dose, see if we can survive taking less." He fought to keep his composure, but his eyes filled with tears when he looked at Shyoli.

Allyv put his hand on Fento's shoulder. "She took something else, didn't she?"

"It's a new way among the youngsters, taking in powdered imbued stones with wine."

"Light bless us!" Allyv's eyes widened.

Fento's shoulders slumped as if, contrary to reason, he'd been expecting words of reassurance, not horror. Yet he didn't look away. "They say it brings something more than just temporary relief. I had my doubts, but Shyoli ignored my words." His voice broke, and he hid his face in his hands. His shoulders shivered with suppressed sobbing. "Maybe if I wasn't so harsh—"

"The sickness pushes our instincts to the surface. The hunger is hard to control," Allyv said softly. No matter what Fento would have done or said differently, he couldn't win with the craving that consumed them all.

Fento looked up at Allyv, eyes red and watery with traces of tears smudged over his unshaved cheeks, and an understanding flashed on his face. "You suffer too, don't you? To think the queen would deny essence for her own son is outrageous."

"I parted ways with my mother, and I don't expect her support." Allyv raised his chin. "Cahala qi'Devanshari is shortsighted and doesn't wish for our people to be cured. All she wants is Hajihali to be replaced, so she can bathe in its light again."

A moment of silence hung between them, and Allyv expected an expression of outrage for such disrespectful and harsh words, but instead Fento regarded him in thought, like he used to do when Allyv presented his skills or knowledge.

"And that doesn't solve the problem," Fento replied. "We were attacked once, so we can be attacked again, and our Light can be taken from us. You've grown, Prince Allyv." Pride rang in his words.

"I'm trying to be the man my people expect me to be." Allyv offered a faint smile and modesty, though Fento's words strengthened his resolve. "But now we need to find a way to help your daughter." No matter the praise, if Allyv couldn't help Shyoli, Fento's respect would quickly fade.

"Can you do it?"

Allyv chose honesty instead of reassuring lies. "I haven't had a case like this so far, but I'm sure I can at least ease her pain. There is a spare room upstairs. It's meager, but she'll be comfortable, and people here are used to helping the sick."

Fento hesitated, but sighed in surrender and picked up Shyoli. No matter how run-down the building looked, he must have realized that here, at the asylum, she would be under the care of those who dealt with similar situations, and who would search for a cure and try new ways to ease her condition. At home, all the servants would do was bring her food and water and change the compress if she needed it.

Allyv asked Hajha to bring his medicine bag while he sifted through his memory, choosing possible treatments. Shyoli might be the first, but he had no doubt his asylum would soon see more of this affliction, because even if other noblemen laughed at his efforts or cut ties upon Cahala's pressure, they would all come to him when everything else failed. If Allyv wanted to ensure their favor, or at least neutrality, he needed to find a way to deal with the condition quicker than more sick would arrive.

At his call, the asylum came to life. Hajha came first. She handed Allyv the bag and darted off muttering about getting a hearty meal for them all, unmoved by Fento's disapproving gaze when she showed no due respect to either of them. Then Gulir took Shyoli from the nobleman, her tiny frame no burden for his massive arms. Another man brought light blankets and fresh linens. As they ascended the stairs, many people stopped to offer their help or words of reassurance and comfort.

Fento's face expressed doubts as he looked past the tattered furniture and shabby walls, but Allyv ignored it. To him, the sight of his people working together like a perfect crew brought an unexpected realization. As poor as the asylum was, it belonged to him. He organized it, oversaw every task, and ensured everyone in need received care. In return, people trusted his decisions and respected him. Following Gulir and Fento upstairs, Allyv didn't even bother to conceal his expression as the understanding poured at him like the blessed Light.

Never in the past, not even in Devanshari, sitting on his father's throne, had Allyv felt so clear what it was to be a king.

8

Kamira yawned as they made their way north, ignoring Veelk's amused glances. They hadn't left at dawn, as she had planned to, and even at noon it seemed too early to get out of bed, but with Yoreus still alive, she didn't want to dawdle.

They had long left the bustling Kaighal streets and its busy outskirts behind, and the paved path led them across the fields and pastures toward the line of trees. As she looked past the woods, her thoughts turned toward home. Further to the north, two weeks of travel, lay Tivarashan. She didn't miss it much, especially not after her last visit, but the sight of woods always made her wonder how things were back with her family. Save for an occasional letter, she rarely heard from them, which suggested her father still couldn't forgive her the scandal she had caused. At that, Kamira smirked. He should have been happy she didn't chose a demonologist way to pay him back for his deception and manipulation, because for Tivarashan families, scandals were a minor transgression, while performing unsanctioned arcane arts caused much more trouble. That thought made her cringe. Yet another point she disagreed on with her father, who dutifully worshiped the Four and believed all arcanists should be controlled by the Temple. But then, a priestess's position would be prestigious enough... more so than a "wandering demonologist for hire," as he'd called her before she turned her back on him.

"So, what did you do last night?" Veelk's words snapped Kamira out of her memories. "You didn't wake up when I came back."

She couldn't tell whether he intended to shift her attention away from grim thoughts or picked the moment to catch her off guard, but they could have been one and the same. He must have been waiting for the opportune moment to ask the question, and at the same time used it to lighten her mood with his usual teasing.

"I took your advice. I had fun," she pretended to fall for his bait.

"Drinking a bottle of wine?" He rolled his eyes. "I think next time I should take you with me."

"Are you sure you want me to spoil your time with the ladies?" she teased. "I can think of so many ways to ensure you'll never insist on my company again."

Veelk grinned, making it clear he was ready to challenge her claim, and before Kamira could control her reaction, he burst out laughing. With a smile, she shook her head. After so many years of traveling together, he still managed to startle her.

When she didn't reply, he gave her a playful nudge. "I don't get why you're so picky when it comes to choosing a lover. Take one, and if you don't like him, find another one."

She pretended her focus was on the forest they were approaching. Yet if he thought she'd given up, he was in for a disappointment, and she threw her own bait. "I did have fun last night," she murmured, mustering some frustration into her voice, as if his remarks had hit the right spot.

"Alone?"

The corner of her lip lifted. "I had company." No need to mention Veranesh's name.

Veelk laughed, and Kamira could swear his deep, gruff voice scared birds off the nearby branches. When he looked back at her, with another tease at the ready, she offered him a smug smile. His eyes opened wider.

"You are serious..." He stepped in front of her, barring the way. "Was he handsome? Was he *good*?" His wide grin made it clear she wouldn't get away with a mere claim.

She pretended to consider his questions. "I guess you could call him handsome." The sheer thought of Veranesh as a romantic partner to anyone made it hard to keep her face straight, but she had to admit the demon had appealing—if inhuman—features. "And by the pact... he was really good." She savored Veelk's dumbfounded expression before adding, "Though I can't tell you anything about his bed skills, if that's what you had in mind."

His shoulders slumped. "I give up. You're hopeless."

As he turned away and resumed their journey, Kamira allowed herself a chuckle of victory. At that, he threw her a playful glance, his face promising the payback to come.

"So, what did you do last night?" he asked when she caught up with him, his casual tone a sign he was done with teasing for the time being.

"Magic."

It would have been obvious, if he hadn't have fallen for her trap, and Veelk nodded. "And the company?"

Her only response was a glance at her wrists as she brushed past the nightflies. Even though the road looked empty, speaking Veranesh's name out loud felt like an invitation for trouble.

Veelk became serious in an instant. "Are you sure? Playing with fire…"

"If I don't, he might grow impatient or suspicious." No matter how many times she tried to find a solution, she couldn't find a good one, and staying on the demon's good side was better than risking his rage. Her vision dimmed at the memory of the severed pact and the pain Veranesh's spell put her through.

Veelk didn't respond, and the mood soured. With all the fears that came from dealing with such a powerful demon, Kamira didn't want to mention what Veranesh had taught her the previous night. As grateful as she was for his lessons, she wouldn't allow herself to forget who he was. With that thought, she picked up her pace, pointing at the crossroad.

The road split, the paved one leading north, toward the Tivarashan border, while the westbound one disappeared within the trees. Their feet hit the dirt as soon as they took the turn. The dry season ensured it remained traversable, but Veelk still eyed it with doubt.

"We should have taken the west road from Kaighal instead."

Kamira rolled her eyes. He knew that getting to the closest river crossing would add at least half a day to their journey. "You can survive a few trees," she said. If Veelk had one weakness, it was his dislike for woods and wet weather. "And Gaunash isn't that far."

"Let's go, then," he announced with a sudden vigor and took off down the path.

Kamira rushed after him, suspicion creeping in her mind.

"We're being followed," he muttered as soon as she caught up. "Four men, since Kaighal."

A huff was her initial response. "You should have said something earlier."

Veelk shrugged. "We couldn't do anything until we got here. They will want no witnesses, and so will we."

He offered a wide grin with his words, and she involuntarily reciprocated it, though in a more restrained manner. Her blood rushed in anticipation of the confrontation to come. Four men meant they didn't mean to spy on them or ask a few questions, but at the same time, it felt odd that there were so few of them if they sought to kill.

"Maybe some thugs who thought I'd be easy target."

She gave an absent-minded nod. "Yoreus wouldn't be such a fool. He'd pay real assassins." One glance over her shoulder told Kamira that the path behind them was still empty. "We should give them time to catch up with us."

"They won't be long," Veelk replied. "If they really are after us, they won't risk us disappearing in the trees, but we better get away from the main road."

As much as she wanted to ensure the thugs didn't give up on them, she made no objections. They were so close to the well-traveled route that they risked innocents getting caught up in the fray. "If I remember correctly, there should be a clearing further down the road."

If she remembered correctly... It'd been too long since the last time she'd walked that path, but traveling with Veelk meant she'd never found time or a reason to visit her former teacher. Quite the contrary: having a mage killer for a companion gave her all the reasons to restrict communication to the letters. But finding Veranesh meant questions she couldn't entrust to paper and messengers, and she couldn't help thinking of Master Tijhran's expression when he told her what he thought about her lack of visits.

Deep in her thoughts, she didn't notice Veelk slowing to match his pace with her until he nudged her in the arm. "I thought the prospect of taking out your frustration on some ne'er-do-wells would cheer you up at least a bit."

With a chuckle, she replied, "We need them alive."

As she'd expected, he didn't give up. "One will be enough to talk, and I'm actually curious to see your new demon in action... in something more than just conjuring dancing flames and lumispheres."

At the remark, her whole body itched in anticipation. Sure, she used magic almost daily, for convenience or practice, but Veelk was right. The true power of the pact manifested in a fight, and that alone made her regret Yoreus had retreated instead of falling into her trap. To battle an archmage, even for those few moments before Veelk took care of him, would tell her more about Veranesh's power than any tale of the Cataclysm could.

Yet she shook her head. "We shouldn't draw attention for as long as we can." A day would come when she wouldn't be able to keep her pact a secret, but until then, it served them better if anyone who knew her still considered her an insignificant arcanist with an insignificant pact.

"You're no fun," he said. "There. Looks like a good spot."

The road wound, taking a sharp turn southward around a hill, and Kamira nodded. If they set up behind it, the thugs wouldn't see them until the last moment. She allowed herself a smile at the thought of confrontation. Veelk was right: they only needed one alive, and she indeed could use some venting of her frustration. Besides, if the men were hired by someone, letting them live would be foolish.

Veelk mirrored her smile, and she once more

appreciated her companion. With so many differences between them, when it came to survival, they thought alike. "Four..." she said. "That's hardly going to be a challenge."

≈

BACK WHEN KAMIRA studied under him, Master Tijhran often found ways to test and build her patience with meticulous studies and tedious tasks, but pointless waiting was different. With nothing to do, she leafed through Gayabal's journal in the desperate hope that a random passage would not only hold her attention but reveal the very secrets Yoreus was after. Instead, all she found was rambling of a frustrated man, jealous of pacts the best arcanists had. Every now and then, she looked up the road. Veelk was hiding nearby, and he wouldn't let anyone sneak up on her, but if she overlooked four thugs approaching, she'd never hear the end of it.

Cringing, she checked the road yet again. Only complete amateurs would keep their distance so far that their marks could freely disappear into the woods. Unless Veelk was wrong, and the thugs weren't after them. She discarded that thought. Veelk's instincts were always sharp, and he wouldn't make her wait for nothing. Holding off a groan of frustration, she glanced at the trees back at the curve of the road where he was hiding. His absence could alarm the thugs, but this way he could ensure no one else was coming and cut off the ones who would try to run.

She sneered. A lonely woman would look like an easy target, and when they rushed toward her, she'd make sure to make them pay for all the pointless waiting.

In the distance, angered voices carried. She could hardly discern the words behind the bickering, but she didn't need to. Hoarse voices and crude accents made it clear it wasn't merchants who were approaching.

The men were local to Kaighal, their copper skin darkened by sun and reddened by the alcohol, but their bodies were hardly those of tavern drunkards. None could match Veelk's muscles, but they would have no trouble instilling fear in common travelers. As they stopped at her sight, their faces unconcerned, first cruel smiles showing, it became clear that no one had told them who their target was.

"What kind of a guard leaves a woman alone in the forest?" one of them said.

"Maybe it was a lovers' quarrel," another added, and they all croaked in a twisted version of laughter.

Kamira didn't let her guard down at their seemingly casual approach. The way they moved suggested that even if they couldn't be sure she was a threat, their instincts tugged on their minds hard enough to force caution, and their carefree act must be meant to distract her.

"The kind of a guard who sets up a trap," she calmly replied.

They understood immediately, she had to give them that much. Two of them spun on their heels, facing to the back, where Veelk was walking out with his keshal stretched to the side, barring the way.

"Tell me, who sent you?" Kamira didn't wait for them to react.

They exchanged glances, but her question remained unanswered.

"Get her," barked the one she couldn't see from behind his companions, and the two thugs closest to her took off without hesitation.

She almost shook her head in disappointment. Even

back when she had much less magic at her disposal, two men were hardly a threat. Magic could make quick work of almost anyone, and even if everything else failed, she only needed her barrier to stay alive until Veelk got to her. With Veranesh's power at her disposal... she was definitely getting some answers.

With years of practice, magic flowed as soon as she stretched her hand forward, but its rush was still new and felt like a river that would never run dry, no matter how much she drew. Veranesh was, indeed, generous, and she took more of his gift than the situation required.

One of the thugs stopped wide-eyed as his companion flew backward, across the road, and smashed against a tree with a thump and crack before sliding down. His limp body showed no signs of life, and Kamira smirked at the other man. His face twisted in fear as he corrected the grip on his knife. She couldn't help wondering whether he'd feel tempted to throw it, but it didn't matter. The barrier had protected her ever since the band came in sight.

"Who sent you?" She might as well start asking questions already.

Farther down the road, Veelk had already disposed of his opponents, his keshal's blades red, but the last thug alive couldn't see it, with his eyes glued to Kamira as if he could see the magic coming before it was too late.

"'Twas... a man. Not from 'round 'ere." The thug swallowed heavily, closing his hands on the cloth of his dirty pants. "But not of them pale wimps."

That didn't tell her much except for confirming that Yoreus didn't have a hand in it. But if it wasn't that hateful Devanshari either, she had a hard time coming up with anyone else who would want her and Veelk dead.

"They got paid quite handsomely." Veelk approached,

displaying several pieces of jewelry. The glint of light the gemstones caught reassured her that these weren't mere trinkets. "Fine craftsmanship. Exotic."

That again suggested the Devanshari man, but Ryell didn't seem like someone who'd have servants to hire thugs for him. With her eyebrows arched, she stared the thug down. "And what were you supposed to do?"

At first, the only reply was silence, but he flinched when Veelk offered him a prod with the tip of his keshal. "We was to kill a woman called Kamira." He avoided her eyes. "And anyone she was going to meet. He told us none about a tribal." He glared at Veelk as if his presence alone made their task impossible. "And of magics." He spat, and his mouth moved voicelessly, but Kamira had no doubt he said something like "demon's gaharra." The tolerance for arcanists waned quickly when they interfered, and the man was no different.

She ignored the veiled insult, so used to hearing it around, and her mind immediately focused on the new piece of information. Ryell wouldn't have cared about killing anyone else, but with him and Yoreus off the list, she couldn't think of anyone else who would send thugs after her and anyone she was going to... Her eyes widened. The thought that struck her suggested the improbable, but with the recent events, she had to take it into consideration.

"So ya know who's after ya." The thug sent her an ugly grin. "He's not goin' to stop. But I could tell him you're dead."

Veelk looked down at him. "He got a name?"

The thug shrugged. "None he told us." He leaned forward with a sly expression, his gaze fixed on Kamira. "I can lead you to him."

He tried to keep her eyes locked, and Kamira huffed,

amused. Even if she missed his fidgeting hand, the knife he threw couldn't hurt her, and to his visible surprise, she didn't even flinch. The blade bounced off her barrier, and the unexpected outcome cost the thug precious time when, instead of reacting, he stared dumbfounded.

Veelk didn't wait, and with one thrust of his keshal's thin blade, he sent the thug to the ground. The unfortunate man dropped the other knife and curled, holding his leg, and his scream scared off nearby birds. "Demons take you both!"

Kamira sneered. "They already did."

Veelk waited for her signal, and as soon as she gave it, he struck once more. As he took the thug's head off with a clean cut, Kamira shivered at the reminder of how sharp his keshal was. In the past, these weapons were meant for arcanists.

"Did he really think he could take us both? He'd have been better off trying to run." He spat while cleaning his blade, and then looked at her. "You really know who hired them?"

"I have my suspicions." She stared at her wrists, and then woke up the nightfly.

"Pactee." Veranesh's voice was every bit formal. "Mage killer."

Veelk muttered a response that could have been a greeting before he headed over to the other dead bodies, and Kamira didn't bother with pleasantries.

"Would other demons have any reason to keep me from freeing you?" It pained her to even ask such question, because she'd rather keep Veranesh in the dark, but she needed to confirm her suspicions.

The first response was amused laughter, and the nightfly hovered over the dead body as if inspecting it. "I expected them to take longer to send someone after you. Though they do seem to have underestimated you."

Kamira did her best to keep the cringe off her face. A bit of forewarning would have been appreciated, but at the same time, she couldn't blame Veranesh. Maybe if she wasn't so reluctant to talk to him, he'd have revealed more.

In a swift move, the nightfly returned to her. "If you learn any names, I'd appreciate you sharing them with me." The malicious undertone made the demon's intentions obvious.

She couldn't help snickering. He must have guessed that if she knew those names already, she would have never asked. "So they want you trapped as you are."

"They aren't your allies, pactee." His voice carried a clear warning.

Reminding him that neither was he didn't seem like a good idea, so she remained silent.

"Is there anything else?" Veranesh asked. "Or all you needed was confirmation that my brethren will try to stop you?"

The sarcastic undertone in his questions was hard to miss, and Kamira smiled. "No, that's all." She hesitated as she lifted her forearm. "Do you want to...?"

"Does it make you feel better about asking questions, pactee?" Veranesh didn't conceal his ire. "Are you treating it as a bargain? Answers for a glimpse of freedom? Because you don't call upon me any other time."

Veranesh might be testing her, but to remind him that having flying and talking crystal nightflies about was hardly discreet felt like allowing him to drag her into an argument. With a huff, she focused her will on the creature, forcing it down to her wrist and pushing the demon's consciousness out. To her surprise, he yielded, and the nightfly curled around her forearm, once more becoming inanimate crystal.

"So, you do talk to your demon." Veelk returned, dragging two of the three corpses. He dumped them by the dead thug.

Her only response was a mean glare. Not that he'd take the warning, but at least she wouldn't give him more ammunition, though this once his teasing could have distracted her from her own thoughts, if only Veelk picked some other topic than the demon. Her offer for Veranesh was an expression of gratitude, but his remark still rang with enough truth to sting.

While she sat silent, gritting her teeth, Veelk hauled over the last body. "I think there was another one. He must have kept behind the others, so we never saw him."

"How can you tell?"

Veelk grinned. "Most of the valuables are gone." He pointed at the dead man's finger that bore a mark of a missing ring. "He probably grabbed them when we were trying to get answers."

"Wise one. Took the trinkets and ran." Anyone who saw three of his companions dead and didn't run would be a fool. She furrowed her brow. "We better hurry, then."

He pointed at the bodies lying at the side of the road, and she got to work. Magic flowed through her without restrictions, making her wonder whether Veranesh cared little about their exchange or tried to convince her of his benevolent nature, but her task required attention. Directing the energy into the ground to create a fissure took all her focus, and she breathed with relief when it didn't cause other effects. Last thing she needed was trees collapsing or underground springs breaking to the surface. As soon as the thugs and their possessions disappeared into the ground, Kamira's magic pushed the moist soil over them. The ground in the spot looked moved, and she couldn't do anything about it, but the corpses were deep enough to ensure no scavenger nor passersby bothered digging.

"Let's go."

To her relief, Veelk didn't offer any comments. He simply nodded, and they resumed their journey.

Late in the afternoon, shadows between the trees lengthened as the canopy filtered out the light, and Kamira sighed. Waiting for the thugs had delayed them more than she liked, and she could only hope that whoever was after her—and she would bet her pact it was an arcanist with a demon who wanted Veranesh trapped—didn't make the connection between her and Master Tijhran. After all, even if she hadn't made a name for herself, it wasn't hard to check the student registry the high mages kept... But at the same time, she couldn't understand why an arcanist would send only a few thugs. Questions came one after another, and each made her pick up her pace. Maybe her teacher would help her find answers... If she got to him before anyone else did.

A SMALL LUMISPHERE accompanied Tijhran through the dark corridor. A cold draft weaved around his bare feet, but he had left no window open in the evening. No sound disturbed the quiet house, but an unwanted guest wouldn't reveal his or her presence so easily, contrary to himself, who didn't bother with silence or lack of light. As he reached the main corridor, a slight breeze made him turn toward the small balcony at the side. Without hesitation, Tijhran called upon his demon, and, guided by the skilled hand of an arcanist, the energy activated the lamps, illuminating the whole space with warm yellow hue and revealing a massive figure in the balcony's open door.

The intruder's bald head didn't look familiar, but Tijhran recognized the weapon strapped behind, and the air hissed between his lips when he took a deeper breath. With all the power his demon offered, he still stood little chance with this opponent. Yet pride would not allow him to run.

"You're in a wrong house, mage killer." He kept his voice and face stern. "Unless your lot is killing indiscriminately now."

"He's in the right house, master." The reply came from behind the intruder. "I apologize for the intrusion."

Tijhran recognized the voice in an instant. "Kamira?" The last person he had expected to sneak into his house was his former best student, but on the other hand, said student always tested the limits of his patience with her approach to many things. "Is there a reason you haven't knocked on the door? And why for all the powers do you keep company with a mage killer?"

She pushed past the man, her face apologetic enough to make it clear that she still was the honest and loyal woman he knew, and Tijhran relaxed.

"Master Tijhran, this is Veelk. A skilled warrior, my friend and guardian." She pointed at the mage killer. "Veelk, this is Master Tijhran, who devoted years to make me a decent arcanist."

The man named Veelk bowed. "It's an honor to meet my friend's teacher."

Tijhran gave him a nod to satisfy courtesy, but his eyes were on Kamira. "I don't recall you ever mentioning in your letters that he's a mage killer."

Her body shifted, and she said in a half-defensive, half-challenging tone, "I didn't think it was relevant in any way, and I wanted to spare you the shock."

Bold as always, she was, and Tijhran almost burst out laughing at the absurd argument, then covered it with a throat-clearing cough. "If you wanted to spare me the shock, you should have used the door," he replied. "What's with all that sneaking in? Are you planning to bring down the Towers?"

The amused and somewhat hopeful glance Veelk shot Kamira didn't escape him, reassuring Tijhran that his student still was levelheaded enough, likely much to the mage killer's disappointment. Yet Kamira wasn't entertained by the notion. She shifted, revealing uneasiness he hadn't seen since he first took her as a student, and Tijhran discarded another jovial remark.

"How greatly will I regret asking what brings you here?" he asked with all seriousness. Whatever reason she had to pay him a visit, it certainly wasn't one born of sentiment.

Her expression was enough for an answer. "I need your help, master. I've stumbled upon something... something unexpected."

Tijhran had no doubt that she wanted to use another word, and gestured at them to come in. "Let's talk in my study. I'll get some food and drink."

She knew the way, and without delay, she headed there with Veelk in tow as soon as Tijhran closed the balcony door. Tijhran froze as she passed him, and a wave of unfamiliar and powerful magic reached him. Her control was unquestionable, but the sheer amount of the energy she must have at her disposal created an aura an experienced arcanist wouldn't miss. Especially not the one who had witnessed her pact-making and knew how meager her demon's power was.

Of course, with her inherently Tivarashan ambition, he'd expected Kamira to make another pact with a more powerful yalari, but it'd been years, and she had never mentioned anything. In the past he suspected no other demon was willing to risk it, since traditionally Tivarashan people only made pacts with the Four, the demon-protectors of their land, and most of their kin were wise enough to keep away.

With growing concern, he rushed to the kitchen. A demon powerful enough to not be bothered by the Four's threat... or maybe one wise enough to know that stealing one Tivarashan arcanist away didn't matter as long as she kept away from her homeland. Filling a tray with cold meat leftovers, pieces of bread, and wine, he laughed at his speculations, because Kamira was in the study and could answer all his questions. Yet, as he carried the tray upstairs and remembered the expression on her face, the one foretelling trouble and dangers, concerns took their place back in his mind.

To SHARE the secret with another arcanist was like a burden lifted, but the silence that fell after Kamira finished speaking weighed heavy on her. Master Tijhran's expression remained inscrutable, and with every passing heartbeat, it was harder to remain calm. In the past, he used to look at her in a similar way when he took his time choosing words of reprimand, as if it was important how he delivered his dissatisfaction with her.

Veelk was sitting on the floor, in the corner, his back

comfortable against the wall, and with his head tilted downward he looked asleep, though she suspected he was listening. Throughout her story he didn't speak even once, letting her deal with her own teacher as she saw best. Yet the lack of his usual comments left no space for levity or distraction, and she longed for a smile that would promise her the familiar teasing would come later.

In search for distraction, she looked toward the bookshelves of Tijhran's private study, along the many leather-bound spines. Few had titles embossed on them, but Kamira remembered the shapes and the placement, and without a doubt could reach out blindly and get the right book. She flexed her fingers before she responded to the urge of delving into their rich wisdom once more.

"When I said you had a promise in you"—Master Tijhran's voice forced her to pull away from alluring visions full of intriguing reads—"I meant I could see you doing well, whether climbing in the Temple's ranks or making a decent living in Kaighal, despite the high mages rule. I didn't expect you to go off into the desert and find secrets that undermine all we know of the past."

Of course, she caught the reprimand in his gentle tone. He didn't expect her to go roaming the desert in search of trinkets like a scavenger instead of becoming a well-respected arcanist, even if in her case this would have involved at least some scandalously rebellious behavior, whether in the service of Tivarashan Temple or spitting in the face of the high mages in Kaighal. She gave him a nod, as it would be hard to claim she wasn't wasting her skills and knowledge, but no guilt crossed her mind, because she'd prepared for Tijhran's disappointment long time ago, when she first agreed to Veelk's offer to wander together.

"Yet you don't seem shocked. Hardly even surprised," she replied.

"Most of the knowledge was lost or destroyed, and the high mages ensured we didn't learn much, but some stories survived all those years." Tijhran pointed at his book collection. "Arcanists questioned the mages' story and speculated on what really happened back then. For all we knew, a demon—whether in his material form or not—couldn't be truly destroyed by humans. And you found a proof."

"A proof I can't use," she retorted. "And a demon who, once freed, might finish what he started four hundred years ago."

Tijhran's expression became serious. "Do you really believe he was the one who started it?"

His question gave her a pause. The way he leaned forward and searched her face made it clear there was more to it, but she couldn't figure out his intentions. "It doesn't matter what I believe. I need to know what really happened." She looked him in the eye. "I need to speak to a demon who had a pact with one of the arcanists back then."

Without hesitation, Tijhran shook his head. "If he knows anything, he's not willing to share even with me."

She suspected he wouldn't let her speak with Beranec, but hoped that the circumstances would make him look at the idea favorably. Yet one glance at her teacher made it clear no argument would change his mind, and she couldn't blame him. Even though some demons made many pacts, the relationship between them and an arcanist often became personal. No one was foolish enough to share their deepest secrets, but when a demon was willing to make that kind of contact, questions and answers were traded, and knowledge was power in both worlds. Beranec wouldn't share such power with anyone but his chosen, and she wasn't one of them.

"You could at least ask him," she said nevertheless.

"And offer what in exchange? The very secrets that might mean your death when they reach the wrong ears?" Tijhran replied sharply. "To get what you need, you'll have to take it, not ask for it."

Hearing these words made her cringe, but in the end, he only said what she'd already been thinking. Unless she decided to go against Veranesh and form another alliance, her pact with the demon had to remain secret, and that meant she would have to resort to blackmail and manipulation. And since she already had planned to kill Archmage Yoreus, she couldn't claim such underhanded methods were beyond her.

"It's going to be hard to find a demon who's knowledgeable enough to be of use and foolish enough to fall for whatever deception I might conjure."

"Have you thought about the temples?"

She blinked. At first, the image of her homeland's exuberant Temples of the Four resurfaced in her mind, but then the understanding came. Even though the true nature of demons had been known long before the Cataclysm, some people still worshiped them as deities, either misguided by desperate priests or convinced the being they followed wasn't like other demons. But even though calling them demons was misguiding, since they had their own name for themselves—yalari—and even though they might be superior in strength and power, living in a world steeped in magic, they were not gods. At least her own people back in Tivarashan openly admitted to worshiping the four powerful demons, and no one ever tried to call them anything else. Her thoughts circled back to Tijhran's suggestion.

"Can I look through your books? Old arcanist records might help in finding the right demon." In the past, the library was hers to peruse, but since she had left Master Tijhran's tutelage, courtesy demanded she asked.

Tijhran lifted from his seat. "Yes, and I have something else that might help you. A new text on the cults around Kaighal. I'm sure it misses quite a few of the more secretive ones, but it might point you in the right direction." It didn't take him long to fetch the right book and pass it to Kamira. "I don't have any students at the moment, so you can take your old room. As for Master Veelk..." He hesitated.

"I can take the floor if there's space," Veelk replied.

It didn't escape Kamira that even though her teacher nodded, his face shifted for a blink. It couldn't be disapproval, because she'd already told him in her letter that Veelk and she weren't lovers, and she doubted Tijhran cared in the first place, but then, she had little idea of what might have caused his grimace.

"My guest room became more of a depository for my books, notes, and oddities, but I do have another student room, if you don't mind," Tijhran offered.

To Kamira's surprise, Veelk shifted, his posture less relaxed. "Floor will be fine."

His reaction made it clear that he'd also picked up on her teacher's concealed animosity, and Kamira bit her lip. There wasn't any reason to keep them apart... Of course, she could ask, but she doubted Tijhran would reply with Veelk present.

A wave of magic traveled through the house, and Kamira looked at her teacher with concern. Somewhere in the house, a circle must have been activated, but with so many years away, she couldn't recognize its purpose.

"Excuse me," he said calmly, "but it seems I have some uninvited guests." He shook his head. "I thought local thieves already learned that my house isn't an easy target."

Veelk was faster. He got up from his spot and headed for the door before Tijhran so much as turned toward it.

"I'll handle it. Whoever it is, they won't expect a mage killer in an arcanist's house," Veelk said and left.

Her teacher didn't object, and instead looked at her inquisitively. "How much do you trust that man?"

She huffed. Back when she was his student, Tijhran had every right to question her judgment, but to do so after she'd left his tutelage expressed distrust in her abilities, and she didn't bother concealing her frustration.

"He's a mage killer, Kamira," he continued when the silence between them grew uncomfortable. "You might consider him a friend, but mage killers serve a demon too. One that might not be too happy when you free Veranesh."

"I didn't say—"

"But you will free him," he said. "You gave your word, and I know you well enough to know you'll keep it. Unless the demon turns on you first, you'll do your part, no matter how much it's going to cost you."

The slight sadness in his voice, as if he regretted the fate that could be awaiting her, made her remain silent. To argue would be pointless, because he knew her well. For the past days she'd been swinging back and forth, between the resolve to break her word if she could outsmart Veranesh and the need to do just the opposite, to keep that word and give him what he wanted, but in the end, she couldn't think of betrayal without an overwhelming amount of self-loathing. As much as freeing a powerful demon gnawed on her conscience, she'd agreed to the demon's terms, and she'd do what was necessary... At least she could hope that one day he'd try something that would free her from that obligation.

Tijhran nodded, his expression softer. "I worry that he will turn on you when he realizes what your true intentions are."

Kamira let out a sigh. Her teacher's concerns were valid, but at the same time, he didn't know Veelk as well as she did. Years of traveling together, of facing danger... and that one time when they wouldn't have survived if he didn't trust her with his life. Yet none of these could put Tijhran's worries to rest, because for him they would be only reassurances that she trusted Veelk too much.

In the end, all she could do was to look Tijhran in the eye with a confident smile. "If I was to make a bet, I'd say he's more likely to go after the demon than me."

"And I might even win, if you care to help." Veelk re-entered the room.

"Against a demon I have a pact with?" She shook her head in disbelief.

"You were eavesdropping." Tijhran's tone made his disapproval clear.

"Let's just say I trust you as much as you trust me," Veelk replied. "A man tried to get into your house, but he fled as soon as he saw me." He glanced at Kamira. "He might have followed us after all."

She stood up from her seat. "It's better if we go, then. I won't put my own teacher in danger."

Tijhran stopped her. "Don't you think that I'm already in danger if whoever is after you knows where I live?" he asked, almost amused. "Stay, rest, and consult my books before you leave. My house is safe, and with your new pact... I'm safer with you here, am I not? Besides, it was likely only one of the local thieves. They do try to get in here every now and then."

Kamira gritted her teeth at his dismissal of possible danger, but he was right that the damage had been already done, and she needed information his books could offer. She gave him a bow. "I appreciate your hospitality, Master Tijhran."

"Anything for my best student," he replied with a smile, then regarded Veelk. "And her friend."

Veelk returned his glare, but his lip curled in a slight smile as if he recognized that, despite his distrust, Tijhran wasn't their enemy, and she allowed herself a breath of relief. At least she could get rest without worrying that her teacher and her friend would try to kill each other while she slept.

9

K aighal greeted Kamira and Veelk with the stench of rotten vegetables. After departing Gaunash early in the afternoon, they'd hardly made it to the city before the guards closed the Gate of the Northern Winds. That entrance, closest to the waterfront, was mostly used by the local farmers and fishermen who lived in the settlements right outside Kaighal, and led to the poor district adjacent to the port.

Her nostrils twitched when the full power of the decay hit them, but she didn't dare complain. If she hadn't insisted on taking the longer, less obvious route, they would have already arrived at the Jagged Swordsman without inhaling all the worst scents Kaighal had to offer. In hindsight, such secrecy was pointless if the night intruder in Master Tijhran's house was indeed the same man who'd avoided the ambush in the woods, but she wouldn't say it out loud; Instead, she picked up her pace. The sooner they made it out to the main streets, the better. Her thoughts still circled around her teacher's safety, and once more she regretted getting him involved. Maybe instead of visiting, she should have written yet another vague letter, asking him to consult his books for her.

The stench grew stronger when they approached at overturned cart with a heap of vegetables by its side. Both the High Towers and Gildya Magna supported the council and paid for maintaining the main streets and squares, as a display of wealth encouraged traders and merchants to do business in Kaighal, but the northern part of the city, left to itself, was rotting away both figuratively and literally. Only one street, leading to the main northern gate further to the west, got the council's attention, because many Tivarashan traders still chose it.

She rarely visited the area, but if she remembered correctly, they would soon reach the street that connected with the main one and would be lit properly with lamps powered by imbued stones. The poor district had hardly a few braziers lit, and she preferred to not draw attention with a lumisphere, but at the same time, walking in the dark when someone was after them was like inviting danger.

A ruckus in a nearby alley alarmed them both, and while Kamira stopped, Veelk took two steps in front of her, readying his keshal.

"We'll teach you a lesson, Devanshari scum!" came a shout from the alley. "Sniffing around Gildya! Fool!"

Veelk relaxed, listening to more shouts as they echoed between shabby townhouses. "At least three or four of them, but they're busy with their prey. Not a threat to us." He glanced at Kamira, and the waning moon caught on his teeth when he gave a wide grin. "But they're from Gildya."

She arched her eyebrow. Personally, she had little care for the Gildya, though at odd times they bought some of the contraptions she and Veelk uncovered in one ruin or another, but Veelk was never happy with those dealings. He never gave her details, so she only knew it involved some Gildya's adept, and whenever an opportunity presented itself, he was happy to antagonize any members of Gildya. An opportunity such as the one they stumbled upon.

"You want to help whoever's in trouble." She didn't even have to ask. "Fine. But I'm not getting dirty." The last thing she wanted was getting in a brawl in a narrow alley with people who hardly deserved Veelk's and her attention.

"I thought you could use some exercise." Veelk grinned again. "Besides, you've hardly had a chance to try your new pact in action. Gildya's henchmen should be a bit tougher than some lowlife thugs."

His enthusiasm for a brawl was contagious, and he was right. All that magic at her disposal, and she'd hardly had any chance to use it. If only Yoreus hadn't retreated at the last moment... That returning thought filled her with sudden longing, because to stand her ground against an archmage would not only prove Veranesh's power but also her skill. Yoreus—likely too cautious after their last encounter—was out of her reach, but the men beating up some poor refugee weren't.

She made an encouraging gesture toward the alley. "Let's see who Gildya's dogs are fussing about."

They entered with caution. The space between the buildings, filled with trash and old crates, was hardly enough for the six men who dispensed generous kicks and strikes to a figure curled on the ground.

"Spirits of the desert bless you on this fine evening," Veelk said with his hand on his keshal.

Kamira held off a snicker, as always, as he pretended to be of the desert tribes. But in the end, those who didn't recognize a mage killer by his weapon didn't have to know of his origins.

"Who's that freak?" said one of the men. His eyes resembled quicksilver in the way they restlessly moved around.

"None of ours." The tallest one shrugged and lifted his club at his victim again.

Veelk took a step closer, as they weren't paying enough attention to his muscular body or his weapon. "I think that man's had enough beating for the night." His voice remained polite, as if the thought of looking for a fight would have never crossed his mind.

"That's none of your business," barked the bulky man. "Get out of here or you'll join him. And we'll play with your gaharra."

Kamira grimaced when several of the men licked their lips, and her fingers moved in anticipation. "Sure, let's play," she muttered.

Veelk still stood motionless, and she waited for his signal. They needed to draw the assailants away from the beaten man, unless they wanted the poor victim to die from a stray spell.

The bulky man spat when neither Kamira nor Veelk left, then turned to his companions. "You four get the muscles, and Hagga with me—we'll take care of the woman."

The eagerness with which they abandoned their previous mark suggested they cared little for the beaten man, so he was either an errand or unfortunate passerby, but with their opponents approaching, Kamira left such thoughts for later.

"Why is it that no one ever deems you the more dangerous one?" Veelk said playfully as he stepped forward to meet his opponents. With his grudge against the Gildya, she wouldn't be surprised if none of the six made it past him.

"It's probably my cheerful and innocent demeanor." The familiar rush of blood before the fight brought a grin to her face.

Veelk didn't reply. Four of the men circled him while the two other slipped by the wall, making their way to Kamira.

The bulky thug didn't bother with caution, while the one he called Hagga kept to the side, away from the mage killer, and with slow, cautious steps, he made his way around Kamira.

The bulky man delivered the first attack exactly as expected, but then again, she couldn't blame the man for not knowing whom he was dealing with. Far gone were the times when people recognized the arcanist's symbol, and to do so in a dark alley was near impossible anyway. His thick palm shot toward Kamira as if he expected grabbing her would be enough to win, and she dodged to the side, placing the attacker between her and Hagga. She channeled the demon's power, and before the thug realized, lightning struck him between the eyes and soon enveloped his whole body as he jolted in the crackling cage of her magic. When the scent of charred flesh reached her nostrils, she cut the energy, aware that more, much more, remained at her disposal.

To her surprise, Hagga lunged at her before his companion's body hit the ground. With no time to react and not enough space between them, she ducked instead of summoning a barrier, and a thin, flat blade cut the air above her head. Another attack followed, and Kamira pushed her opponent away with a burst of magic.

He spun to the side, getting out of the violent stream. As she conjured a ball of flame, he smiled, looking into her eyes, making it clear he'd dodge any attack.

Kamira smiled back at him. He might have had some

experience fighting an arcanist, but she had a trick or two up her sleeve as well, and she threw her fire projectile almost nonchalantly.

He was expecting deception, she had to give him that, but he still had to dodge the fire, and while he searched for any cue to her next spell, a winged spike pierced his throat. He died with disbelief on his face, and when his corpse collapsed to the ground, the nightfly lifted from the wound. It spun in the air, slinging blood and tissue, and then flew back to Kamira. It hovered in front of Kamira for a heartbeat as if Veranesh intended to say something, then coiled around her right forearm without a word.

Veelk was still fighting. One of his opponents already lay on the ground in a dark pool, but three others still circled Veelk like cats playing with a mouse. They leapt at the same time. The one at the front feinted, which many inexperienced warriors would fall for, while the other two attacked from the sides.

Veelk ignored the trap and didn't bother defending himself from the two flanking thugs. As the men advanced, his keshal came to life and cut through the attacker to the right. Accompanied by the crack of bones, the wide blade made its way through the body. At the same time Veelk grabbed the other opponent by the throat. In one move he lifted the thug off the ground and thrust him against the wall, crushing his skull, and the man's body went limp.

The remaining assailant stared at Veelk with wide eyes and took a step backward. A dark patch spread on his pants, and the sound of the urine trickling down his own legs snapped him out of the stupor. He ran. Driven by panic, he didn't register at first that the only person between him and the alley's exit was a woman, and when he saw the corpses on the ground, it was too late.

Kamira locked him in a cage of lightning, and not long after, he dropped dead.

"They weren't just Gildya's errand boys." Kamira stepped over the thug. "They had some skills."

"We killed them all anyway, didn't we?" Veelk cleaned his blade before strapping the keshal across his back.

"I just wonder what kind of trouble your grudge has gotten us into." She glanced at his handiwork. "Six trained men beating one down doesn't look like a chance encounter to me. And because we did kill them all, there's no asking questions."

They both looked at the man lying deeper in the alley.

"If he's still alive," Veelk said, "he might have answers."

Kamira conjured a lumisphere, and its warm light revealed an unconscious man curled up in a pool of his own blood. Part of his face resembled pulp, but they still recognized him.

"Out of all the Devanshari in Kaighal, we had to save that one." She cringed, contemplating the luck that had made her help the man who'd interrupted her confrontation with Yoreus. Yet the sight of his beaten body didn't provide the satisfaction she expected, even if she was far from feeling compassionate.

Veelk leaned over him, checking the extent of his injuries. "Why would Gildya Magna want to kill a Devanshari? I heard their queen is generous with the adepts working for her."

"I wouldn't be surprised if his acquaintance with the archmage brought that upon him. Yoreus likely used him, and the poor fool just paid for it." She didn't join Veelk in his inspection. "I guess we don't really *have* to know."

"No, we don't." Veelk stood up.

They owed nothing to that—she made an effort to recall

his name—Ryell, but there was a difference between killing a threat and leaving a helpless man to die, a man she didn't like, but one who, in the end, didn't pose a threat that would justify his death.

She looked down at him. Even with the extent of his wounds, he could pull through if he had enough will to live and if other local thugs didn't get to him before he woke up. He didn't have to know to whom he owed his life. But then, the memory of his hateful expression resurfaced, and Kamira hesitated. Maybe he should know who had saved him. And if he changed his mind about arcanists, or at least about her, maybe she could glean Yoreus's plans.

"Can you carry him?" she asked.

"I didn't know you had that soft a heart." Veelk leaned over and hefted the wounded man with ease, though there was little gentleness in the way he slung him over his shoulder. "The Jagged Swordsman?"

Kamira nodded. Taking Ryell to their inn could be risky, but she wasn't keeping it secret where she lived anyway, and at least the innkeeper knew them enough to never ask any questions they didn't want to answer.

Without any more words, they left the alley, carrying one body and leaving six behind.

THE SOUND of shuffling tore through the shroud of silence and darkness, and when someone leaned over him, Ryell's arm snapped forward before his eyes opened. And when they did, Ryell looked up at the woman he'd least expected to see. The same demonologist who'd challenged Archmage Yoreus was sitting beside him with a displeased expression on her face. Her name escaped him, but then, he hadn't made an effort remembering it.

"Do you mind?" She tried to pull her wrist free from his grip, her voice expressing impatience, not hostility. "It's just a cold compress."

He let go and chose his next words carefully. "I didn't expect... to wake up like this."

In fact, he hadn't expected to wake up at all after the thugs cornered him in the alley. With no way to escape and outnumbered, he knew he wouldn't make it out of there alive. Yet he did, and it seemed that the demonologist had something to do with his survival. His body ached in many places, and even though most of the fight remained a blur, he recalled some of the blows that matched the pain.

"I didn't expect it either," she mumbled.

"She hoped you wouldn't wake up before we were gone." The mage killer was sitting on the other bed, watching Ryell.

Lifting himself on his elbows, he took in the room. Two beds, two chests, and a table, but no personal trinkets or decorations. They had to be in an inn, and a good one judging by the room's size, brightness, and cleanliness. He hid his surprise that a shady demonologist could afford such lodgings, especially after he'd met her in one of the cheapest taverns in the port.

"It would save us the embarrassment of trying to make conversation, wouldn't it?" she said to the mage killer, though without viciousness, as if it was their routine. Ryell caught a note of amusement in her voice, but her expression was serious. "If you would please lie down, I'll put the compress where it belongs and check your other wounds."

Ryell obeyed. "Broken?" He pointed at his left arm, sore and bandaged.

"Veelk set it while you were out, so it'll heal nicely." She put the compress on his forehead, and Ryell smelled various herbs. "This should reduce swelling."

She was gentle with sore areas, but didn't lack confidence: no fainting or fussing over the sight of blood, and her focused eyes, though black instead of brown, reminded Ryell of the women from the Devanshari borderlands. At the same time, this memory contrasted with the pendant around her neck, and the way she wore her hair, and Ryell grimaced. The ones like her had helped the demons destroy his homeland.

"I might need to open this one again if it's painful," she said. "I apologize. I should have paid more attention cleaning it."

Guilt rushed blood to his cheeks when she misread his reaction. No matter what other demonologists had done, this one had saved his life. "No, the wound is fine," he said. "I was just... I thought you'd have enough reasons to leave me to die."

The corner of her lips tipped upward, though there was no warm smile to follow. "Because I'm a corrupted and malicious demon worshiper?"

He looked away before she could read in his eyes that this was exactly what he thought of her, but Veelk's burst of laughter drew his attention.

"Don't mind her," the mage killer said. "She teases everyone like that. One would think she almost wants them to believe it."

She huffed, clearly amused. "I think I convinced a person or two."

"Including our unfortunate guest, though he might be grateful enough to let you be." Veelk lifted himself from his spot. Ryell flinched when he picked up his keshal, but the mage killer headed for the door, not him. "I'll be at Hircifa's." With these words, he left.

Ryell looked at the demonologist, confused. He might be new to Kaighal, but some names came up often enough. "Isn't Hircifa the woman who runs the Peony Garden brothel?"

"She is. Veelk's quite friendly with her girls," she replied in such a casual manner that Ryell stared at her wide-eyed. His reaction gave her pause, and then she burst out laughing. "Veelk isn't my lover," she said, still chuckling.

He liked how she laughed and how it softened her sharp features, but with her neck arched as she leaned back, the demonologist's symbol reminded him that a woman like her couldn't be trusted. With a sudden idea to expose her deception, whatever it might be, he asked, "But you do know what he is, don't you?"

The lie he'd expected didn't come, and she never hesitated. "Of course I do. But I'm not fool enough to admit it in front of Yoreus. No high mage would do business with me again."

"Business?" He vaguely remembered that she and the archmage were discussing some arrangements back in the tavern, but he hadn't committed details to memory. Back then he'd cared little for her and her undoubtedly underhanded dealings.

"I fetch things high mages are too lazy or scared to get themselves."

There had to be more than that, but he didn't pry. Even the archmage, when they spoke on their way to High Towers, spoke very little of his reasons for contacting the demonologist.

"What about you?" she asked. "What made Gildya's thugs go through so much trouble over you?"

Ryell smiled with the half of his face that wasn't swollen, and even if the pain didn't affect him, it still would have been a rather bitter grimace. "I'm not sure it's the Gildya who's after me. I have a powerful enemy, and she likely learned that, despite her efforts, I'm still alive. It would be like her to make others do what she needs done."

"She?" A teasing smile curled her lips for a heartbeat. "Though I admit, you got me curious. I can't think of a woman powerful enough to commandeer Gildya's—"

Ryell watched her face dawn with understanding. She was smart enough to draw conclusions, and after all, a scheming demonologist would likely have no trouble in seeing through other people's plots. He shifted in the bed. Saving his life must have been a part of some scheme of hers.

"I better get going," he said. "The least I could do to thank you for saving my life is making sure they don't come after you."

For a reason that eluded him, she seemed amused by the idea, and when he fought his aching body to sit upright, she gently pushed him back onto the pillows.

"Going? In this state?" She shook her head. "All you'll do is make me work that much harder to help you back into the bed. Besides, no one will come, so you needn't worry."

Ryell was about to protest when the meaning of her words dawned on him. They must have killed them all, she and the mage killer, and it shouldn't have been a surprise to him. A wave of memories from Devanshari flooded him: images of demonologists engaging in acts as vicious as the ones done by the demonlings they commanded. Yet the woman in front of him didn't look like someone relishing in cruelty, and for this once, he hoped it to be true.

"I guess I have more to thank you for." Reining in his

distrust, he exercised gratitude. Until he could leave, he'd rather not enrage her. "Do you never leave anything to chance?"

"Not if I can help it," she said. "I like to stay alive, and a good plan, no heroics, and Veelk by my side is the way to go. Doesn't always work, but has gotten us through a lot," she added with forced cheerfulness. "What about you? Survival doesn't seem high on your list."

He laughed and ignored the pain of his chest wound. "You sure have a way of making things sound bad. There are things more important than that. Honor. Duty. Defending the weak."

He waited for her reaction, but she didn't ridicule him. Her eyes dimmed a bit, and for a moment Ryell couldn't help wondering what had happened in her past that pushed her onto the path of a demonologist. Her familiarity with the archmage and the offer she'd made him back in that tavern suggested she used to be a high mage, and he had trouble conjuring a reason that would make her leave the High Towers. The images of the demon worshipers who invaded his country still haunted him, reminding him of how treacherous demonologists were, but this one... She seemed different. She wasn't rotten with evil yet, just misguided. He could repay her for saving his life by helping her find the right way.

He couldn't tell whether his face changed, reflecting some of his thoughts, or if she snapped out of her recollection on her own, but she shook her head. "If honor gets you dead, you won't defend anyone."

"If you have no honor, you won't defend anyone either," he retorted.

"Is that so? I know of a demonologist who might have done so last night, no honor involved."

He narrowed his eyes, his suspicions and doubts resurfacing in an instant. "She sure went through a lot of trouble for someone she doesn't like."

"I was convinced the feeling of dislike was rather mutual."

Of course it was, but anger forbade him from admitting it, and it didn't help that he was indebted to her, no matter the motives she'd had to save him. "You're playing games, demonologist. You admitted that you lied to the archmage" —he grasped for the one argument she couldn't discard— "and now you're trying to deceive me. Use me against him."

This remark should have gotten him the upper hand and forced her to admit her scheme, but instead she looked him straight in the eye. "Do you really think I'm fool enough to try to kill the second archmage and have High Towers chase me down? I simply hoped for the satisfaction of dragging his face through the mud and wiping away that condescending smile of his." Her lips twisted in contempt. "But I don't think you, with all your fancy words about honor and duty, can understand the lowly need for revenge."

Ryell looked away, because her words struck the right chord. He couldn't claim to follow all those noble concepts when all it took was the mere thought of Cahala for him to toss his ideals for the same desire as hers. "I understand," he whispered, clenching the bed cover with his healthy hand. "I'd do anything to bring our queen, Cahala qi'Devanshari, down for what she did." He paused, then exhaled heavily. "She's the reason my country fell, and she knows I witnessed her betrayal."

Imparting that secret turned out easier than he'd thought. Maybe because that demonologist could gain nothing out of it, and telling her was of no consequence. She couldn't use it against him, because Cahala was already aware of Ryell's knowledge, and if the queen learned Ryell had shared it with someone else... He almost smiled at the thought that the queen would go after the demonologist to ensure her secret was safe.

"There's still honor in trying to make the traitor pay," she said, sounding almost caring.

He bit his tongue before remarking that a demonologist couldn't possibly know of honor, but she must have read his face, because she huffed and shook her head.

"The name's Kamira, if you bother to remember it." She walked over to the table and returned with a mug. "Here, drink this."

Ryell inspected the liquid, and the faint smell suggested that it wasn't water. "Poison?" He did his best to make it sound like a jest.

Her expression softened. "You could say so. This concoction should help you sleep. The sooner you heal, the sooner we'll both be on our way and free of each other's company."

Even if she didn't mean them that way, her words still stabbed him with guilt. No matter his personal feelings toward demonologists, he should express at least some gratitude. "Thank you... Kamira. For saving my life and seeing to my wounds."

He cherished the surprise on her face, and then drank the liquid without hesitation. It tasted like the sleep medicine his mother used to give him when he fell ill as a child. Resting back on the pillow, he watched Kamira return to the table and pick up a book. When she started reading, focus on her gray face, he could almost forget that she worshiped a demon and likely wasn't much better than the scum that had pillaged his homeland. If she was, she wouldn't have become an arcanist. But she'd saved his life, so there must be some good left in her.

The mixture she gave him was stronger than expected, and his eyelids became heavy. Before Ryell let sleep take him in its embrace, he remembered the archmage was willing to teach Kamira. Maybe once he got back on his feet, he should ask Yoreus about it.

Maybe Kamira could be saved too.

10

Days went by in that slow and quiet manner that Tijhran used to appreciate, engrossed in his studies of the old arcane grimoires, but Kamira's short visit had reminded him how reinvigorating the conversations with a like-minded person were. Yet to take another student seemed too much of a distraction, and nowadays gifted people rarely sought an arcanist's tutelage, so he'd risk another mediocre pupil who'd waste his time. A much better solution would be a short trip to Kaighal, to meet with a few of his old friends, and maybe even check on how Kamira was doing if she was around.

That thought brought the memory of her companion, Veelk. As much as Tijhran wanted to believe the mage killer's intentions, he'd read enough of their deeds to nurture doubts. What was worse, Veelk wasn't one of those knaves who simply fashioned keshal-like weapons and took the mage killer name to gain respect or instill fear, but one of those whom Tijhran considered a fading legend. The intricate net of Veelk's scars might be concealed to an unsuspecting eye, but an arcanist could hardly miss it if he knew what to look for. A shiver ran down his spine when he remembered how those marks responded when the intruder activated circles in Tijhran's home. If needed, those scars could sap all the magic in the house with ease, and it left no doubt of how effective Tijhran's spells would be should it come to a confrontation.

With a sigh, he rubbed his eyes, looking around his study. Meeting Kamira meant meeting Veelk as well, and the mage killer had made it clear he disliked Tijhran. At least he seemed bound to protecting Kamira from everyone else, so she only had to worry about him... if she ever did worry, given her unyielding trust in Veelk.

A wave of magic disturbed Tijhran's thoughts, and he smiled when he realized it was one of the protective circles again. It was either Kamira, stubborn as she was to sneak into his house instead of knocking on his door with some ill-conceived need to keep him safe, or the local thieves had a new recruit who didn't understand there was a reason thugs kept away from Tijhran's house. Both would provide an interesting distraction, so he stood up from his desk and followed the magic's trail.

The balcony door was open, but the tall and bulky silhouette against the midnight sky didn't belong to Veelk, and Tijhran stopped, veiling himself in magic, which Beranec, as always, offered in abundance.

The intruder stepped inside, his frame hardly fitting the door, and Tijhran gasped. The light revealed dark, nearly black skin, and an elongated face with a nose that looked much like a beak, and behind the stranger, a tail swung. Of course, Tijhran had heard of demons attacking the Devanshari kingdom on the other continent, so someone must have succeeded in summoning something more powerful than mere demonlings to the human world, but he'd never expected such a being in Tyorane, let alone in his own house.

"How much does she know?" The demon's voice carried a promise of cruelty. "How much do *you* know?"

Tijhran didn't respond, and instead took a step back like a frightened person would. Several steps more, if he could manage, and he'd be safe in one of the protective circles every arcanist had in his or her house.

"Answer me, human!"

Contrary to his own words, the demon didn't wait for a reply and dashed toward him. Tijhran stumbled backward, his eyes glued to the charging creature, and in a desperate attempt to buy himself enough time, he sent a wave of magic, but it did not stop the demon's motion. Even though in his life he'd had few opportunities to fight, his instincts and long-practiced skill guided his hands more than his mind, and when the first attempt failed, he forced the energy to solidify into a volley of ice spikes. Most shattered upon contact with the demon's body, but several dug into his skin, and one hit the maroon eye. The demon stopped, and his scream of pain was mixed with anger.

Tijhran glanced at the circle behind him and took another step back, but his movement drew his opponent's attention. The demon ignored the blood trickling down its face, reaching toward him. One swipe of the tail, and Tijhran was on the floor, away from the safety of his circle.

"Never mind. If you're dead, it matters not how much you know." The demon offered a cruel smile as he raised his hand, claws extending from the thick fingers.

Pinned down, and unable to reach the circle, Tijhran hesitated only for a heartbeat. A barrier could buy him a few more breaths, but with the demon so close, it would be hard to get it between them. He could die nevertheless, and his killer would go after Kamira. His second choice didn't give him a chance to live, but he could take the demon down.

As the clawed hand struck, Tijhran allowed himself a smile of satisfaction. With the focus of his will, Tijhran woke all the magic stored in the circles across the house, activating all the defenses. The luminous lines came to life and intensified into a blinding light the moment the magic reached its full potential.

Demon or not, only a fool attacked an arcanist in his own home.

THE TAVERN SMELLED of smoke and sweat, but the beer was cheap, and nobody bothered Hafnis. Sailors and dock workers exchanged stories and songs, clutching either wooden mugs or women's curves, and the waitresses carried around heavy jugs of ale.

He grimaced but ordered another drink, pondering his choices. Staying in Kaighal was not one of them, if he wanted to save up some coin and settle down. No arcanist, especially one as unskilled as he, could make money easily in the town governed by the high mages. One wrong step, one mistake, and he could be accused of conspiring with demons or some other ridiculous deed. But Gildya Magna paid enough for imbued stones to get by, while going north or west meant changes, and Hafnis liked a stable life, even if it comprised cheap beer and a dirty basement room in the poor district. If only he could charge more for the stones... He discarded the thought. Negotiating with Gildya required a better position than he had, or better skills. A grimace twisted his face at the reminder of how limited his power was. He rubbed his temples. Finding a better demon would be a solution to his problems, but countless failed attempts to make a better pact had left him bitter.

"You look troubled, my friend." A man approached his table with a jug. He was bulky, with his fat oddly misaligned on his tall body, and he wore the plain clothes of a minor noble, an outfit chosen by those wealthy men and women who wanted to spend their pleasure time undisturbed and unrecognized. The only distinct part of his look was a leather patch over his left eye.

Before Hafnis could tell the stranger to go where even demons didn't look, the jug had already found its way to the table, and the man carried no mug for himself. In this part of Kaighal nobody offered beer unless they wanted something, so instead of discouraging the unexpected companion, Hafnis grumbled, "Life is trouble."

Uninvited, the stranger sat in front of him, the wooden stool protesting his weight with a creak, and the smile on his thin lips was both teasing and cunning. "They say it also has its brighter sides: women, good wine, nice clothes...."

Hafnis inspected the man's face, but its long features and pointy nose didn't look familiar. The subtle aura of magic suggested the stranger was either an arcanist or a high mage, and Hafnis could hardly conjure a reason for someone like that to have any dealings with him, but on the other hand, no one would bother to go all the way to the poorest of taverns only to mock him. Unless... Unless the matter was underhanded or illegal. He almost smiled at that thought. Such things often brought a lot of coin, paid not only for the work itself but also for silence.

Focusing back on the stranger, he kept the disgruntled expression on his face. "These things come with power and money, and I have little of either, so unless you're here to share your wealth with me, I might never taste that good side of life." If he could convince the stranger he was after his money, he could learn secrets that would later help him gain the upper hand when it came to negotiating his pay.

"I could share it," the stranger said, "in exchange for a favor from a skilled arcanist."

Hafnis leaned forward, curiosity fighting with suspicion. "What kind of favor? And what do you offer in return?"

The stranger regarded him with another cunning smile. "The kind better discussed in private. The kind for which I would be very generous... I could even offer you the thing you probably desire the most."

Hafnis burst out laughing. "No man can give me that. But money will do if you have enough."

"I'm no man."

The stranger's eyes lit up, and the magic around him intensified, filling Hafnis with longing and jealousy. To have such power at his disposal... Why would a man like this would even bother to ask him for a favor? Wrapped in his thoughts, he almost missed the subtle change in the stranger's face, as if waves of energy affected his features. Hafnis blinked several times, but the blurry image disappeared, and he couldn't help glancing at the jugs on the table. He wasn't that drunk, but at the same time, he couldn't bring himself to admit that he saw something more than an alcohol-induced delusion. Yet, at the sheer possibility that what he glimpsed was real, his pulse rushed. Even though the voice of reason whispered that some things were too good to be true, and the offer was likely one of them, his treacherous heart controlled his lips as he said, "Let's go somewhere more discreet, then."

The man led him upstairs, where the tavern keeper rented rooms to lascivious sailors. They stepped over drunken men lying in the corridor and pushed their way past several others who fondled half-dressed women. Hafnis's companion found and unlocked the room, and they walked in to be greeted by the heavy stench of sweat and alcohol. Hafnis hurried to the window to let the evening breeze in while the man closed the door.

"You have a job for me, don't ya?" Hafnis asked when they faced each other. "Something you don't want the high mages to know about."

The man nodded. "Something only a pact... an arcanist can do. I need someone to summon demonlings to this world. As many of them as possible."

"Here? In Kaighal?" Hafnis gave him a dubious glare. Nothing so far suggested his companion was insane. "Right under the eye of Gildya and archmages?"

Not that he'd be able to fulfill such a request anyway. With the power he had, he'd be lucky to summon more than one, since the pact with a minor demon was hardly enough to produce imbued stones. But the odd request sparked his curiosity, and even if he couldn't meet the man's demands, there was no harm in asking. Any piece of information could prove useful later.

"No, not here. Outside the city, but I don't know the place yet. You'd have to travel with me."

Hafnis pretended to consider, though with each new detail the request became odder and more suspicious. "That could be arranged. I have no pressing matters here." He rubbed his chin as if in thought. "But why would you need so many demonlings? Scaring a business partner? Teaching someone a lesson? There are better ways to—"

"There is a woman I need dead."

Hafnis whistled. In the past, he'd been asked to summon demonlings for menageries, for pit fights, and even for medical experiments, but to kill someone? The man either held a serious grudge, or the woman he wanted dead had a small army at her disposal. No matter the truth, it was way above Hafnis's head anyway, because the stranger didn't look like someone who'd settle for one or two demonlings and a few cheap tricks. One more question remained before he refused the job and went downstairs to drown newfound regrets in a sea of cheap beer. "How much are you offering?"

The man smiled, and Hafnis finally remembered where he'd seen similar magic. As the stranger's body expanded, his clothes ripped by the tail he kept wrapped around his body, his skin darkened and turned into feathers, and Hafnis stared in awe instead of terror. His unexpected companion and future employer spoke truth. He was, indeed, capable of giving Hafnis what he desired most, something no man could give—something only a demon, a higher demon, could grant.

Hafnis held his breath as he awaited the answer, his whole body tense in anticipation of the word he had dreamed of for years.

The demon, now in is true form, not veiled anymore by the subtle illusion magic only his kin wielded, widened his smile as if responding to Hafnis's unvoiced hopes. "I offer you a pact."

CHAINS WHISPERED in protest when the prisoner shifted. They didn't allow much movement, stretching his arms, and a collar enhanced with imbued stones weighed on his neck, forever reminding him of the betrayal his fellow inventors and friends had committed. So many years and the memory remained as fresh as on that day, that last day of his freedom.

He didn't want to recall the event, but images swarmed him nevertheless, as if they knew he had nothing else to do in his prison.

Experimenting on himself meant maintaining a careful balance between remaining conscious and easing pain with mind-numbing concoctions, and that last stone blending had left him dazed. His neck muscles ached, and the skin itched where the imbued stones freshly connected with his body, so he didn't thought much of a knock on the door. Even if other adepts frowned at his research, not once nor twice they'd come asking for help with their own inventions, and he was always happy to lend a hand. But when several of them barged in, leaving him fighting for balance, he should have known better than to appeal for a peaceful solution.

They didn't give him a chance to speak or to leave—they attacked.

His world blurred when they released an incapacitating drug in his face, but he still tried to push his way through without violence. After all, they were all men of science, and there had to be a way to solve it.

The prisoner huffed in the darkness at his own naivety. Other adepts gave him reasons to abandon the foolish notion of peaceful conversation, and he clung to it even when masked guards brought in more drug and snapped a heavy collar around his neck. He remembered the humiliation of being chained like a common criminal, and each link of his bindings erupted with magic from imbued stones, stifling his own abilities. Overwhelmed and barely conscious, he couldn't fight anymore even if he chose to do so, and putting imbued cuffs around his wrists and ankles was a matter of time.

He vaguely remembered the sentence announced after he fell to his knees. Imprisonment, not death, as if they were offering him mercy. Then more drug, and he didn't even know where they took him, though he recalled seeing a forest, so it must have been away from Kaighal.

They left him bound and immobilized, and were he an ordinary man, he would have died within weeks of the torment. He often wondered whether this was the adepts' intent: to have him die on his own, so their hands remained dirt-free, even if they weren't clean to begin with. Maybe they hoped his body would give in, but the imbued stones kept him alive. Year after year, he stared into the darkness, pondering his own mistakes. He shouldn't have been deceived by the adepts' interest in his studies and their invitation to work in the Gildya Magna. He shouldn't have trusted their reassurances. And he shouldn't have let them bind him.

That last thought returned to him often. His research wasn't about gaining power or exerting it over others, and he always believed he could only prove his goodwill and devotion to science by words, not violent actions, but if other adepts made the first move, he shouldn't have hesitated. Yet he had, and he'd paid with his freedom. Over the years, he'd questioned his choice so many times that he had a hard time remembering why he'd even bothered trying to talk. Instead, he should have killed them all, every single man or woman that raised their hands to him after feeding him so many lies.

In the beginning, he'd hoped the adepts would return, question him, or maybe even try to find a way to remove the stones from his body, but no one ever visited, save an old man who once a week came to check his vitals, and before he'd leave, the drops of water from his hip flask brought moisture to the prisoner's lips. But the water, though a comfort of sorts, was not necessary for his survival, as the stones' power never faded, feeding his body with the energy it needed. As long as they remained, he'd live.

After the hope, anger came, and the prisoner restlessly pulled on the chains and fought against the magic binding him. His imbued stones burnt, as did his rage, but after weeks of futile attempts to rip the chains out of the walls, or at least weaken the links, he gave up. Whichever adepts had designed his binds, they knew what they were doing, and the way to his freedom didn't lie in an outburst of anger, but in patience. They might have used the strongest alloys and most powerful stones, but nothing man-made lasted forever, and the magic within the chains would fail sooner or later.

The sound of footsteps outside distracted him, though in the slow and steady pace he recognized one of the two men who guarded the door to his cell. He used to talk to them, ask questions about his sentence or even the outside world, but they always remained silent, as if their orders forbade them any interaction. One of them never seemed to react, while the other banged on the door whenever the prisoner spoke, drowning his words in the echo ricocheting within the empty cell.

The two men spoke to each other no more than they spoke to the prisoner, and as soon as the relieved guard walked away, the tormenting silence returned, leaving the prisoner to continue his obsession.

If he could turn back time... The allure of an alternate choice pulled him in, but it meant he would have become a different man, one he would possibly loathe, because as much as he wished to wring the life from each adept that played part in his imprisonment, he'd never been one to kill in cold blood.

But when the darkness and chains yet again reminded him of his fate, he wasn't so sure anymore he would let them live.

RYELL TOOK a deep breath before knocking on the door. The student who'd led him to the archmage's quarters had already left, her absence bringing an end to the Towers' formalities. The first time he'd come here, he'd entered in company of Yoreus, so the overzealous mages left him alone, but this time he wasn't so lucky, and high mages took their time contacting the archmage to confirm whether he, indeed, was expecting a Devanshari guest, while Ryell had to wait in the reception area.

The frustration of the time wasted didn't help when he thought of the reason he was seeing Yoreus in the first place. The previous visit had had its consequences, since even though the archmage considered himself indebted to Ryell, he'd somehow gotten Ryell to run a simple errand for him, and the nature of that errand left him torn. He'd promised to share with the archmage what he'd learn about Cahala's dealings with Gildya, and even though he loathed the queen, he couldn't help wondering whether, by helping Yoreus, he was becoming a traitor himself.

That brought a cringe to Ryell's face, and the grimace reminded him his wounds were hardly healed—the outcome of said errand. And if it wasn't enough, there were also those two long days in a demonologist's presence...

The memory of the gray-skinned Tivarashan woman made him pause mid-move, even though his knuckles were already at the door. As much as he wanted to loathe Kamira for who she was, it seemed that the Light had sent her on his path to remind him that not all people were the same. Just like Cahala qi'Devanshari was nothing like other noble Devanshari, Kamira didn't match the image of demonologists he'd met during his homeland's siege. Sure, she had a sharp tongue and spoke her mind without reservation, but during the two days he got to spend with her, she'd never searched for an opportunity to deliver a jab unless he provoked her.

He chased away the image of her confident, slightly playful smile, even though it was Kamira who'd advised him to keep close ties with Yoreus for as long as he could. He suspected ulterior motives, but she shrugged his accusations off in her usual manner, and he had to admit that even if she wanted, there was no way she could use him against Yoreus. That thought gave him pause when he realized that the archmage would likely do the same if he saw the opportunity, and being indebted to Kamira made Ryell reluctant to do anything that could be considered betraying her.

He shook his head. As soon as he delivered the promised information, he should find a way to sever the acquaintance and keep away from High Towers, leaving the archmage and the demonologist to their own games.

With that thought, Ryell knocked on the door.

In less than a heartbeat, it opened, and Atissa's brown arms surrounded his neck. "Ryell!" She kissed his cheek, and her breasts, covered only with the thin cloth of her gown, pressed against his chest. "I was starting to worry! I missed you!"

He swallowed hard, because in all his frustration, he'd forgotten about her. To conceal his embarrassment, he kissed her on the neck and inhaled the smell of her brown curls. The scent of cinnamon mixed with magic made him say, "I missed you too," but he pulled her arms away and grimaced when his body reminded him of his recent beating.

"Oh!" Atissa put her hand to her mouth. "You're hurt! What happened?!"

"Just some Devanshari-hating thugs. Nothing worth mentioning." Ryell forced a smile. "I'm almost healed anyway." As if a broken arm could heal within days... But Atissa didn't have to know.

"You don't look healed. Come, I have bandages and salves."

The way she pursed her lips made him want to kiss her, and a familiar craving, a mixture of physical desire and hunger for magic, twisted his bowels. Atissa could sate them both, and he fought with his own body to resist the need to follow her to her room.

"I need to speak to the archmage first," he said with wavering confidence. His instincts demanded he surrender to that beautiful woman.

She gave him a sigh of disappointment and turned her head around. "Father! Ryell is here to see you," she called out.

Ryell shifted uneasily, because as Yoreus stepped out of his office, Atissa shamelessly gave him another kiss and whispered, "Come see me when you're done."

Upon the archmage's gesture, Ryell followed him to the office, once more pondering how little the most powerful men in Kaighal needed. Cahala qi'Devanshari alone had a whole palace wing devoted to her needs, and many of her officials enjoyed similarly extravagant living. Compared to them, Yoreus's accommodations were comfortable but meager: a bedroom, an office, a day room, and a student's room, though the last was occupied by his daughter. From what Ryell gathered, all the archmages had similar lodgings at their disposal, and he had to admit, he liked the Towers' way better. It encouraged humbleness that his queen and her noble subjects would benefit from.

"Was there any trouble?" Yoreus asked as soon as he closed his office's door. "I hope I didn't put you in harm's way with my request."

"It's a bit of a story." While they took their seats in deep, comfortable armchairs, Ryell considered how much he wanted to tell the archmage. He wanted to talk about Kamira with Yoreus, and maybe find a way that would lead her away from the demonologist's path, but mentioning her name could cause distrust. "Whatever the queen was doing with the Gildya, it's finished. She set off with her adviser and the most loyal servants, leaving others behind. I tried to follow, but Gildya's men were waiting for me near the Gate of Northern Winds."

Yoreus rubbed his chin. "We had a complaint from Gildya, two days ago. Six of their men were found dead, and they claimed a high mage had a hand in it. Ridiculous, of course. Our students and teachers don't roam the beggars' quarter searching for trouble."

"They weren't entirely wrong," Ryell replied. "Our mutual acquaintance and her mage killer were passing by. Gildya's men weren't happy about witnesses, and when they engaged them, I ran."

Yoreus huffed, amused. "I didn't expect Kamira to have such... violent inclinations, but perhaps she simply defended herself. With a limited pact like hers, she might have not had a choice but to ensure the attackers are dead."

"Are you going to let Gildya know?" With his own words,

Ryell might have gotten Kamira in trouble... Not the way one should repay a life debt.

Yoreus gave him a long look, and Ryell could hardly remain still under his evaluation. "I'd rather not get Gildya arguments against magic in general. It wouldn't help that Kamira used to be a High Towers student, and the archmages have more important things to do than bother with the adepts' squabbles. I'd rather deal with her myself, especially as I still don't know why she would try to kill me."

Ryell swallowed. He still hadn't decided whether he trusted Kamira's claims about the events in the tavern, but either way, he couldn't admit he had more insights without revealing their second meeting had been much longer than a brawl in an alley. With everything he said and did, the tangle tightened, and soon he would be caught with no way out. That thought reinforced the decision he'd made before entering Yoreus's chambers. He'd keep away from them both, and find another way to repay Kamira, though she didn't seem interested in collecting on the debt. Instead, he'd find work. If he ensured his own survival, he could focus on exposing Cahala's betrayal.

"There's something I wish to discuss with you," Yoreus continued, pulling Ryell back to reality. "It's about Atissa. It's seems that she has taken to you."

Ryell blushed. He'd met Atissa the first time he visited High Towers, when she generously gave him her bed, and he wasn't sure whether Yoreus knew that, the following night, she'd visited him in his inn. The memory of the night spent together once more woke up his craving, but he said, "If you disapprove..."

Yoreus laughed and waved his hand in a dismissive manner. "Quite the contrary. I'm glad she'd found someone she can trust." He sighed. "Being an archmage's daughter isn't always easy, and other students tend to assume she enjoys privileges because of that. I'd like to ensure her safety, especially when she leaves the Towers, but she insists on being treated like any other student." Yoreus looked him in the eye. "I'd be happy to know she's safe spending time with you. And if it turns out there are feelings invested..." He offered a gentle smile. "She's a mage, so she won't be married off for anyone's gain. She's free to choose as her heart desires."

Ryell kept his face straight. The one night he'd spent with Atissa was of no consequence; she'd simply sought an adventure in the arms of a man different to the ones she was surrounded with. Devanshari boasted their bright skin, and he had no doubt that his blond hair also looked exotic to her.

He looked at the door, but it remained closed, and he had no way of checking whether Atissa was tempted to eavesdrop. "My feelings for Atissa... don't run as deep as you might be expecting," he confessed in a quieter voice.

"I'd be surprised if they did," the archmage replied. "But your honesty tells me I needn't worry. Either you two will grow closer, or part ways when... the novelty wears off. Until then, I hope she'll have someone to confide in, and if you notice anything that might threaten her, you'll let me know. I don't think Kamira would go after my daughter, but being an archmage means I've made enough enemies to be concerned."

Ryell nodded. With the matter put like that, he didn't have much room to refuse without risking the archmage's anger for turning down Atissa. A man like him must be used to getting what he asked for, and as Ryell remembered Atissa's face, he had to admit he wasn't ready anyway. The craving twisting his guts intensified at the mere thought of her and the magic that surrounded her.

Yoreus smiled. "You should go to her, then. I'm sure she's waiting for you."

"Thank you, archmage." Ryell bowed.

"No need for that." Yoreus made a dismissive gesture. "I still remember I owe you for saving my life, and if you make my daughter happy, that's an even larger debt in my eyes. So please, indulge me in those meager ways of repaying you, and making your own life comfortable. I'll be happy to ensure your lodgings are paid for, and speak with our overzealous guards to ensure you can visit any time."

"I appreciate that," Ryell replied. "But please, don't concern yourself too much. It's hardly saving your life if I all did was offer words of advice."

Yoreus stood up as well, and led him to the door. "Nonsense! I will not dismiss what you did, nor will I refrain from expressing my gratitude." He looked at Ryell with eyes narrowed. "Unless, of course, this makes you uncomfortable? I'm not well read in Devanshari ways."

"No, that's fine," Ryell said. Despite the noose of the dependency he was willingly putting around his neck, he needed what the archmage was offering. With no money and no work, he couldn't turn down such a gift. "I just wanted to make sure you don't feel obliged to do more than my deed was worth."

Yoreus smiled. "Then let's not speak about it again. Now, I believe my daughter is waiting for you..."

The archmages apparently dismissed their guests in a similar way to the Devanshari nobles, and Ryell understood the conversation was over.

The day room was empty, but the door to Atissa's room remained cracked open like a teasing invitation, and when he knocked on it, it opened wider. Without a word, Atissa pulled him inside, shutting it behind him, and he exhaled with relief when her subtle magic aura surrounded him along with her arms.

But when they lay in bed, and Atissa's fingers traced the bruises on his body, Ryell couldn't chase another image from his thoughts. No matter how much he tried to focus on returning Atissa's kisses and caress, the face of a black-haired woman and her dry, sarcastic smile accompanied him through the evening.

11

They made their way southwest along the desert's edge at the steady pace of seasoned travelers. Even over rough terrain, they should make it to their destination faster than if they took the westbound road from Kaighal, and Kamira liked the solitude of the wilderness. After two days with Ryell, her well-honed patience was wearing thin, and she was on the verge of seeking refuge in another inn, forever cursing herself. If she really had to save his life, a decision that in hindsight could have been different, she should have left him in the first place they'd passed on the way to Jagged Swordsman, doing as little as paying for his room before disappearing.

He wasn't a bad patient, obediently staying in bed, but after the first time, he'd refused the sleep concoction and bothered her with endless questions, few of which were worth replying to, as if he wasn't really interested in her answers but simply trying to fulfill the need for courtesy and polite conversation. Once or twice, she thought to have sparked his curiosity, but of course, before they could discuss anything meaningful, he would make a remark about "vile demonologist ways" or some other absurdity, and she would give up. She had better things to do than to argue with an arcanist hater, and Gayabal's journal, among other books, provided enough excuses to avoid talking to Ryell, but after two days of torment, she was ready to finish what Gildya's men had started back in the alley.

"So, was he worth saving and all that hassle?" Veelk's question startled her.

Mage killers didn't have the gift of reading people's minds, but he knew her well enough to read her face instead, and she never bothered concealing her frustrations, providing him plenty of opportunities to study. And it couldn't have been hard to guess what was on her mind, since she'd openly rejoiced at Ryell's departure from the Jagged Swordsman.

Veelk was watching her intently with a teasing smile across his lips, and she gave him a mean look. For most of the two days he'd left her alone with Ryell, seeking pleasure in the arms of Hircifa's girls, and Kamira had no doubt about his ulterior motives.

"Why don't we discuss something more interesting than the men I didn't sleep with?" she said, cutting to the chase. They've been traveling together for too long for her to claim she was oblivious to the true meaning of his question.

"We won't have such a talk until you finally sleep with one." Veelk looked over his shoulder, but she didn't expect anyone would dare to follow them so openly. Not after the last time. "So, why not that Devanshari? Handsome, muscular, exotic...?"

She couldn't hold her laughter at Veelk's merchant-like tone. "And an arcanist hater?" she added.

"Two days with you, and he still babbled about evil

demons? You're slipping." He expressed his disapproval with a shake of his finger.

Kamira rolled her eyes. "I wasn't really trying. It's hard to persuade someone who is convinced all evil comes from demons." She grimaced. "As if humans are all pure and good... Even though he knows otherwise. His own queen betrayed her people."

Veelk arched his eyebrows. "I think he might like you more than he lets on if he shared a secret like that."

"It's not like it has any value to me." She shrugged. "And you're trying too hard. With his objections to arcanists and his ties to Yoreus, we might as well discuss the possibility of me seducing the Tivarashan prince."

The smirk Veelk gave her suggested he'd find such a topic entertaining, but to Kamira's relief, he didn't pursue it.

"You could show him that not all arcanists are evil, and spend some time more pleasantly than staring at your own magic," he replied. "Otherwise, you'll die a virgin, and I'm not going to oblige if you have any near-death regrets."

Kamira burst out laughing at the image he conjured. As much as she enjoyed Veelk's company, and they'd been through a lot together, sharing secrets and everything else, their friendship had never taken a romantic turn. "If you did oblige, *that* would be a regret," she said, still chuckling.

As she expected, Veelk had a response ready. "And that's coming from a woman who used her magic to burn my clothes just to see me naked."

The truth was that Veelk had actually walked into her fire spell, back when they weren't used to working together, but, of course, he claimed to have been backstabbed. Not that her magic could hurt him unless she made the energies something more solid, but his clothes suffered, and Kamira had no doubt he'd never let this one go.

Veelk looked over his shoulder again, and her mood shifted instantly. Joking brought a temporary distraction, but she couldn't ignore that someone had sent murderers after her. A shiver ran down her spine when she reaffirmed to herself that her adversary likely wasn't human, and even with all the power Veranesh offered her, an arcanist couldn't be an equal match for a demon.

To stay alive, she needed knowledge, and this one wasn't easy to find. And in the end, she also needed to trust Veranesh enough to work with him, before he decided he'd waited long enough for her success.

"Your new demon makes you double the grumpy you were," Veelk remarked lightheartedly.

"I can't solve my problems by killing them like you do," she muttered.

"I could kill them for you."

She couldn't help but smile, appreciative of his attempt to pull her away from the whirlwind of concerns and questions that could drive her into the depths of insanity.

"I almost want to see you try," she said, "but dead demons don't talk any more than humans do."

"Neither do living ones. Did you find anything that could help you in your teacher's books?"

She shook her head. The volumes she'd leafed through didn't deal with gossip and secrets, if humans had such knowledge about the demon world to begin with. All her hope lay in finding a demon who had a pact when the old Towers fell, and then question him or her about the events, but the details of how to make one talk still eluded her. Master Tijhran was right: she couldn't ask or bargain for such knowledge.

"Pardayi must have secrets, or maybe a weakness of sorts," she replied. "Veranesh might know."

"Last time you spoke to him, it didn't seem to go well."

Kamira clenched her fists and looked away, as if, in the rolling hills they traversed, she could find an excuse to change the topic. "I'll have to try. If I can convince him I trust his words and need his help, he might be willing to be more patient... I don't want to learn one day that I've run out of time, even if it means I risk being manipulated." She didn't mention that she was already spending too much time thinking about all the traps the demon could set and all the lies he could feed her.

Veelk reached out and pulled her closer, wrapping his arm around her. "Any other arcanist would jump on the chance of a pact with one of the most powerful demons known to humankind. And you are still trying to figure out what's right... and whether it wasn't better to die in the tunnels under the desert." He held her tighter. "Get what you need from your demon. You'll worry about how evil he is when he's free."

An amused huff escaped Kamira's mouth before she could scold him for treating Veranesh's freedom so lightly. There was no telling what a demon who'd caused the Cataclysm would do when he broke free from his prison... Images of her continent or even the whole world ravaged swarmed her mind, and she pushed them away. There had to be something she could do to prevent such destruction while still keeping her word to Veranesh.

She sighed. Questions, always more questions, and no answer in sight. But at least, perhaps, speaking to her demon would help her with Pardayi.

Veelk gave her a glance before letting her go, as if to make sure she wasn't going to succumb to her grim thoughts, and she did her best to keep her expression worry-free.

They walked the paths between the hills. Veelk kept looking back, but his lack of concern suggested no one followed them, and Kamira allowed herself to relax. Even though she mostly focused on choosing the words best suited to talk with Veranesh, once or twice, her thoughts drifted toward Ryell. She'd never admit it out loud, but she'd entertained a thought of meeting the Devanshari again and trying to convince him that not all arcanists were demon-worshiping spawns of evil.

Veelk's playful teasing reminded her that she hadn't had a lover in quite a while, and if Ryell could see past his hatred, she would consider him. A glance at the nightflies coiled around her forearms reminded her with whom she'd made her pact. Most people might agree that some demons were less evil than others, though none should be trusted, of course, but one mention of Veranesh would likely swipe such notions away. She doubted whether there was a single person in Tyorane who didn't consider "her" demon a vile, malicious creature.

Only when Veelk stopped did she realize the sun was already descending toward the uneven horizon.

"We'll sleep here tonight." He looked her up and down with a knowing smile. "Well, *I'll* sleep here. For all I know, you might spend the whole night arguing with your demon."

THE NIGHTFLY LIFTED from her forearm without a sound and hovered just above the flames of the campfire. Its crystal eyes stared at Kamira, ignoring Veelk, who was already asleep.

"More questions, pactee?"

She could swear there was a coldness to his words, but without seeing his face, she couldn't be sure. "I found the name of a demoness who had a pact back then," she chose her words carefully, "and I want to talk to her." Thin branches crackling in the fire was the only reply, and Kamira preferred it to the suggestion that she was about to strike a bargain with another demon. "She had a pact after the old Towers fell, so if the arcanists who survived knew anything, Pardayi likely knows it too."

"Pardayi..." Veranesh huffed. "She's one of the last yalari I'd trust with anything." There was displeasure in his voice, as if he was considering her motives or suspected deception.

"I agree." Kamira allowed herself a wry smile. She was far from trusting any demon, but some were less scrupulous than others, and Pardayi counted among the scheming ones. "That's why I need something to make her talk... without offering too much in return."

"A game of wits with Pardayi? Now that's a bold move, but one I'd expect from my own pactee." His voice changed, dissatisfaction replaced by a trace of approval. "But nothing I know about her will guarantee any answers. Only fear ever worked on her... Yes, fear would be good."

Kamira couldn't help staring at him, puzzled. The mere idea that a human would be able to frighten a demon was absurd. Unless he intended to use himself as the threat— but even then such words would be empty until he regained his freedom. Of course, she could bluff that Veranesh was free, but the questions she needed answered could reveal the truth to Pardayi.

Veranesh's voice pulled her away from her thoughts. "You'll like that, pactee." He chuckled, and that sound crawled down Kamira's spine. "I'll teach you a spell to destroy a higher yalari."

Gaping, she waited for him to admit he was trying to play her, but only silence followed. Apparently, she had to take the bait first. "I appreciate the attempt at humor, but I find it hard to believe you'd share such a secret with a human, any human." Veranesh was neither foolish, nor careless, nor insane, yet all these words fitted his offer.

"Why wouldn't I?" he replied, amusement lingering in his words. "You're doing my bidding, and the spell could serve you well. You also display an unusual amount of distrust. I'd wager you trust your fellow humans as much... or rather as little as you trust me, so you wouldn't share such knowledge with anyone else. And if Pardayi proves too stubborn and you destroy her... I couldn't care less."

Kamira breathed in slowly as she took in his words. Veranesh wasn't jesting, and he intended to share the spell with her. He must have some other motive to do so, but she couldn't conjure anything worth such a risk. "What if I overcome my distrust? Several skilled arcanists could destroy all of your kind." Not that she'd risk sharing it, but she had to prompt him to reveal more.

Veranesh's hearty laughter made her think of a benevolent father amused with a child's play. "I'm sure you could wipe them all out alone, if your body could endure so much power. If you'd like to try, I won't stop you. I'd even warn you that destroying a yalari releases a lot of energy. You should ensure you seek to fulfill such goal away from any humans you find... worth keeping alive."

The image conjured by his words resembled the one she had of a Cataclysm, but the pieces of the puzzle remained scattered, unfitting and confusing. Veranesh had been imprisoned, and not destroyed, and the Cataclysm had started before the high mages intervened to stop it. She furrowed her brow, grasping for any thread that could link those two images. She needed more information, but to ask Veranesh's part of the story, she had to be certain he would share the truth with her, no matter how unfavorable it could be to him.

"Besides," he continued, "killing all yalari would bar magic from your world forever."

She almost laughed, because Veranesh truly knew how to get her attention. "What do you mean?" Even if he intended to fill her head with lies, she had to risk the question. Any scrap of knowledge could prove useful in the future, and she could sift the truth out of his words once Veranesh wasn't around.

"No more yalari equals no more magic," he replied with confidence. "Except maybe for the scraps that so-called high mages used to tear out through the void between worlds." He let out a dry chuckle. "I'm sure you'd be happy in such a world, wouldn't you, pactee? But I'll teach you the spell, and you'll do with it as you please."

Blatant lies, then. She almost sighed with disappointment that it was all Veranesh had to offer. At the same time, trapped in his crystal for so many centuries, he might not know any better. In the past, high magic might have been what he described, but during the Cataclysm, high mages found another way and their arts flourished.

Her eyes widened when she remembered their conversation back in his chamber. He promised she'd see the high mages fall, so he could know how they gained their power. She had to consider that Veranesh was actually telling the truth.

"I like that expression." Veranesh didn't hide his satisfaction. "You are already discovering things, pactee, aren't you?"

She gave him a restrained nod, one that could barely

suffice for confirmation. Her discoveries were her own to ponder, at least until she was ready. "Some."

Veranesh said, his voice colder all of a sudden, "I'm starting to learn you, pactee, and I see you're shielding yourself with your distrust again. I'd commend such approach, worthy of a yalari, but it makes our... cooperation difficult. The less trust you show me, the more inclined I am to assume you're going against my will."

The threat hidden between the lines was clear, and she couldn't blame him. "Yet you were offering to teach me a spell I could use to destroy you."

"Could you now? I'd like to see you try to destroy a yalari using the energy he channels for you. That could turn out very interesting. But I think you've figured out as much already, and your words are nothing but a distraction."

Kamira clenched her fists as she looked down. No human was a match for a demon like Veranesh, and she'd been foolish if she thought such a childish trick would work. "Apologies," she muttered.

"I believe that you'll do your best to learn the truth, and maybe then you'll exercise some trust." To her relief, there was more frustration than anger in Veranesh's voice. "I'm willing to give you more time, and I'll help you to deal with Pardayi, as I said I would."

She looked the nightfly in the eye, though its crystal body didn't convey any of Veranesh's features. "And what if the truth I find doesn't match your words?"

"Then it'll mean you haven't found the truth yet," Veranesh replied, his confidence lined with returning amusement. "Now, pactee, before we lose more time discussing your distrust, I'll teach you the spell." The nightfly moved away from the fire. "Come. Even the mage killer is not to hear what I'm about to share with you, and I'm not certain he's as asleep as he appears to be."

Kamira glanced at Veelk, but she didn't argue. For all she knew, her friend was listening all the time, be it out of curiosity or concern. She stood up and followed her crystal guide into the night. Its body lit up with gentle blue glow, so reminiscent of how Veranesh's prison lit up, so she didn't need her own lumisphere. Veranesh led her until sand crunched under her boots, and the dark shapes of desert dunes emerged against the starlit sky.

"There are three stages of the spell," Veranesh began while she sat down, her legs crossed, like she used to when studying with Master Tijhran. "First is the binding, so a yalari can't escape. Second is the ripping, when a yalari is taken apart. The third disperses their energy, so a yalari can't be reborn. You must be close to a yalari for the spell to work. Since you're a human, Pardayi can't try to bind you in return, but I suggest you protect yourself with a circle. Even if summoned only in an ethereal form, yalari are capable of killing you, especially when threatened like that."

She gave him a nod, grateful for the warning. No matter whether he spoke the truth on other matters, he did seem honest when it came to teaching her.

He then spoke in the arcane tongue, teaching Kamira all the syllables and how to weave a yalari's name into the binding. The wind from the desert cooled her skin while she repeated parts of the spell over and over to Veranesh's satisfaction. A tedious task, but she committed every single word to memory, too afraid to write any of them down even if Veranesh allowed it.

Even though she was focusing on his lesson, thoughts circled at the edge of her mind. Of his own volition, Veranesh was giving her a powerful weapon—one she could use how she saw fit, and once more she gave in to concerns for the future. If she managed to free him, what reason would he have to keep her alive? Such knowledge in the hands of a human would be a risk to him and other yalari, and even if he cared little for his brethren and she couldn't destroy him, he still had to take into consideration that she'd find another arcanist to do the deed.

"Not bad, pactee, but there are still parts you should practice."

"It's a long spell." She muffled a yawn. As a skilled arcanist who could change the nature of her magic during channeling, she considered spells limiting, but for once, her brief training in the High Towers proved useful, as high mages also relied on memorizing their spells.

Veranesh chuckled. "If you want to kill a yalari quickly, you resort to other methods. The spell is used for the pleasure of torture, and as a final solution."

"You relish in cruelty?" she asked, though the notion didn't surprise her.

"Not more than humans do. Killing quickly is effective and limits the threat, at least until yalari are reborn, and sometimes longer, if they are wise enough to keep away. But some enemies should experience death for much longer, don't you think?"

She looked away. To answer would mean to reveal something about herself, something Veelk and she never spoke about. On bad nights, she still dreamed about Garivan's screams as he begged for the mercy of a quick death, and in her dreams, she walked away never hesitating —as if her instincts tried to reassure her that she had made the right choice back then. She shivered at the vivid memory.

"You don't have to answer that, pactee. I'm sure you

understand," Veranesh said, and she would swear he was smiling. "Don't wipe out a town by accident, if you can help it."

His laughter echoed in her ears long after the nightfly coiled onto her wrist.

～

PARDAYI'S TEMPLE towered over Jenara, its walls reaching high into the blue. Other buildings around the main square cowered in its shade and clung to one another like a crowd of scared peasants in the presence of a king. Kamira walked across the cobblestones with her eyes fixed on the temple, and Veelk followed at a slower pace, looking around and inciting anxiety in the eyes of townswomen gathered by the main well, while the tattered rascals pointed at his keshal and whispered in awe.

Kamira glanced at him, hardly containing amusement. "Stop scaring children. We have more important things to do."

Veelk caught up with her. "Like scaring demons." As she'd suspected, he had listened in on her conversation with Veranesh until the demon led her away. "I thought we'd wait till nightfall."

"Too much hassle," she replied, though summoning Pardayi had already turned out a hassle. At first, she tried it out in the hills, and the demoness wouldn't answer. Most demons wouldn't, unless it was a pact summoning or they were answering their own arcanist's call, but Kamira hoped Pardayi would be different or at least curious enough, given her scheming nature. With no result, the only other way was to find her temple. If in the past she'd responded to her priests, Kamira had a chance of drawing her attention. "The temple might be closed, and I don't want to get in trouble with local guards. The less attention we draw, the better." She looked the temple over as they approached. "And if we're lucky, there won't be anyone in there now, save maybe some priests."

The moment her mouth closed, the temple's wind chimes rang and their eerie sound carried through the town like a spirit's whisper. A nice touch, Kamira had to admit, though usually such tricks made no impression of her, since she knew the so-called deities were nothing more than demons. But people around them stirred and tore away from their conversations and tasks, trickling toward the temple's wooden doors.

"If we're lucky, you say?" Veelk sneered and pointed at the inn. "Come, let's get something to drink and wait out the boring parts."

Kamira shook her head, a sarcastic smile curling her lips. "I want to have a look at their local customs." Jenara's townsmen likely had no idea they unwillingly served a demon, and even if enlightening them wasn't her goal, learning of their worship could give her an advantage in dealing with Pardayi. And if not, it surely would be more entertaining than staring at the patrons of an inn.

They entered the temple after all the faithful had gathered inside, and Kamira motioned to the back, where the shade of massive columns concealed them well enough, but some of the locals still noticed the newcomers, and when neither she nor Veelk raised their hands at the beginning of the prayer, several heads turned. Curiosity mixed with suspicion in their eyes, so Kamira bowed her head ever so slightly and smiled gently, hoping her foreign looks would grant her some leniency. She didn't want to miss the show due to some over-vigilant townspeople.

A tall and surprisingly scrawny priest stepped in front of the altar and bowed to the enormous statue behind it. The woman depicted in stone had pleasant features and a veil of locks that would make any girl jealous. Her dress was modest, with a high neckline, but the carver had emphasized the feminine features of the statue. The goddess's tilted head forever watched her followers, and she held a single desert rose in her right hand, while the other stretched out with blessing.

"He looks famished," Veelk whispered, leaning toward Kamira. "Don't they feed their priests here?"

"Hush you! You're disturbing a sublime ceremony!" She waved a finger at him, but the corners of her lips already trembled in a suppressed chuckle.

Several people looked at them again, and Kamira sent them the kindest and most inconspicuous of smiles. Back in Tivarashan, her compatriots treated their worship with a bit less reverence, and no one had illusions of what kind of beings they directed their prayers to. No Tivarashan in their right mind expected divine miracles, and priests wielded their arcane magic without trying to conceal its nature.

The priest started his incantations, and the congregation refocused on him, leaving Kamira and Veelk alone.

"Hear us, oh, hear us, Pardahaji! Listen to our prayers and look into our hearts! Grant us your wisdom and your gifts, and we shall forever praise thy name."

Kamira resisted cringing at the exalting speech, and stood on her toes to whisper into Veelk's ear. "He should use the arcane language, that's obvious, but he's not standing in the center of the circle. He should keep it in better shape, too. Master Tijhran would have me scrub all the floors if I ever let one become so damaged."

"He also got the name all wrong," Veelk whispered.

"That's a *minor* problem…" She suspected that the name had been deliberately changed in the times following the Cataclysm. Back then, all "demon worship" was persecuted, so a different name was supposed to convince the arcanist haters that people prayed to some vague deity with no power, or a long-dead local patron. "With a good circle and spell, he'd actually have a chance of summoning *some* demon."

An elderly woman turned her head toward the duo. The grimace and squinted eyes sunken deep in the wrinkles made her look unpleasant, and Kamira resisted responding with a sneer. It took much more to scare a demonologist. The hag pointed a finger at them, and her lips moved, but no words followed.

"I think you've just been cursed." Veelk kept his voice down, but the playful undertone still carried.

"I'm sure she was pointing at you."

The priest lowered his arms and turned toward his congregation, and Kamira could swear he was mildly disappointed that his prayer had no effect. "My friends! You come here every day to pray and show your devotion to Pardahaji. Your hearts are untouched by doubt and strong in faith!" Exaggerated gestures accompanied each sentence. "I'm sure the goddess sees it, and soon she'll grace us with her presence. She'll speak to us in person and give her blessing to the people who worship her with such piety."

"I bet he's trying to figure it out," Kamira said. The man was no arcanist, but his predecessors must have left some notes hinting that one could summon the so-called deity.

"The summoning?"

Kamira grinned at a new thought. "I think we could have a bit of fun, don't you?" She stepped out of the shadow, walking into the main aisle. "Why can't it be today, then?"

Her voice carried through the temple, ensnaring everyone's attention. "Didn't these people wait long enough for their goddess to speak to them?"

The priest swallowed. He had the pleasant face of a young man who knew neither malice nor deception, and Kamira thought his eyes were silently pleading. Whatever his motives were to become a priest, it couldn't have been for power or personal gain, and contrary to her impulse, she gave him a warmer smile.

"The goddess will bless us with her presence whenever she deems fit. It's not up to us to hasten her arrival," the priest replied, and Kamira bet he'd mustered all his willpower to sound confident in front of other worshipers.

"Or maybe it's not the right prayer?" Kamira stepped in front of him, her feet firmly in the middle of a forgotten circle people must have considered nothing more than a decorative mosaic. "Would you allow a meager traveler to pray in her own way for the goddess's guidance?"

The priest stared at her with wide eyes while a murmur of discontent rose from the congregation, as if he was unsure whether agreeing to her request would help him maintain the control over the gathered.

"I promise to teach you my prayer," she whispered.

The priest was quick to catch on, his eyes now evaluating her with curiosity, and he raised his palm to the people. "Calm, everyone! The goddess rejects no honest follower and receives all prayers, even if they come from distant lands and unfamiliar lips," he called out. "Let us show graceful Pardahaji that we welcome everyone in her abode!"

With these words, he stepped to the side, but Kamira didn't take his place. Instead, she inspected the mosaic around her, recognizing the lines and noticing the missing tiles. Its ruined state urged her to kneel down and reinforce the pattern with carefully woven magic, but she didn't know how much time she had before the priest or his flock called her a blasphemer. So she fished out a piece of chalk from her bag and, with a few quick moves, repaired the most damaged lines. This had to do, because the priest was already narrowing his eyes at what he must have considered a disputable action.

She couldn't help pondering some mockery of a prayer and hand-waving to accommodate the onlookers, but the time for her little enjoyment of the farce was up, and she turned her focus to the task at hand.

Few of the arcanists' arts required spells, but summoning a manifestation of a demon was one of them, and Kamira rushed to mutter the words and focus her magic on the statue. It had to be the demoness's link to that place, allowing priests untrained in arcane ways to summon her easily enough, with mere chants and the strength of their faith to create a bridge between the worlds. In a way, their ways still reflected the workings of a pact-making, and Kamira had no doubt that, in the past, the more ambitious among the priests and priestesses became powerful arcanists... much like it still happened in Tivarashan.

People in the temple gasped when the statue stirred. A townswoman let out a yell of panic, but it wasn't the statue that moved. Instead, the goddess's ghostly figure stepped forward through the altar and down the wide steps, toward the circle. She had the looks of a beautiful human, but Kamira noticed her long, curled fingers undoubtedly concealing demonic claws with a subtle illusion demons could conjure, and the veil of locks must be covering her folded wings. Her face, though, longer and sharper than the statue's features, complete with an unflattering, beaklike nose, revealed Pardayi's true nature clearly enough for anyone who studied demons.

The townsfolk fell to their knees, and the walls echoed with their fiery prayers, but Kamira just bowed her head. As much as she believed no demon deserved any kind of worship, a bit of courtesy could make the conversation easier. In the corner of her eye, she spotted the priest: motionless, as if he fought to keep his composure, but with his wide eyes taking in all the details.

"You've called upon me, my child?" Pardayi asked. Her voice carried the softness of delicate wind chimes.

"I seek your wisdom," Kamira played along.

"Then my wisdom you will have. What bothers you?"

"Look into my eyes, yalari, and you'll know all my troubles." The corner of Kamira's mouth twitched with a sarcastic smile. No demon could read minds, but the word demons used as the name of their kind should have been both a hint and a challenge enough.

Pardayi didn't falter, returning the stare, though her benevolent expression faded, replaced by caution and cunning. "I see," she replied. "You did well to come to me, and I'll help you. But first let me speak to the people who turn their thoughts to me every day." She looked above Kamira's head. "Let me bestow my blessing upon you, good people! Know that no prayer goes unheard, and nothing pleases me more than when you direct your thoughts to me. I wish I could speak to you longer"—a trace of regret and sadness marred the beauty of her face, though Kamira had no doubt the emotions were faked—"but this traveler brought news of matters I need to look into for the good of all the faithful."

The priest stepped before the congregation, his expression full of eagerness and anticipation. He must be looking forward to a discreet chat with his "goddess" as well. "Go and bring the good news to all!" he commanded, raising his hands in what Kamira considered an overdramatic gesture. "Let them know your prayers came to fruition, and the goddess walks among us."

People reluctantly vacated their pews. Whispers of excitement mixed with their shoes scuffing as they left, and the priest readied to bar the wooden door behind them.

"Me? I'm with her." Veelk's voice echoed within the temple as he replied to the priest's urging gesture.

Once the door was closed, both men made their way to the altar, while Pardayi inspected Kamira, no longer hiding a grimace of discontent.

"You've got some nerve summoning me in front of others, pactee," she said.

At that, the priest dashed toward Kamira. "Pactee? You're a pactee? A priestess of the highest order?"

While he looked at Kamira with anticipation, Pardayi stared at him with disbelief on her face.

"Amusing, isn't it?" Kamira said. "So many things get lost with the passage of time. The knowledge is forgotten, and the truth is warped."

"Indeed, pactee. So many things." Pardayi turned to her confused follower. "Priest, I'll speak with you later. Leave me alone with the woman." She offered Veelk a dismissive glance. "And take the man with you. His presence is an affront to me."

Veelk gave a bow with a sarcastic flourish of one hand— a wasted effort, since the demoness wasn't looking at him any longer. "Sentiment reciprocated," he said, and that earned him a glare of contempt. Grinning at Pardayi, he placed his palm on the priest's shoulder. "Come. I'm sure I can answer at least some of your questions."

Kamira held back a snicker. The last thing the demoness must want was a mage killer explaining to her most faithful servant that she wasn't a goddess but a being from another world, using human faith to strengthen herself.

"Nicely played," Kamira said when the temple's door closed behind Veelk. "A flock of people praying to you, nothing in return, and you don't have to bother making pacts. I'd say you were quite lucky that no arcanist had ruined it."

"Veiled threats won't work in your favor, pactee," Pardayi said. "Nor having Suzhaul's dog around. Tell me who sent you, and what they want. If you're swift and honest, you might leave unscathed."

"And your threats aren't even veiled, demon." Kamira didn't so much as twitch. Even such a short exchange with Pardayi reminded Kamira why she hated dealing with her kind. Most of them were condescending toward humans, though she had to admit that Veranesh seemed different enough. If his behavior was honest, his ire stemmed from her distrust, not from having to deal with an inferior being, and if he was deceiving her, at least he knew how to do it well. "I'm a bit disappointed, since the old texts spoke highly of your cunning. But bluntness will work, since I'm not here to play word games. I need information. As soon as I get it, I'll be gone, and I might even teach your priest the summoning spell, so you can keep your little flock's faith strong and unwavering."

Pardayi grimaced. "You don't lack confidence, that's for certain. But you're clearly not used to dealing with powerful yalari. Humility would serve you well."

Kamira stood unmoving. Humility was the last thing she'd offer any demon. "I don't have time for all those things that would make you feel superior. I need to know what happened four hundred years ago in the old Towers."

The demoness's laughter filled the temple with multiple echoes. "You're talking to the wrong yalari, then. I've never been one to remember historical facts."

That might be the truth, but it was still a convenient one. "You had a pact with Eloran at the time, your last pact with one of the most esteemed arcanists of his time and one who survived the Cataclysm, so don't even try telling me you don't remember."

The swiftness with which Pardayi's face changed, from dismissive to fear-lined hate, revealed her volatile nature. "Who sent you? Was it Suzhaul? Speak, pactee!"

Kamira shook her head. In the end, Master Tijhran was right: there would be no bargains or exchange of information. "Just tell me what I need to know, and I'll be gone."

"Oh yes, you'll be gone." Pardayi bared her teeth, and her hands unfurled, revealing needlelike claws. "This is your last chance, human. Speak!"

Pardayi couldn't do much in her incorporeal form, but Kamira had no doubt that the demoness had her past priests, the ones who actually had an idea of their goddess's true nature, make necessary preparations. If they enabled Pardayi to affect the physical world, the half-shattered circle wouldn't offer much protection.

With a bittersweet realization that Veranesh might have been right as well, and only fear worked on Pardayi, Kamira gave no final warning. When Pardayi raised her hand to strike and magic around the temple condensed in response, the spell words were already dancing on Kamira's lips, slipping into waves of power one after another. No syllable came too late, and no syllable was mispronounced, and her magic surged within her.

Pardayi shrieked and fell back, but too late. Strings of energy surrounded her, clutching her hair and biting into her intangible skin. A scream of pain carried through the temple. The demoness twisted and turned, fighting the bind, but the magic barred her escape.

"Don't make me use the second part," Kamira said once the spell was finished.

"You humans were never taught the second part. No yalari would be foolish enough. This is as much as you can do, little gaharra."

With narrowed eyes, Kamira considered her words—a new piece of information and a proof that the demoness knew more than she claimed. But asking questions would mean engaging in endless arguments. So instead, Kamira spoke the first syllable of the second part, elongating the vowel, as Veranesh taught her, and suffered through the shriek she provoked. "Start speaking, demon. Or I'll make sure you feel every word of this spell. Right up to the end of the third part." To issue such a threat was easy, but the very thought of acting on it made Kamira's stomach twist. As much as she agreed with Veranesh that some deaths deserved to take longer, Pardayi had done nothing to justify such treatment.

"Then you'll kill me regardless. No one would teach you the full spell to leave me alive." Pardayi's grim tone carried more than words. "Go ahead, torture me if it pleases you, but I see no reason to tell you anything."

It might be a bluff, but one Kamira wasn't eager to call. If Pardayi's shrieks were any indicator of how painful the spell was, prolonged torture would lure the priest back, or even the townspeople if the sound carried outside, and ultimately, torture wasn't Kamira's goal. Using fear could only get her so far, so she had to throw a lure as well.

"If you tell me what I need to know, we'll perform the ritual of peace," she offered. "I know enough to tell when you lie, and if you try, forget about the ritual."

Pardayi's eyes lit up, and Kamira could tell which way the demoness's thoughts were going, but she kept her expression neutral. Either the old books were wrong about Pardayi's cunning or she'd been away from humans too long —but on the other hand, her own brethren should have kept her on her toes. The demoness could have revealed her emotions on purpose, weaving a net of her own.

"Swear on your pact," Pardayi demanded, "that you'll perform the ritual of peace."

Any moment of hesitation could convince the demoness that Kamira was scheming against her, so she quickly recited the promise in the arcane tongue, submitting to an oath no arcanist would dare break. If she did, she'd be branded forever, and no demon would ever make a pact with her. She almost smirked at that. For a plotting, lying, and manipulating species, demons surely were attached to keeping their word... at least when it suited them.

A smile of satisfaction appeared on Pardayi's smug face. "Very well. I'll tell you what I know and what Eloran suspected." She paused, her eyes dimming as she recalled the past. "Back then, the arcanists were working on a way to invite yalari to this realm in material form, and they were supported by those of my kind who were interested in strengthening the relationships between the worlds. Pointless endeavor, if you ask me, but some claimed your world had a lot to offer ours." She shrugged dismissively. "Either way, Veranesh was supposed to be the first one to cross."

"Why him?" Kamira's curiosity spiked at the chance to learn more about her demon.

"Because he didn't have a pact, and he was interested in the research as well. He was also thought powerful enough... I think he just wanted to be the first, that arrogant hoyve, and no one was fool enough to stand in his way. But even high mages, insignificant as they were back then, supported that choice."

"What interest they had in it?"

Pardayi regarded her with caution. "This is the knowledge you really seek, isn't it, pactee? For whatever ends you need it." She offered a wide, satisfied smile. "I think you're going to love that little tidbit. The summoning was a success, but before anyone could celebrate, the high mages in Kaighal started their own spell, trapping Veranesh. In the three-way power struggle, the Towers collapsed, and your lands were destroyed, though Eloran wasn't sure how exactly that happened. No wonder, really, because surviving that day was a strain... for both of us."

Kamira took a deep breath, her fingers curling into fists and her teeth gritting. "They blamed arcanists for it."

"Very crafty, wasn't it?" Pardayi smiled with delight. "In one smooth move they got rid of the competition, ensured pactees became insignificant, and took all the power for themselves."

"Too smooth of a move for someone with no magic and influence, which means they had help."

"Eloran suspected as much, but never found anything solid. He wasn't the same after the Cataclysm." Sadness flashed on Pardayi's face, but she regained her composure quickly.

"But you had more than guesses, didn't you?" Kamira

asked. "You said only the binding part of the spell was taught to humans, so you had to know more."

"Veranesh was always a pain, and many would have loved to see that hoyve fall." Pardayi grimaced. "I wasn't surprised someone finally decided to act. As for what I said... I can think of only one thing that would make any yalari react with desperation resulting in such a destruction." She looked Kamira in the eye. "Had I known you could bind me, I'd have killed you the very moment you had summoned me. Nothing would be worth risking the bind."

"But why only bind him? Why not destroy him?"

Pardayi shrugged. "Whatever the reason, it came from the mages. Any yalari would prefer Veranesh destroyed... You don't humiliate someone like him and let him live. Maybe they feared teaching humans the full spell, and with that hoyve trapped in this world, no one could finish the deed. But I had a pact at the time, and I wasn't in on the conspiracy, so your guess is as good as mine." Even though the magic binds held her tight, Pardayi leaned her head forward. "Tell me, pactee... You know the spell, the whole spell. Are you going to finish him?"

Kamira grinned. "So, he's still alive, isn't he? That's good to know." A little deception could throw Pardayi off the right path and suggest she'd been played into revealing more than she intended.

Pardayi's face shifted with barely contained anger. "Are you done? I'm growing tired of your questions."

"I'm done." As much as Kamira craved knowledge, more questions could guide the demoness to the truth or prompt her to ask questions of her own. "Let's perform the ritual and be done with each other."

Already within the circle, Kamira added several more

symbols to it and began the chant. Pardayi chimed in at the right parts, and her voice lost the contempt-filled undertone always present when she spoke.

As magic sealed the ritual, forever restraining them from attacking one another, the demoness narrowed her eyes. "You've shown cunning and resourcefulness, so I'd be willing to offer you a pact."

Kamira smiled, because were Pardayi a human, she'd do well in Tivarashan. Not everyone would be able to swallow pride in an attempt to gain a useful pawn. "Thank you," she replied honestly. In the past, she'd at least consider the offer, even if the demoness's methods felt too underhanded for her liking. "But I have no need for a pact with you." She stepped out of the circle. With the ritual protecting them both and the bind still in place, she had nothing to fear.

"Haven't you now?" In so few words, Pardayi made it clear that another blow to her pride hadn't gone over well. "I didn't take you for a fool."

Kamira stood motionless though focused. If the demoness had a trick up her sleeve, the time was coming to reveal it. "I think I'm wise enough."

"If you had any wisdom, pactee, you wouldn't have entered a ritual of peace with me. You would have known that the most powerful among yalari can break such rituals when they're made with those of inferior strength. Whatever pact you have, it doesn't protect you, because there are few who are a match for me." Pardayi's eyes glowed, and her face hardened into a mask of cruelty. "I could have some use of you, so I'm being generous with my offer. But if you aren't wise enough to accept it, you aren't worth my time."

Kamira allowed herself a wide smile. After all, there was no deeper scheme, and Pardayi had gotten sloppy. "What makes you think I don't know all the rules of the ritual?" She savored each word.

Pardayi's expression changed, with fear stretching her face, and Kamira took the time to taste her victory. It was not every day that she got to win a battle of wits with a higher demon.

"So, in the end, you are just a puppet," the demoness whispered. "But whoever is pulling the strings, you dance on them very well."

"Save your insults. I have no intention of breaking the ritual." Kamira allowed herself a show of contempt for Pardayi's pettiness, even though her motives for keeping the demoness alive were of a pragmatic nature. Using the spell's full power could mean the destruction of the town, and she neither wanted innocent lives on her conscience nor the attention such a deed would draw. If she chose to only kill Pardayi, once the demoness was reborn in her realm, she could cause a lot of trouble.

With no more words, Kamira walked toward the inner temple.

"Where are you going?" Pardayi called out.

Kamira looked over her shoulder, never breaking stride. "To keep my promise and teach your priest the summoning."

"You have to unbind me first!"

That made Kamira stop, and she turned back toward the demoness. Undoubtedly, Pardayi would free herself after some time, because magic waned when the caster wasn't around, but waiting meant more humiliation, especially if the priest witnessed her like that. But as far as Kamira was concerned, the condescending creature deserved that bit of cruelty, so she smiled and said, "Oh. I'm sorry. The puppet wasn't taught *that*."

12

Ryell sat motionless on Atissa's bed as she wrapped her arms around him. Her breasts pressed against his bare back, and her lips traveled across his skin, waking up a faint feeling of desire and hunger for magic. "You seem worried," she muttered the moment her tongue stopped drawing lines on his body. "I don't like it when you worry."

Ryell put his hands on hers, searching for the right words or an apology, but his mind could focus neither on the woman behind him nor the pleasures she used to distract him. "It's nothing."

His thoughts were still bound to Cahala. Archmage Yoreus had mentioned that high mages had their own interest in finding the whereabouts of the Devanshari queen, and promised to keep Ryell informed. But what then? The question always returned. He still had no plan, and no way to prove her guilt. To dream of bringing her to justice accomplished nothing, and he had yet to take any steps to make it happen.

"If it's nothing, then let's focus on more important

things," Atissa said, offering both the warmth of her skin and the faint aura of magic. "Or I'll feel forlorn."

No less distracted from her caress than he was before, he kissed her hands. "I'd never want you to feel like that." The words left his mouth with an ease and confidence he didn't feel, reminding him of the times when protocol required him to dispense such pleasantries to the women at the queen's court. The memory stung with an unexpected power, as if it tried to tell him he was wasting time in the arms of a woman he cared little about, while the traitor of his nation, the woman with the blood of countless innocents on her arms, remained free and perhaps plotted another betrayal of the very people she was supposed to protect.

To Ryell's relief, knocking disturbed them, saving him from continuing the conversation.

"Mistress Atissa, there's a letter for Master Ryell," a servant said through the door. Ryell and Atissa must have missed him knocking earlier, and with no response, he let himself into Yoreus's chambers.

"Leave it on the table!" she called.

"The man who brought it insisted it was urgent. He's in the waiting area," the servant replied.

Ryell freed himself from Atissa's embrace and, without a word, picked up his garment from the floor.

Still in the same spot on the bed, naked and inviting, Atissa pouted while he threw his pants on. "You're no fun sometimes."

He didn't bother with a shirt, because he doubted the fact that he slept with an archmage's daughter was a secret to anyone in High Towers. Yet before he creaked the door open, he indicated the bedsheets, and she covered herself up, the dissatisfaction on her face spoiling her youthful beauty.

With her modesty assured, Ryell stepped out. The servant was waiting in the day room, the plain envelope with a merchant's seal in his hand, and he seemed relieved he could hand it off. He left before Ryell even tore the letter open.

The message inside, chaotic and written in an unsteady hand, left Ryell confused, but it was enough to recognize the word "help" and Tyddes's shaky signature.

"I need to meet a friend." Ryell looked at Atissa.

She cocked her head with an eyebrow slightly arched, and let the covers slide down and reveal her body, luring him back. He turned his gaze away from the small but perky breasts that demanded his attention.

"I have a debt to repay," he added when Atissa offered no reply.

A sigh of disappointment escaped her, and she pulled the sheets back up, but when she looked at him, her expression was playful rather than angry. "Hurry up, then, or you'll have debts to pay here as well!"

He offered her a charming smile and a bow of the Devanshari court. "This one I'll be sure to pay with interest, my lady," he promised.

Her face brightened, and, leaving, Ryell felt a hint of guilt. Atissa wasn't a lady, and any Devanshari noble, even as minor one as he was, would look down on her, but she loved both the title and compliments, and they ensured her good mood when Ryell needed it.

He rushed down the countless corridors and stairways of the maze the High Towers were. Most students and teachers ignored him or threw him a passing glance of curiosity before returning to their own tasks, but Ryell caught several sneers as well. He had no doubt these stemmed from jealousy or contempt, and it was best if he ignored any remarks, lest he be pulled into the high mages' politics and petty games.

Tyddes was still in the reception area. His face made it clear he had troubles other than the essence starvation, though the hunger for magic had devastated the merchant's body even more than Ryell remembered. In comparison, thanks to Atissa's frequent company, Ryell hardly experienced the lack of the Light's presence.

"What happened?" Ryell didn't waste time on greetings.

"It's Gann. He needs help beyond the healer's expertise." Tyddes's eyes filled with tears. "I brought him to the asylum, but Prince Allyv says a demon is consuming my boy, and he can't help. I heard you have contacts among the high mages... Maybe they could do something?"

"A demon?" Ryell said, fears feeding his imagination with dreadful visions. Apparently, the demons wouldn't stop at destroying the Devanshari kingdom—they also wanted to destroy its people. "How's that possible?"

"I think he took an imbued stone. The hunger grows strong among our people, and they resort to desperate measures," Tyddes said in a shaking voice, a blush coloring his otherwise pale face. "One of them is mixing the powder of imbued stones with water. Those who use it say it's almost like Hajihali."

Ryell kept his face neutral. Even though the sheer idea made his stomach revolt, Tyddes didn't need a lecture. "But it has side effects?"

Tyddes shrugged. "It's supposed to be safe if you follow the instructions, or so they say. Prince Allyv thinks they took too much of the powder and only from one stone, from one demon. That's why they suffer."

Cold sweat gathered on Ryell's skin. "They? It isn't only your son?"

"No, there's several more. They all have similar symptoms."

Ryell paced in thought. He didn't even bother asking about Cahala. The queen had disappeared, and even before that, she'd lacked any interest in her people's plight. Some still clung to her promise of rebuilding Hajihali, but so far the Gildya had nothing to show for it. "I'll see what I can do, but high mages don't deal with demons. I'm not sure if they'll be able to help." He hesitated before asking the next question. "Did you ask an arcanist for assistance?" Someone like Kamira, someone not entirely rotten, could possibly know how to cure such suffering.

"Arcanist?" Tyddes's face went white, even though Ryell would've sworn it couldn't get any paler than it already was. "You mean... a demonologist?" He spoke the last word as if he was ready to spit it out with bile.

"Some call them that." Not so long ago, Ryell also did so without hesitation. "But over here, they seem to have earned some respe—"

"Why would we do such a thing?" Tyddes's voice rose as he cut Ryell off. "They're evil! They're the ones who helped destroy our lands. The same that had a hand in slaughtering our people? No good nor help would come from them, no matter what foolishness people in Kaighal want to believe."

"I see." Ryell swallowed, giving a nod, even though when he thought of Kamira, he had trouble picturing her as a bloodthirsty demonologist who summoned demonlings and slaughtered innocent children. If he shared such an image with her, she'd surely laugh at it. But an attempt to convince Tyddes would be a waste of time his son might not have. "I'll try to get some help. Wait for me in the asylum. I'll be there as soon as I can."

Tyddes's eyes glistened with unshed tears, and he

squeezed Ryell's hands. "Thank you, my friend. I knew you'd help. We'll wait for the good news."

Ryell stood in the reception area, looking at the merchant who hurried out of the Towers, regretting he didn't have Tyddes's confidence. With the high mages' lack of knowledge about demons and their noblemen-like attitudes, he could only hope that indeed he'd bring some good news.

"WAKE UP, MY SWEET CAHALA," a voice whispered into her ear. "You're starving again, my dear. It can't be this way."

Cahala's eyes snapped open, and she stared at the cloth of her tent. She turned on her bedroll, searching for the person who had spoken, but in the faint light of the lantern, she found no one. The Gildya's contraption stood on the table right where Cahala had left it, and its magic wavered as it waned. Another stone was gone, and each lasted only a couple of weeks. Anger filled her veins, as it reminded her of Gildya's greed and their half-made inventions that would make all Devanshari broke within a year, if not sooner. That feeling brought clarity and lucidity, and she remembered what had woken her up. She listened carefully to every sound that reached her tent, but nothing was out of the ordinary. Several guards on duty, some servants who were finishing their tasks, and one or two hushed conversations by the crackling campfires... None sounded like the voice she'd heard.

Her eyes were fixed at the artifact, so she replaced the imbued stone. The device stabilized, and steady waves of magic soothed her senses, but even though her fear faded, there was no getting back to sleep.

She reached for her robe and stepped outside.

Above her, the star-filled sky and dark canopies weaved into a patchwork pattern. The night creatures' calls carried within the black around her, reminding her how foreign this land was and what she'd lost.

"Is something wrong, my queen?" Phuran stepped out from the shadows.

"Do you ever sleep?" She would not answer his questions outside, where others could see her distress.

"Sometimes I do." He bowed. "Did something startle you, my queen?"

Cahala stepped back into her tent, holding the flap for Phuran to follow. "I thought there was someone here... speaking to me," she replied once they were alone.

His eyes narrowed as he scanned the surroundings, and she had no doubt that her loyal servant would notice anything that could have escaped her, any sign of an intruder's presence. "I haven't heard anything, but I might have been too far away. Did you recognize who it was, my queen?"

She wrapped her arms around her body, but a shiver shook her nevertheless. "It was *him*, Phuran. It was him again."

Even the faint light couldn't conceal his suddenly pale face. "It's impossible. He's still in Devanshari. He never followed us across the sea."

"I heard him, right by my ear!" Her voice, too high-pitched, accompanied her to the verge of panic. If someone was to believe her, it had to be Phuran. "He must have found me again."

Her adviser came closer, and she hid her tears in his chest. "If he did, my queen, then I'll kill him this time." He brushed his hand through her hair, and Cahala sobbed for a while, allowing herself a moment of weakness. No one else could ever see her like this, but Phuran knew all her secrets already. "I'll have the watch doubled with a few more fires, and I'll stand guard by your tent, my queen."

"No." She moved away and wiped her face with her robe's sleeve. "Stay inside tonight, please."

"As you wish." He bowed again. "I'll make necessary arrangements and find someone to bring you some wine, my queen. Shall I call someone to come here while I'm away?"

"That won't be necessary." She took a deep breath and her voice returned to normal. Her people needed a strong queen to lead them, and she'd endure a brief solitude if that meant no one else would witness her misery. "I'll be fine."

When Phuran left, so did Cahala's confidence, and her eyes swept the tent once more. The faint echo of the voice in her head brought back memories from the siege, sending another shiver through her body. She'd rather bury those images forever, but they kept resurfacing in a never-ending cycle of torment. All the nights she had woken up, cold and craving magic, and that very voice had guided her out of the royal chambers, down the stairs and through the empty halls to the little garden. She remembered her hands shaking to the rhythm of her trembling heart while she stole Hajihali's magic... She remembered well when the attack on the capital became so fierce that all the artifact's power was used to sustain the protective barrier, and her husband ordered rationing the essence in preparation for the prolonged siege, refusing to give more even to his own wife and son.

Just a little bit. The thought returned, and she couldn't tell anymore whether it was her own justification or the voice's suggestion. Those tiny bits missing wouldn't hurt anyone, and they didn't count. But then the barrier protecting the city fell, and demons swarmed Devanshari, taking away her home and her husband in one long, nightmarish attack.

"It wasn't my fault," Cahala whispered while the cruel laughter rang in her ears as if she'd heard it just moments ago, not months earlier. "Tell me it wasn't my fault. Tell me, Myrkan."

No reply came from the dark corners of the tent or from her own heart.

13

The land southwest of Jenara rose toward the mountains far in the west, and the hills overtook the flatlands Kamira and Veelk had journeyed over so far. The mage killer had insisted they didn't stay at an inn for the night, and she'd obliged, glad to put some distance between them and Pardayi. The scrawny priest had taken in the news of having worshiped a demon with moderate shock, though how he muttered about the Four, the official religion of Tivarashan, sounded like a lot of rationalization. To Kamira, all demons were just demons, but she couldn't blame him for searching for something more. After all, throughout his whole service to Pardayi, or rather "Pardahaji," he genuinely believed he'd prayed to a sublime higher being, not just another demon who wanted the power of human will to strengthen her. At least now he had somewhat of an equal footing, and Pardayi would have to give him a pact or reward him in some other way if she wanted to ensure he kept looking after his flock in Jenara.

But thoughts of the priest brought the memory of the conversation with Pardayi, and Kamira flexed her fingers when her anger surged. Even if she didn't want to believe the demoness, her words had matched scraps of knowledge Kamira already had and echoed Veranesh's claims, painting him in a much brighter light: betrayed and lured into a trap, not a demon who threatened humankind and was defeated by high mages. He was still ready to kill her and destroy half of the world to regain his freedom, but—Kamira bit her lip —so far Veranesh had spoken openly about his intentions and was willing to help her if she found another way to free him. After Pardayi's revelations turned the world's history upside down, she couldn't stubbornly claim he was lying to her... at least not about everything.

"You'll think yourself to death." Veelk, who had been scouting ahead, now matched his pace with hers. "Ever consider that Veranesh might not be hiding anything? Demons might have their own goals, but some are honest in their pursuits."

"Don't do that. It makes me feel like you're in my head."

He displayed his lack of concern with a wide grin. "It wasn't hard to figure this one out. You've been talking and thinking about it since we left town. But you're avoiding my question. Pardayi quite mercilessly dealt with the history the high mages wrote."

"I'm still digesting that." It wasn't as easy as simply learning that high mages had yet again lied. She used to be one of them, and she'd hardly bothered to question anything they did, at first too trusting, then too determined to climb their ranks. Studying with Master Tijhran had rekindled her inquisitiveness, but even to him the story of the Cataclysm, as told by the high mages, was the truth.

She sighed when Veelk's insisting stare made it clear he wouldn't let go. "I'm afraid that if I start trusting Veranesh, I'll miss something important."

"You might also miss something if you don't."

She huffed, her mood lifted, and waved a finger at him. "I'm not discussing it with you. You were too keen on sealing the deal in the first place."

"Which got us out of there alive. And this is what we'll keep doing instead of trying to outsmart everyone. You've beaten one demon with your wits. That should be enough."

A meager smile was all she could offer in return, as, in her thoughts, she was already questioning herself again. If at least she could tell how much of her distrust was justified, and how much was nurtured by the stories she'd heard during her studies in High Towers, she could make a well-informed decision.

"So, how far do we have to go? It's almost dark now," she changed the subject.

"The message I received back wasn't precise, but over there should be good." Veelk pointed toward the dark line of the hills, much further away than Kamira liked.

Darkness was embracing the world when they finally stopped. Her lumisphere's light revealed exactly the same landscape she had been watching all afternoon, and nothing explained the difference Veelk apparently saw between the place they stood in now and the one three or four hills away.

"We could use a fire." He mowed down the nearby vegetation with his keshal and gathered an armful.

"They're fresh. They won't burn well."

"That's why I'm asking you for the fire."

Forcing the twigs to burn took time, but with her new pact, feeding magic to the flames until they took the wet wood was child's play, and she enjoyed the warmth and the familiar crackling of the fire. Veelk sat down at a distance, scouting the dark, and Kamira fished out Gayabal's journal.

The high mage's notes bored her, and she cared little for the frustration about failed attempts to make high magic more powerful that he'd vented generously on the journal's pages.

"Still digging through that old book?" Veelk asked.

"I have to. There has to be an answer there, otherwise Yoreus wouldn't drool at the very thought of getting his hands on it." That, of course, led her to ponder again whether Yoreus knew that Veranesh was alive.

"And what if there's nothing in there? What will you do?"

"There has to be something," she replied with determination, as if she could make it real instead of her own desperate hope. "Think of it. He didn't take his journal before leaving the old Towers. He was in Kaighal during the Cataclysm, and he likely knew the book would be buried forever."

"Why didn't he destroy it, then?"

"Why raise suspicion by destroying your life's research if you know it's going to be lost anyway?" She wasn't as confident as she wished to be. Even if high mages expected the arcanists and Veranesh himself to counter their ritual, they couldn't predict the Cataclysm, and with all the magic in the Towers, Gayabal couldn't have been certain the journal would perish... unless it was a part of their spell. A drop of cold sweat ran down the spine. It was one thing to hide the truth of the battle with Veranesh, and another to knowingly cause the demise of a whole kingdom.

Veelk shrugged in reply and returned to scanning the darkness, so she focused on the journal again. Once more, she skimmed through the basics, finding no motivation to slog through the praises of the ideas upon which high magic was based on, especially given that they hardly held after centuries had passed, but halfway through, her curiosity grew when Gayabal focused on the topic of enhancing the powers of the non-arcanist mages.

It is said that magic can be transferred to our world only through the means of a pact with the inhabitant of the other plane, a yalari. Human willpower strengthens the yalari in his world while the so-called demon serves as a medium through which magic travels to the arcanist. But what if there was another way of drawing the power that would not be dependent on making a pact? Unrestricted, always available power that wouldn't rely on pleas to an unwilling entity? The Devanshari artifact, which they call Hajihali, proves that magic can be channeled into our world without the yalari intermediary. If high mages were to pursue a similar path, we would be able to draw power more easily than we do now.

Kamira paused as the ideas congealed. Gayabal seemed reluctant to put his real thoughts into writing, but with the knowledge of both schools of magic, she could read between the lines well enough. All she had to do was to find the thread that connected all the pieces she had.

"What are you doing?" Veelk's shout disturbed both the silence and her thoughts, and she looked up confused, but he was staring at the darkness. "Come out already. You couldn't sneak up on the dead."

"And you're as pleasant as a hog in mating season," came from the darkness, and a woman stepped out into the circle of light.

Kamira thought no one would ever match Veelk's height and build, but the stranger was at least half a head higher and as muscular as him. Her face had similar features to his, but she boasted a mane of dark hair that flashed with deep red strands when they caught the campfire's light. Time had left its marks on her skin, so she must be considerably older than Veelk, but still in her prime years. She wore simple clothing, similar to Veelk's, dusty and bearing the marks of a long journey, but her keshal's blade reflected the flames with no trace of dirt.

"It's good to see you, Zee."

"You too," replied the woman. "But I see no new scars, which means you must have grown lazy. I dare not think I've trained a coward."

Veelk laughed. "Or I'm just more skilled than you ever were."

"As bold as usual." Her smile mirrored that of Veelk. "Maybe I should whack your hide once or twice." Despite the playful threat, they hugged, and then she inspected Kamira. "And who's that skittish arcanist? Your captive? I thought you had better taste in women."

Kamira couldn't help smiling at the comment. "He does, to our mutual content. I'm Kamira."

"Zelna." A short nod. "If Veelk keeps you around, you must be worth something, and I assume you and your demon behave."

Kamira swallowed. Veelk might be a mage killer, but they'd been traveling together long enough for her to lose most of her instinctive fear, and there was a life debt he claimed to still owe her, but Zelna was another matter. The tribal woman looked every bit unforgiving, and Kamira could imagine Zelna's shiny keshal springing to action at the mere mention of Veranesh.

"You didn't ask to meet me because you're bringing her over, are you?" Zelna looked down at Veelk. "Because I'm not killing our mother with news you're marrying some sickly arcanist."

Kamira stared with her lips parted, wordless as her mind bounced from the idea someone would think she'd marry Veelk to the fact she was staring at his sister. He'd never bothered mentioning he had a family, and she assumed he spoke little about his tribe because he protected secrets she wasn't to know.

Veelk burst out laughing. "No, sis. We need information only Suzhaul might know."

Zelna huffed, displeased. "No knowledge is exclusive. There are many means to obtain it, and if you're asking on the arcanist's behalf, I see no reason to grant her audience. She's not of the tribe."

Kamira bit her tongue and hid her disappointment. As much as she reasonably knew that Veelk's tribe would not allow an outsider to confer with Suzhaul, she'd hoped that Veelk's word would be enough to convince Zelna.

"You're not one to pass a rushed judgment." Veelk looked his sister in the eye. "And I wouldn't have sent the message if I didn't think you'd see my reasons. So come, sit with us, and we'll answer your questions. Then decide."

Zelna hesitated and eyed Kamira. "I'll stay till dawn."

Veelk opened his mouth, but instead of speaking, he looked past Zelna into the darkness. "You brought other kinsmen with you?"

Zelna's surprised expression sufficed for an answer, and both mage killers reached for their keshals.

"Barrier!" Veelk called out.

Kamira's instincts responded before her mind comprehended the meaning. Magic surged around her and formed a protective cocoon the moment the first creatures leapt from the darkness. Small beasts with claws longer than their snouts attacked Veelk and Zelna, but two keshals spun in retaliation. They turned their backs to Kamira and made their stand with the barrier behind them.

Kamira stared in horror at the twisted creatures pouring in from the dark. Part of her studies required her to read up on them, the lowest and the least sentient among demon kind, but she'd seldom gotten to see any demonling alive. The last time was, if she recalled correctly, when she'd met Veelk for the first time, and the demonlings were hardly living at that point.

She sat behind her barrier, unable to do anything unless she lowered it, but until Veelk and Zelna needed her help, she wouldn't interfere. Two mage killers could likely dispose of a small army of such creatures, and Veelk wouldn't appreciate it if she gave up on her barrier and put herself at risk.

Zelna's massive body impaired her agility, but the wide arcs of her keshal made up in strength what she lacked in speed. One of the creatures leapt, and its flexible legs pushed it high up in the air toward the mage killer, but as it descended, Zelna's keshal was thrust quickly between the demonling's ribs. She slung the body from the thinner blade she'd impaled it on into the crowd of oncoming creatures then stepped on another's head before it could sink its teeth into her leg.

To the side, Veelk spun with the weapon's broad blade, interrupting the smooth movements with sudden thrusts. His fighting was fluid and introduced many demonlings to Kamira's barrier face-first. She cringed when the creatures' skulls crushed against the magic shield and slid down, leaving smears of blood hanging in the air, trickling down the barrier in surreal morbidity.

Kamira scanned the battlefield tirelessly. The attacks were too coordinated, with waves of demonlings leaping toward the defenders, for it to be a stray band that had killed its own summoner. She narrowed her eyes and pressed her lips together, but deep within, anticipation rose. The arcanist who'd summoned them had to be nearby, and once she found him, he'd get a taste of her magic. The barrier flickered when she sent the lumisphere high above the skirmish. Shadows scattered as the growing light poured over the combatants, and Kamira reinforced her barrier just in time to prevent a demonling from entering it. The tips of the creature's claws that had breached the wavering field fell to the ground, cut cleanly off. Kamira cursed her lack of experience: holding two spells required not only focus but also power, and with her previous pact she could hardly have a lumisphere and a barrier going together.

One of the shadows just outside the light's edge moved, and Kamira fixed her gaze on the shining eyes of the arcanist controlling the creatures. With so many of them, he should be already burning out and losing focus.

"Got him!" she called out, hoping her voice would carry over the screeches and howls.

Zelna spun and planted her elbow into a demonling's stomach, and the creature was sent reeling, but not before burying its claws into her arm. She groaned, turning her wounded side to the barrier and raising her keshal for protection, but the demonlings continued their assault, two lunging for her throat, and three more trying slip beneath her defenses.

Kamira watched the scene with eyes wide, because even with her limited knowledge of physical battles, it was clear that Veelk's sister was going to fall.

Yet she ducked, at the same time striking down her keshal. The broad blade tore through three demonlings' snouts, crushing their skulls and slinging blood, but the claws of leaping creatures dug deep into her back. She lunged backward and crushed their bodies against the barrier, then regained her footing.

With more of them coming, Kamira knew better than to

allow herself a breath of relief. Instead, she gave the battlefield a quick look. The demonlings focused their attacks on Veelk and Zelna, and only a few were trying to get through the barrier. With a bit of luck, she would be able to extend it.

"Stay close!" she shouted. Another pack darted at the wounded Zelna, leaving her little time. "Now!"

The barrier flickered and disappeared, emerging farther away a moment later. At Kamira's signal, Veelk turned his back to the new barrier, ready to fight any creatures caught inside, while Zelna stared at the demonlings outside, scratching at the flickering dome.

"Duck!" Veelk threw his keshal.

Taught by previous experience, Kamira immediately pressed her face to the cold ground, and the blade cut the air right above her. A screech of pain told her that Veelk's keshal had found its mark. She sighed with relief, since the weapons were not crafted nor balanced for throwing. Veelk's steps thumped the ground beside her, and Kamira rose while the mage killer picked up his keshal and charged the two remaining demonlings within the barrier.

The thin blade caused the first to leap. Veelk spun, using the dead body's weight for extra momentum before it slid off, and the wide blade cleaved the other creature in half.

"That was foolish." Zelna sat down with a sigh of pain. "Now we're trapped."

"But we have time to see to those wounds." Veelk eyed his sister with concern. "I see you finally accepted Suzhaul's gift."

She gave him a half-sour sneer, but when she spoke, her voice rang with amusement. "Could beat you silly without them. But Suzhaul gives, and we accept." She looked at Kamira. "I suppose some gratitude is in order. My duties as a kallan don't offer many opportunities to fight, and it seems I got rusty."

Veelk shook the blood from his keshal, inspecting the blade closely for nicks. "You couldn't possibly have a look at her wounds, could you?" He paid no attention to the growing horde of demonlings clawing at the barrier now that their opponents were out of reach.

"I can have a *look*, but no chance of using magic. The barrier won't hold, or I'll have to get rid of the light." Kamira would prefer not to perform any healing by the fading light of the campfire.

Of course, it also meant she had to move, and even one step could destroy her barrier, so she drew hasty symbols on the ground, and her lumisphere flickered while she poured magic to reinforce her makeshift circle. Then, cautiously, she linked it with their protection, ensuring the circle channeled the magic to the barrier and allowing her to move freely within it.

Zelna shook her head and took off her ripped shirt and breast binds. "Back in the day, arcanists could hold three if not more spells at the same time," she remarked dryly while Veelk inspected the wounds on her back. "They used to provide some challenge, while now they hide behind barriers or summon demonlings to aid them."

"Speaking of which..." Kamira stood up. "I should have a conversation with someone that does the latter." As she approached the barrier, the demonlings doubled their efforts, but she ignored them. With all of Veranesh's power at her disposal, the barrier would sooner fall when she died than from any attack. "I know you're there!" She stared straight in the stranger's eyes. "Drained of all the strength and trying to crawl away before you lose control over what you've summoned."

The darkness shifted and a man stepped forward just within the lumisphere's light. His pale face and the dark circles under his eyes betrayed the strain, but he still stood on his own. Several demonlings looked back at him, growling, but to Kamira's disappointment, none attacked.

"Long time no see, eh, Kamira?" the man said, and his voice carried over the screeches and howls.

He did look familiar, but only when he spoke did she recognize the voice—and the lazy accent of Kaighal's docks. "Not long enough, Hafnis."

"An old enemy of yours?" Veelk asked from behind.

"He's the master's other pupil." She didn't break eye contact with Hafnis. "Rejected by five demons before one made a pact." Words allowed her to play for time and figure out what was happening, because the Hafnis she knew would never be able to perform such a straining summoning. The demon desperate enough to make a pact with him was weak and insignificant, even compared to her previous pact, and so was the magic he offered. "Still running your petty schemes, Haf?"

Hafnis smiled, and his thin lips resembled a worm crawling across his brown but pale face. "The teacher's pet trying to be mean? It's not me who's trapped."

Kamira cocked her head to the side. "I'm pretty sure I can hold this barrier longer than you'll keep your creatures leashed." Since Hafnis didn't know she had a new pact, Kamira hoped that such a bold claim would unbalance him enough to lose his grip on the demonlings. He'd never had good control, either of his magic or his emotions.

"I'll summon more, and they'll crush your pathetic protection," Hafnis spat.

Kamira kept her expression neutral and waited for his slip. With so much confidence, he must have gotten a new pact, but she could hardly think of any demon that would bother with such a lousy arcanist. "That's a bold statement for an arcanist who can't even draw a circle," she said casually.

"Shut up! You'll beg for mercy! I'll listen to your screams while I watch you being eaten by—" Hafnis suddenly paused and curled up like a scolded dog. He knelt down, and with his eyes closed started mumbling. Kamira didn't hear the words, but recognized the rhythm of the summoning spell.

"I see." Kamira grinned. Hafnis's servile behavior told her enough. "He's going to kill you when it's done. If you don't die of exhaustion first."

"Shut up!" Hafnis cried. "Shut up, gaharra!"

It gave her no pleasure to torment him like that, but if he wanted her dead, she'd use his own weakness against him.

Veelk walked up to her. "Zelna will live, but I don't want her to fight," he said in a hushed voice. "Can they break through?"

The demonling in front of her snarled as she stared at it with contempt. "The barrier should hold, but I'd rather not fight and protect Zelna at the same time." Alternating between a barrier and offensive magic was easy enough, but not when she had to take another person into consideration, and when it was only Veelk, he could take care of himself. "And there's also someone stronger here pulling Hafnis's strings."

"A demon?"

Until his question, she hadn't pondered such a possibility, but he had a point. No matter how jealous Hafnis might be, if he'd made a better pact, he wouldn't have wasted it chasing after her, but rather made it work for his own gain, no matter what underhanded dealing it might have meant. "Most likely," she replied.

Another wave of demonlings headed toward the barrier, almost trampling the creatures that were already at it.

"Scared now?!" Hafnis yelled, his eyes crazed. "I can summon many more!"

Kamira grimaced at the taunt. "We need to wear him down. Demon's help or not, there's only so much a human body can take."

"I'll go and play, then." Veelk corrected the grip on his keshal. "You keep talking."

"Don't die. I'd hate to be stuck with your sister." As much as she wanted the teasing to sound playful, the countless demonlings reminded her of when she'd met Veelk, in a forest clearing and surrounded with dead bodies. He might have killed them all back then, but if she hadn't happened upon him, he wouldn't have survived either.

She took a step back, and with a little focus her barrier erupted into ice shards. As they flew at demonlings, Veelk leapt forward, and his strikes added to the howls of pain her magic had already induced. As soon as he was out, Kamira recalled her protection and, with a glance, ensured no demonling had made it through. Veelk was already running along it, cutting down surprised creatures.

Hafnis started summoning again, and Kamira tensed. If he kept it up, he could swarm Veelk, so she had to keep Hafnis distracted.

"You're just a pawn, Hafnis. You'll be tossed away when you've served your purpose." Her mockery succeeded. Hafnis gritted his teeth in anger, and the summoning was interrupted. "Oh dear, he can't even keep the spell going when someone talks! Your master will scold you again!"

"I think it's time you stopped talking, pactee." A demon

walked out from the dark. "You're upsetting my lackey, and I need him to work."

He was taller than a human, of slender build, and had a long face with a beaklike nose. He had one eye missing, and the wound looked fresh, sparking Kamira's curiosity. He wore a plain outfit she'd seen around Kaighal, which suggested he had the means to mingle with humans, likely through the gossiped-about illusion magic. She couldn't see wings, which was uncommon for higher demons, but she took notice of his massive legs and a tail swaying in the dark.

"I thought higher demons chose their pactees a bit more carefully," she threw her bait. Without knowing anything about the demon, she was at a disadvantage. Dealing with him would be more difficult than outsmarting Pardayi, and he'd kept too far away for her to try binding him, even though she needed his name anyway.

"Carefully picking a tool I'm only going to use once is a waste of time. Humans are to serve their purpose and die." He looked at Veelk, fighting at the far side of the barrier, and suddenly all the demonlings shrieked and backed away, gathering around Hafnis and the demon, making it clear it wasn't the arcanist who controlled them. "We have time. We'll summon many more and crush your little barrier. How much longer can you hold it anyway, pactee?"

Kamira accepted the challenge. Her barrier disappeared in a flash, and the arcs of lighting she sent jumped between the demonlings, throwing the creatures into disarray, but the demon stepped in front of Hafnis before her attack reached its real target. She didn't risk another attempt and instead restored the barrier.

"Not bad," Zelna muttered behind her back, closer than Kamira thought she was. Veelk's sister, no matter the disregard she might have for arcanists, still cared enough to protect Kamira if needed.

"You were saying?" Kamira couldn't help grinning at the demon. The magic rushing through her body reminded her that, with Veranesh's help, she could be a match equal to even a demon.

"As impudent as I expected. You should know your place, pactee."

The demonlings attacked again, some of them wearing down the barrier and ensuring she wouldn't be able to take it down again, while others circled Veelk and cut him off.

"I thought it was to serve my purpose?" She needed to get the demon talking.

"I was told that you didn't serve your purpose well, and you'd caused disturbance instead." The demon took several steps forward, and the way he eyed Hafnis told Kamira that he didn't trust his tool. Yet he still kept close enough to prevent her from trying another spell.

"I had good intentions, but there were complications." Kamira pretended to be regretful. "Our mutual *friend* interfered. You know, the one you fear." If the demon was after her, he must have been involved in Veranesh's trapping.

The demon's face twisted. "Watch your words, pactee!"

No matter how intimidating he might look, his reactions made him an easier opponent than Pardayi. Despite her shortcomings, the demoness was adept at playing games and could hold her emotions at bay, while this demon gave in to his instincts much easier. Kamira smirked at the thought that maybe, in the end, Hafnis and he were a good match.

"Am I not right?" she taunted him. "You wouldn't be chasing after me and trying to kill me if you didn't fear him."

A thunderous growl carried through the hills and sank into the night. The demon leapt toward the barrier, and it trembled under the pounding of his fist.

Kamira hushed her instinct that demanded her to back away. With him so close, she would be able to bind him if only she knew his name. There had to be a way to force him to reveal it. "Whether I live or die, he has already won. But I don't think your strength matches his power. You won't get through."

"Your lies will get you nowhere," the demon said. "Humans are but a curiosity to him, a toy to play with. He might have promised you a pact, but he'll never make one."

Steady strikes of his claws, supported by his magic, forced Kamira to focus on the barrier and energy flow, but she still paid attention to the battlefield.

"My words got me exactly where I wanted to be," she muttered with satisfaction.

The triumphant expression faded from the demon's face, replaced by suspicion.

"Uganel, help!" Panic overflowed in Hafnis's words.

The demon turned to see what Kamira was already looking at: Veelk making his way through the last of the demonlings and closing in on the arcanist. At Uganel's growl, the creatures at the barrier turned, and the demon leapt to protect Hafnis, but Veelk was too seasoned in battles to lunge forward and expose himself to attack. He faced the monsters, taking a defensive stance as he loosed his dagger. Within a heartbeat, the crystal blade was buried in Hafnis's eye.

The arcanist dropped dead, and Uganel roared, turning toward the mage killer. Veelk leapt backward, reaping the blood of several demonlings, and his eyes shone with battle fervor.

"You're not thinking of taking me on, are you, human?" A malicious smile curled Uganel's lips, and his claws flexed.

"No. She will." Veelk pointed at Kamira. "Your pactee gave her all she needed."

The demon glanced back at Kamira, his eyes narrowed.

Kamira smiled, grateful for those few moments Veelk had bought her, so that she could weave Uganel's name into the spell. Without delay, she started the binding incantation, letting her lumisphere fade as she focused on it. The energy extended through the barrier as if it was nothing, and its tendrils touched Uganel.

He roared and pulled away, breaking the bind, and as magic chased after him, he dashed into the dark.

Kamira muttered a curse. She should have known binding a demon who could move freely wouldn't be as easy as capturing one who was immaterial and therefore tied to her summoning place.

With his departure, the demonlings fell into disarray. A few attacked Veelk, but the rest started fighting amongst themselves. Kamira removed the barrier, turning its energy toward the creatures, and channeled some more, letting the freezing wind spread. The creatures began moving sluggishly, and some turned to ice. One by one, Veelk crushed the ones that survived the infighting.

"Why not bolts of lightning? I can't freeze, but I do feel that flerra of a cold." Veelk approached after the last demonling shattered.

"Because I'm fed up with the smell of charred bodies and burnt fur. Besides, ice is more difficult to conjure, so I need to practice."

"We'll have to move the camp anyway." Zelna's face remained placid, but her stiff movement told of her wounds. "Whatever magic you did scared that demon mindless, and it won't likely come back, but I'd rather not be seen with a lot of dead demonlings."

As Kamira packed her belongings, her eyes stopped at the forgotten journal, and she sighed after tucking it away. Veelk packed up the rest of the bags, but kept his keshal at the ready, and they walked away from the battlefield, darkness swallowing them.

"IF YOU CAN'T HOLD MORE than one spell, how were you going to bind the demon without lowering your barrier?" Zelna asked while Kamira looked over her wounds.

They stopped to rest after the night's trek toward the mountains, away from the slaughter site. The campfire flames provided warmth but not enough light, and dawn was slow to come, so a small lumisphere floated by Kamira's face. "I can hold two spells," she muttered, focused on her task. "Otherwise I'd be fixing you in the dark."

The gashes on Zelna's back still bled, and Kamira pushed the skin closer together, watching the scar lines. She'd learned enough from Veelk to know they didn't need to be aligned, but the healing worked better when they were. Of course, she'd never openly admit to having knowledge of his tribe's workings and that they put powdered imbued stones into their skin. Some secrets were meant to be left unspoken, even if she had no doubt that Zelna had a good idea of the extent of Kamira's knowledge.

Zelna let out a growl of frustration when Kamira mistook a battle scar for the one with Suzhaul's powder in it, and after checking the marks on Zelna's skin, she released her magic in short, controlled bursts, then as a wave. Zelna's scars lit up and absorbed it, sending it partially back into the demon realm, but a part of it remained within the skin, hastening the tissue's mending.

The process of enhanced healing always mesmerized Kamira, since the art of actual healing with magic had mostly been lost after the Cataclysm. What was left behind required lengthy preparations and an intricate circle, and didn't compare to the mage killers' quick recovery.

"No one will patch you up as good as an arcanist." Veelk sat by the fire. "But now you owe her, sis."

"Or you could add it to the debt you've been so generously repaying for the past years." Zelna gave him a mean look. "But I'll call for Suzhaul, if that's what you had in mind. I've seen and heard enough."

Kamira leaned forward, pretending to have a closer look at Zelna's wound as she hid a smirk. Veelk's sister had a lot of questions, and didn't miss a single detail as they laid out their explanations during the short journey. Even if she at first considered keeping some secrets safe, Veelk's insistent glare made it clear she shouldn't avoid answering, and in the end, Zelna learned all about Veranesh.

"There," Kamira said when a fresh scab covered the last of three gashes. "Try not to stretch it for a couple of days."

Zelna's expression told her how much Veelk's sister cared about such health recommendations, and Veelk's similar stare resurfaced in Kamira's memories. If she ever had a doubt they were family, that reaction put it to rest. Both siblings were as stubborn and full of disregard for their own wellbeing.

"Do you need to rest, or should I start the ritual?" Zelna asked.

"I'll be fine." Kamira withheld a yawn, her tiredness chased away by both the promise of answers and curiosity of how the most reclusive and unresponsive demon was summoned.

Zelna took out arm bracelets and a circlet made of a metal Kamira had never seen, then sat away from fire with her legs crossed, one hand in the other. With her eyes closed, she inhaled and exhaled in an irregular pattern.

Kamira's eyes widened as she studied the arc of Zelna's arms. Her body, her own flesh served as a circle! No wonder no one else had ever managed to summon Suzhaul, neither through the pact offering nor any other means.

"No one can summon Suzhaul the traditional way," Veelk said, catching her stare. "He only responds to our priests, as you'd call them."

"That I do." A ghostly figure stepped forward, forming from Zelna's breath. Suzhaul shared his kin's birdlike facial features, and massive wings towered over his broad shoulders. The size of his claws paled in comparison to other yalari, but blade-like growths reaching out from his elbows toward his shoulders suggested the demon's prowess in combat.

Veelk lowered his head, and Suzhaul reciprocated the gesture. Then his eyes turned to Kamira.

Sitting on her heels, she leaned forward, touching her forehead to the ground. If any demon was worth respectful treatment, it was the one before her. "Etay shannev," she said, using the traditional greeting. "I'm Kamira—"

"I don't speak with pactees." Suzhaul looked back at Veelk. "Why did you bring her to me?"

"Because of a demon who claims to have known you in the past." Veelk's unwavering gaze met Suzhaul's eyes.

Suzhaul grimaced. "I give you my strength, and you are free to make your own judgments. If she misuses the power given to her, you kill her, and if she acts forced by the yalari's will, you make sure she breaks the pact."

Kamira let out a sigh, ready to give up, because she'd expected as much from the unyielding demon with an equally unyielding sense of justice, but speaking out loud could enrage him. Veelk's attention remained focused on Suzhaul, so she couldn't let him know to cut this short, before Suzhaul's patience ran out.

"She can't break the pact," Veelk replied. "Veranesh won't allow it."

Suzhaul's eyes lit up, resembling liquid gold, and he turned to Kamira again. "Now that's an interesting name to hear. I'd like to know why you lied to my warrior about the yalari you have the pact with. Speak, pactee, and choose your words carefully." The demon's posture relaxed, but Kamira had often seen Veelk in a similar stance, and she remembered how quickly he could strike. Even if the demon was immaterial, he undoubtedly had the means of killing her if her response didn't satisfy him.

"We'd been exploring the ruins in the desert." She kept the story short, hoping he wouldn't take it as concealing things. "This is where I met Veranesh, trapped in a crystal, and made a pact at his... insistence."

"Veranesh was destroyed four hundred years ago. And he never granted a pact to all those who begged him, let alone coerced someone into it." Suzhaul reached out, and his claw pushed on Kamira's chin, forcing her head up until their eyes met. His touch, emanating with concentrated magic, made it clear that he had enough power to kill, even across the worlds. Yet the strike did not come, and instead he inspected her face. "But you seem to believe it true... Whomever you made a pact with, he or she deceived you." He let go of her, rubbing his chin.

"Demons tend to do that a lot." Kamira's habitual response got the better of her, but to her surprise, Suzhaul burst out in laughter, not anger.

"And yet you seek my counsel?" he asked with slight amusement.

"Veelk trusts you. I'm here on his advice."

Suzhaul nodded as he moved away, a promise of life for her. "Tell me of this yalari you met. Veranesh was my friend, if my kin had such a thing, and I won't allow anyone to use his name for their own purposes."

"He's trapped in the bowels of the desert, in the place where Veranesh was said to have been summoned," she replied. Even if Suzhaul doubted her story, all the pieces fit to confirm the demon was who he claimed to be. "He mentioned your name, saying that you sought his advice when you... created the mage killers." She kept her face neutral, hoping he'd miss that she knew of such secrets.

With the sudden change in Suzhaul's expression to a stony glare, she could swear he was trying to conceal something as well. "Did he say anything else?" Suzhaul's voice wavered.

Kamira shook her head. "Not much. Whoever he is, he's very powerful. He broke my pact with a lesser demon in an instant."

Her words set off a reaction she didn't expect. Suzhaul clutched his fists, and a grimace of anger twisted his face. "The events of the past were kept from me," he said. "And I'll make sure they'll pay for that." His voice hinted at the fury that boiled within, and Kamira couldn't help admiring the demon's control over the rage. When he looked at her, his gaze was almost amiable. "It's me who's been deceived, not you. I know of only one yalari capable of what you speak." For the first time, Suzhaul smiled as he leaned forward, inspecting her again. "So, he finally made a pact? You must have impressed him, pactee."

She meant to argue Veranesh didn't have much choice, but he'd had enough of it. With the destruction spell he'd put on her, he didn't have to bother with a pact and waiting. Unless his hidden motives required having someone do his bidding.

With Suzhaul's mood lighter, Kamira risked a question. "Why would he never make one? There must have been some people in the past worthy of his attention." Back when the arcane arts were flourishing, when an arcanist like her wouldn't be worth a second glance.

"What do yalari get from it? What do they get in return for channeling magic to your world?"

"Our will strengthens them and protects them like a shield." The simple explanation she'd learned as a student felt naive, but if there were any deeper understandings, they'd been long lost after the Cataclysm.

"It's an accurate understanding." Suzhaul nodded. "Veranesh has no need of what humans have to offer, so he never bothered. Either this changed, or he had another reason for entering a pact."

"He wants me to find a way to free him."

Suzhaul narrowed his eyes. "Explain."

"A trap crafted by yalari and high mages imprisoned him." Since Suzhaul wasn't known for his affinity toward his own kin, Kamira omitted her source of information. In his eyes, Pardayi likely wouldn't be a reliable source.

To her relief, the brief response sufficed, and Suzhaul nodded. "Once she wakes up from the trance, you'll tell my kallan how to find Veranesh. I wish to hear his account of it all."

"I can arrange it much quicker," she said, glancing at Zelna. "If you have more time here."

"The trance doesn't strain her," Suzhaul said. "Can you summon Veranesh while he's trapped?"

Kamira shook her head. "He gave me other means." She lifted her arm, indicating the crystal nightfly coiled around it. The demon gestured for her to proceed, and she woke it up, letting Veranesh take control.

The creature circled as the demon within made himself aware of his surroundings. It didn't fly up to Suzhaul's manifestation, as she'd expected, instead hovering in front of her.

"Calling my bluff again?" The way he asked carried both his dissatisfaction and a warning.

The nightfly spun in the air, and without waiting for her answer, it approached Suzhaul. Words of arcane tongue, spoken too quickly for her to understand, flowed like an ancient song between the demons. Their voices carried little emotion, giving no indication of the relationship between the two. While they conversed, Kamira glanced at Veelk, but he watched the exchange as if he could actually follow it, and paid no attention to her.

Finally, the nightfly went silent and descended, coiling back at her wrist.

"He *is* Veranesh," Suzhaul said. "I won't interfere with his plans, nor will I aid him." He turned to Veelk. "Do you intend to travel with this pactee?"

The mage killer nodded. "I have a debt to pay."

Kamira knew his reasons were more complicated, and their friendship beyond mere repayment of debt, but simple answers worked best with both humans and demons. One could argue the strength of a relationship, but not the power that a life debt held.

"Very well. See to her survival as long as you see fit." Suzhaul gave Kamira one more glance. "I should warn you that he wasn't happy with your display of distrust and coming to me... to put it lightly. Yalari like him or me value their word above all, so whatever he promised you for your services, he'll give you. If his word is not good enough for you, you shouldn't have entered an agreement."

"I appreciate the warning." As much as Suzhaul's reprimand stung, risking Veranesh's displeasure had turned out worth it. Kamira's demon already knew she was distrustful, so he shouldn't be too unhappy that she'd sought confirmation from another of his kind who could vouch for him. At the same time, her Tivarashan nature made her relate to the hurt pride. "I'm in no position to repay you for your counsel, but I won't forget it." She bowed.

Suzhaul laughed dismissively. "I told you I don't deal with pactees. Debts with my people are settled when and how I see fit."

She could hardly contain the grimace that twisted her lips, since he'd made it clear that Veelk would have to pay whatever price was set. Not trusting her own composure and unable to argue with the demon, she offered another bow, and when she lifted her head, the demon had disappeared.

Zelna stretched her limbs. "Did you get what you were seeking? Suzhaul is just, but he can be difficult sometimes."

As far as Kamira was concerned, "difficult" didn't even begin to cover it, though—in the end—he did provide answers. "I did. I appreciate your help." She looked Zelna over. "You didn't hear anything?"

"No kallan ever does," Zelna replied. "We're to let others speak to him, not manipulate his words. Whatever answers you got, they belong to you. I can neither influence your understanding nor alter it."

"This... feels foreign to me." Back in Tivarashan, hardly anyone conferred with the Four, even though Kamira had no doubt that the arcanist priests sought their counsel and kept them informed of the happenings in the kingdom. "To summon a demon and never speak to him... It's the opposite of what arcanists do." Not that she used to summon her demoness often, but when she did, it was for the purpose of talking to her.

"Oh, she does speak to Suzhaul when someone else serves as a kallan," Veelk added, amused. "She would have never gotten the scars if that demon didn't convince her she should."

Zelna huffed, but her disgruntlement rang with concealed amusement. "I wouldn't have had to if you hadn't run off to die in some distant land." She looked him up and down. "Our mother still believes that one day you'll be back home, with all your exotic lovers in tow."

Kamira arched her eyebrow. To her knowledge, Veelk didn't stay in contact with his tribe, yet Zelna knew of his habits.

Her voiceless prompt earned no reaction from Veelk, and Zelna responded with laughter. "He's always been like that," she said. "Seducing merchants' daughters when we set out to trade or luring traveling healers."

"He hasn't changed, then," Kamira replied with a chuckle.

Veelk regarded them with a wide grin. "Why would I fix what's not broken?" He leaned forward, his expression turning to a snide smile. "And you're the one to talk?"

They both laughed, and Kamira couldn't help smiling. If she could, she'd love to spend more time with Veelk's sister, get to know her, and learn all the stories her brother was unwilling to share. But as much as Kamira's two companions lightened the mood, the recent confrontation with one demon and a conversation with another pushed her toward considering the future.

"We should get some rest." As always, Veelk caught her mood shift. "With the demon likely on our trail, we don't have much time."

Zelna shifted. "Did Suzhaul...?"

Veelk shook his head, and before she could argue, he said, "Go home, sis. As much as I'd love to fight by your side, you're needed there, not in a battle that isn't yours. Besides..." He offered a wide grin. "I don't think you need any more lovers to haul home."

Zelna leaned back, her own self-satisfied smile matching his. "I suppose so." Her grin faded and she became serious. "You made Suzhaul give you permission, though?"

"Live debts seem to do the trick." Veelk shrugged. "But I'd best not come and visit before it's all over in case he changes his mind." He glanced at the horizon. "You two should get some sleep. It's been a long night, and we best be on our way before the demon finds another foolish arcanist to serve him. I'll keep watch."

Kamira didn't argue, the strain of the events taking its toll, but Zelna waved him off.

"You're not getting off that easily. I want to hear all about your exploits," she said.

Veelk sighed, and Kamira snickered as she set down the bedroll she'd fished out of his pack. Her lumisphere dispersed as she rested her head, but the sky was already brightening in the east. Thoughts swarmed her, but before she could focus on any of them, tiredness and the quiet murmur of the siblings exchanging stories and news pushed her over the brink of sleep.

~

VEELK DISAPPEARED into the dark to scout the perimeter, and Kamira sighed.

They'd been traveling for three days since parting with Zelna, and he'd insisted on speed, pushing Kamira's body to its limits. In the evenings all she wanted was to sleep, not talk to a demon, but she'd be lying if she claimed she wasn't avoiding Veranesh. Waiting until they reached Kaighal seemed the best choice, since at least she'd have the energy and mindset of dealing with him, but as time passed, so might the demon's patience. And, after all, she was the one constantly testing the boundaries of their agreement.

Acting on impulse, she woke up the nightfly before tiredness took over.

It spun around as if the demon indulged in the substitute freedom, and she couldn't help wondering whether Veranesh would speak to her at all, but the crystal creature finally hovered in front of her. "Pactee. Do you need my assistance?"

She swallowed before taking the leap. "I think I've learned enough for us to talk."

"I suspected Suzhaul's insight might change your perspective," he replied lightly.

Her eyes widened. "You're not angered."

Veranesh laughed. "Why would I be? You did exactly what I expected you would do, with the distrust you've been displaying, and I knew that if you were persistent enough, you would uncover the truth that I would never be able to convince you of."

As a memory of Suzhaul's remark resurfaced, Kamira offered him a sour smile. "You made Suzhaul say what you wanted me to hear." And she'd fallen for it, naive like a beginner arcanist, giving in to the guilt the demon had elicited. "Well played."

"No one *makes* Suzhaul do anything, but he was kind enough to oblige my curiosity as to how you would react." Veranesh chuckled. "And what will you do now, pactee? Resort to your distrust again?"

Kamira shook her head. If he wanted to deceive her, he wouldn't have admitted to having played her, and his message was clear: she had no way of seeing through his manipulation. After all, the very mention of Suzhaul back in the Towers might have been intentional, designed to lead her down the path she'd gone. "I'm no match for you. Besides, like you said, I did uncover the truth. Pardayi proved very helpful."

"Tell me about it."

At first, she thought Veranesh was being sarcastic, but his voice rang with genuine interest, so she relayed the meeting with the demoness, and as a reward, she received Veranesh's hearty laughter.

"I couldn't have done it better myself," he said. "I'd give a lot to see the look on that gaharra's face. Beaten at her own game by a human." Veranesh let out another chuckle, and Kamira couldn't help picturing the demon in his prison, laughing like that maybe for the first time in centuries. "And in the end, you even managed to convince her that there is another player, and she'll be chasing shadows... You played it well, pactee."

Kamira acknowledged the compliment with a nod. Perhaps Veranesh was still playing her, first begetting her guilt, then reminding her of her place, and, finally, by offering praise, all actions calculated to make her abandon her distrust. The Tivarashan in her demanded caution, but the arcanist within reminded her that pacts didn't work without at least a pinch of mutual trust. Besides, something in Suzhaul's voice when he'd claimed she was unworthy of the agreement if she kept doubting Veranesh made her think that he wasn't only delivering the message but also speaking his mind, and that alone was a jab to her pride.

"Will you answer my questions?" she asked humbly. "What I've learned, and what I've deduced... It contradicts all I knew."

She expected Veranesh to remind her that his very existence undermined the truth she used to know, but instead he said, "Let's hear what you know, then."

Her inborn distrust made her hesitate only for a heartbeat. It was her chance to prove she was worth the pact and the agreement. "The other yalari would prefer you dead, but you're alive. At first, I thought that maybe they didn't trust high mages enough to show them how to destroy you. But then, the book that archmage Yoreus was after made me understand why the high mages wanted you alive." She took a deep breath as the thought of sharing the most blasphemous realization made her body stiff, even if she was about to tell it to a demon who would not laugh her off. "High magic is a lie. Using their spells, they channel energy through you... like a twisted, forced pact."

At first, the only reply was silence. As the nightfly hovered in the air, only its wings alive, Kamira second-guessed her decision to share that discovery. How humiliating it would be for the higher demon to admit he was no better than a slave to the high mages.

"All that from a few scraps Pardayi offered and scribbles of a frustrated human?" he finally said. "I'm impressed, pactee. Though, I admit, I'm also surprised you aren't more... shaken by such a revelation."

A bitter smile crossed her face. "I appreciate you're not

openly accusing me that I knew beforehand." She looked to the side, but Veelk wasn't within sight. Perhaps he'd heard the conversation from afar and was offering her time to deal with the demon. "I had three days to think about this and other things, and I had no love for the high mages to begin with." The memory of the moment when she discovered she'd have to sleep with her teacher, amongst other things, to pursue more in-depth knowledge brought back the familiar taste of disappointment, and she chased it away. "Learning that all their power comes from deception is just another reason to loathe them. And if I free you, they'll fall."

"They'll lose their power," Veranesh confirmed. "But freeing me is not going to be easy."

Her eyes widened as she stared at the nightfly. "You know how, don't you?" She ignored the voice in her head, frustrated that Veranesh hadn't shared that knowledge before. Back in the old Towers, she wouldn't have listened anyway.

"I had four hundred human years and countless failed attempts at research," Veranesh replied. "My powers are restricted for as long as the high mages cast their spells, and my prison, which I expected to crumble decades ago, remains as solid as in its first days. I can't be certain, but it leads me to believe that the key is in the High Towers. A device, perhaps, or a circle."

His words sparked a memory. "The initiation circle!"

A place that every aspiring mage had to enter once, becoming a subject of the simple ritual everyone considered nothing more but a tradition. But if what Veranesh said was true, the circle could serve another purpose as well, and if high mages used it to allow their students to access the demon's power, it also explained why the High Towers were the only place one could learn high magic. Without it, all knowledge passed on remained but a theory, and drawing energy was as difficult as it used to be before the Cataclysm.

"It won't be easy, but I can find a way." If needed, she would deceive the high mages or bribe the students to gain access to the circle, and if that failed, Veelk would likely applaud a more direct and violent approach. She could almost picture the glimmer in his eye at such an offer, and that brought a smile to her face.

"In due time, pactee. There's much left to discover, and you still need to learn how to wield what I offer you."

The mention of the power at her disposal cooled her excitement. As promised, Veranesh had ensured she didn't draw too much, despite the eagerness to give her more that she sensed every time she channeled magic, but a ritual capable of freeing him would require more than she could handle, at least for now. "If I die, you'll be free anyway," she said.

Veranesh huffed his displeasure. "I didn't make a pact to see you die when magic burns through you. And I thought the whole point of these efforts was to ensure you stay alive. Unless you changed your mind?"

She had to chuckle. "I'd still prefer to survive," she said. "But that brings me to another matter..." The one she initially hadn't intended on discussing with him, but his insights could prove valuable. "We've been attacked by a demon summoned to this world. Does the name Uganel tell you anything?"

"One of the weaker yalari, but still counts among kanyalari... higher demons, as you call them. Ambitious and conniving, but not a match for ones like me or Suzhaul. Cunning enough to never act against us openly, but I doubt he'd be capable of devising any elaborate plan alone."

"Which means there will be more coming..." Kamira bit

her lip. Uganel alone was problem enough, and the prospect of facing more higher demons made her survival look slimmer and slimmer.

"I wasn't aware that my kin could now be brought to your world so easily," Veranesh said.

Kamira shook her head. "In Tyorane, no one has even considered it since the Cataclysm... this is what we call what happened when you were imprisoned. But recently, there's been a war in Devanshari. Armies of demonlings attacked, and the refugees claim higher demons were involved." She grimaced at the few demands she'd overheard back in Kaighal that arcanists were to be banned from the city in case they plotted a betrayal. So far, High Towers and Gildya Magna had refused to give in, since fearing a handful of arcanists would undermine their position, but she could easily imagine how demon sightings could turn things around. "They slaughtered a lot of people and destroyed the artifact that protected the kingdom. Maybe Uganel and others had a hand in that too."

"So they finally did something about that nuisance," Veranesh said, amused. "Yalari discussed the destruction of the artifact for centuries before my imprisonment, but we're not quick to unite, and we had to wait for a way of traveling between the worlds. It seems both issues were resolved."

"What do you mean? Why would yalari want the artifact destroyed?"

"When we don't channel the energy through the pact, when it's drawn without our acceptance, it causes pain. Nothing excruciating, but it can be... distracting. The artifact pulled the magic indiscriminately and randomly, making us suffer when we least expected it. Which, as you might guess, isn't good when you're at war with all the others."

A vision of the world where no friendship or trust existed overwhelmed Kamira, even though she'd already read similar accounts in books. Chasing the images away, she focused on the problem. "Does it mean you suffer the same pain whenever a high mage casts a spell?" Demon or not, it was nothing more than torture, but at the same time, most high mages were unaware of it. She narrowed her eyes, trying to guess how many of them were involved. Some of the archmages, that was certain. Her thoughts turned to Yoreus, and with the new revelations, she had no doubt that he knew of Veranesh. Unless... She had to consider that none of the mages knew, and the secret had died with those who imprisoned the demon.

"Nothing I can't endure, though I admit it's frustrating. Like an itch you can't scratch." The way Veranesh said it made Kamira picture him flexing his claw... and the flesh, human mages' flesh, it would reach if given the chance. "But we strayed from the problem. What about Uganel? Where is he now?"

"He fled when the arcanist who served him revealed his name." Kamira grimaced at the memory of the failed binding. "He might be looking for another arcanist to summon demonlings for him, or plotting some other way to get me. If he asks other demons to aid him, it's going to get difficult... Too much commotion will draw the high mages' attention as well."

"He won't ask for help," Veranesh said with certainty. "To do so would damage his position among others, and you're nothing but a weak human to him. He'll deal with you alone, so lure him out to the desert and use the spell I taught you. And remember to shield yourself, or the energy released in the last part of the spell will be your undoing. If needed, I'll help you."

"Do you know anything else of him?" She chose not to mention that this was exactly what she and Veelk had planned as soon as they made it back to Kaighal for supplies.

The nightfly danced in the air while Veranesh thought. "Yalari are cunning, but proud. In that, we're similar to humans. Hurt his pride, and he'll forget his wits. Ones like him never have enough control over their rage, especially if their target is within sight. Or..." The crystal insect hovered in front of her. "Try to play him. Beg for your life or promise to betray me. He'll like to have power over you, and he'll be tempted by the thought of taking something from me. If you play him as well as you played Pardayi, we might learn something of value before you destroy him."

Her eyes widened at his response, but then she nodded and smiled. "How much power will be released?" she asked to conceal her thoughts. "How deep into the desert we need to go?"

"I'd say half as much energy as four hundred years ago," Veranesh replied after consideration.

She gasped, her mind barely conjuring a relevant image, and the nightfly shifted in the air in something that looked like a nod.

"It will be your test, pactee," he continued, "and I expect you to pass it. I have plans for us that require you to survive."

Survive. Always the word, the rule she and Veelk lived by. Her thoughts drifted. When did making a pact with Veranesh become something more than just surviving? When had she gotten involved in the plots of demons and high mages, trying to outsmart all the opponents in the game? When did it become something more than buying time to find a way to free herself from his spell? She could lie to herself that it was the discovery of the truth that led her to change her mind, but there was more to it. The taste of power that came with a pact that had no limitations pushed her into the game, and her Tivarashan nature, no matter how much she would deny it, enjoyed the feeling of facing both Pardayi and Uganel. Being a threat to them brought confidence she'd never had before, and woke up the ambition she'd buried long ago.

Her own body disrupted her thoughts, and she yawned.

"You should get some rest, pactee." The nightfly hovered over Kamira's arm, just by the dormant bracelet. "Wake up the other one too. I'll keep guard, and you can both rest."

Kamira preferred not to guess how Veranesh's argument would go with Veelk, but she did what the demon asked. With Uganel out there, refusing help would be foolish. "Veelk should be somewhere around." A quick look around didn't reveal the mage killer, who preferred to stay in the dark. Many thugs and robbers were lured by a lone woman sleeping by the fire, only to meet with his keshal before they made it close.

"Suzhaul's magic makes it easy to find him. Until dawn, pactee."

With that, both nightflies took off.

14

At midday, the inn was empty and Ryell found himself looking at the door every time it opened. The innkeeper's daughter, Lefna, brought him another mug of ale and gave him a comforting pat on the shoulder.

"Don't worry. They'll come back soon," she said. "They're never gone for long, and this time they didn't take many supplies."

Ryell forced himself to reciprocate her smile, but frustration fueled his thoughts as they once more circled Atissa. Her mocking words when she refused to help him still rang in his ears, but he couldn't blame her. A high mage, a future archmage, had no interest in helping insignificant refugees. Yet he'd still hoped she might do it for him...

Ryell took a sip of ale. After the fruitless and scathing conversation with Atissa, one that ended with them fighting and Ryell leaving, there was no point in discussing the matter with Yoreus, and Ryell couldn't think of any other high mage who would be interested. When he'd inquired, both mages and students referred him to yet another mage, and he wasted a lot of time running in circles. But giving up was hardly an option when he thought of young Gann's suffering, and the note sent to Tyddes contained only two words—"still searching"—though having run out of options, Ryell was waiting, not searching, and hoping that the arcanist whom he'd wronged would be more helpful than the woman who supposedly was affectionate toward him.

But the question of Kamira's willingness to help was irrelevant if she didn't come back in time. He'd waited for three days already, and Lefna said they'd been gone for over two weeks. He closed his fingers on the mug. *Demons curse it, Kamira. Where are you?*

The door opened again, and Ryell lifted his head, expecting to see another patron, but instead Veelk walked inside, his shoulders barely fitting through the doorway. His dirty and stained clothes told of the journey and its dangers, and it didn't escape Ryell that some of the patches looked like blood splatters. Kamira followed him with her eyes half-closed and dragging her feet.

"You're back!" Lefna called out, beaming. "I was starting to worry you'd never come back!"

Veelk leaned over the counter with a predatory smile. "I'd say a proper goodbye if that was to happen. If you get me some food, I'll tell you all about our adventures."

"I don't know where you get the stamina," Kamira muttered. "I'm going straight to bed." She took the key Lefna handed her, and only then spotted Ryell.

He stood up, covering his uneasiness with a bow. Her state made it clear she needed rest, and he reconsidered his request. She wouldn't be able to go right away, so he could wait to ask her as well.

"You were waiting for me?" She offered him a tired smile.

Ryell looked down, desperate for an excuse, but Lefna didn't shy away from explaining, "He's been here for the last three days."

At such a blunt remark, he couldn't bring himself to lie. "I need your help," he confessed.

Kamira released a heavy sigh, and before she opened her mouth, Ryell was certain she'd refuse, but she pointed at the stairs. "Very well. Come."

As they passed Veelk, the mage killer eyed him with a mix of curiosity and suspicion, and only at Kamira's gesture did he stay at the counter. Ryell offered her his arm as they approached the steps, but she shook her head.

"At least let me carry your bag," he offered, desperate to provide some courtesy to the woman who had every right to tell him to wither in the dark, or whatever curses Tivarashan people used to send away their enemies.

Reluctantly, she handed the bag over and led him upstairs, to her room. It looked exactly as Ryell remembered, save the made beds and even fewer personal items she and Veelk must have taken with them.

"Drop my bag anywhere." She headed straight for the basin. After rinsing her face off, she glanced at him, still standing in the middle of the room. "And tell me what you need. You wouldn't have been waiting for so long if it wasn't important."

Ryell set her bag beside the bed, but reluctantly gave up the idea of sitting on it. Back when she took care of him, it was his to sleep in, but to claim it after they'd parted ways would be rude, even if he hoped it would create some familiarity between them, rekindling the cautious friendliness of that time. With some regret, he took the chair.

"Shouldn't I start with courtesy and ask you about your trip?" A pang of guilt dug into his thoughts. After all she'd done for him, he'd offered her little in return and come back only to ask for more.

"No. I'm tired. I want to be done with whatever you need and then rest." She sat on the bed and stretched her legs. "I swear Veelk intentionally set the pace to murder me."

Ryell hesitated, but he'd already wasted some of her time, and his own was short. "It's my people. Are you aware of the... affliction the Devanshari suffer from?"

"You're talking about the addiction to magic, aren't you? The artifact affected your bodies, and you can't live without it."

He gave a nod, hiding his grimace at her crude explanation. She was right, but to hear his people described as addicts, as if they were some lowlifes, spread his composure thin. "It's difficult, and many of us suffer. Prince Allyv is searching for a cure to free us from this... affliction. But some can't bear the hunger and they turn to questionable alternatives."

"So I've heard," she replied. "Several substances and mixtures are recently in high demand. Though it's nothing you'd need an arcanist for."

"I... They..." He took a deep breath. "Some youngsters drank water with powdered imbued stones."

"They did *what*?!" Kamira tensed. "I'd think that after what you've all been through, that's the last thing any Devanshari would do. Haven't you people had enough dealings with demons?"

Her tone surprised him so much that he silently suffered

through her lecture. Kamira was a demonologist, but the way she'd reacted made it clear that she wasn't about to defend demons. He'd never thought that someone willingly serving one would express such distrust.

"The young ones don't understand the dangers," he gave in to the need to explain his people's actions. "I don't think they even understand what the stones are. The recipe requires mixing powder from several stones, but Prince Allyv thinks those who suffered failed to follow it and used only one stone. They are expensive and hard to get."

"And now they have a demon stuck in their bodies, trying to break free." Kamira got off the bed and headed for the trunk. "I might be able to help." She fished out some clothes, crumpled but clean, and glanced over her shoulder. "Wait downstairs, if you don't mind."

Ryell pictured Kamira changing, his imagination filling in what the clothes concealed, and rushed to the door, hoping to hide any blush. He stopped short of turning the door handle. "I'm not sure if they'll all be able to pay," he said. "But I'll try to cover any of your expenses."

"I guessed that much. And don't worry about it." She waved him off.

Arguing would only delay them, so Ryell nodded and left. Even if Kamira didn't want money, he'd find a way to repay her, maybe with a gift or a service. He already owed her, and the thought of being even more indebted to a demonologist... He paused. No, not demonologist. Arcanist Kamira. She deserved to be called by her name and the true title.

Veelk's laughter filled the downstairs room, contrasting with Lefna's soft chuckle, and Ryell hesitated before descending the stairs. He wasn't in the mood for the mage killer's company, even if it was watching from afar as the broad-shouldered man flirted with the innkeeper's daughter. So instead, he leaned against the wall and allowed himself to drift in thought as he waited.

Sooner than he expected, the door to Kamira's room opened and she stepped outside, her clothes fresh, her hair brushed, and her bag visibly lighter. He arched his eyebrow, because with the time it took Atissa to simply put her clothes in the morning and see to her beauty powders, he'd expected Kamira to take at least half of that time. Yet the arcanist was ready, and even though tiredness marked her face, she offered him a smile as they headed downstairs.

"I'll be back in a while," she said in passing.

Veelk gave her one of his grins in return, the ones Ryell had learned were meant to tease her. Sudden jealousy clutched his heart, because Kamira always responded to Veelk's quips with laughter or a witty remark, and in such moments the bond the two shared became apparent. This time she simply threw a small spark in Veelk's direction, like a teacher issuing a warning, and he caught it with his bare hand.

"Have fun!" the mage killer said before they left, and that earned him an amused shake of her head.

Ryell swallowed hard, trying to conceal his feelings. Kamira seemed amiable enough, no matter what Veelk claimed about her moods, so the distance between them was Ryell's fault. At the same time, the way she'd refused his arm in the inn and kept a step or two away as he led her through Kaighal's streets suggested that she was content with their relationship. He suspected she wouldn't welcome any attempts to fill the gap he'd created. Yet he had to try. It wasn't even the debt he owed her, because the further away she kept, the less likely she'd bother chasing him down for collection. He had to admit that Kamira fascinated him. She was different from the Devanshari noblewomen Ryell used to be surrounded with, with a sharp mind and even sharper tongue when he provoked it, and she also contradicted all the images of an evil demonologist he'd harbored.

"You were tired, you don't like me, and yet you agreed to help without asking for anything in return," he finally said. If he wanted to change something between them, he couldn't resort to conversations about the weather or how exotic Kaighal still felt to him. "Why?"

"I like the thought of proving your ideas of an arcanist wrong." Her lighthearted smile made it clear that it wasn't up for discussion.

"But you already did it, didn't you?"

To his surprise, she didn't deflect again, but became serious. "It's how I was taught. Arcanists always traveled and helped others, especially with anything demon-related. I like to think it's what sets up apart from the high mages, but..." She shrugged. "Like with everyone, there are some good high mages and some pretty nasty arcanists out there."

"You sound like you know one or two. Is that why you were away?" he guessed. "To help Veelk hunt down a demono... a rogue arcanist?"

She laughed. "Veelk's a mage killer, but he's not on a glorious quest to kill every wrongdoer out there. If he were" —her lips stretched into an evil grin—"don't you think he'd start with the High Towers?"

"But you did fight with one, didn't you?" he asked, remembering the stains on Veelk's clothing.

It didn't escape him that she hesitated before replying, "It was a man who threatened us."

The way she said it made Ryell think there was more to

the tale, and he couldn't imagine Kamira resorting to violence only because someone taunted her... But at the same time, whenever he recalled the unclear situation with Yoreus, he doubted whether he knew her well enough to be certain.

"And that's why he deserved to die?" he couldn't help asking.

She narrowed her eyes, and a grimace twisted her lips. With that look, he could almost believe she was an evildoer, and the way she wore her hair, pinned up, with small bones and feathers braided in, didn't help either. "Should I have seen him off and wished him better luck killing me next time?"

If Ryell could, he'd smack himself on the head. Of course it wasn't an insult or taunt thrown in passing, but something more serious. "I didn't know you had that kind of enemies."

"I don't," she replied. "It's just a sad tale of a jealous fellow student who thought he'd found a way to right all the wrongs done to him."

"Just like you?" Words escaped his lips faster than he could consider their effect.

Kamira slowed down, inspecting him, and he felt a sudden rush of blood to his cheeks. The question verged on a discourteous one, but she didn't express anger. "Whatever I'd say, I'd make myself defensive and prove you right. I guess the answer would depend on one's perspective," she said, but Ryell could swear she had another reason to avoid answering.

"And what's yours?"

They had already left the crowded streets behind as they entered the slums. Locals knew better than to stare at strangers, especially the odd duo of a Devanshari man and a

Tivarashan woman, and they moved out of the way, hiding in the shadows of half-crumpled townhouses, but Ryell still eyed them with wariness. The memory of the thugs beating him nearly to death was still vivid, and he wouldn't forgive himself if he got Kamira mixed up in his trouble.

She shook her head. "That's not a story to be told when we're about to reach a place full of Devanshari refugees. Speaking of which, how did you convince them to seek my help? I wouldn't think your people would trust an arcanist."

Ryell was sure Kamira's responses were meant to hide something she didn't want to share, but the way she skillfully changed the topic prevented him from more prodding. He'd heard that Tivarashan women were adept at word games and intrigue, and his companion seemed no different. Not only had she stopped his questions, she'd put him in the position where he was the one being asked about things he'd rather not share.

"They wouldn't." He looked away. "So I didn't tell them who you were, or that you'd be coming."

"I see." She looked him up and down. "I do hope to come out of there alive."

She didn't hide her distrust, and as much as he wanted her to believe he wasn't scheming against her, no matter his feelings toward demonologists, he couldn't blame her for it. He also couldn't reassure her that no harm would come from his people. Stricken with grief after losing their home and—often—family members, driven to the edge by the lack of essence, they could react in the way he couldn't predict, but he could hope to prevent.

"I asked you for help, so I won't allow them to do anything," he replied with all his confidence.

Kamira was polite enough to not express her doubts out loud, but looking at her face, Ryell could read all the concerns. He couldn't help wondering why, with all the possible danger, she simply didn't turn back and walk away, but as they rounded the corner and the asylum came into view, the time for asking questions was up.

⁓

"WHO RUNS THIS PLACE?" Kamira asked when they entered the building.

No detail seemed to escape her inquisitive eye, but as she looked at the paint peeling off the walls and the worn-down wooden floors, she expressed no disgust, only curiosity, putting Ryell at ease. He'd much rather walk her into the finest of Devanshari gardens than into a run-down building, and it reminded him of how much his people had lost. As always, his thoughts turned toward Cahala qi'Devanshari, his own enraged heart reminding him that so far he'd done nothing to make her pay, but this time Ryell reined in his anger. He needed to focus to ensure no harm would come to Kamira, and the queen could wait if it meant Kamira eased the pain of the suffering youngsters.

"Prince Allyv qi'Devanshari started it shortly after our people arrived in Tyorane," Ryell replied. "While the queen is trying to recreate Hajihali, our Light of the Land, her son is determined to find the cure, so we won't need a new one."

She gave a nod of respect to that, and returned to watch their surroundings, though he noticed how she avoided prolonged eye contact with any of the people around. They walked up the stairs, and Ryell caught the whispers that followed them. Concern and anger sounded in those exchanges, almost too quiet to be heard. At least the man he'd asked for directions earlier was too busy to pay attention to Ryell's companion, so he told them where to find the prince instead of raising alarms that a demonologist was trying to meet the Devanshari heir.

"But your artifact did more than just feed you with magic, didn't it?" Kamira asked.

"That's true." Ryell focused back on the conversation. If he acted casual enough, maybe they'd draw less attention. "It created a protective barrier along our borders, shielded us from disasters, and protected us from sicknesses. But it also bound us to our land and itself. Its loss revealed how vulnerable we were."

In those rare moments when Ryell allowed himself to consider the future and foolishly hope that one day all his people would return home, he shared Prince Allyv's dream. No more artifacts, no more crippling affliction... There were other ways to protect their land and its inhabitants, even if the Devanshari would never turn to demons. For a glimpse, he pictured inviting Atissa to travel with him to Juamha and maybe even become the first archmage of the rebuilt Devanshari kingdom. He hoped she'd like it.

In a small room, Prince Allyv stood by the window, talking to Hajha. Ryell had heard gossip of the old caretaker becoming the superintendent of the asylum, carrying out the prince's orders and seeing to everyone's needs and duties, while the prince himself focused on his research.

"Your highness." Ryell bowed when the prince gestured for them to approach. "I brought someone who could help."

To Ryell's surprise, Kamira bowed. Her body moved smoothly as if she had practiced court manners for years.

"It's an honor to meet you, your highness," she said with her head still bent. "I've heard of the work you've done here, and it's remarkable. The people of Devanshari are lucky to have a ruler who cares so deeply about them."

Ryell put all his effort into not gaping at her. Her

smooth, diplomatic remarks were exactly what court etiquette would require, and she'd still managed to say her lines without making them sound like blatant flattery.

"I do what I can for my people," Prince Allyv replied. "Are you a healer?"

"An arcanist, your highness." Kamira finally looked into the prince's eyes, but her expression was that of kindness, not challenge. "Kamira Altrainne, at your service."

The prince's body tensed, and so did Ryell's when he expected to be ordered out immediately, but if Prince Allyv was unhappy with Kamira's presence, he did not reveal his feelings, and Ryell had to admire his composure.

"Altrainne..." The prince rubbed his chin. "That's an influential name in Tivarashan, isn't it?"

"We do have a bit of land, but saying my family is influential is surely exaggeration." She offered a courteous smile like a noblewoman accepting a compliment. "I've heard that your people might be in need of my services, your highness. With your permission, I'd like to see them right away."

"I'd appreciate that. Come." Allyv led them both along the corridor. "I trust Ryell told you about our problem?"

"He did. I came as soon as I could."

A woman in the corridor let out a short scream muffled by her own hand, and she was looking at Kamira's arcanist pendant in horror. Others stepped out of the way or gestured toward the prince, ready to dash to his defense, and Ryell let out a sigh. Only the prince's presence stopped them from questioning Kamira's right to be there... or even worse, he realized.

They entered a room, leaving the crowd outside, but Tyddes stood by one of the beds, and as soon as his eyes fell on Kamira, a mask of fear and anger overtook his face. He moved, standing between his son and the woman he perceived as a threat.

"She's here to help." Ryell reached out to the merchant.

"Help? A demonologist?!" With disregard to the royalty present, Tyddes spat. "How dare you bring her here?! It was her kind that helped destroy our home, and you let her walk among the most vulnerable of our people?"

Behind him, Gann thrashed in the bed, and only then did Ryell see the binds tying all the patients. Things had gotten much worse since he'd last heard.

Kamira noticed them too. "How long have they been like this?"

"Why would you even care?!" Tyddes shouted, his whole body trembling. "Get out of here, gaharra! Get away from my son!"

"Calm yourself, Tyddes," Allyv demanded, his voice and posture suddenly more imposing. "She came here to help. If you do not wish her to look at Gann, so be it, but I won't allow you to insult my guest."

Tyddes clenched his teeth but bowed. "I apologize, your highness."

Ryell grimaced; the merchant did not look at Kamira or offer an apology to her, but to bring it up would mean antagonizing him even more, and Kamira herself didn't seem bothered by what had happened. She might have, Ryell realized, experienced such treatment far more often than she deserved.

"I'll need the room emptied of onlookers," she said. "What I'm about to do is not to be disrupted by emotions."

Prince Allyv looked at her for a long moment. "Very well. Though for the peace of mind of all involved, would you mind Ryell or me offering you assistance? I can assure you that neither of us will give in to unnecessary reactions."

"I think your highness should speak to those concerned and put their worries to rest, but I'd welcome Ryell's help."

The glance, smirk, and arched eyebrow she gave him made Ryell think she was silently questioning his ability to control his emotions. Yet her words seemed honest, and he couldn't help reciprocating with a smile.

Prince Allyv nodded, grabbed Tyddes by the arm in a not very royal gesture, and forced him out of the room. Unfriendly faces were gathered in the corridor with clearly directed disdain, and Ryell rushed to close the door.

"I apologize for my friend. It's his only child."

"I've seen and heard worse." Kamira walked over to the young man jerking violently in her bed. "High mages ensured arcanists are despised and distrusted."

"But after the role they had in causing the Cataclysm—"

Ryell went silent when she spun in place and looked at him. There was no anger, but Ryell didn't miss the subtle grinding of her teeth, and he had no doubt Kamira was about to lecture him on his beliefs, even though the Cataclysm was a fact known to all, even the people overseas. Yet she stared for a moment, and then turned away with a small shake of her head as if arguing was a waste of time.

"Let's get to work before someone outside decides to... 'give in to unnecessary reactions,' as your prince put it. I'll need your help."

"But I know nothing of demons." He didn't expect her to take the prince's offer literally.

She glanced over her shoulder, a smile softening her face. "I'd take you know how to kill one."

Ryell nodded, his hand reflexively resting on the hilt of the short sword at his belt. The picture of countless skirmishes during the siege of Devanshari resurfaced in an instant. "What do you intend to do?" he asked.

"I can sense demonlings trapped within their bodies," Kamira replied. "A good imbued stone contains only a part of a much stronger demon, but there's always demand for cheaper solutions, and some arcanists imbue stones with demonling power, basically trapping their immaterial being within. A demon trapped within an imbued stone is bound to our world even if it doesn't have a physical body here. Ingesting a stone simply changes one trap to another."

"Do you mean to say they're possessed?" Ryell went cold, and he fought to keep his hands from trembling.

She huffed. "There's not even a single documented case of possession. It's all child's tales." She waved her hand dismissively. "But with the imbued stone powdered, there's no spell binding it anymore, so the demon fights to get free. I'll try to pull them through to our world. You kill them."

"Try? Is there any risk?" The last thing he wanted was to tell Tyddes that Gann didn't make it.

She gave him a look of uncertainty. "I've never summoned a demonling in the flesh."

"I'd think all arcanists know how to do that."

"Know—yes, we all know," she replied. "But not many do so. A demonling has no mind of its own. Arcanists who summon them wish to use them to cause harm. Few deliver them to fight pits and other places that use them... well, to cause harm as well."

"Why not sent them back instead?" He had nothing against killing those vile creatures, but the thought of having them in the middle of the asylum didn't sit well with him.

Kamira sighed. "Because it's easier to summon them, and I don't want to risk making a mistake." She glanced at the boy, still moaning and fighting the binds. "And I never had to deal with a demonling's essence trapped within another body. I'd rather not risk the possibility I send the patients back as well."

He shuddered at the thought, but the way she spoke made Ryell think there was another reason behind it, one the arcanist wouldn't share. And with the voices outside becoming stronger than Prince Allyv's calm explanations, they didn't have much more time, so he gave up on pressing for more answers, and while Kamira drew arcane circles on the floor in front of each bed, he readied his sword.

Her chalk scratched against the wood, leaving fine white lines, and then she looked up at him.

"Ready?"

At his nod, Kamira closed her eyes and muttered words in another language. The line between her eyebrows creased, and dust gathered in the air within the circle. It thickened, drew closer, and before long, a creature stood on the floor: small, with a snakelike body, two short limbs, and the snout of a lizard. It stared at Ryell in surprise and then lunged forward, lashing out with its claws. Ryell struck instinctively, cleaving the creature in half.

Kamira opened her eyes and glanced at the body by her feet. Then she inspected the boy tied to the bed, now calm and breathing slowly. "Good. Next one." She walked to the next circle and, without delay, repeated the summoning.

Ryell waited for the creature to materialize and without hesitation struck at the limbless, fanged, cat-sized leech. "These things are disgusting." He cleaned his sword as they walked to the last circle.

"They're worms of the demon world. The pettiest and most powerless creatures, but they still contain some magic," she replied. "That's why unskilled arcanists trap them within the stones."

Ryell lifted his sword one more time, but paused when Kamira didn't begin the summoning. "Is something wrong?"

"I'm just tired. Unfocused." She rubbed her temple and gave him a forced smile. "Let's be done with it, so I can go and rest." With eyes closed, she chanted the spell.

The demonling appeared within the circle, and Ryell struck, but the creature leapt to the side. It bounced around on four limbs, and Ryell pushed Kamira out of his way, trying to keep the demonling away from the people in the room. The arcanist cursed when she stumbled backward and fell onto the nightstand, but, focused on his target, Ryell didn't pay attention.

Cornered, the creature hissed at its attacker and scratched the floor in anger. Its behavior offered Ryell no tells, and again he relied on his instincts to catch the leaping demonling in flight. The sword's level swing buried the blade deep in the vile body and the wall behind it.

"Are you hurt?" he asked when the creature stopped twitching and its dark blood tricked down the wall.

"Just a bruise or two," she reassured him.

The door swung open, and a Devanshari noble stormed into the room, followed by several other people.

"What's going on here?!" the man shouted. "Why was a demonologist let close to my daughter?"

Prince Allyv pushed his way through the crowd as their anger turned to fear at the sight of horrid bodies in pools of blood, but Ryell was wrong to expect Kamira to wait for the prince to calm them down. Instead, she faced the nobleman with confidence, her expression closely matching his rage.

"The demonologist pulled *that*"—she pointed at the demonling—"out of your daughter." She gave a challenging glare to all the gathered. "Have a good look, people, before you decide to take the powder of an imbued stone."

Whispers rose among the Devanshari, but the man didn't waver. "What sort of trickery is that?"

Kamira stared him down, blatantly ignoring the question, but Ryell's frustration peaked.

"The sort that saved your daughter's life, Lord qi'Aytrella," he blurted out as soon as he fished out the nobleman's name from his memory.

The crowd, still full of whispers and angry mutters, stepped to the sides, finally letting Prince Allyv through, and Kamira turned to him. "They'll need care and time to recover, your highness," she said wearily. "But what ailed them is gone now."

"You have my most sincere gratitude, Lady Kamira." The prince's head dipped, and Ryell hoped that it would sent the right message to any who might have harbored ill ideas.

"I'm glad I could be of service, your highness." She reciprocated the bow, though longer and deeper. "Unfortunately, duties elsewhere require my attention, and I beg your forgiveness, your highness, but I'll have to leave sooner than would be considered courteous."

"I understand," Prince Allyv replied, gratitude in his eyes clear, and Ryell had no doubt that Kamira had saved him from an invitation that would stir the uneasy mood in the asylum even more. "Allow me to send my royal guard to accompany you back. It's the least I can do."

The corner of Kamira's lip curled, as if she knew the prince wanted to ensure her safe departure from the asylum, not a safe arrival to where she was heading.

Ryell retrieved his sword, and several people jerked when the demonling's body fell to the floor. "I'd be honored to do so, your highness." He cleaned the blade and sheathed it.

As he stepped forward, the crowd parted, allowing them

both to pass, but many glares and grimaces bore people's unspoken emotions, and Ryell clenched his fists. Those foolish people couldn't appreciate help given willingly and for free, because they were blinded by their hate. It didn't help that not long ago, he was one of them.

Kamira walked slowly. Ryell caught stiffness in her gait, and even though she must be doing her best to keep her expression neutral, he could see the strain in it. Yet, when she caught him staring, she offered a smile.

"I'd appreciate it if you discreetly helped me down the stairs," she muttered when they got out of earshot. "I'd like to keep up appearances."

Ryell offered his arm, and she accepted in the courtly manner. He held her tight as they descended, enjoying her closeness and the subtle magic around her. They left the asylum undisturbed, and he refused to let go until she did, but she didn't move away.

"So, care to tell me what a Tivarashan noblewoman is doing wandering as an arcanist in foreign lands?" he asked to break the silence.

"Earns her living or gets in trouble," she replied, tiredness and amusement in her voice. "Most of the time both."

Ryell laughed. "It seems a polite way of telling me to be quiet."

He might have meant it as a friendly tease, but Kamira nodded. "I'd appreciate it," she said almost pleading. "I'm about to collapse and don't feel like dwelling on my family history, which is not, by any stretch, even half as interesting as my arcanist life."

"Maybe some other time, then?" Ryell held on to that feeling of familiarity and cordiality, desperate to make it last past that single event, and as they took a turn, leaving the asylum behind, he let go of her and wrapped his arm around her waist instead, pulling her even closer.

With her eyes half-closed, she took the offered support, her black hair teasing the skin on his neck as she rested her head on his shoulder, and he smelled the faint scent of dust and herbs he didn't recognize.

"Maybe," she muttered.

15

Yoreus could hardly contain his frustration as he watched his three students work, and once again he cursed the High Towers' rules that expected every archmage to tutor the most promising among the future mages. The two young women and a teenage boy seemed focused on trying to impress him by any means available... except for excelling in magic. Of course, Yoreus couldn't expect much from students who'd so far only attended lectures in overcrowded groups and most likely did little outside of given assignments, but he hoped at least one of them would reveal a spark of brilliance.

The teenage boy shot a nervous glance at his fellow student, a long-haired woman with a deep copper tan who behaved as if she desired to become an arch-seductress, not an archmage. Yoreus caught a grimace on the boy's face, a hint of jealousy, and that emotion broke the young man's focus. His so far perfectly executed spell degraded into slurring.

Yoreus rolled his eyes while his third student threw innocent glances at him, each followed by batting eyelashes.

The archmage gritted his teeth, because the woman couldn't be any more obvious, and subtlety was a trait that could get any mage far... whether in the manipulation of magic or of people.

A knock on the door drew everybody's attention, and silence fell in the small classroom as Ryell walked in, only to stop when his eyes found the three students.

"The lesson's over for today," Yoreus announced, ending the torturous tutoring before Ryell, in his courtesy, could offer to come another time. "Tomorrow I expect you to recite all the spells without a single stutter," he added as he gestured Ryell to come closer.

It turned out a pleasant surprise that the Devanshari approached casually but with a confidence the archmage didn't expect from a man in his position.

"My daughter came crying and complaining about you," Yoreus said as soon as the door closed behind his students. They knew better than to eavesdrop on the archmage, and he couldn't help his curiosity about Ryell's response.

"I'd expect as much. I didn't even send a message that I was busy," Ryell replied.

Yoreus arched his eyebrows. No apology, no explanation, and no attempts by Ryell to paint himself in a better light—not how things usually went when Atissa's lovers confronted her father. It seemed that Ryell might have been less prone to her manipulation that Yoreus had expected, or perhaps Atissa was foolish and overconfident... as always. "Drinking in a tavern, or so I've heard," he said, though it did reveal that he had checked on Ryell's whereabouts.

"I can't deny that." Ryell remained relaxed, as if no words could throw him off balance. "Though it was more of a pastime than anything else."

"Was it now? Trying to outlast my daughter's rage?"

Ryell smiled as if Yoreus had told a joke. "After three days without an apology, she's probably angrier now. I take it she's refused to even see me? There was no one upstairs."

At least he cared for her enough to visit... Yoreus offered a smile, hiding his satisfaction. Ryell might not have been of much use so far, but the archmage rarely got rid of tools that could be useful in the future, and Atissa needed to practice manipulation, for which the Devanshari, addicted to magic, was perfect.

"I sent her away," Yoreus replied, gesturing for Ryell to sit down. The benches in the teaching room weren't comfortable, and he'd prefer to have such a discussion in his own chambers, but he didn't want to risk losing control over the conversation while they walked through the busy corridors of the Towers. "She's at a small temple to the north, doing the chores of an apprentice priestess."

Ryell stared at him, and for the first time, his confidence wavered. "That's something I didn't expect."

Yoreus allowed himself a rather theatrical sigh. "Atissa is spoiled, and although it's not easy to admit, I had a hand in it." He did his best to play a regretful father. Of course Atissa was spoiled, and rightly so, being the daughter of an archmage, the one child he'd taught and acknowledged as his own, and her punishment had nothing to do with that, but Ryell didn't have to know. "I wanted the best of everything for her, but I couldn't give her the wisdom that comes with age, and her pride had grown too much. I thought it was time to remind her that high mages gain their power through hard work and meticulous studying." He wasn't even lying, because some of them indeed worked hard and achieved mediocre success, but the ones who wanted true power knew how to balance the studies with other opportunities the High Towers offered.

"Not every father would be ready to do so for his daughter. Most wouldn't speak of their problems so readily, let alone try to mend what's broken."

Yoreus shook his head. "I wasn't quick enough if Atissa became so petty that she'd refuse a small request from a man she... has a passion for." He chose his words with caution, hoping the anger within them would give the right impression. His daughter was foolish enough to refuse Ryell when Yoreus expected her to accommodate him. "If you still need assistance, I'll be happy to provide it. Am I right that there was some affliction your people suffered from?"

Ryell nodded. "I appreciate the offer, but it's been dealt with already."

"Oh?" Any other time, Yoreus would consider the topic resolved, but for the first time since entering, Ryell looked uneasy, and it sparked the archmage's curiosity. The servants claimed Ryell hadn't been in the High Towers for three days, and Yoreus's spy insisted the Devanshari spent that time drinking, so he couldn't have approached any other mage for help.

"I was quite desperate," Ryell replied to the unvoiced question, "and I asked the arcanist for help."

The arcanist, not the demonologist... The word choice didn't escape Yoreus. "You mean Kamira?" He expressed his surprise, while he was already adjusting his plans. Atissa's foolish refusal could bring some unexpected benefits. For days he'd thought about a way to get information out of that stubborn arcanist and tried to find someone who'd be able to gain her trust. Ryell wasn't perfect, but she'd helped him, and he'd changed his view on demonologists enough to address her differently. That was more than Yoreus could hope for from himself or any of his usual spies and henchmen.

"Yes." Ryell paused. "This makes me think that I might have misjudged her during our first meeting, doing both of you a disservice."

Yoreus nodded, pretending to consider his words, while he tried to figure out the game. He wouldn't put it past Kamira to use Ryell to deliver the message or even manipulate Ryell so he could change his mind. That Tivarashan gaharra might have expressed her loathing for the High Towers, but her own lineage was hardly better, full of manipulative and power-thirsty women.

"I remember her as a good and dedicated student, one who could've achieved a lot," he said as a new plan formed in his head.

"But she got expelled, didn't she?"

Yoreus almost smiled, because Ryell's tone suggested he didn't know what had happened, and that served the archmage well. There was no need to enlighten Ryell on how many teachers abused their position to get what they desired. "Indeed. For insulting one of the archmages. She had a tendency to be quite... undiplomatic with her comments. If you ask me, I'd say the old hoyve got a bit of honesty he rightly deserved." He faked a laugh, and then became serious again as he added, "But the rules are strict, and she had to leave. I think she's bitter about it."

"Then what happened at the tavern?" Ryell asked. "She seemed so set on challenging you."

Yoreus shrugged. "I don't know. There was some deception there, but as for her motives... I'm not sure if she really wished me dead. She might have been simply trying to prove her worth. Or maybe she reached her limits as an arcanist and devised this plan hoping I would defeat her and indeed take her as a student?" He hoped his words came across as honest, though deep in his heart Yoreus couldn't help believing that Kamira did plan to kill him. When he'd sent her to the old arcanist Towers, he considered the risk, but Gayabal's journal was worth it, and Veranesh was supposed to have been sealed off. "I wish she'd resume her studies, and I'm sure I could convince the first archmage she's been remorseful over her behavior, but all of our conversations end up the same way." He forced out a sigh of disappointment.

"She seems quite stubborn," Ryell remarked politely, but a stray note in his voice told Yoreus that the Devanshari had experienced this trait firsthand.

"That's putting it lightly." A little exaggeration could help. "She won't listen to any high mage anymore. But I've just had a thought..." Yoreus leaned closer as if an idea had struck him. "I know that your first meeting wasn't friendly, but she did help your people. Maybe you could influence her? Her talent goes to waste as she is now."

Ryell looked at him with surprise and, Yoreus could swear, taken aback. "I don't think I'm the right person. Royal guards are not trained in the arts of manipulation and deception."

"No, nothing like that!" The archmage might have pushed too hard, and his tool was slipping away from him. "I hope that if she warms up to you, she might listen and see reason. I think she could achieve so much here, but whenever I try to speak about it, she only sees evil intent. And that mage killer thug... He might be filling her head with hate." As he watched Ryell's expression, Yoreus knew the last remark had hit the right spot, so he shook his head as if giving up on the idea. "But I don't want to press you. It was just a thought."

Ryell paced. "I don't mind talking to her, if I get a chance. After all, it's for her own good." The way he was trying to convince himself made Yoreus swell with satisfaction. "But I don't think she'd trust me. She's not a fool, and knows of our acquaintance."

"Maybe if..." Yoreus pretended to consider. "No," he murmured as if discarding it. "I couldn't ask that much." He shook his head and brightened up as he looked at Ryell, pretending to give up on the topic. "I'm sorry for what happened between Atissa and you. I'm sure she would take her words back if she could. Her exile will last for a couple more weeks, but I see no reason why you wouldn't be welcome here in the meantime, and later."

"I'd... I'd like to speak to her and apologize. I've said words I'd like to take back too," Ryell said. "Please, feel free to send word when she's back, if she's willing to meet with me."

"I most definitely will." Yoreus headed for the door, the smile of a satisfied man on his face. "Now that's all been discussed, maybe you'd like to join me in my chambers? I have some fine wine, and I'd be glad to hear more of your people. You're part of Kaighal now, so us archmages should take proper interest in your problems, fears, and hopes."

"I'd be happy to oblige, but..." Ryell hesitated. "You had some idea, didn't you? About Kamira?"

"I thought that if the rumors of your argument with Atissa spread, it would appear you had fallen out of my favor," Yoreus said in a dismissive manner. "But as much as I'd love to help Kamira, I can't ask you to be deceitful."

Ryell's face showed his inner struggle, and Yoreus waited patiently. The ones like Ryell, honest and full of honor, were the easiest to manipulate, because they rarely noticed deception. Yoreus could see how the idea of lying repelled Ryell, but at the same time, he wanted to help Kamira, and maybe even repay Yoreus for the hospitality. As Ryell wasn't looking at him, too deep in his own thoughts, the archmage took a deep breath, enjoying the moment. Playing others, manipulating them into acts and words that weren't their own, always proved satisfying. Nothing else, not even using magic, gave him a greater sense of power.

"Atissa and I *did* have an argument," Ryell muttered. "And it'd be a shame not to at least try to help your noble intent to get Kamira back onto the path of good."

Yoreus hid a smile. "Don't bother yourself too much with it. I'd hate to see you uneasy about speaking to her. And, of course, in gratitude for your help, let me cover all your expenses. I'll make sure the coin gets to you in a discreet way." Gold was expendable and easy to replace, and finding a useful tool remained worth every coin. "Now, let's go and drink to a hopeful future."

Yoreus led his companion through the corridors, but his mind hardly bothered with the small talk that circled some trivial Devanshari matters. Atissa's disobedience had borne an unexpected benefit, and even though his daughter deserved punishment for not fulfilling his wishes, things were turning in the right direction. Yoreus had no doubt that Kamira was the key to understanding recent events, and whoever got the information from her would have the upper hand in any future dealings with Uganel and other demons. More so, if Yoreus was wrong about her malicious intentions, and Kamira willingly accepted him as her teacher, sharing her knowledge and maybe insights into demonic matters, he'd be perceived as more capable of solving problems, and even more influential that the current leader of the High Towers. It could provide a chance to remove Irtan and replace him with someone more suitable.

First Archmage Yoreus.

A thought he enjoyed and allowed to linger.

～

KAMIRA GROANED as she tried to get up, and dug her elbows deep into the pillow in a vain attempt to lift herself from the bed. The muscle pain from the days of arduous marching was enough to keep her in it, but by helping Ryell, she'd added mental strain. Channeling magic wasn't necessarily too strenuous on its own, but the focus it required at the brink of exhaustion took its toll as well. Yet not even for a moment did she regret helping the Devanshari, even if she had no illusion that any of them would change their minds about demonologists. She could only hope that the prince would call for her again if more of his people suffered.

"If it's so bad you slept past noon, you should stay in bed." Veelk glanced at her from the table. "And don't tell me you're fine."

"I'm not, but we need to go." She tried once more, and her body dutifully rebelled, but the more time they spent in Kaighal, the greater the chance Uganel would catch up to them. He'd lured Hafnis already, and she had no doubt a demon like him would find more followers, be it a power-hungry arcanist without morals or equally immoral thugs with a thirst for gold.

"And we will... when you can go, not crawl."

Kamira dropped back onto the pillows. "I could still kill you now, lying here." She couldn't help trying to fight her own tiredness, but couldn't deny one more day in bed might be a necessity.

"You meant to say you could have Veranesh try to kill me." Veelk grinned as he brought her wine. "Here, it'll help you rest. We can spare a day or two before we set out."

She pushed his hand away, her frustration fighting for the reins with reason. "If we get attacked here, we can't destroy Uganel." Not to mention the unwanted attention of the mages and Gildya's adepts that she'd prefer to avoid. The longer she stayed in the shadows, the more she could learn, and her chances for success grew.

"If you pass out on the way, we can't kill him either." Veelk held the mug to her lips, and Kamira gave up and drank.

"Just one more day," she muttered. It eased her concerns that, in a densely populated city, the demon wouldn't come for them himself, likely too afraid to be exposed in a fight, and both she and Veelk could deal with some more hired thugs.

Knocking made them look at the door, and Kamira couldn't help wondering if her thoughts had lured the first assailants. She discarded such a thought as childish, but nevertheless made an attempt to get up. Veelk helped her sit against the headrest, and she placed her hands on the bed cover, ready to summon the nightflies or channel magic as necessary, while Veelk moved silently to the wall.

"Come in," she said.

The door creaked open, and Ryell stepped in, hesitant, but then he smiled at her. "I hope I'm not disturbing. Veelk's not in?"

Kamira could swear his question was hopeful, as if he didn't wish her friend to be around, and she gestured to his side with her chin.

"You expect trouble?" He eyed them both as he stepped into the room.

Veelk looked at him as if surprised, then grinned. "You don't? I've heard you were the one who pushed Kamira to exhaust herself, so you should be the one to convince her to rest."

Kamira bit her tongue before reminding Veelk that the

pace he'd set for their journey back to Kaighal had played its part in her sorry state as well. Without being certain how much of what Ryell heard would be shared with Yoreus, she preferred not to give the archmage any clues. It was better if Ryell believed she was simply not used to Veelk's traveling speed and didn't dwell on it.

"I hope you're not here because something happened?" she asked. The thought of dragging herself out of the bed and to the Devanshari asylum caused almost physical pain, and as much as she wanted to offer help when it was needed, she preferred to keep away from a place full of people who hated arcanists. At least until she was rested enough to stand her ground if needed.

"I came to see how you were feeling," Ryell replied, glancing at Veelk.

"As if a demon chewed on me and spat me out," she replied.

His hesitation didn't escape her. Whatever he wanted, he wasn't comfortable saying it around Veelk, and that spiked her curiosity. With all his talk of honor, she didn't expect Ryell to turn into an assassin while he was still indebted to her, but maybe the archmage was using him in some other way.

She gave Veelk a blunt stare. "Weren't you heading out?"

He gave her a wary look, so she brushed her hands against the nightflies coiled on her forearms. If it came to assault, she had magic and Veranesh for her defense, and Ryell would regret his deception.

At that, the mage killer put away his keshal. "I was. I'll be downstairs, talking to Lefna. And you better stay in bed."

She chuckled as he closed the door behind him, leaving her alone with Ryell, who visibly relaxed. She couldn't be sure, but he might consider Veelk a threat only because he saw a crude barbarian—an image far from the truth, but it served her better to maintain such a misconception.

She shifted on the pillow, but Ryell approached her and sat on the bed before she managed to get up.

"You shouldn't." The intense gaze of his hazel eyes locked on her, and she couldn't help noticing his expression wasn't that of constrained hate.

"We have things to do that can't wait."

Ryell stretched for the mug on the table and offered it to her. "Veelk seems to think otherwise."

"Veelk always thinks otherwise." She swirled the wine, but didn't drink it.

He laughed, not taking his eyes off her, and Kamira resisted the urge to pull the covers tighter. Her shirt, undone for the night, revealed more than she wanted to show, at least to a stranger. Veelk had seen enough when tending to her various wounds, so she'd gotten comfortable around him, but Ryell wasn't even a friend.

"So, why are you really here?" she said, cutting to the chase.

To her surprise, he looked away before replying, and his moves became stiff. "To apologize," he said before meeting her eyes again. "My misjudgment caused you a lot of trouble, but you saved my life and helped my people anyway. And don't say it was just arcanist duty."

Silence was a better option, because his words stung, even if that wasn't his intention. The way he leaned forward, his eyes shining with what she considered genuine affection, made her want to admit that he wasn't wrong back in the tavern. But her cautious nature held her emotions at bay before she revealed anything.

Ryell's feelings might be honest, but his sudden confession and apology were not. He had already thanked for the help in the asylum, and even when she'd saved his life, he was far from apologizing for interfering in the tavern. With all the earlier remarks, it seemed odd he'd changed his mind about arcanists so suddenly. Unless...

An understanding struck her. Unless he hadn't. She couldn't tell how close his ties with Yoreus were, but she couldn't discard the possibility that Ryell was doing the archmage's bidding, and it mattered little whether he did it willingly or was a victim of deception.

She almost smiled. Two could play that game, and having grown up in Tivarashan, where intrigues and political manipulation were acceptable means of social advancement, had made her confident that she'd at least be able to keep her footing. If Ryell wanted to deceive her, she'd have no regrets repaying him with the same.

"I have to confess, I envy Veelk," Ryell said. "Even when you two argue, you seem to remain... close."

"He's a friend." Kamira thought of the mage killer downstairs, flirting with Lefna. "Making friends takes time."

"And trust." A bitter smile twisted Ryell's lips. "And you don't trust me."

The disappointment in his voice sounded genuine, but she didn't know him enough to tell for certain. "You smell of high magic," she replied, unable to resist baiting him. The way he reacted, and whether he denied his connection to Yoreus or not, could make his intentions clear.

He didn't avoid her eyes, and she took it as a good sign. "I'm of Devanshari. Our bodies crave magic and absorb it." He leaned forward. "But if I spend enough time around you, I could smell of your magic."

Kamira shifted on the bed under the intensity of Ryell's stare. It had hunger within, and her instincts pushed to respond, since she understood the nature of his addiction. The memory of those moments after Veranesh severed her old pact was enough to bring out her compassion, and she also could understand how Yoreus could keep Ryell under his thumb. If she shared her magic with him, he'd be free from the archmage's influence, and maybe he'd even reveal what he knew of Yoreus's plans.

"I might be able to help you." It would have to wait till she was rested and would require finding the best way to sate his hunger, but at least she could offer it.

He brightened. "I'm glad."

Before she could ask about the nature of his addiction and the ways to remedy it, he leaned forward even more, his face in front of hers. He pressed his lips against hers with the intensity of a famished man, but he also seemed ready to back away at any sign of discomfort. To her surprise, she experienced no drain of magic. Instead, the subtle magical aura that always surrounded arcanists soaked into him like water into desert sand.

Surprised by the kiss, she didn't push him away, and as Ryell's scent filled her nostrils, she parted her lips, letting his tongue slip in. He tasted of sweet wine, and she allowed herself to forget that he was trying to play her. It'd been a long time since she'd had a lover, and her body responded with eagerness to his caress.

"I didn't mean this way," she said when they stopped.

"I did," he replied with disarming sincerity. No matter what his other motives were, his interest in her wasn't a lie. "But it doesn't mean you have to share all your secrets," he added.

When she didn't reply, Ryell ran his fingers along her chin, a gentle but enticing touch, and lower onto her neck. She closed her eyes, enjoying his fingertips on her skin, but when his hand slipped down to her cleavage, she held his wrist.

"Making friends takes time." It was one thing to find a little pleasure in the game of deception, and another to get tangled in a net of lies with a lover who could use her feelings or attachment against her.

If Ryell was disappointed, he didn't show it. He offered her a playful smile. "I heard you're not going anywhere today, so you should have enough of it to at least start, don't you think?"

An arched eyebrow was her only response, and he took it as invitation. She didn't stop him when he went for another kiss. As long as she didn't let things go too far, there was no reason she couldn't enjoy the game a little more, and with his lips on hers, she wouldn't have to dodge uncomfortable questions.

16

After an arduous two-week march through the desert, Kamira could hardly drag her feet. Veelk set an unforgiving pace again, committing every night and most days to traveling with only a few hours of rest when the sun was highest. Kamira didn't argue. The farther they got away from civilization, the less likely the destruction would reach it, so she endured the trek, even though every breath she took burnt as if the air itself was fire. At the same time, with every dune they scaled, she questioned why that dune didn't suit their needs, and each time Veelk replied with a mention of particular ruins that were ideal for an ambush, so they kept going. There was no denying that solid ground would be better to ensure their plan succeeded, and regardless of the heat, she shivered at the thought of what they intended to do. Going against a higher demon was an insane idea already, and she needed to destroy him too. Veelk, no matter what support he could offer, was no arcanist, so the final spell depended on her, and so did the protection from its aftereffects. Every now and then, she considered the plan was leading them to their deaths, not only because they were sure Uganel and his henchmen had plenty of opportunities to learn when she and Veelk were headed—be it through spying or other means—but also because, for all she knew, Veranesh had lied to her about how the spell worked.

She discarded that last thought. Sure, the demon likely kept things to himself, and she couldn't ignore that leading her to death in a clash with another demon might have been his plan all along, but she remembered the pain and the magic flow of the spell he'd put on her back in the ruined Towers. The more she considered it, the more she believed Veranesh was convinced this was his way out, and he had the means to enact it. He wouldn't have pitted her against Uganel to break free from his prison, and it brought some comfort. At least she was against one demon, not two.

"We're here." Veelk's voice brought her back to reality.

As they circled a dune, the ruins emerged from the side. The crushed remains of city walls stuck out from the sand like the broken teeth of an elderly man. Their rusted color brought a picture of bloodstains to Kamira's mind, and she couldn't help thinking of all the people who'd perished with the city centuries before. The desert might have initially swallowed the lands, but winds worked their way through the dunes, uncovering what was once lost and then concealing it again in endless cycles.

Kamira's trained eyes searched for cave-ins and intact buildings while she allowed herself to wonder about the old artifacts they could find, but Veelk unstrapping his keshal reminded her that they hadn't come to explore. Regret settled in her heart when she realized that, if their plan succeeded, the city would be lost forever. She couldn't blame Veelk for bringing them here, because the ruined streets would provide solid ground for her to draw the circle on, one that would endure more than any markings on magically hardened sand.

"We made good time," he said. "It should allow us to rest and prepare."

She nodded, as so far, they'd seen no one following them, and she couldn't help questioning whether the news of their departure had even reached Uganel. He must have enough spies to keep track of her in the city, so his absence concerned her, even if it meant they'd have plenty of time to set everything up. She picked up her pace, refreshed by the mere promise of solid stone under her feet and a sliver of shadow by the crumbled stones.

Built on a plateau, the ruined city overlooked the area, and the last stretch of their journey led up the sandy incline that leaned against what must have once been fortified walls. The jagged line of collapsed rocks told of the its once powerful defense, and Kamira's thoughts once more wandered into the past. Questions of the city's people and their culture, their history and magic, filled her mind while her feet sank into the sand. Some of the knowledge and records had survived in Kaighal, and her homeland kept chronicles as well, but those texts lacked all the details their authors deemed unnecessary, letting her imagination roam. She pictured the guards on the battlements looking to the southeast and squinting to recognize what they saw on the horizon: a flash of light and a dark wind that followed. That was how the books of old described the day when the high mages fought Veranesh and half of the continent became a barren land.

Kamira grimaced at all the teachings hammered into her head. Stories of the arcanists' fall, of the powerful demon's rage, and of the courage and sacrifice of the first high mages who'd supposedly risked their own lives bringing down the monster. Part of her still believed these tales, ingrained in her mind for so many years, and even though she knew the truth was far from them, she couldn't help questioning her own allegiance and motives. Others might have confirmed what Veranesh had told her, but with her limited knowledge she could have been asking the wrong questions, and if the demon had kept any knowledge from her, even the smallest detail, it could pivot the truth once more.

She chased away those thoughts. It wasn't the time to hesitate, and no matter how much she wanted to doubt Veranesh, according to Suzhaul's words, he'd keep his promise. Once all was done, she'd be free and alive, and the continent wouldn't crumble under the demon's spell.

She allowed herself a grim smile. Unless, of course, she died much sooner, at Uganel's hand or in the outburst of magic that was supposed to follow his destruction.

Doubts distracted her, but she still caught a glimpse of a shadow on the battlements, a moving shadow. It might be an old rag pulled by the wind or a desert creature skittering through the rocks, and she focused too late to catch more of it. She looked at Veelk, but he was already charging.

"Get to solid ground!" he yelled on his way up.

His voice faded amongst the growing din of demonlings' shrieks, burying her hopes that those were some bandits or rogues from desert tribes. The creatures poured out from around the crumbled walls, leaping into the sand.

She wasn't going to make it. The swarm descended upon her as her feet sank into the sand, but putting up a barrier meant she'd trap herself, and without a circle, it might not endure such an onslaught.

At her summoning, magic took the shape of gales that swept up and carried the sand toward the oncoming swarm, concealing her for a few precious moments, and she scrambled to the side, along the dune. Veelk had already reached the breach in the battlements, and his keshal saw limbs rent, blood reaped, and bodies tumbling through the sands. Heads rolled as the dead fell, but the creatures kept coming, and if she tried to stay around him, without the protection of her circle she'd only be a hindrance.

The veil of windswept sand was settling, but the creatures were confused enough to go after Veelk instead. Taking advantage of their shifted focus, she crawled desperately upward. The sand swallowed her hands as it did her feet. She needed something to hold on to, but the dune sifted through her fingers like golden grains in an hourglass. Even the desert was telling her that time was running out.

An idea arose from a glimpse at the nightflies. With no other options, Kamira woke them up, quickly seizing control of both. She grabbed their long bodies with both hands as they left her wrists, and ran across the sands, relieved with the sudden lightness of her step as the crystal creatures lifted her.

She reached the ruined fortifications just before a stray group of demonlings caught up with her.

Unleashing another gust of wind halted the monsters' advance in a blast of sand, and Kamira let Veranesh take control of the nightflies.

"I hope you know how to draw a protective circle," she said, breathing heavily. "I'll need one."

She pointed at the opening amongst the ruins, and one of the crystal fliers took off without a word while she channeled magic, shaping it into fire. The demonlings down the slope died in the flames, and no more were coming, all focused on the whirlwind of death that had Veelk at its center.

A shadow moved to her side, and she ducked

instinctively, narrowly avoiding the bite of a saber. Its wide blade rang against the stone, while the man wielding it resorted to a dagger and lunged forward, forcing Kamira to reel and back-pedal. She threw magic at him, but he dodged and continued his attack. Her second nightfly darted toward the assailant's veiled face, and he lost his footing, lifting his arms to defend himself.

With a heartbeat-long focus, she forced magic into the shape of an icy thorn, and threw it at him while he was distracted. She didn't wait for the outcome. As soon as she got back on her feet, she ran. Taking sharp turns around the corner to lose her pursuer, she thought frantically. There had to be at least two of them, because the one who'd attacked her was not the one controlling the demonlings. She needed to find the arcanist before he summoned more of these wretched things.

The rock maze muffled the sounds of battle, but the echo still carried the shrieks and howls of demonlings, and their cries reassured her that Veelk still stood his ground.

Around another corner, a tall, dark figure rose in front of her, and the strong backhand sent her flying. She cushioned herself from the fall, but a quiet crunch in her left arm, accompanied by a piercing, sharp pain, rendered her limb useless. Moaning, Kamira lifted herself.

"That's much better, pactee." Uganel approached. "If you stay on your knees, you might live through this. I knew you would try to return to his prison, but I didn't expect you'd walk straight into my trap."

Two more steps and the demon was by her side, so Kamira braced herself for the next assault. If he kept hitting that hard, his lies about her survival would lose any credibility, and without a circle to protect her, she couldn't dream of having enough time to bind him. Uganel lifted her by the throat and drew a deep gash through her calf with his claw, while his other fist's razor-like talons closed around her neck.

Kamira pressed her lips together, but a shriek gurgled in her throat, fighting to get out. When the demon slung her to the ground, her body crushing her already broken arm, her vision blurred and another wave of pain made her fight for consciousness.

"You're nothing without Suzhaul's lap dog." Uganel spat. "Crawling in the dirt and bleeding. Worthless."

Kamira coughed, grateful her throat had survived the demon's grip. As long as he talked, he wasn't about to kill her, so she needed to play for time. In the corner of her eye, she spotted her nightfly not far away, hovering over the ruined street's cobblestones. Flashes of magic suggested Veranesh was making a circle for her, so she needed to keep Uganel's focus.

"That must be very frustrating." She hardly recognized her own voice, rough and raspy. "To see me like this and to know that if I die, Veranesh will be freed."

The demon stopped, but smiled. "It's not the time for lies, it's the time for begging, pactee."

She rested on her good arm and looked up. "Then beg."

Like Veranesh had said, Uganel could hardly contain his rage. He darted forward and sent Kamira rolling across the ground with a rib-cracking kick, adding to the pain of her broken arm and smearing sand into the wound on her calf. "You still don't know your place, do you?"

She lifted her head with all the weariness one would expect from a bleeding, broken adversary, taking the time when Uganel couldn't see her eyes to check the circle's progress. The nightfly was gone, so she hoped Veranesh had finished his work, but getting there would require time she didn't have with the demon looming above her. "I serve my purpose, demon." Better if she didn't remind him she knew his name. As long as he believed he was in control, she could try to outsmart him. "I just refuse to die."

Her time and options were running out. Veranesh must have decided to keep away, and she couldn't blame him. Crystal nightflies would not survive Uganel's grip.

A blurry figure smashed into Uganel and threw the demon off his feet. Wide-eyed, Kamira watched Veelk leap back, readying his keshal.

"Your henchmen are dead, demon," he said. "So is your arcanist and most of the critters she summoned. Will you run again?"

Uganel bared his teeth, and his tail swung in anticipation. "No. First I'll kill you, and then I'll take my time with the pactee. She'll keep screaming long after your blood dries in the sun."

They attacked at the same moment, neither waiting for their opponent's move. Veelk sidestepped with a wide swipe of his keshal. Its arc barred the demon from his frontal assault, but Uganel was quick to adapt, launching himself into the air. Even without wings, his leaps gave him the advantage of height. The aerial attack forced Veelk to roll and recover to a defensive stance, and the demon pressed his offense. Parrying, feinting, and timely evasion left Veelk unscathed until Uganel's constant flurry finally drew first blood.

Kamira refused to let her eyes off the fighting, but she crawled away nevertheless. Getting inside the circle was the only way she could save Veelk... save them both.

Veelk recovered and squatted down, thrusting the thin blade at the demon's side. The attack missed as Uganel leapt over him. Veelk rolled from the demon lunging from behind, and Kamira screamed her desperation as Uganel's claws caught Veelk across the chest as he came to his feet, but it was a traded assault. The keshal snapped through the demon's arm, striking bone, but Uganel advanced unfazed. The demon suffered the bite of Veelk's weapon only to strike his arm. Veelk's bones broke with a loud crack, and his keshal spun away through the air, but the mage killer's off hand darted forward, and a lizard-shaped dagger found Uganel's eye.

The demon roared and pulled away. Veelk dove, rolled, and snatched up his keshal with his good arm as Kamira finally dragged herself completely within the circle.

Uganel yanked the dagger from his skull, and dark blood shot across the sand. With his other eye already gone, she hoped for a moment of respite, but the demon lunged at Veelk, swiping in a mad rage. Despite Veelk's attempts at defense, Uganel's claws slung his blood repeatedly over the ruins. His death was a matter of time under the demon's relentless attack.

Kamira took a deep breath, and as soon she'd poured on the magic that activated the circle, she began the incantation, her blood already cold with the fear of being too late.

Uganel roared when the binding pulled him away from his target, but he let the energy carry him, using the momentum to strike at her. The circle, burnt into the stone and fed with steady magic, held even when her voice wavered, and before the demon could breach her protection, he was trapped.

"So you've been taught the binding," Uganel said in an ice-cold voice. "And what are you going to do now? Let me watch you bleed to death? The moment you pass out, I'll be free again. You can't win this, pactee."

Kamira hissed when shifting her weight caused more pain than relief. Behind the demon, Veelk leaned on his keshal to stay on his feet, and she realized the possible truth behind the demon's words.

"I think I can finish the other two parts of the spell before that. So I'll take you with me." She tore some ripped cloth off her trousers and wrapped it around the wound. It had to do until she had time for a proper dressing.

The demon's expression changed and the eyebrows over his eye sockets arched. Even though he was blind, Kamira could swear he was looking at her. Maybe he sensed the magic within her, or maybe demons had a better sense of smell than humans. "He taught you all of it, didn't he?" There was no surprise in his voice. "So you are nothing but his puppet, and you'll die serving." A mean smile twisted his face. "If you end me, you won't survive."

Instinctively, she wanted to proceed to the reaping part of the spell, but Veelk needed time to get to her circle, which meant she had to put up with the demon's insults and threats. At the same time, she could use it to learn more and maybe get Uganel to spill a useful tidbit or two. The nightfly hovered nearby, its idleness suggesting that Veranesh was leaving it up to her.

"I want to live as much as you do," she said. "But for that, I need the help of those that devised Veranesh's prison. If you tell me how to find them, I'll leave and you'll be able to free yourself from the bind."

Uganel's face shifted, his eyeless sockets narrowing as if it could help him see her. "Why the sudden change of heart? You were ready to fight to the death moments ago."

"Veranesh can't hear us anymore," she replied, staring straight at the nightfly that hovered nearby and sending it a crooked smile. After all, the betrayal idea was his. "His power is greatly limited, and the only thing he really controls is my life. As long as he believes I serve him, he won't kill me to free himself." Lies flowed seamlessly, fueled by her Tivarashan ancestry. As much as she despised the petty games her compatriots played, the skills they'd equipped her with came in handy in the least expected situations.

While she spoke, Veelk collapsed to his knees but pulled himself back up. Crimson patches on his clothes grew, and she looked away before fear swallowed her whole. To outsmart Uganel, she needed a clear head.

"Why would he wait?" the demon asked.

"I think he isn't as confident as he tries to appear," she said. Part of her kept wondering what Veranesh thought of her words, but he knew better than to speak. "I think he's unsure whether my death will be the key to his freedom."

A mocking smile stretched Uganel's face. "He was always all mouth. I knew it was the mages' lousiness, not his doing, that weakened the prison."

The nightfly remained silent, but Kamira could swear Veranesh laughed in the distance of his prison, an echo of his emotions traveling through their pact to her, and that alone spoke of the control and power he had. A higher demon belittling him was nothing but amusement to him.

"Do you know how his prison works?" She let hope into her voice. "Do you know how to strengthen it?"

Anything the demon could tell her of the trap could prove useful, but to her disappointment, Uganel shook his head. "It's the others' doing. Release me, and I'll take you to meet them."

Even though he couldn't move in his bind, Uganel's body tensed, and Kamira recognized the cue in an instant.

"You won't," she replied. "You'll try to kill me the very moment I free you."

Uganel laughed and relaxed. "I was never good at deception. That's Myrkan's domain. So what now, pactee? The smell of your blood is getting thicker. Do you think you can finish destroying me before your strength fades?"

"I only hoped to get some names, and you gave me one, but I'm sure there's more you could share."

"Take your time, pactee." Uganel's hissing voice sent a shiver down her spine. "It is my ally, not yours."

He was right. The longer she asked questions he wouldn't answer, the less likely she'd have time to destroy him. And even if the ripping part was as excruciating as she suspected, he'd still be reborn back in his realm.

Veelk took his last steps toward her, and she let the barrier flicker, letting him in. He collapsed inside, but didn't let go of his keshal. The nightflies made it in as well, but Veranesh kept them hovering silently, so she paid no attention.

"Well, pactee? Are you still alive?" Uganel taunted her. "I can't hear the spell... Maybe you don't know it as well you claim to."

Kamira ignored him, ripping Veelk's shirt open. Most of his wounds demanded attention—and magic—and she hesitated before picking the one that looked the biggest.

Veelk pushed her hand away. "Save your strength. You'll have to keep the barrier up."

It wasn't the time to argue. Powering the protective circle and keeping the demon bound took all of her focus already, and it would be a strain to pour magic into Veelk even without his objections.

"You better start crawling, pactee. It's not going to be long." Uganel pulled on the bind again, and she countered with her magic. He wouldn't break free that easily. "I'd be disappointed if you died before I got to you."

"Her name is Kamira," Veranesh said all of a sudden. "And her life is mine to dispose of, not yours."

She allowed herself an ugly smile as she savored the bound demon's terrified expression. Blind, he could not see the meager nightflies, and Veranesh's voice alone was enough to send him into panic.

"Impossible!" Uganel squealed. "We trapped you! You can't be here! It's just some human trick."

Veranesh laughed with ominous cruelty, making Kamira's instincts urge her to flee. Then he started his own incantation, and his spell, even channeled through the small crystalline creatures, overwhelmed that of hers, and Uganel broke free from Kamira's bind only to find himself trapped by the other demon.

With a sigh of relief, she refocused, pressing her hands to Veelk's body. Energy flowed, obeying her will, strong and steady, as if what she drew meant nothing to Veranesh working his own magic.

"Save your strength," Veelk repeated. "Consider it repayment of my debt."

A quiet growl was the only sign of her frustration at his foolish insistence. Throughout the years, he'd paid his debt of life a hundredfold. "Just heal."

"Give me the names, Uganel," Veranesh said.

"You can't offer anything in return, hoyve," the other demon said. "I don't know how you got out, but the others will imbue you back into the crystal."

"I can make it quick. Or slow." Veranesh resumed the incantation.

Uganel's scream flooded the landscape, and Kamira found the sound more satisfying than she'd expected.

Cruelty itself didn't excite her, but the payback for what she and Veelk had suffered, and Veranesh's need for revenge, justified it this once. She didn't savor the demon's torment long, instead focusing on her friend. If he was to survive and heal, he needed much more of her magic. As soon as she channeled it, her trained ear recognized that Veranesh was already halfway through the ripping part of the spell, his chanting twice the pace he'd taught her to use. Her eyes widened at the realization that he couldn't hold the spell through the nightflies, not for long, so no matter how much he might want to torture Uganel, be it for information or the sheer pleasure, he had to destroy him without any delays.

"Your leg?" Veelk muttered.

"It's going to be fine. The pain helps me stay conscious." She forced a smile.

Veelk regarded her with narrowed eyes. "You worry."

"I always worry." This time her lips obeyed and curled with the ease she didn't feel. Were the situation less dire, she'd have given him an appropriate scolding for not worrying enough and enjoyed his snappy ripostes.

Uganel kept screaming. "I beg you, stop! Stop!"

Countless wounds marked the demon's body, as if an invisible assassin lashed at him. Pieces of skin, flesh, and even bone littered the ground, and dark blood oozed from the wounds. Kamira watched the spectacle with morbid fascination as the name of that part of the spell, the ripping, proved more accurate than she'd expected.

"Give him the names!" she called out, not certain if Uganel heard it over his own scream. "Tell him of others!"

Veranesh paused the incantation. "You'll die here. But you don't have to be destroyed."

Kamira gasped, glancing at the nightfly, but the crystal body couldn't give her any clues about Veranesh's intentions. Supposedly, he always kept his word, but she couldn't see any reason to risk Uganel going after them again. It was also possible that Veranesh couldn't perform the last part of the spell through the nightflies and was masking it behind his offer.

"Trupyad. Fyertash." Uganel's words came between wheezing breaths. "Myrkan."

To her surprise, Veranesh spoke another syllable of the ripping incantation, and as it echoed with power, the other demon screamed.

"I'm not going to waste my time on you listing every insignificant yalari there is," Veranesh said. "Give me the names that matter."

Uganel clenched his jaw, holding back both a howl of pain and the names while the other demon resumed the spell.

"Names!" Veranesh demanded between syllables.

The way he controlled his voice, weaving conversation into the spell, reminded Kamira of the high mages. Tied with their incantations to produce intended results, the best of them could merge three or even four spells together, controlling their barriers while attacking their opponent. With Veranesh being adept at something so similar, she would bet that the archmages had stolen that art from demons—like anything else related to their magic.

The ripping was near to its end, and she doubted Uganel would speak, unless they changed their tactic.

"Destroy him," she said with conviction, but shook her head as she stared at the nightfly. "He's no use to us. I'll get you the names, all of them," she added, as a loyal servant would.

"Very well."

Uganel called out, "No! I'll tell you!" Immobilized, he

still struggled to break free, and more pieces of his body fell onto the sand as Veranesh continued the spell. "Don't destroy me! It's Derazin—"

The demon's voice died out when his flesh burst from within and collapsed into a heap of entrails, muscles, and bone. Two nightflies hovered beside her. "Well done, pactee. I couldn't hold it longer, but you did get us a name of worth." Veranesh paused and sighed. "I have to destroy him."

She swallowed but nodded. Letting Uganel be reborn meant unnecessary risk, and he wasn't the only demon they had to face. "Will this circle hold?" The circle *would* hold, at least for as long as she could channel her energy into it, but she had to ask to overcome the cold feeling paralyzing her body while her imagination conjured images of the Cataclysm. Some of the arcanists of old had survived it, but that brought little comfort. They counted among the most powerful of their kind, and she was...

Kamira clenched her fists, her Tivarashan pride demanding she claimed her worth as an arcanist.

Veranesh ignored her question as if he knew she didn't need an answer. "Be ready to activate the circle."

She took a deep breath as if such a simple thing could ease the raging fear, but when Veelk's large palm rested on her trembling fists, she was at least focused and determined.

The last part of the spell was much shorter than the previous one. After all, no torture was possible when the opponent already lay disembodied, and she imagined demons might be bored with the cleanup part, as she'd nicknamed it. She gasped when the heap of body parts caught fire, and she recognized the pattern of magical flames shivering and coiling against the nonexistent wind. Her barrier was up, and her veins were filled with equal parts anticipation and fear as Uganel's flesh charred, turned to embers, and then finally melted into pure energy.

Its wave hit the barrier harder than Kamira had expected, and she focused on maintaining it, resisting the need to pour more magic into it. She needed it to last as long as possible, and both the taxing journey and wounds from the ambush had taken their toll on her body.

A stronger gust of energy burst through, hitting Veelk and slashing her face. The gashes burnt and bled, but the pain forced her mind to clarity, enough to stabilize their protection.

"Steady, pactee. Hold it." Veranesh's voice reminded her of lessons with Tijhran. "The energy will grow for a while."

She clenched her jaw, gritting her teeth. It was one thing to maintain a steady flow of magic, and another to respond to random surges, and the thought of channeling even more power through her body made her heart pound all the more fiercely. Even if the cataclysmic outburst didn't kill her, she still could die from exertion, because the human body could only endure so much magic, and both outcomes meant Veelk would die as well. Part of her wondered whether the energy surrounding them would burn out the spell Veranesh had put on her, and whether the demon wanted her to live only because he'd lose his chance for freedom if she didn't, but she had enough self-preservation instincts to put it to the test. Besides, if she died, she'd never know anyway.

The oncoming surge proved more than she'd expected, and her barrier cracked. She screamed when spikes of power pierced her, disturbing the channeling, but she forced herself to pour out even more magic. Before she could repair the barrier, another wave of magic broke through. The nightflies darted forward, absorbing most of it.

Veranesh groaned, but the crystal creatures survived, and she used the time to seal the barrier shut.

"How much longer?" Wounded and exhausted, she was nearing her limits.

"One more rising wave, and then it'll start dying out," Veranesh replied.

The barrier wavered again. No energy broke through, but Kamira's arms went limp, and she couldn't hold her body straight anymore.

Veelk's strong arms pulled her into the cradle of his body. "Lie down."

She didn't even have strength to argue, her all focus going to maintaining the flow as the energy outside kept coming harder and harder. With her face pressed against his chest, she inhaled the mix of sweat and blood, and the smell brought unexpected comfort, steadying her heart and clearing her thoughts. She sensed the waves of energy, felt the rhythm, and adjusted the flow of magic while preserving as much of her own strength as she could. The surge came —a steady influx of power pushed to crush her protective shell—and she didn't yield. When the wave finally broke, Kamira's body gave up.

Her mind slipped into unconsciousness, but before the barrier collapsed, Veelk curled on the ground, around her.

17

T hree archmages sat in Irtan's chambers sipping wine and trying to conceal their fears. Yoreus leaned back in his chair, taking pleasure in watching Loktra tremble. The third archmage clenched both the wine cup and the armrest to hide her reaction, but her face, tight and unnatural, revealed what she tried to hide, while the Towers' leader, Irtan, made the wine swirl in his cup and watched it, deep in thought. Yoreus knew Irtan enough to know that the elaborate expression of mild concern masked a whole array of other feelings, and he could only hope he didn't look as desperate as the other two archmages.

His thoughts returned to the echo they'd felt earlier. Powerful magic released in the desert had stirred many students and raised questions the archmages had to address without knowing the answers themselves. And even if they knew, they wouldn't share the truth, because none of them had any doubt the event had to be linked to their deepest secret.

"At least we know it wasn't Veranesh breaking free," Yoreus said, only to break the silence.

"We do?" Loktra looked up.

"You still have your magic, don't you?" Yoreus allowed himself a hint of sarcasm. "Or haven't you used it lately?"

The third archmage choked, and her riposte went unspoken. Instead, she downed her wine.

"We still don't know what happened," Irtan spoke for the first time since they'd gathered, and Yoreus hid a cringe. The first archmage could make even admitting his lack of knowledge sound like a reprimand. "Such immense power could only come from a higher demon."

"Uganel's doing?" Loktra suggested, all too eager to blame the only demon she knew, but Yoreus couldn't fault her. The third archmage preferred to keep away from anything that threatened her comfortable life. "We don't even know if he has a pact."

"It's possible." Irtan nodded, but his voice had expressed skepticism. "Yoreus, did you manage to gather any information?"

Yoreus revealed no emotions as he replied, "All I know is Kamira left for the desert, so she might be involved. Or she might be trying to get to the old Towers again."

"Or it might be just a coincidence." Loktra sent the second archmage a challenging glare. "There are many ruins hidden within the sands that recent winds might have uncovered, and she might be doing what she's best at: scavenging."

Yoreus held off a smile. If the third archmage was stupid enough to ignore possibilities in the name of undermining an opponent, there was no need to cure her ignorance, and he let Loktra have her little victory. "That's possible too." The less the other mages knew, the easier it would be for him to control the flow of information and, perhaps, ultimately gain an upper hand. "I have someone trying to learn more, but Loktra is right. Kamira might be a dead end."

To Yoreus's disappointment, Irtan shook his head. "We can't afford to overlook anything. I'll send an expedition of the Towers' best researchers to the desert, and maybe they can find that energy's origin. Loktra, you reach out to your spies in Gildya Magna and determine whether they had anything to do with it. And Yoreus"—the first archmage looked straight at him—"you learn what you can from that arcanist, or I'll question her myself."

Yoreus bowed his head, more to conceal his displeasure than out of respect. He needed to push Ryell a bit harder once Kamira came back, before Irtan interfered. As the first archmage concluded their meeting, Yoreus stood up and exchanged hollow courtesies, but his thoughts were on the problem. Maybe he should cut Atissa's punishment short, since she had better influence over Ryell. Walking out of Irtan's chambers, Yoreus considered how much he should tell his own daughter. With the stakes so high and some knowledge forbidden to anyone but the three archmages, he weighed all the options. He had to reveal enough to make her take the task seriously. He could only hope her punishment sufficed for a cure for her childish whims, and she'd be ready to join the game that only the best in the High Towers played.

Myrkan stood at the pier of the ruined port that was once the Devanshari capital's pride, staring at the sea and beyond the horizon. His claws closed and opened in rhythm with the gritting of his teeth. Uganel had failed. They'd taken such an outcome into consideration, but none of them had expected him to be destroyed. The echo of the power released upon the spell's completion carried through both worlds and sent shivers down Myrkan's spine. He tried to keep calm, but his thoughts circled back to Veranesh. The infallible trap they had devised centuries ago was failing, and he couldn't help wondering about the consequences. The wind from the sea whipped his skin with both salt and remnants of the energy, reminding him that they knew nothing of what had transpired on the other continent. They were planning an invasion and had become blind. But Veranesh hadn't broken free yet, no matter how Uganel's destruction had happened, so they had time to fix their mistakes.

"The long-lost player has rejoined the game."

Arujhan's voice made Myrkan flinch, and the yalari fought off the urge to leap away as his instincts demanded. Instead, he turned slowly, letting his muscles relax, and watched his opponent with narrowed eyes. He forced a casual tone and said, "You don't seem too concerned." More so, Arujhan hadn't expressed any doubt that it could have been someone else who destroyed Uganel.

"He's trapped and weak. And whenever humans use magic, they weaken him and reinforce the binds." Arujhan walked up next to Myrkan at the edge of the pier and looked at the sea. "He's a concern, but not a threat yet. We have time."

Myrkan watched the other yalari out of the corner of his eye, focusing all his effort on defying his instincts to fight or flee, reminding himself that either would fail if Arujhan intended to kill him, because only a few were a match for a kanyalari of such power. "You're not here to talk about Veranesh, are you?"

Arujhan didn't turn his gaze from the sea, clearly

indicating he perceived Myrkan to be no threat. "No." The waves broke against the pier, filling the silence between them. "I came to offer you what you desire."

Myrkan laughed. "And what is that?" He expected an offer, but Arujhan couldn't have discovered his real desire.

"To rule over humans." Arujhan smiled with satisfaction while Myrkan fought to keep his face straight. "I admit, it's a smart move. In our world you'll always be in the middle, forced to serve those like Derazin and constantly threatened by other mediocre but ambitious yalari, but over here... Here you can be the strongest."

Myrkan swallowed. Pride demanded he shove the insult back down Arujhan's throat, but reason whispered of the jagged truth hidden behind the words. He might be considered a kanyalari, but those more powerful would always see him as... mediocre indeed. He almost spat the word out as it stained his thoughts. At least Arujhan considered him strong enough to bargain with. "Let's hear it, then."

"The only one to object to your stay in this world would be Derazin. And I want Derazin's domain. If you help me destroy him, I'll give you the human domain to rule and ensure no other yalari questions it... including the Four."

That got Myrkan's attention. The four kanyalari who'd made an unlikely alliance in a bid for the worship of a whole nation of humans could see him as a threat, but if Arujhan was willing to negotiate on his behalf, he wouldn't have to worry about them. "What about others?" He hid his readiness to jump at the offer.

"Trupyad's not stupid. Unless cornered, he'd sooner run away than take sides." Arujhan snorted. "The only reason he's still alive is that nobody cares enough to destroy him."

"And Fyertash?" Myrkan would rather not make an enemy of that weak but cunning yalari.

Arujhan grinned, giving his first emotional display since they'd started the siege, and Myrkan had to question the sudden openness of someone so powerful. "I feel tempted to test your limits and tell you to destroy him."

"That would be a waste," Myrkan replied. Loyalty meant nothing to him, but fighting was always a risk, and for all he knew, Arujhan could use it to get rid of them both. "Fyertash is resourceful, and just like me, he's no threat to you. Let him take my domain, or whatever small part you weren't planning to take for yourself, and he'll receive more than he'd ever achieve by going against you." He froze when a thought crossed his mind. *Us.* He'd almost said *us.*

The smile faded from Arujhan's face. "Very well. We'll ensure the reinforcement of Veranesh's prison and destroy Derazin. Then I'll return with Fyertash to our realm while you remain here to do as you please."

"I'd rather see Veranesh destroyed." Myrkan grimaced. Of course, seeing as it'd taken a risky conspiracy and the help of human mages to even imprison that powerful kanyalari, he'd rather see *someone else* try to destroy him. Keeping Veranesh trapped might not have been ideal, but it was safer than any attempt to get rid of him... if they managed to find a yalari foolish enough to try.

"So would I, but we'll find no one willing to do the deed." Arujhan donned a dry smile. "So, do we have an alliance?"

Myrkan pretended to consider and finally replied, "We do."

The other yalari nodded and spread his wings, then lifted into the air without a word.

Myrkan turned to watch the sea again, but movement in

the ruined port caught his attention. Not revealing his awareness, he stared at the waves while his body tensed muscle by muscle, readying for a battle.

His wings shot open, and he darted above the rubble toward the ruined building. In a heartbeat, he struck with his talons, burying them deep into the victim's body.

"Don't kill me!" Trupyad twisted in his grip. "I won't tell anyone!"

"But you heard, didn't you?" Myrkan offered him a cruel smile. The pitiful, sly yalari had been testing Myrkan's patience since the beginning of the siege, and the thought of finally doing something about it filled his mind with anticipation. "Including the part how no one cares enough to destroy you?"

Trupyad nodded eagerly, his eyes pleading.

"Good." Cruelty flowed through Myrkan's voice. He clenched his talons, and the other yalari's bones cracked, forcing out a squeal of pain. "Then remember, if you try to come back to this world or warn Derazin from our realm, I'll care enough to hunt you down and finish this."

Trupyad opened his mouth, but before he could utter any reassurances, Myrkan ripped his tongue out. Then he plunged his talons into his victim's eyes, deeper and deeper, savoring the kill, until Trupyad twitched, gurgled, and died.

Myrkan stood over the other yalari's body, the rush of power coursing through his veins. Soon, he'd have even more. With all its limits, the world of humans also had a lot of offer. So many ways to kill them, to manipulate them, to make them praise him as their ruler... and the vast lands he could claim as his own without the need to constantly guard them from greedy neighbors. Once they were done with Veranesh and Derazin, he'd return to this continent, keeping away from the Four's lands. The Devanshari kingdom may lie in ruins, but Juamha swarmed with humans and their petty domains. One by one, he'd crush them, building his own domain, his own empire.

One day, his power would be equal to that of Arujhan, or maybe even the Four, and he'd show them how mediocre *they* were.

He smiled at the thought.

18

K amira woke up like a drowning person who finally reaches the water's surface: with a desperate gasp. Her whole body ached from overexertion, as if the magic she had channeled had burnt it inside out, but with enough rest, she'd recover, and that alone brought a sigh of relief. Yet at the scent of burnt flesh, her eyes snapped open and all the concerns returned. Veelk still kept her close, but his clothes were gone, and his skin was covered with deep burns, the price he had paid for protecting her. She'd seen him heal from worse, but his scars, pulsing with intense red, made her scramble to get up. Putting her weight on her broken arm sent her back to the ground with a groan, so she resigned to resting on her healthy limb and looked Veelk over.

The blisters on his skin brought tears to her eyes, but she clenched her teeth and reached out to him. She might be exhausted, but she'd endure channeling a bit more.

"He's had enough magic already." The nightfly hovered by her face. "His body is fighting to stay alive, and trying to heal him is only going to cause further imbalance. And you are in no better shape. More magic might kill you."

She shook her head, refusing to acknowledge it. Veelk had been in worse states before, and her magic always helped. "I have to at least try."

Veelk opened his eyes, his gaze unfocused. "No, you don't." His coarse voice was so quiet that Kamira almost missed it. "I didn't save your life so you could waste it trying to help me. The debt is paid."

She shook her head violently, scattering the tears that flowed down her cheeks. The debt had already been paid, hundredfold or more, and if anyone owed anything, it was her.

"Kam..." His expression softened, and he struggled to speak. "Don't make it all go to waste. See this through to the end. Ask Ryell for help. He knows how to fight and... seems to have taken a liking to you. Or Zelna. She won't say no. And she's almost as good as I am." His breath became shallow and slower, and he closed his eyes with a sigh.

Pain coursed through her body when Kamira drew energy, reminding her of her own limitations, but she would not sit idly by while her friend, her only friend, died. No matter what Veelk claimed, there was no replacing him, no matter how skilled Ryell or Zelna could be.

The nightfly wrapped around her wrist and pulled her hand away from Veelk. "If you do it, you'll kill him, pactee."

She let out a cry of anguish. "There has to be something... There has to be something I can do." The overwhelming feeling of helplessness clouded her thoughts, and she fought for clarity. If only she could think straight, she'd find a way.

"No, *you* can't."

Her eyes wide, she stared at the nightfly, the demon's

words sinking in. "But you can," she whispered when it dawned on her. Anger and desperation flooded her. Veranesh knew how to save Veelk, but had instead taken his time toying with her. Yet she had no time for fighting with him. "Name your price."

The demon laughed, his amusement at her reaction more than clear. "Very well, then. I'll take your trust, pactee."

"My... trust?" The payment was both so ridiculous and low that it had to be yet another game. All that while the red scars on Veelk's body pulsated more and more violently.

"I can try to save his life, but such a thing has never been done before. I could just as well fail," Veranesh replied. "I will not make such an attempt if that means I'll have to deal with your accusations. More so, if I don't succeed, you'll still keep your part of our other agreement. Don't worry, I'll make sure you'll get a fitting revenge."

She nodded, swallowing hard. "Just save him," she pleaded. Veelk's life was worth any price.

The nightflies darted toward her friend, and their long tails straightened. Before she could react, both lunged downward, digging deep into Veelk's chest, and the mage killer didn't react in the slightest, making her wonder whether it was already too late. Veranesh explained nothing, but she knew better than to protest. Even if her trust in the demon was at best limited, she had to keep her part of the deal.

The red of Veelk's scars faded, but the nightflies lit up with the same hue, and Kamira could swear that Veranesh's low moan came through the creatures. The amount of magic that emanated from both nightflies made her eyes go wide. The demon was trying to sap the energy Veelk must have absorbed during Uganel's destruction, but it was destroying the nightflies. Tiny cracks appeared on their crystal bodies.

"Pactee." Veranesh's voice revealed his strain. "These creatures won't survive. You'll have to pay me another visit if you want new ones."

Kamira pulled herself closer and eyed Veelk, his scars returning to their natural hue and glowing slightly, as always when he was healing, but the nightflies remained embedded in his body, and by the fluttering of their wings, she could tell Veranesh was struggling to break free. With every attempt, more cracks appeared.

Without hesitation, she reached out to them. Her broken arm rebelled at the strain, but as long as she could close her fists around the crystals, the pain didn't matter.

"No, you foolish—"

Her hands closed on the nightflies before Veranesh could finish, and a blast of energy hit her, reigniting the pain of her broken arm, but she refused to let go as it carried her into the air, and the crystal creatures ripped out of Veelk's body. The descent was quick, and as she fell onto the hard surface of glassy sand, the impact sapped her consciousness.

19

Days dragged the same way Ryell dragged his feet on his way back to the Jagged Swordsman every evening. He filled them with helping Prince Allyv in the asylum, but his mind constantly circled back to Kamira. He should have gone with her. The way she spoke about her journey into the desert, with determination and concern, had made it clear that she was about to face danger, and he couldn't help wondering what kind of trouble Veelk had gotten her into. He clenched his fists at the memory of her refusal, adamant that he couldn't accompany her, and at the sudden sting of jealousy he'd felt back then. A couple of weeks alone with Veelk would poison her mind again, and Ryell would never convince her to return to high magic studies. He shook his head in a vain attempt at chasing away the unwanted thoughts that crowded his mind.

Kamira had said that the journey through the desert would take at least a couple of weeks, and he tried to be patient regardless of his frustration, but without her around, every moment seemed longer, like months.

Ryell sighed, relaxing his muscles, but the tension still

lingered. *Withdrawal.* The one word Prince Allyv had mentioned in passing, and whenever Ryell's mind was clear enough, he couldn't help wondering whether he really missed Kamira, or if it was her magic that he craved. But it was her and not Atissa he kept thinking about, even though Kamira openly distrusted him and kept her distance. He clung to the thought and picked up his pace in a sudden rush of hope that the demonologist had already come back to the inn. His common sense whispered, condemning him to suffer disillusionment, but like every other evening, Ryell didn't care.

The back alleys he walked were already drowned in the dark, and the guards lit the streetlamps in the square ahead. With the Jagged Swordsman around the next corner, a familiar scent and a faint aura of magic surrounded him like a cloud of smoke. He turned with a mix of hope and joy, and looked at the person who stood behind him. When his eyes met with Atissa's, he had to fight his own body to conceal his disappointment.

"It's only me, silly." Her laughter sounded a thousand silver bells in his ears, and it came as a relief that she misread his reaction. A simple temple outfit, wide pants and a vest, made her look young and innocent, unlike the proud and spoiled mage he saw the last time they'd seen each other. "I missed you!"

She came at him, and Ryell opened his arms instinctively.

"Your father is not angry anymore?" He kissed her cheek, inhaling the flowery scent of her skin. The relief her presence brought was both immediate and overwhelming.

"It took him long enough to forgive me." She giggled, but then became serious. "I'm just glad he didn't punish me by having you sent away."

Ryell brushed his fingers against her skin. "I missed your sweet voice."

He felt the fingertips and nails against his bare skin and took a deep breath, making Atissa smile with triumph.

"Looks like it isn't only my voice you missed," she teased. Her eyes shone when she looked at him, while her soft and willing lips teased his neck. "So, you live around here now?" Atissa's tongue tickled his skin while she whispered into his ear. "Maybe we should go there?" Her hand traveled down his spine, and she pushed her fingers under his belt, pulling his shirt out.

Ryell slid his hands to the curve of her hips and pulled her closer. "Still in the same room in an inn." His lips played with her ear, and Atissa's breath sped to shallow quickness. "I'm here at your father's request."

"Oh?" She looked into his eyes, excitement replaced with concern. "I hope he wasn't too harsh on you because of me. The argument... It was my fault, not yours."

This had to be the closest she'd get to an apology, and Ryell took it. With her magic so generously flowing to him, he wasn't about to dwell on the single argument they'd had. "It's just a favor for him. Dealing with a... demonologist."

Atissa frowned. "Is it about the woman who tried to kill my father? Isn't that dangerous?"

"We're not sure anymore whether she really wanted to kill him." Ryell knew he spoke too quickly, but couldn't resist defending Kamira. He bit his tongue before mentioning she'd helped him with the trouble at the asylum. He'd spoil the mood mentioning Kamira had agreed to what Atissa refused. "But there's something more at play, and I'm helping your father uncover the plot," he offered a quick lie that would match whatever Yoreus had told his daughter about their arrangement.

Her forehead furrowed, as if she didn't like that idea, but then she smiled at him. "I hope you'll still find some time to visit me."

Ryell's blood rushed when her voice hit the low tone and carried a promise his body longed for. He slid his hands under Atissa's silk vest and stroked her breast while pressing a kiss to her lips. Before she had a chance to reciprocate, he pushed her gently against the wall, and, after lifting the cloth, he buried his face in her cleavage while moving his hands along her waist and curves. His tongue traced around her nipples, and he could feel her fast-paced heartbeat through her soft skin.

"Always." His hands made their way below her waist, again sliding under her clothes. He didn't care if she pushed him away or reminded him they were standing in a back alley, which was hardly an appropriate place for lovemaking. Until she did, he'd enjoy every bit of her body and the magic lingering around her.

And Kamira... Guilt bit into his thoughts at the memory of the Tivarashan woman. But she was away, traveling with her best friend, and she'd pushed him away, keeping both distance and secrets. Perhaps there was a way to save her from demon influence and from the mage killer's poisonous words, but until her return, she was as good as lost to him. He'd be a fool to choose her over a woman who had both magic and affection for him.

When Atissa pulled Ryell closer and searched for the buckle of his belt, her reply became clear, and the last thought Ryell had was surprise that he could have ever thought about anything or anyone else but her.

～

AFTER ALL THE years bound in the dark, the prisoner had learned to recognize the hidden melody of his prison: the guards' heavy steps, water trickling down the wall, flames crackling from the torch outside his cell. Everything had its place within the unvoiced song, and he grew to appreciate it, even though it spoke of his captivity. The routine soothed him, helping him remain in torpor, so when the distant echo of unknown sounds distorted the melody, the prisoner stirred in his slumber.

As his consciousness resurfaced from the dreamless depths, he listened intently. Strangers' voices, clanks of steel, and shrieks of the dying interrupted the sound of water dripping in his cell, and they spoke of change coming. The prisoner moved, pulling on his binds. Strangers had come to the prison, and they were killing along the way.

For all he knew, he was meant to become part of the slaughter. He couldn't imagine Gildya adepts, the only ones who wished him dead, would send assassins to wipe out everyone along with their main target, but his knowledge of the outside world had been limited for years. Things could have changed, and for the first time since he'd lost his freedom, he wondered how. Maybe adepts had become as hated as the arcanists... Or the high mages had decided to destroy Gildya in a struggle for power. Of course, it could also be some thugs who didn't know better than to attack a place guarded by Gildya's adepts.

The guard outside the door died with a gurgle, and the prisoner attempted to break free, but the chains held as strong as ever. He had no choice but to remain kneeling, helpless and defenseless when the intruder made it inside his cell.

Bright light forced his eyes shut, and he blinked several times until he could see as he stared at the entrance.

The man who entered wore a gray robe stained with blood. He carried a torch, and two long sabers hung at his sides. He was not of the tribes, but like them, he had the moves of a killer. His light hair and fair skin, so unusual on Tyorane, caught the prisoner's attention.

"Are you the man whom they call Alluvendran?" the stranger said, his soft accent distorting some of the words. Or perhaps this was how people communicated nowadays.

The prisoner grimaced. Alluvendran. He hated the very sound of this name, but saw no reason to conceal the truth. "Some call me that, yes." His voice, coarse and dry, bore no resemblance to the deep tones that once came from his mouth.

The man nodded. "There's a woman who wishes to speak with you. You will not speak without being asked a question, and when you speak, you will address her as 'my lady,' do you understand?"

Alluvendran narrowed his eyes, reserving a grimace. The formal approach meant nobility, and they mostly came from Tivarashan, a place of lush woods and devoted priests. This couldn't possibly be good, and he couldn't help wondering whether the northern kingdom had finally conquered Kaighal. Instinct urged him to try breaking free once more, but he had tested the chains countless times already.

"I understand," he said. If that woman wanted to talk, maybe she had some sort of an offer for him and not a death sentence.

The stranger turned toward the entrance and nodded to someone Alluvendran couldn't see, but he heard the footsteps rushing away.

They didn't wait long, and when a woman stepped into the cell, the prisoner's eyes widened in surprise. He'd expected to see one of the gray-skinned, dark-haired crones who wore ceremonial robes adorned with the symbols of the Four, not a mature, attractive lady dressed in what he recognized as fine clothes. Her jewelry glimmered in the light of the torch, and colorful stones contrasted with her fair complexion. These people weren't from Tivarashan... But then—from where?

"Thank you, Phuran," the woman said, and then turned to the prisoner. "We were told that a man by the name of Alluvendran is a skilled adept. An adept who's not afraid to break rules and reach beyond their boundaries, a brilliant inventor. Is that correct? Are you such a man?"

"Some say so, my lady," he replied. The plural pronoun she'd used didn't escape his attention, but she couldn't be of Tivarashan royalty. "Though most Gildya Magna adepts would brand me as blasphemer and insane, hence my imprisonment here."

The woman stepped closer, and the warrior named Phuran readied to protect her at any sign of danger.

"We have a need of an inventor to help rebuild an artifact lost to our people. Someone who can match the genius of ancient creators," she said. "We need it done by any means necessary, outside of the rules that Gildya Magna uses to bind its adepts' minds. We will ensure you have a discreet place to work and all resources at our disposal. In return for your services, upon completion of the task, you will be free to go, and you will receive generous amount of coin as well."

"What was the artifact? Is there any information on how it worked? Any blueprints?" Alluvendran asked, and Phuran grimaced. "My lady?" Alluvendran added, though a small tone of sarcasm sneaked into his voice.

"We have very little," the woman said. "Several

scriptures and a failed prototype constructed by some of Gildya's adepts. Our people didn't know the workings of Hajihali, only its effect."

"Hajihali." Alluvendran fished through his memory, since the word seemed familiar. "It's something overseas. In... Devanshari, I think."

The woman nodded with approval. "We see that you are aware. Do you accept our offer, then?"

Alluvendran almost snorted. Trapped in a cell, chained to a wall, and stripped of all the power he possessed, and with all the prison guards dead, leaving him as the only witness of what had transpired, it was hardly a choice. He glanced at Phuran. The warrior shifted his stance slightly, and his narrowed eyes watched Alluvendran's every move, every grimace. If he wanted to live, he had to agree. "I accept... my lady."

The woman motioned to Phuran, and with one of his unsheathed blades, he struck the chains at Alluvendran's wrists, cleaving them to dangle, clinking against the stone. The blade shone magic for a blink, then it faded.

Alluvendran's muscles screamed in pain as his arms dropped, and he wavered while standing up for the first time in years. His body, motionless for so long, responded with stiffness and numbness, but the gems embedded in it were already pumping their magic through him. They'd kept him alive for what seemed an eternity, and now they'd give him the strength to stand on his own.

"We will have the shackles and the collar removed once you complete the artifact." The woman couldn't be clearer on how little she trusted him. "We have days to travel." She turned to Phuran. "We trust you to organize everything. We can't suffer any more delays."

The warrior bowed, and both men watched her leave.

"Come, adept." Phuran gestured at the door. "I'll get you some food and fresh clothes."

"So, to whom do I owe my release?" Alluvendran asked while he followed Phuran to the surface. As they stepped over bodies and pools of blood, the adept recognized some of the faces, and the bliss of being able to walk again ebbed. They didn't deserve such deaths. But then again, he didn't deserve imprisonment, yet he'd spent ten years chained.

The presence of Phuran walking in front of him reminded Alluvendran that he'd just agreed to swap one prison for another, and if the people who'd come for him were ready to kill indiscriminately, trusting their words was asking for betrayal, and Alluvendran had had enough of betrayal.

"To her majesty Queen Cahala qi'Devanshari," Phuran replied. "The last to sit on the throne of Devanshari before the demon invasion, and our people's only hope."

Alluvendran raised his eyebrows. *Demon invasion?* These two words made him wonder all the more about the outside world. "I'm not aware of these events."

"There'll be plenty of time for you to learn, adept." Phuran looked over his shoulder. "The queen has trusted you with the reconstruction of the artifact lost during the war, and you'll be provided with all the knowledge we have."

They stepped out of the dungeon, and fresh air filled Alluvendran's nostrils with the long-forgotten smells of the woods. The overcast sky hung low, but the abundance of light still hurt his eyes, and he squinted to look around. Several servants helped Cahala onto the oxen-drawn carriage, and she departed, throwing one last glance at the men ascending from the prison's entrance.

"We have a camp nearby." Phuran pointed to the woods, but didn't indicate Cahala's trail. "Will you be able to walk?"

"For a while. Then I'll need food and rest." The gems' power, greatly limited by the shackles and collar, still supported Alluvendran's body, and with every step, years of imprisonment became irrelevant as the magic pumped into his veins and muscles, but he was still a human and needed to remedy years of starvation and his motionless state. He longed to take off the restraints, to taste his full strength and endurance again.

Phuran looked over the gems melted into Alluvendran's forearm. "I didn't expect you to walk at all," he said. "We were told that your... inhuman abilities were restricted by the collar."

Alluvendran couldn't help laughing at that. "The adepts who captured me hoped to make me powerless, and I don't think they'd ever readily admit they failed. But 'restricted' is an accurate word, so you don't have to fear."

"I don't fear you, restricted or not." Phuran stopped and looked Alluvendran straight in the eye. "But you should fear me if a thought of betraying the queen even crosses your mind."

"Duly noted." Alluvendran met the warrior's gaze calmly, and they resumed their walk through the wood.

Men who issued such threats were rarely as powerful as they claimed, and their strong words often concealed their weaknesses and fears, but he knew better than to make any remarks about it. Minor men with big egos were often just as dangerous as the truly powerful ones. The sooner Alluvendran was done with his part of the agreement and parted ways with those Devanshari, the better.

20

Sharp pain pulled Kamira back to reality, and she moaned, reflexively trying to fight back, but found herself unable to move. The low-hanging sun blinded her when she opened her eyes, but then she recognized Veelk's face above her and relaxed. His copper skin, darker than usual, had a distinct red hue to it, but nothing else spoke of his injuries. His leg was pressing against her chest, while the nightfly pinned her healthy arm to the ground.

"Don't move. I just set your broken bone," Veelk said. "And don't speak, because if you say something foolish, I swear I'll break your other arm."

Kamira smiled faintly, overwhelmed by relief while Veelk stabilized her limb. "I'm glad you're alive."

"More than you are," he said with a hint of anger as he stood up. "What in demon's guts made you think I'd want you to kill yourself? Have you no self-preservation instincts?"

He didn't await her reply, only turned and walked away, so Kamira looked at the nightfly that finally released her arm. "What did you tell him?" It was unlike Veelk to express so much frustration and in such a serious manner.

"The truth." Veranesh's reply indicated the outburst he'd witnessed didn't move him. "That, against my better judgment, you saved his life. I got to hear what a 'lousy demon' I am for not stopping you."

"That's not true." Kamira sat up, holding her broken limb still. The last thing she wanted was more scolding from Veelk. Her leg was already bandaged.

"Is it not?" Veranesh asked. "I wouldn't have done anything if you hadn't pressed. So he's been saved by your persistence."

Kamira gave the nightfly a long, considering stare. "Thank you," she said. "I appreciate it." It didn't escape her that, despite the earlier strain, the nightflies looked unscathed. Veranesh must have found a way to repair them, and that raised the question of what else he was capable of, but since he'd bound and destroyed a higher demon through them, she could assume there weren't as many limitations for him as she might have believed.

"I might be a yalari, but I'm not of Uganel's kind. A pactee is not a slave or a tool, and the pact is to be of mutual gain."

The way he said it made it clear that the difference really mattered to him, and his talk of mutual gain stung her. So far, she'd taken what Veranesh offered, magic and knowledge, but even though she'd agreed to free him, even when her discoveries confirmed his story, trust wasn't something she gave. Instead, the demon had to trade for it. Guilt pressed her conscience.

"I haven't been a good pactee, then."

"I have no reasons to complain. You did what I expected and succeeded. And I suppose after what transpired, I don't have to concern myself with thoughts of your betrayal."

She nodded. For saving Veelk's life, Veranesh had her loyalty, and if the circumstances were different, she'd almost consider it a part of his play. But in the end, it wouldn't matter.

Veelk returned and dropped a bag, pointing a finger at her. "Don't you dare stand up."

The nightflies fluttered around and coiled on her wrists, demonstrating Veranesh's lack of support in dealing with Veelk's anger.

"I couldn't even if I wanted to." Her lips stretched into a teasing grin. "Which means I'll need help."

He stared at her. "Maybe you should ask your demon to carry you around." Yet he knelt and lifted her. "You know you're stuck with me? I have a debt to pay again."

The softness and playfulness in his voice brought a smile to her face. "I hoped you'd say that."

He helped her stand and walk through the ruins, since swept clean of sand to reveal the soot-covered cobblestones of what had once been the street of the old city. Parts of the walls crumbled, charred and reduced to rubble in the recent outburst of magic, but a few stood proudly, jagged teeth of the forgotten culture, and all was covered by sand melted into solid glass. No traces of their adversaries remained, not even a single bone trapped in that glass, and her eyes widened at the thought of the power they'd endured. Back in the circle, too focused on holding the wavering barrier, she'd never had time to fully consider the amount of energy released.

"What about our supplies?" she asked with little hope.

"Some survived. I dropped my bag by the wall as soon as the fighting started, and the stones shielded most of it." He led Kamira to a collapsed building and set her down in its foundations. "Most food got soaked in demonlings' blood, but we have enough water." He looked over his crumpled clothes, stained with dark blood. "And I have something to wear." He offered a grin, as if he knew her mind would wander to that one time she'd accidentally set his clothes aflame, to lighten the mood. "Seems that the magic was strongest by Uganel's body, so next time you decide to go against a higher demon, get away from him before the destruction starts."

This remark made her snicker. If she could help it, she'd never fight another demon again, and that thought made her serious again. "That much power must have drawn attention. We should get away from here." Back to Kaighal, to rest and resupply, but then what? Nothing she'd learned so far offered clues on how exactly she was supposed to free Veranesh.

She moved to get up, but Veelk held her back. "No standing up. I'll help you walk, but first you need to eat and rest. With your injuries, you only have magic when it comes to fighting."

No lighthearted comment could ease his concerns, and Kamira remained quiet. Uganel might have set his trap here, but he could have also sent more henchmen to scour the desert in case they picked another route. She shook her head in bitter amusement. If they hadn't set out to prepare their own trap, Uganel could have been waiting in the ruins for weeks, without interfering in their plans... She discarded that thought. They needed to confront the demon one way or another, and only bad luck decided on who had the upper hand. All things considered, they'd still succeeded, even if nothing went the way it was supposed to.

"I'll try to catch something edible," Veelk said. "You get

some rest and wake up your demon. He better keep you alive until I get back."

The nightfly lifted from Kamira's wrist before Veelk was out of sight. "Yalari never sleep."

"But they do eavesdrop?"

"Knowledge is a way to gain power over someone, isn't it?" the demon replied lightly. "Speaking of knowledge, you played Uganel well. I regret we didn't have time to press him more."

"Do you know the names he spoke of?" she asked.

"In the past, none of them alone held any significant power, but allied, they'd have some leverage." Veranesh paused. "Still, there has to be someone leading them. A powerful yalari, undoubtedly."

Kamira reached for her bag, tattered from the beating she'd suffered from Uganel and showing minor burns, but otherwise intact. Its lighter weight suggested Veelk had already rummaged through it in search of supplies. She pulled out her journal and wrote down the names, though she doubted the memory of Uganel's final moments would ever fade from her mind. "And which one be the weakest?"

"Trupyad. He's nothing without others, never had real power, and even if things have changed over the centuries, he'd be the least likely to rise to it. He's cunning enough to recognize the strongest yalari around and work his flattery, but otherwise hardly a threat." The nightfly hovered by her side. "Are you thinking of summoning him?"

As much as she liked the idea of gaining knowledge from another demon involved in devising Veranesh's prison on her own terms, with all the preparations made and precautions taken, she was safer if she didn't draw any more attention. She savored the image, but not long enough for it to dim her common sense.

"Not anytime soon," she replied. "I don't even know if I want to take the risk again. Trupyad would have to be destroyed too." Her body rebelled at the very thought of surviving such immense power again.

"You did well," Veranesh said. "With little training, you survived longer than many master arcanists did when the Towers fell."

They both knew she'd need a lot more skill to free him, but she wasn't about to dwell on it. As long as she kept practicing, she'd be capable of channeling more and more magic. "Did they really imbue you into that crystal?" she asked.

"It grew around me after I was summoned. Imbuing would explain how they did it."

She scribbled a note into her journal. "That's something I can look into."

"All in due time," the demon replied. "You need to heal. What we did here won't go unnoticed, but you have time before other yalari gather the details."

"That leaves the high mages to worry about, but I don't think they'll try anything openly. They don't know enough." Kamira leaned against the crumbled wall and relaxed. "I could mislead them too. If I asked Ryell whether this event was Yoreus's plot or mentioned we had to run from the outburst of magic... The archmage might believe I had nothing to do with it."

"The lie is only as good as the liar," Veranesh said. "But you're resourceful. You'll handle it."

Before she got to reply, Veelk approached from around the corner. "Demon magic charred everything around, so the food will have to wait until we get away from here." He looked her up and down, then picked up her bag and slung it over his shoulder along with the one he was already carrying.

Then he lifted her, cradling her in his arms like a child, and she smiled at the special treatment. In any other circumstances, he'd have slung her across his shoulder, adding comments about her lack of exercise or endurance.

"I'll scout ahead," Veranesh said, and the nightflies darted through the air, disappearing around the corner.

Veelk followed at a slower pace, but seemingly not bothered by his additional burden.

Kamira looked up at him, her instincts responding to the safety of his embrace, the dread of the previous hours slowly fading. Even if she'd never forget the horrors they'd faced, and despite their all-too-close brush with death, her mood was lifted simply by her friend's presence.

He looked down with a grin. "So, we survived again."

His lighthearted voice left no space for concerns about the future, for outwitting the high mages, fighting more demons, and the insane attempt at freeing Veranesh from his centuries-long prison.

They survived, they always did, and as long as they stuck together, they always would. That thought offered her more comfort than she'd expected.

Veelk turned the corner, and the vast desert opened before them. In the distance, nightflies flashed in the setting sun, and for once, the red hue of the sand didn't make her think of rust. Instead, she found hope in its rich color.

"We survived again," she echoed Veelk's words with a smile.

Thank you for reading! If you enjoyed the book, please consider leaving a review.
Kamira's and Veelk's adventures continue in

Scars of Stone

If you'd like to know how Kamira and Veelk met, sign up for the author's newsletter and receive your complimentary ebook of **Scourges, Spells, and Serenades** – a collection that contains two stories featuring Kamira and Veelk as well as other short stories:
authorjm.com

ABOUT THE AUTHOR

Joanna might be a bit too cautious to do anything even remotely daring or dangerous herself, so she writes about daring adventures and dangerous magic instead. Yet, she found enough courage to abandon her life in Poland and move to Ireland, and then some years later, she abandoned her life in Ireland to move over to the US. She's determined to settle there, once she finally chooses which state to reside in.

When she's not writing or thinking about writing, she plays video games or makes amateur art. She lives the happy life of a recluse, surrounded by her husband, a stuffed red monkey, and a small collection of books she insisted on hauling across two continents.

You can find the full list of her publications and more about her at:

http://authorjm.com

and connect with her via social media:

- facebook.com/AuthorJMac
- instagram.com/authorjmac
- indiepocalypse.social/@AuthorJMac
- bsky.app/profile/authorjmac.bsky.social
- threads.net/@authorjmac
- x.com/AuthorJMac
- goodreads.com/authorjmac
- bookbub.com/authors/joanna-maciejewska

ACKNOWLEDGMENTS

Even though writing itself is a rather lonely endeavor, a writer is rarely alone.

If it wasn't for my husband, Inq, I would have never made the leap to writing in English, and ever since then, he encouraged me every step of the way. He listened to me reading out rough drafts of my chapters, corrected my wonky grammar, and helped me solve plot issues and streamline my fight sequences. In a way, this book is as much his as it is mine.

A very special thanks goes to Piotr Schmidtke who has read By the Pact several times already, in its various iterations, and is always willing to have a look at early drafts to provide feedback and allow me to discuss any doubts or issues.

I was also very lucky to have wonderful beta readers who read through the first version of By the Pact—a mammoth of a novel before it became two books. Anna Suseł, J.R. Bee, S.L. Saboviec, Kamil Jach, Mikołaj Kamiński, Mariusz Kubiński, and others: your feedback made By the Pact so much better, so I'll be forever grateful to you.

Another group I received a lot of support and encouragement from were my writer friends: J. Morgyn White, L.A. McGinnis, Chesley Cox, and Sara Marschand. Without your cyber-whips and virtual cookies, I would probably still be writing and revising one book.

Last, but not least, a heartfelt thank you to my editor, Arran McNicol, who did a great job tracking down all the issues I missed in my manuscript, and to my cover designer, J. Caleb, who not only took my vision and made it reality, but also ensured it looks badass.